The Tom Swift Omnibus #8

The Tom Swift Omnibus #8
By Victor Appleton

Tom Swift and His Air Scout
(Or Uncle Sam's Mastery of the Sky)

Tom Swift and His Undersea Search
(Or the Treasure on the Floor of the Atlantic)

Tom Swift Among the Fire Fighters
(Or Battling with Flames from the Air)

Tom Swift and His Electric Locomotive
(Or Two Miles a Minute on the Rails)

Tom Swift and His Air Scout
Or Uncle Sam's Mastery of the Sky

TABLE OF CONTENTS:

A Sky Ride

"Oh Tom, is it really safe?"

A young lady—an exceedingly pretty young lady, she could be called—stood with one small, gloved hand on the outstretched wing of an aeroplane, and looked up at a young man, attired in a leather, fur-lined suit, who sat in the cockpit of the machine just above her.

"Safe, Mary?" repeated the pilot, as he reached in under the hood of the craft to make sure about one of the controls. "Why, you ought to know by this time that I wouldn't go up if it wasn't safe!"

"Oh, yes, I know, Tom. It may be all right for you, but I've never been up in this kind of airship before, and I want to know if it's safe for me."

The young man leaned over the edge of the padded cockpit, and clasped in his rather grimy hand the neatly gloved one of the young lady. And though the glove was new, and fitted the hand perfectly, there was no attempt to withdraw it. Instead, the young lady seemed to be very glad indeed that her hand was in such safe keeping.

"Mary!" exclaimed the young man, "if it wasn't safe—as safe as a church—I wouldn't dream of taking you up!" and at the mention of "church" Mary Nestor blushed just the least bit. Or perhaps it was that the prospective excitement of the moment caused the blood to surge into her cheeks. Have it as you will.

"Come, Mary! you're not going to back out the last minute, are you?" asked Tom Swift. "Everything is all right. I've made a trial flight, and you've seen me come down as safely as a bird. You promised to go up with me. I won't go very high if you don't like it, but my experience has been that, once you're off the ground, it doesn't make any difference how high you go. you'll find it very fascinating. So skip along to the house, and Mrs. Baggert will help you get into your togs."

"Shall I have to wear all those things—such as you have on?" asked Mary, blushing again.

"Well, you'll be more comfortable in a fur-lined leather suit," asserted Tom. "And if it does make you look like an Eskimo, why I'm sure it will be very becoming. Not that you don't look nice now," he hastened to assure Miss Nestor, "but an aviation suit will be very—well, fetching, I should say."

"If I could be sure it would 'fetch' me back safe, Tom—"

"That'll do! That'll do!" laughed the young aviator. "One joke like that is enough in a morning. It was pretty good, though. Now go on in and tog up."

"You're sure it's safe, Tom?"

"Positive! Trot along now. I want to fix a wire and—"

"Oh, is anything broken?" and the girl, who had started away from the aeroplane, turned back again.

"No, not broken. It's only a little auxiliary dingus I put on to make it easier to read the barograph, but I think I'll go back to the old system. Nothing to do with flying at all, except to tell how high up one is."

"That's just what I don't care to know, Tom," said Mary Nestor, with a smile. "If I could imagine I was sailing along only about ten feet in the air I wouldn't mind so much."

"Flying at that height would be the worst sort of danger. You leave it to me, Mary. I won't take you up above the clouds on this sky ride; though, later, I'm sure you'll want to try that. This is only a little flight. You've been promising long enough to take a trip with me, and now I believe you're trying to back out."

"No, really I'm not, Tom! Only, at the last minute, the machine looks so small and frail, and the sky is so—big—"

She glanced up and seemed to shiver just a trifle.

"Don't be thinking of those things, Mary!" laughed Tom Swift. "Trot along and get ready. The motor never worked better, and we may break a few speed records this morning. No traffic cops to stop us, either, as there might be if we were in an auto."

"There you go, Mary !" exclaimed Tom, as if struck with a new thought. "You've ridden in an auto with me many a time, and you never were a bit afraid, though we were in more danger than we'll be this morning."

"Danger, Tom, in an auto? How?"

"Why, danger of a wheel collapsing as we were going full speed; or the steering knuckle breaking and sending us into a tree; danger of running into a stone wall or a ditch; danger of some one running into us, or of us running into some one else. There isn't one of these dangers on a sky ride."

"No," said Mary slowly. "But there's the danger of falling."

"One against twenty. That's the safety margin. And, if we do fall, it will be like landing in a feather bed! There, don't wait any longer. Go and get ready."

Mary sighed, and then, seeming to summon her nerve to her aid, she smiled brightly, waved her hand to Tom, and hastened toward his home, where Mrs. Baggert the matronly housekeeper, was waiting to help the girl attire herself in a flying-suit of leather.

Mary Nestor, who had a very warm place in the heart of Tom Swift, had, as he stated, some time since promised to take a trip in the air with the young inventor. But she had kept putting it off, for one reason or another, until Tom began to despair of ever getting her to accompany him. Today, however, when she had called to inquire about his father, who had been slightly ill, Tom had, after the social visit, insisted on the promise being kept.

He had his mechanic get out one of the safest, though a speedy, double machine, and, with Mary to watch, Tom had taken a trial flight, just to show her how easy it was. It was not the first time she had seen him take to the air, but now she watched with different emotions, for she was vitally interested.

Tom had sailed down from aloft, making a landing in the aviation field he had constructed near his home, and then he had insisted that Mary should keep her promise to take a sky ride with him.

"Don't be too long now!" called Tom to the girl, as she hurried toward the house. "Never mind about your hair, or whether your hat's on straight. You're going to wear a cap, anyhow, and tuck your hair up under that. It's hot down here, but it will be cold up above; so tell Mrs. Baggert to see that you're warmly dressed."

"All right," and gaily she waved her hand to him. Now that she had made her decision, and was really going up, she was not half so frightened as she had been in the contemplation of it.

As Tom climbed out of the machine, to give it a careful inspection, though he was certain there was nothing wrong, an aged colored man shuffled toward him.

"Yo'—yo'll be mighty careful ob Miss Nestor now, won't yo', Massa Tom?" asked the man.

"Of course I will, Eradicate," was the young inventor's answer.

"Case we ain't got many laik her no mo', an' dat's de truf, Massa Tom," went on the old man. "So be mighty careful laik!"

"That's what I will, Rad! And, while I'm up in the air, don't you and Koku have any trouble."

"Ho! Trouble wif dat onery no-'count giant! I guess not!" and the colored man limped off, highly indignant.

Satisfied, from an inspection of his machine, that it was as nearly mechanically perfect as it was possible to be, Tom Swift finished his trip around it and stood near the big propeller, waiting for Mary Nestor to reappear. Presently she did so, and Tom gaily waved his hand to her.

"You're a picture!" he cried, as he saw how particularly "fetching" she looked in the aviator's costume which was like his own. Because of the danger of entanglement, Miss Nestor had doffed her skirts, and wore the costume of all aviators—men and women.

"I wish I had my camera!" cried Tom. "You look—stunning!"

"I hope that isn't any comment on how I'm going to feel if we have to make a—forced landing, I believe you call it," she retorted.

"Oh, I'll take care of that!" exclaimed Tom. "Now up you go, and we'll start," and he helped her to climb into the padded seat of the cockpit, behind where he was to sit.

"Oh, Tom! Don't be in such a hurry!" expostulated Mary. "Let me get my breath!"

"No!" laughed the young inventor. "If I did you might back out. Get in, fasten the strap around you and sit still. That's all you have to do. Don't be afraid, I'll be very careful. And don't try to yell at me to go slower or lower once we're up in the air.

"Why not?" Mary wanted to know, as she settled herself in her seat.

"Because I can't very well hear you, or talk to you. The motor makes so much noise, you know. We can do a little talking through this speaking tube," and he indicated one, "but it isn't very satisfactory. So if you have anything to say—"

"In the language of the poets," interrupted Mary, "if I have words to spill, prepare to spill them now. Well, I haven't! Now I'm here, go ahead! I shall probably be too frightened to talk, anyhow."

"Oh, no you won't—after the first little sensation," Tom assured her. "You'll be crazy about it. Come on, Jackson!" he called to the mechanician. "Start the ball rolling!"

Tom was in his place, his goggles and cap well down over his face, and he was adjusting the switch as the mechanic prepared to spin the propellers.

Suddenly a man came running from the Swift house, waving his arms not unlike the blades of an aircraft propeller, he also shouted, but Tom, whose ears were covered with his fur cap, could not hear. However, Jackson did, and stopped whirling the blades, turning about to see what was wanted.

"Why, it's Mr. Damon!" exclaimed Tom, as he caught sight of the excited man. "Hello, what's the matter?" the youth asked, pulling aside one flap of his head-covering so he might hear the answer.

"Tom! Wait a minute! Bless my mouse trap!" exclaimed Mr. Damon, "I want to speak to you!" He was panting from his run across the field. "I just got to your house—saw your father—he said you were going up with Miss Nestor, but—bless my dog biscuit—"

"Can't stop now, Mr. Damon!" answered Tom, with a laugh. "I have only just succeeded, by hard work, in getting Mary to a point where she has consented to take a sky ride. If I stop now she'll back out and I'll never get her in again. See you when I come back," and Tom pulled the covering over his ear once more.

"But, Tom, bless my shoe laces! This is important!"

"So's this!" answered Tom, with a grin. He saw, by the motion of Mr. Damon's lips, what the latter had said.

Around swung the propeller blades. The gasoline vapor in the cylinders was being compressed.

"Contact!" called Tom sharply, as he pressed the switch to give the igniting spark at the proper moment. The mechanic had stepped back out of the way, in case there should be a premature starting of the powerful engine, in which event the blades would have cut him to pieces.

"Wait, Tom! Wait! This is very important! Bless my collar button, Tom Swift, but this is—"

Bang! Bang! Bang!

With a series of explosions, like those of a machine gun, the motor started, and further talk was out of the question. Tom turned on more gas. The propellers became almost invisible blades of light and shadow, and the aeroplane began moving over the grassy field. The mechanic had sprung out of the way, pulling Mr. Damon with him.

"Come back! Come back! Wait a minute, Tom Swift! Bless my pansy blossoms, I want to tell you something!" cried the little man.

But Tom Swift was away and out of hearing. He had started on his sky ride with Mary Nestor.

A New Idea

Any one who has taken a flight in an aeroplane or gone up in a balloon, will know exactly how Mary Nestor felt on this, her first sky ride of any distance. For a moment, as she looked over the side of the machine, she had a distinct impression, not that she was going up, but that some one had pulled the earth down from beneath her and, at the same time, given her a shove off into space. Such is the first sensation of going aloft. Then the rush of air all about her, the slightly swaying motion of the craft, and the vibration caused by the motor took her attention. But the sensation of the earth dropping away from beneath her remained with Mary for some time.

This sensation is much greater in a balloon than in an aeroplane, for a balloon, unless there is a strong wind blowing, goes straight up, while an aeroplane ascends on a long slant, and always into the teeth of the wind, to take advantage of its lifting power on the underside of the planes. The reason for this sensation—that of the earth's dropping down, instead of one's feeling, what really happens, that one is ascending—is because there are no objects by which comparison can be made. If one starts off on the earth's surface at slow, or at great speed, one passes stationary objects—houses, posts, trees, and the like— and judges the speed by the rapidity with which these are left behind.

Going up is unlike this. There is nothing to pass. One simply cleaves the air, and only as it rushes past can one be sure of movement. And as the air is void of color and form, there is no sensation of passing anything.

So Mary Nestor, as she shot into the air with Tom Swift, had a sensation as though the earth were dropping from beneath her. For a moment she felt as though she were in some vast void—floating in space—and she had a great fear. Then she calmed herself. She looked at Tom sitting in front of her. Of course, all she could see was his back, but it looked to be a very sturdy back, indeed, and he sat there in the aircraft as calmly as though in a chair on the ground. Then Mary took courage, and ceased to grasp the sides of the cockpit with a grip that stiffened all her muscles. She was beginning to "find herself."

On and on, and up and up, went Mary and Tom, in this the girl's first big sky ride. The earth below seemed farther and farther away. The wide, green fields became little emerald squares, and the houses like those in a toy Noah's ark.

Down below, Mr. Wakefield Damon, who had hurried over from his home in Waterfield to see Tom Swift, gazed aloft at the fast disappearing aeroplane and its passengers.

"Bless my coal bin!" cried the eccentric man, "but Tom is in a hurry this morning. Too bad he couldn't have stopped and spoken to me. It might have been greatly to his advantage. But I suppose I shall have to wait."

"You want to see Master?" asked a voice behind Mr. Damon, and, turning, he beheld a veritable giant.

"Yes, Koku, I did," Mr. Damon answered, and he did not appear at all surprised at the sight of the towering form beside him. "I wanted to see Tom most particularly. But I shall have to wait. I'll go in and talk to Mr. Swift."

"Yaas, an' I go talk to Radicate," said the giant. "Him diggin' up ground where Master told me to make garden. Radicate not strong enough for dat!"

"Huh! there's trouble as soon as those two get to disputing," mused Mr. Damon, as he went toward the house.

Meanwhile, Mary was beginning to enjoy herself. The sensation of moving rapidly through the air in a machine as skillfully guided as was the one piloted by Tom Swift was delightful. Up and up they went, and then suddenly Mary felt a lurch, and the plane, which was now about a thousand feet high, seemed to slip to one side.

Mary screamed, and began reaching for the buckle of the safety belt that fastened her to her seat. She saw that something unusual had occurred, for Tom was working frantically at the mechanism in front of him.

But, in spite of this, he seemed aware that Mary was in danger, not so much, perhaps, from what might happen to the machine, as what she might do in her terror.

"Oh! Oh!" cried the girl, and Tom heard her above the terrific noise of the motor, for she was speaking with her lips close to the tube that served as a sort of inter-communicating telephone for the craft. "Oh, we are falling! I'm going to jump!"

"Sit still! Sit still for your life!" cried Tom Swift. "I'll save you all right! Only sit still! Don't jump!"

Mary, her red cheeks white, sank back, and the young inventor redoubled his efforts at the controls and other mechanisms.

And that Tom was perfectly qualified to make a safe landing, even with engine trouble, Mary Nestor well knew. Those of you who have read the previous books of this series know it also, but, for the benefit of my new readers, I shall state that this was by no means Tom's first ride in an aeroplane.

He had operated and built gasoline engines ever since he was about sixteen years old. As related in the initial volume of this series, entitled, "Tom Swift and His Motorcycle," he became possessed of this machine after it had started to climb a tree with Mr. Damon on board. After that experience the eccentric man —blessing everything he could think of—had no liking for the speedy motorcycle and sold it to Tom at a low price.

That was the beginning of a friendship between the two, and also started Tom on his career as an inventor and a possessor of many gasoline craft. For he was not content with merely riding the repaired motorcycle. He made improvements on it.

Tom lived with his father in the town of Shopton, their home being looked after, since the death of Mrs. Swift, by Mrs. Baggert. Mr. Wakefield Damon lived in the neighboring town of Waterfield, and spent much time at Tom's home, often going on trips with him in various vehicles of the land, sea or air.

As related in the various volumes of this series, Tom was not content to remain on earth. He built a speedy motor boat, and then secured an airship, following that with a submarine. He also made an electric runabout that was the speediest car on the road. Sending wireless messages, having thrilling experiences among the diamond makers, journeying to the caves of ice, and making perilous trips in his sky racer took up part of the young inventor's time.

With his electric rifle he did some wonderful shooting, and in the "City of Gold" made some strange discoveries, part of the fortune he secured enabling him to build his sky racer. It was in a land of giants that Tom was made captive, but he succeeded in escaping, and brought two giants, of whom Koku was one, away with him.

Following this achievement Tom invented a wizard camera and a great searchlight, which, with his giant cannon, was purchased by the United States Government. Work on his photo-telephone and his aerial warship, the problem of digging a big tunnel, and then traveling to the land of wonders, kept Tom Swift very busy, and he had just completed a wonderful piece of work when the present story opens.

This last achievement was the perfecting of a machine to aid in the great World War and you will find the details set down in the volume which immediately precedes this. "Tom Swift and His War Tank," it is called, and in that is related how he not only invented a marvelous machine, but succeeded in keeping its secret from the plotters who tried to take it from him. In this Tom was helped by the inspiration of Mary Nestor, whom he hoped some day to marry, and by Ned Newton, a chum, who, though no inventor himself, could admire one.

Ned and Tom had been chums a long while, but Ned inclined more to financial and office matters than to machinery. At times he had managed affairs for Tom, and helped him finance projects. Ned was now an important bank official, and since the United States had entered the war had had charge of some Red Cross work, as well as Liberty Bond campaigns.

Somehow, as she sat there in the craft which seemed disabled, Mary Nestor could not help thinking of Tom's many activities, in some of which she had shared.

"Oh, if he falls now, and is killed!" she thought. "Oh, what will happen to us?"

"It's all right, Mary! Don't worry! It's all right!" cried Tom, through the speaking tube.

"What's that? I can't hear you very well !" she called back.

"No wonder, with the racket this motor is making," he answered. "Why can't something be done so you can talk in an aeroplane as well as in a balloon? That's an idea! If I could tell you what was the matter now you wouldn't be a bit frightened, for it isn't anything. But, as it is—"

"What are you saying, Tom? I can't hear you!" cried Mary, still much frightened.

"I say it's all right—don't get scared. And don't jump!" Tom shouted until his ears buzzed. "It's all nonsense—having a motor making so much noise one can't talk!" he went on, irritatedly.

A strange idea had come to the young inventor, but there was no time to think of it now. Mentally he registered a vow to take up this idea and work on it as soon as possible. But, just now, the aeroplane needed all his attention.

As he had told Mary, there was really nothing approaching any great danger. But it was rather an anxious moment. If Tom had been alone he would have thought little of it, but with Mary along he felt a double responsibility.

What had happened was that the craft had suddenly gone into an "air pocket" or partial vacuum, and there had been a sudden fall and a slide slip. In trying to stop this too quickly Tom had broken one of his controls, and he was busily engaged in putting an auxiliary one in place and trying to reassure Mary at the same time.

"But it's mighty hard trying to do that through a speaking tube with a motor making a noise like a boiler factory," mused the young inventor. Tom worked quickly and to good purpose. In a few moments, though to Mary they seemed like hours, the machine was again gliding along on a level keel, and Tom breathed more easily.

"And now for my great idea!" he told himself.

But it was some time before he could give his attention to that.

THE BIG OFFER

Working with all the skill he possessed, Tom had got the aeroplane in proper working order again. As has been said, the accident was a trivial one, and had he been alone, or with an experienced aviator, he would have thought little of it. Then, very likely, he would have volplaned to earth and made the repairs there. But he did not want to frighten Mary Nestor, so he fixed the control while gliding along, and made light of it. Thus his passenger was reassured.

"Are we all right?" asked Mary through the tube, as they sailed along.

"Right as a fiddle," answered Tom, shouting through the same means of communication.

"What's that about a riddle?" asked Mary, in surprise at his seeming flippancy at such a time.

"I didn't say anything about a riddle—I said we are as fit as a fiddle!" cried Tom. "Never mind. No use trying to talk with the racket this motor makes, and it isn't the noisiest of its kind, either. I'll tell you when we get down. Do you like it?"

"Yes, I like it better than I did at first," answered Mary, for she had managed to understand the last of Tom's questions. Then he sailed a little higher, circled about, and, a little later, not to get Mary too tired and anxious, he headed for his landing field.

"I'll take you home in the auto," he cried to his passenger. "We could go up to your house this way—in style—if there was a field near by large enough to land in. But there isn't. So it will have to be a plain, every-day auto."

"That's good enough for me," said Mary. "Though this trip is wonderful—glorious! I'll go again any time you ask me."

"Well, I'll ask you," said Tom. "And when I do maybe it won't be so hard to hold a conversation. It will be more like this," and he shut off the motor and began to glide gently down. The quiet succeeding the terrific noise of the motor exhaust was almost startling, and Tom and Mary could converse easily without using the tube.

Then followed the landing on the soft, springy turf, a little glide over the ground, and the machine came to a halt, while mechanics ran out of the hangar to take charge of it.

"I'll just go in and change these togs," said Mary, as she alighted and looked at her leather costume.

"No, don't," advised Tom. "You look swell in em. Keep 'em on. They're yours, and you'll need 'em when we go up again. Here comes the auto. I'll take you right home in it. Keep the aviation suit on.

"I wonder what Mr. Damon could have wanted," remarked Tom, as he drove Mary along the country road.

"He seemed very much excited," she replied.

"Oh, he almost always is that way—blessing everything he can think of. You know that. But this time it was different, I'll admit. I hope nothing is the matter. I might have stopped and spoken to him, but I was afraid if I did you'd back out and wouldn't come for a sky ride."

"Well, I might have. But now that I've had one, even with an accident thrown in, I'll go any time you ask me, Tom," and Mary smiled at the young inventor.

"Shucks, that wasn't a real accident!" he laughed. "But I do wonder what Mr. Damon wanted."

"Better go back and find out, Tom," advised Mary, as they stopped in front of her house.

"Oh, I want to come in and talk to you. Haven't had a chance for a good talk today, that motor made such a racket"

"No, go along now, but come back and see me this afternoon if you like."

"I do like, all right! And I suppose Mr. Damon will be fussing until he sees me. Well, glad you liked your first ride in the air, Mary—that is, the first one of any account," for Mary had been in an aeroplane before, though only up a little way—a sort of "grass-cutting stunt," Tom called it.

Waving farewell to the pretty girl, the young aviator turned the auto about and speeded for his home and the shops adjoining it. His father had not been well, of late, and Tom was a bit anxious about him.

"Mr. Damon may bother him, though he wouldn't mean to," thought Tom. "He seemed to have his mind filled with some new idea. I wonder if it is anything like mine? No, it couldn't be. Well, I'll soon find out," and, putting his foot on the accelerator, Tom sent the machine along at a pace that soon brought him within sight of his home.

"Is father all right?" he asked Mrs. Baggert, who was out on the front porch, as though waiting for him.

"Oh, yes, Tom, he's all right," the housekeeper answered.

"Is Mr. Damon with him ?"

"No."

"He hasn't gone home, has he?"

"No, he's around somewhere. But some one else is with your father. Some visitors."

"Any relations?"

"No; strangers. They came to see you, and they're rather impatient. I came out to see if you were in sight. Your father sent me."

"Are they bothering him—talking business that I ought to attend to when he's ill? That mustn't be."

"Well, I suppose it is business that the strangers are talking over with your father, Tom," said Mrs. Baggert, "for I heard sums of money spoken of. But your father seems to be all right, only a trifle anxious that you should come."

"Well, I'm here now and I'll attend to things. Where are the strangers, and who are they?"

"I don't know," answered the housekeeper. "I never saw them before, but they're in the library with your father. Do you think they'll stay to dinner? If you do, I'll have Eradicate or Koku catch and kill a chicken."

"If you let one do it don't tell the other about it," said Tom with a laugh, "or you'll have a chicken race around the yard that will make the visitors sit up and take notice."

There was great rivalry between Eradicate Sampson, the aged colored man, and Koku, the giant, and they were continually disputing. Each one loved and served Tom in his own way, and there was jealousy between them. Koku, the giant Tom had brought with him from the land where the young inventor had been made captive, was a big, powerful man, and could do things the aged colored servant could not attempt. But "Rad," as he was often called, and his mule "Boomerang" had long been fixtures on the Swift homestead. But old age crept on apace with Eradicate, though he hated to admit it, and Koku did many things the colored man had formerly attended to, and Rad was always on the lookout not to be supplanted. Hence Tom's warning to Mrs. Baggert about letting the two be entrusted with the same mission of catching a chicken for the pot.

"Better get the fowl yourself and say nothing to either of them about it," Tom advised the housekeeper. "Mr. Damon will stay to dinner, as he always does when he comes, and as it's near twelve now, and as I may be delayed talking business to these strangers, you'd better get up a bigger meal than usual."

"I will, Tom," promised Mrs. Baggert. And then the young inventor, having seen that one of the men took the automobile to the garage, went into the house.

"Oh, here you are!" was his father's greeting, as he came out into the hall from the library. "I've been waiting anxiously for you, my boy. I couldn't think what was keeping you."

"Oh, I had a little trouble with the air machine—nothing serious."

A moment later Tom was standing before two well-dressed, prosperous-looking business men, who smiled pleasantly at him.

"Mr. Thomas Swift?" interrogated one, the elder, as he held out his hand.

"That's my name," answered Tom, pleasantly.

"I'm Peton Gale, and this gentleman is Boland Ware," went on the man who had taken Tom's hand. "I'm president and he's treasurer of the Universal Flying Machine Company, of New York."

"Oh, yes," said Tom, as he shook hands with Mr. Ware. "I have heard of your concern. You are doing a lot of government work, are you not?"

"Yes; war orders. And we're up to our neck in them. This war is going to be almost as much fought in the air as on the ground, Mr. Swift."

"I can well believe that," agreed Tom. "Won't you have a chair?"

"Well, we didn't come to stay long," said Mr. Gale with a laugh, which, somehow or other, grated on Tom and seemed to him insincere. "Our business is such a rushing one that we don't spend much time anywhere. To get down to brass tacks, we have come to see you to put a certain proposition before you, Mr. Swift. You are open to a business proposition, aren't you?"

"Oh, yes," answered Tom. "That's what I'm here for."

"I thought so. Well, now I'll tell you, in brief, what we want, and then Mr. Ware, our treasurer, can elaborate on it, and give you facts and figures about which I never bother myself. I attend to the executive end and leave the details to others," and again came that laugh which Tom did not like.

"You came here to make me an offer?" asked the young inventor, wondering to which of his many machines the visitors had reference.

"Yes," went on Mr. Gale, "we came here to make you a big offer. In short, Mr. Swift, we want you to work for our company, and we are willing to pay you ten thousand dollars a year for the benefit of your advice and your inventive abilities. Ten thousand dollars a year! Do you accept?"

Mr. Damon's *Whizzer*

Characteristic it was of Tom Swift that he did not seem at all surprised at what most young men would call a liberal offer. Certainly not many youths of Tom's age would be sought out by a big manufacturing concern, and offered ten thousand dollars a year "right off the reel," as Ned Newton expressed it later. But Tom only smiled and shook his head in negation.

"What!" cried Mr. Gale, "you mean you won't accept our offer?"

"I can't," answered Tom.

"You can't!" exclaimed the treasurer, Mr. Ware. "Oh, I see. Mr. Gale, a word with you. Excuse us a moment," he added to Tom and his father.

The two men consulted in a corner of the library for a moment, and then, with smiles on their faces, once more turned toward the young inventor.

"Well, perhaps you are right, Tom Swift," said Mr. Gale. "Of course, we recognize your talents and ability, but you cannot blame us for trying to get talent, as well as material for our airships, in the cheapest market. But we are not hide-bound, nor sticklers for any set sum. We'll make that offer fifteen thousand dollars a year, if you will sign a five-year contract and agree that we shall have first claim on anything and everything you may patent or invent in that time. Now, how does that strike you? Fifteen thousand dollars a year—paid weekly if you wish, and our Mr. Ware, here, has a form of contract which can be fixed up and signed within ten minutes, if you agree."

"Well, I don't like to be disagreeable," said Tom with a smile; "but, really, as I said before, I can't accept your very kind offer. I may say liberal offer. I appreciate that."

"You can't accept!" cried Mr. Gale.

"Are you sure you don't mean 'won't'?" asked Mr. Ware, in a half growl.

"You may call it that if you like," replied Tom, a bit coolly, for he did not like the other's tone, "Only, as I say, I cannot accept. I have other plans."

"Oh, you—" began the brusk treasurer, but Mr. Gale, the president of the Universal Flying Machine Company, stopped his associate with a warning look.

"Just a moment, Mr. Swift," begged the president. "Don't be hasty. We are prepared to make you a last and final offer, and I do not believe you can refuse it."

"Well, I certainly will not refuse it without hearing it," said Tom, with a smile he meant to make good-natured. Yet, truth to tell, he did not at all like the two visitors. There was something about them that aroused his antagonism, and he said later that even if they had offered him a sum which he felt he ought not, in justice to himself and his father, refuse, he would have felt a distaste in working for a company represented by the twain.

"This is our offer," said Mr. Gale, and he spoke in a pompous manner which seemed to say: "If you don't take it, why, it will be the worse for you." He looked at his treasurer for a confirmatory nod and, receiving it, went on. "We are prepared to offer and pay you, and will enter into such a contract, with the stipulation about the inventions that I mentioned before—we are prepared to pay you—twenty thousand dollars a year! Now what do you say to that, Tom Swift?

"Twenty-thousand-dollars-a-year!" repeated Mr. Gale unctuously, rolling the words off his tongue. "Twen-ty-thou-sand-dol-lars-a-year! Think of it!"

"I am thinking of it," said Tom Swift gently, "and I thank you for your offer. It is, indeed, very generous. But I must give you the same answer. I cannot accept."

"Tom!" exclaimed his aged father.

"Mr. Swift!" exclaimed the two visitors.

Tom smiled and shook his head.

"Oh, I know very well what I am saying, and what I am turning down," he said. "But I simply cannot accept. I have other plans. I am sorry you have had your trip for nothing," he added to the visitors, "but, really, I must refuse."

"Is that your final answer?" asked Mr. Gale.

"Yes."

"Don't you want to take a day or two to think it over?" asked the treasurer. "Don't be hasty. Remember that very few young men can command that salary, and I may say you will find us liberal in other ways. You would have some time to yourself."

"That is what I most need," returned Tom. "Time to myself. No, thank you, gentlemen, I cannot accept."

"Be careful!" warned Mr. Gale, and it sounded as though there might be a threat in his voice. "This is our last offer, and your last chance. We will not renew this. If you do not accept our twenty thousand dollars now, you will never get it again."

"I realize that," said Tom, "and I am prepared to take the consequences.

"Very well, then," said Mr. Gale. "There seems nothing for us to do, Mr. Ware, but to go back to New York. I bid you good-day," and he bowed stiffly to Tom. "I hope you will not regret your refusal of our offer."

"I hope so myself," said Tom, lightly.

When the visitors had gone Mr. Swift turned toward his son, and, shaking his head, remarked:

"Of course, you know your own business best, Tom. Yet I cannot but feel you have made a mistake."

"How?" asked Tom. "By not taking that money? I can easily make that in a year, with an idea I have in mind for an improvement on an airship.

And your new electric motor will soon be ready for the market. Besides, we don't really need the money."

"No, not now, Tom, but there is no telling when we may," said Mr. Swift, slowly. "This big war has made many changes, and things that brought us in a good income before, hardly sell at all, now."

"Oh, don't worry, Dad! We still have a few shots left in the locker—in other words, the bank. I'm expecting Ned Newton over any moment now, to give us the annual statement of our account, and then we'll know where we stand. I'm not afraid from the money end. Our business has done well, and it is going to do better. I have a new idea."

"That's all very well, Tom," said Mr. Swift, who seemed oppressed by something. "As you say, money isn't everything, and I know we shall always have enough to live on. But there is something about those two men I do not like. They were very angry at your refusal of their offer. I could see that. Tom, I don't want to be a croaker, but I think you'll have to watch out for those men. They're going to be your enemies—your rivals in the airship field," and Mr. Swift shook his head dolefully.

"Well, rivalry, when it's clean and above board, is the spice of trade and invention," returned ~Tom, lightly. "I'm not afraid of that."

"No, but it may be unfair and underhand," said Mr. Swift. "I think it would have been better, Tom, to have accepted their offer. Twenty thousand a year, clear money, is a good sum."

"Yes, but I may make twice that with something that occurred to me only a little while ago. Forget about those men, Dad, and I'll tell you my new idea. But wait, I want Mr. Damon to hear it, too. Where is he?"

"He was here a little while ago. He went out when those two men came and—"

At that moment, from the garden at the side of the library, the sound of voices in dispute could be heard.

"Now yo' all g'wan 'way from yeah!" exclaimed some one who could be none other than Eradicate Sampson. "Whut fo' yo' all want to clutter up dish yeah place fo'? Massa Tom said I was to do de garden wuk, an' I'se gwine to do it! G'wan 'way, Giant!"

"Ho! You want me to get out, s'pose you put me, black face!" cried a big voice, that of Koku, the giant.

"There they go! At it again!" cried Tom with a smile. "Might have known if I told Rad to do anything that Koku would be jealous. Well, I'll have to go out now and give that giant something to do that will tax his strength."

But as Tom was about to leave the room another voice was heard in the garden.

"Now, boys, be nice," said some one soothingly. "The garden is large enough for you both to work in. Rad, you begin at the lower end and spade toward the middle. Koku, you begin at the upper end and work down. Whoever gets to the middle first will win."

"Ha! Den I'll show dat giant some spade wuk as is spade wuk!" cried the colored man. "Garden wuk is mah middle name."

"Be careful, Rad!" laughed Mr. Damon, for he it was who was trying to act as peacemaker. "Remember that Koku is very strong."

"Yas, sah! He may be strong, but he's clumsy!" chuckled Eradicate. "You watch me beat him!"

"Ho! Black man get stuck in mud!" challenged Koku. "I show him!"

Then there was silence, and Tom and his father, looking out, saw the two disputants beginning to spade the soil while Mr. Damon, satisfied that he had, for the time being, stopped a quarrel, turned toward the house.

"I was just coming to look for you," said Tom. "Sorry I had to go off in such a hurry and leave you, but I had promised to take Mary for a ride, and as it was her first one, for a distance, I didn't want her to back out."

"That's all right, Tom, that's all right!" said Mr. Damon genially. "Ladies first every time. But I do want to see you, and it's about something important."

"No trouble, I hope?" queried Tom, for the manner of the eccentric man was rather grave.

"Trouble? Oh, no! Bless my frying pan, no trouble, Tom! In fact, it may be the other way about. Tom, I have an idea, and there may be millions in it! That's it—millions!"

"Good!" cried the young inventor. "Might as well bite off a big lump while you're at it. So you have a new idea! Well, I have myself, but I'll listen to yours first. What is it, Mr. Damon?"

"It's a new kind of airship, Tom. I haven't got it all worked out yet, but I can give you a rough outline. On my way over I got to thinking about balloons, aeroplanes and the like, and it occurred to me that the present principles are all wrong."

"So I evolved a new type of machine. I'm going to call it the Damon *Whizzer*. Maybe Demon *Whizzer* would be more appropriate, but we won't decide on that now. Anyhow, it's going to be a whizzer, and I want to talk to you about it. There is an entirely new principle of elevation and propulsion involved in my *Whizzer*, and I—"

At that moment there came a crash and clatter of steel and wood from the garden, out of sight of which Tom and Mr. Damon had walked while talking. Then followed a jangle of words.

"They're at it again!" cried Tom, as he ran toward the side of the house. "I guess it's a fight this time!"

Tom's Project

Curious was the sight that met the gaze of Tom Swift and Mr. Wakefield Damon as they rounded the corner of the house and looked into the newly spaded garden. There stood the giant, Koku, holding aloft in the air, by one hand, the form of the struggling colored man, Eradicate Sampson. And Eradicate was vainly trying to get at his enemy and rival, but was prevented by the long-distance hold the giant had on him.

"Yo' let me go, now! Yo' let me go, big man cried Eradicate. "Ef yo' don't I'll bust yo' wide open, dat's whut I'll do! An' 'sides, I'll tell Massa Tom on yo', dat's whut I'll do!"

"Ho! You tell—I let you fall!" threatened Koku.

His threat was dire enough, for such was his size and strength that he held the colored man nearly nine feet from the ground, and a fall from that distance would seriously jar Eradicate, if it did nothing else. The colored man's eyes opened wide as he heard what Koku said, and then he cried:

"Let me down! Let me down, an' I won't say nuffin!"

"An' you let me scatter dirt?" asked Koku. for such was the giant's idea of working in the garden.

"Yes, yo' kin scatter de dirt seben ways from Sunday fo' all I keers!" conceded Eradicate. Then, as he was lowered to the ground, he and the giant turned and saw Mr. Damon and Tom approaching.

"What's wrong?" asked the young inventor.

"'Scuse me, Massa Tom," began Eradicate, "but didn't yo' tell me to spade de garden?"

"I guess I did," admitted Tom Swift.

"An' you tell me help—yes?" questioned Koku.

"Well, I thought it would be a little too much for you, Rad," said Tom, gently. "I thought perhaps you'd like help."

"Hu! Not him, anyhow!" declared the colored man in great disgust. "When I git so old dat I cain't spade a garden, den me an' Boomerang, we-all gwine to die, dat's all I got to say. I was a-spadin' my part ob de garden, Massa Tom, same laik Mr. Damon done tole me to, an' dish yeah big mess ob bones steps on my side ob de middle an—"

"Him too slow. Koku scatter dirt twice times so fast!" declared the giant, whose English was not much better than Eradicate's.

"Yes, I see," said Tom. "You are so strong, Koku, that you finished your part before Eradicate did. Well, it was good of you to want to help him."

At this the giant grinned at his rival.

"At the same time," went on Tom, winking an eye at Mr. Damon, "Eradicate knows a little more about garden work, on account of having done it so many years."

"Ha! Whut I tell yo', Giant!" boasted the colored man. It was his turn to smile.

"And so," went on Tom, judicially, "I guess I'll let Rad finish spading the garden, and you, Koku, can come and help me lift some heavy engine parts. Mr. Damon wants to explain something to me."

"Ha! Nothing what so heavy Koku not lift!" boasted the giant.

"Go on! Lift yo'se'f 'way from heah!" muttered Eradicate as he picked up his dropped spade. And then, with a smile of satisfaction, he fell to work in the mellow soil while Tom led Koku to one of the shops where he set him to lifting heavy motor parts about in order to get at a certain machine that was stored away in the back of one of the rooms.

"That will keep him busy," said the young inventor. "And now, Mr. Damon, I can listen to you. Do you really think you have a new idea in airships?"

"I really think so, Tom. My *Whizzer* is bound to revolutionize travel in the air. Let me tell you what I mean. Now cast your mind back. How many ways are now used to propel an airship or a dirigible balloon through the air? How many ways?"

"Two, as far as I know," said Tom. "At least there are only two that have proved to be practical."

"Exactly," said Mr. Damon. "One with the propeller, or propellers, in front, and that is the tractor type. The other has the propeller in the rear, and that is the pusher type. Both good as far as they go, but I have something better."

"What?" asked Tom with a smile.

"It's a *Whizzer*," said the eccentric man. "Bless my gold tooth! but that is the best name I can think of for it. And, really, the propeller I'm thinking of inventing does whiz around."

"But are you going to use a tractor or pusher type?" Tom wanted to know.

"It's a combination of both," answered Mr. Damon. "As it is now, Tom, you have to get an aeroplane in pretty speedy motion before it will rise from the ground, don't you?"

"Yes, of course. That's the principle on which an aeroplane rises and keeps aloft, by its speed in the air. As soon as that speed stops it begins to fall, or volplane, as we call it."

"Exactly. Now, instead of having to depend on the speed of the aeroplane for this, why not depend on the speed of the propeller —in other words, the whizzer?"

"Well, we do," said Tom, a bit puzzled as to what his friend was trying to get at. "If the propeller didn't move the airship wouldn't rise—that is, unless it's of the balloon type."

"What I mean," said Mr. Damon, "is to have an aeroplane that will move in the air the same as a boat moves in the water. You don't have to get the propeller of a boat racing around at the rate of a million revolutions a minute, more or less, before your boat will travel, do you? If the engine turns the screw, or propeller, just over say fifty times a minute you would get some motion of the boat, wouldn't you?"

"Why, yes, some," admitted Tom.

"And what causes it?" asked Mr. Damon, anticipating a triumph.

"The resistance of the water to the blades of the screw, or propeller," answered Tom.

"Exactly! And it's the resistance of the air to the blades of an airship propeller that sends the craft along, isn't it?"

"Yes. And because of the difference in density between air and water it becomes necessary to revolve an aeroplane propeller many times faster than a boat propeller. It's the density that makes the difference, Mr. Damon. If air were as dense as water we could have comparatively slow-moving motors and propellers and—"

"Ha! There you have it, Tom! And there is where my *Whizzer*— Wakefield Damon's *Whizzer*—is going to revolutionize air travel!" cried the eccentric man. "The difference in density! If air were as dense as water the problem would be solved. And I have solved it! I'm going to turn the trick, Tom! One more question. How can air be made as dense as water, Tom Swift?"

"Why, by condensation or compression, I suppose," was the rather slow answer. "You know they have condensed, or compressed, air until it is liquid. I've done it myself, as an experiment."

"That's it, Tom! That's it!" cried Mr. Damon in delight. "Compressed air will do the trick! Not compressed to a liquid, exactly, but almost so. I'm going to revolve the propellers of my new airship in compressed air, so dense that they will not have to have a speed of more than seven hundred revolutions a minute. What's that compared to the three to ten thousand revolutions of the propellers now used? The propellers of Damon's *Whizzer* will be of the pusher type, and will revolve in dense, compressed air, almost like water, and that will do away with high speed motors, with all their complications, and make traveling in the clouds as simple as taking out a little one-cylinder motor boat. How's that, Tom Swift? How's that for an idea?"

To Mr. Damon's disappointment, Tom was not enthusiastic. The young inventor gazed at his eccentric friend, and then said slowly:

"Well, that's all right in theory, but how is it going to work out in practice?"

"That's what I came to see you about, Tom," was the reply. "Bless my tall hat! but that's just why I hurried over here. I wanted to tell you when I saw you going off on a trip with Miss Nestor. That's my big idea—Damon's *Whizzer* —propellers revolving in compressed air like water. Isn't that great?"

"I'm sorry to shatter your air castle," said Tom; "but for the life of me I can't see how it will work. Of course, in theory, if you could revolve a big-bladed propeller in very dense, or in liquid, air, there would be more resistance than in the rarefied atmosphere of the upper regions. And, if this could be done, I grant you that you could use slower motors and smaller propeller blades—more like those of a motor boat. But how are you going to get the condensed air?"

"Make it!" said Mr. Damon promptly. "Air pumps are cheap. Just carry one or two on board the aeroplane, and condense the air as you go along. That's a small detail that can easily be worked out. I leave that to you."

"I'd rather you wouldn't," said Tom. "That's the whole difficulty—compressing your air. Wait! I'll explain it to you."

Then the young inventor went into details. He told of the ponderous machinery needed to condense air to a form approximating water, and spoke of the terrible pressure exerted by the liquid atmosphere.

"Anything that you would gain by having a slow-speed motor and smaller propeller blades, would be lost by the ponderous air-condensing machinery you would need," Tom told Mr. Damon. "Besides, if you could surround your propellers with a strata of condensed air, it would create such terrible cold as to freeze the propeller blades and make them as brittle as glass.

"Why, I have taken a heavy piece of metal, dipped it into liquid air, and I could shatter the steel with a hammer as easily as a sheet of ice. The cold of liquid air is beyond belief.

"Attempts have been made to make motors run with liquid air, but they have not succeeded. To condense air and to carry it about so that propellers might revolve in it, would be out of the question."

"You think so, Tom?" asked Mr. Damon.

"I'm sure of it!"

"Oh, dear! That's too bad. Bless my overshoes, but I thought I had a new idea. Well, you ought to know. So Damon's *Whizzer* goes on the scrap heap before ever it's built. Well, we'll say no more about it. You ought to know best, Tom. I wasn't thinking of it so much for myself as for you. I thought you'd like some new idea to work on."

"Much obliged, Mr. Damon, but I have a new idea," said Tom.

"You have? What is it? Tell me—that is, if it isn't a secret," went on the eccentric man, as much delighted over Tom's new plan as he had been over his own *Whizzer*, doomed to failure so soon.

"It isn't a secret from you," said Tom. "I got the idea while I was riding with Mary. I wanted to talk to her—to tell her not to jump out when we had a little accident—but I had trouble making myself understood because of the noise of the motor."

"They do make a great racket," conceded Mr. Damon. "But I don't suppose anything can be done about it."

"I don't see why there can't!" exclaimed Tom. "And that's my new idea—to make a silent aircraft motor—perhaps silent propeller blades, though it's the motor that makes the most noise. And that's what I'm going to do—invent a silent aeroplane. Not because I want so much to talk when I take passengers up in the air, but I believe such a motor would be valuable, especially for scouting planes in war work. To go over the enemy's lines and not be heard would be valuable many times.

"And that's what I'm going to do—work on a silent motor for Uncle Sam. I've got the germ of an idea and now—"

"Excuse me," said a voice behind Mr. Damon and Tom, and, turning, the young inventor beheld the form of Mr. Peton Gale, president of the Universal Flying Machine Company.

Making Plans

Tom Swift had drawn pencil and paper from his pocket, and, as he and Mr. Damon were sitting on the steps of one of the shops, the young inventor was about to demonstrate by a drawing part of his new project, when the interruption came in the shape of one of the men who had, an hour before, made a business offer to Tom.

"Excuse me," went on Mr. Peton Gale, "but Mr. Ware and I got to talking it over on our way to the station—the matter of having you in our company, Mr. Swift—and we concluded that it was worth twenty-five thousand dollars a year for us to have you. So I came back—"

"It isn't of the slightest use, Mr. Gale, I assure you," said Tom, a bit heatedly, for he did not like the persistency of this man, nor did he like his coming on the factory grounds unannounced and in this secret manner. "I told you I could not accept your offer. It is not altogether a matter of money. My word was final."

"Oh very well, if you put it that way," said Mr. Gale stiffly, "of course there is nothing more to say. But I thought perhaps you did not consider we had offered you enough and—"

"Your offer is fair enough from a financial standpoint," said Tom; "but I simply cannot accept it. I have other plans. Jackson!" he called to one of his mechanics who was passing, "kindly see Mr. Gale to the gate, and then let me know how it was any one came in here without a permit."

"Yes, sir," said the mechanic, as he stood significantly waiting.

"There was no one at the gate when I came in," said Mr. Gale, and his manner was antagonizing. "I wanted to speak to you—to ask you to reconsider your offer—so I came back."

"It is against the rules to admit strangers to the shop grounds," said Tom. "Good-day!"

The president of the Universal Flying Machine Company did not respond, but there was a look on his face as he turned away that, had Tom seen it, might have caused him some uneasiness. But he did not see. Instead, he resumed his talk with Mr. Damon.

"Tom, your idea is most interesting," declared the eccentric man. "I hope you will be able to work it out!"

"I'm going to try," said the young inventor. "I hope that man— Mr. Gale—didn't hear anything of what I was saying. He sneaked up on us before I was aware any one was near but ourselves."

"I don't imagine he heard very much, Tom," said Mr. Damon. "He may have heard you mention a silent motor—"

"That's just what I wish he hadn't heard," broke in Tom. "That's the germ of the idea, and once it becomes known that I am working on that—

Well, there's no use crying over spilled milk," and he smiled at the homely proverb. "I'll have to work in secret, once I've started."

"Do you think the government would use it, Tom?" asked his friend.

"I should think it would be glad to. Consider what a wonderful part airships are playing in the present war. It really is a struggle to see which will be the master of the sky—the Allies or the Germans—and, up to recently, the Huns had the advantage. Then the Allies, recognizing how vital it was, began to forge ahead, and now Uncle Sam with his troops under General Pershing is leading everything, or will lead shortly. We have been a bit slow with our aircraft production, but now we are booming along. Uncle Sam will soon have the mastery of the sky."

"I hope so," sighed Mr. Damon. "We must beat the Germans!"

Briefly, Tom spoke of what Pershing's men were doing with their aeroplanes in France, and mention was made of what the French and British had done prior to the entrance of the United States into the World War.

"While we were yet neutral, Americans had made gallant names for themselves flying for France, and with my silent motor they ought to do better," declared Tom.

"Is silence its chief recommendation?" asked Mr. Damon.

"Yes," replied Tom. "Or rather, it will be when I have it perfected. Aeroplane motors now are about as compact and speedy as they can be made. It is only the terrific noise that is a handicap. It is a handicap to the pilots and observers in the craft, as they cannot communicate except through a special speaking tube, and this is not always satisfactory or sure. Then, too, the noise of an airship proclaims its approach to the enemy, sometimes long before it can be seen.

"With a silent motor all this would be done away with. With my new craft, in case I can perfect it, the enemy's lines can be approached as silently as the Indians used to approach the log cabins of the white settlers. That will be its great advantage— not that conversation can be more easily carried on, for that is, after all, an unimportant detail. But to approach the enemy's lines in the silence of the night would be a distinct gain."

"I believe it would, Tom!" exclaimed Mr. Damon. "And I should think, too, that Uncle Sam would be glad to get such a motor," he added.

"Well, he'll have one to take if he wants it, if I can make my plans a success," declared Tom. "That is, unless those other fellows get ahead of me."

"What other fellows?" asked Mr. Damon.

"Gale, Ware and their crowd," was the answer. "I fancy they are provoked because I wouldn't agree to work for them, and now, that Gale overheard—as he must have—what I propose working on, they may try that game themselves."

"You mean try to turn out a silent motor?"

"Yes. It would be a big feather in their cap for their company, so far, hasn't been very successful on government orders. That's why they came to me, I guess."

"I shouldn't be surprised, Tom," conceded Mr. Damon. "Since the government accepted your giant cannon and your great searchlight, you have come into greater prominence than ever before. And those two things are a wonderful success."

"Yes," admitted Tom, modestly enough, "the big electric light seems to have been of some benefit on the European battle front, and though they haven't been able to make and transport as many of my giant cannons as I'd like to see over there, it is progressing, I understand."

And this is true. For the details of these two inventions of Tom Swift's I refer my readers to the books bearing those titles. Sufficient to state here that the government was using these two inventions, and there had been no necessity for commandeering them either, since Tom had freely offered them at the declaration of war with Germany.

"Well, since I can't help you with my '*Whizzer*,'" said Mr. Damon, with a smile, "let me do what I can toward your silent motor, Tom. What are you going to call it?"

"Oh, I don't know—hadn't thought of a name. I guess 'Air Scout' would be as good as any. That's what it will be—a machine for silently scouting in the air. And now to get down to brass tacks, as the poet says, I believe I will—"

"Gentleman to see you, Mr. Swift," interrupted Jackson.

"Bless my penwiper!" cried Mr. Damon. "More visitors! I hope it isn't Gale or Ware come back to see what they can spy on!"

A Problem in Sound

Tom Swift looked up with a distinct appearance of being annoyed that was unusual with him, for he was, nearly always, good-natured. But the frown that had replaced the pleasant look on his face while he was talking to Mr. Damon about the projected new air scout was at once wiped away as he looked at the card Jackson held out to him.

"Bring him in right away!" he ordered. "He needn't have stood on that ceremony."

"Well, he said it was a business call," returned the mechanician with a cheerful grin, "and he said he wanted it done according to form. So he gave me his card to bring you."

"Who is it?" asked Mr. Damon, with the privilege of an old friend.

"It's Ned Newton," Tom answered; "though why he's putting on all this formality I can't fathom."

Jackson went back to the main gate and told the man on guard there to admit Ned, who had so formally sent in his card.

"Ah, Mr. Swift, I believe?" began the bank employee with that suave, formal air which usually precedes a business meeting.

"That is my name," said Tom, with a suppressed grin, and he spoke as stiffly as though to a perfect stranger.

"Mr. Tom Swift, the great inventor?" went on Ned.

"Yes."

"Ah, then I am at the right place. Just sign here, please, on the dotted line," and be held out a blank form, and a fountain pen to Tom, who took them half mechanically.

"Huh? What's the big idea, Ned?" asked the young inventor, unable longer to carry on the joke. "Is this a warrant for my arrest, or merely a testimonial to you. If it's the latter, and concerns your nerve, I'll gladly sign it."

"Well, it's something like that!" laughed Ned. "That's your application for another block of Liberty Bonds, Tom, and I want you, as a personal favor to me, as a business favor to the bank, and as your plain duty to Uncle Sam, to double your last subscription."

Tom looked at the sum Ned had filled in on the blank form, and uttered a slight whistle of surprise.

"That's all right now," said Ned, with the air of a professional salesman. "You can stand that and more, too. I'm letting you off easy. Why, I got Mary's father—Mr. Nestor—for twice what he took last time, and Mary herself—hard as she's working for the Red Cross—gave me a nice application. So it's up to you to—"

"Nuff said!" exclaimed Tom, sententiously, as he signed his name. "I may have to reconsider my recent refusal of the offer of the Universal

Flying Machine Company, though, if I haven't money enough to meet this subscription, Ned."

"Oh, you'll meet it all right! Much obliged," and Ned folded the Liberty Bond subscription paper and put it in his pocket. "But did you turn down the offer from those people?"

"I did," answered Tom. "But how did you know about it, Ned?"

"First let me say that I'm glad you decided to have nothing to do with them. They're a rich firm, and have lots of money, but I wouldn't trust 'em, even if they have some government contracts. The way I happened to know they were likely to make you an offer is this," continued Ned Newton.

"They do business with one of the New York banks with which my bank—notice the accent on the my, Tom—is connected. The other day I happened to see some correspondence about you. These flying machine people asked our bank to find out certain things about you, and, as a matter of business, we had to give the information. Sort of a commercial agency report, you know, nothing unusual, and it isn't the first time it's been done since your business got so large. But that's how I happened to know these fellows contemplated dickering with you."

"Do you know Gale or Ware?" Tom asked.

"Not personally. But in a business way, Tom, I'd warn you to look out for them, as they're sharp dealers. They put one over on the government all right, and there may be some unpleasant publicity to it later. But they're putting up a big bluff, and pretending they can turn out a lot of flying machines for use in Europe. Why don't you get busy on that end of the game, Tom?"

"I know you've more than done your bit, with Liberty Bonds, subscriptions to the Y. M. C. A. and other war work, besides your war tank and other inventions. But you're such a shark on flying machines I should think you'd offer your factory to the government for the production of aeroplanes."

"I would in a minute, Ned, and you know it; but the fact of the matter is my shops aren't equipped for the production of anything in large numbers. We do mostly an experimenting business here, making only one or two of a certain machine. I have told the government officials they can have anything I've got, and you know they wouldn't let me enlist when I was working on the war tank."

"Yes, I remember that," said Ned. "You're no slacker! I wanted to shoulder a rifle, too, but they keep me at this Liberty Loan work. Well, Uncle Sam ought to know."

"That's what I say," agreed Tom, "and that's why I haven't gone to the front myself. And now, as it happens, I've got something else in mind that may help Uncle Sam."

"What is it?"

"A silent flying machine for scout work on the battle front," Tom told his friend, and then he gave a few details, such as those he had been telling Mr. Damon.

"Then I don't wonder you turned down the offer of the Universal people," remarked Ned, at the conclusion of the recital. "This will be a heap more help to the government, Tom, than working for those people, even at twenty-five thousand dollars a year. And if you get short, and can't meet your newest Liberty Bond payments, why, I guess the bank will stretch your credit a little."

"Thanks!" laughed Tom, "but I'll try not to ask them."

The friends talked together a little longer, and then Ned had to take his departure to solicit more subscriptions, while Mr. Damon went with him, the eccentric man saying he would go home to Waterfield.

"But, bless my overshoes, Tom!" he exclaimed, as he departed, "don't forget to let me know when you have your silent motor working. I want to see it."

"I'll let you know," was the promise given by the young inventor.

"And watch out for those Universal people," warned Ned. "I'm not telling you this as a bank official, for I'm not supposed to, but it's personal."

"I'll be on the watch," said Tom. And, as he went into his private workshop, he wondered why it was his father and Ned had both warned him not to trust Gale and Ware.

The next few days were busy ones for Tom Swift. Once he had made up his mind to go to work seriously on a silent motor, all else was put aside. He sent a note to Mary Nestor, telling her what he was going to do, and, asking her to say nothing about it, which, of course, Mary agreed to.

"Come and see me when you can," she sent back word, "but I know you won't have much chance when you're experimenting with your invention. And I shall be working so hard for the Red Cross that I sha'n't get much chance to entertain you. But the war can't last forever."

"No," agreed Tom with a sigh, as he put away her letter, "and thank goodness that it can't!"

The young inventor threw himself into the perplexing work of inventing a silent motor with all the fervor he had given to the production of his war tank, his giant cannon, his wonderful searchlight and other machines.

"And," mused Tom, as he sat at his work table with pencil and paper before him, "since this is a problem in acoustics, I had best begin. I suppose by going back to first principles, and after determining what makes an aeroplane engine noisy, try to figure out how to make it quiet. Now as to the first, the principle causes of noise are—"

And at that instant there broke on Tom's ears a succession of discordant sounds which seemed to be a combination of an Indian's war whoop and a college student's yells at a football game.

"Now I wonder what that is!" mused the young inventor as he hastily arose. "Better solve that problem before I tackle the aeroplane motor."

Through the Roof

Tom rushed from his private office, and when he reached the outer door he heard with more distinctness the sounds that had alarmed him. They seemed to come from a small building given over to electrical apparatus, and which, at the time, was not supposed to be in use. It had been Tom's workroom, so to speak, when he was developing his electric runabout and rifle, but of late he had not spent much time in it.

"Somebody's in there!" reflected the young inventor, as he heard yells coming from the open door of the place. "And if it isn't Koku and Eradicate I miss my guess! Wonder what they can be doing there."

He crossed the yard between his private office and the electrical shop in a few rapid strides, and, as he entered the latter place, he was greeted with a series of wild yells.

"Good volume of sound here, at all events," mused Tom. "Almost as much as my motor made when I was trying to talk to Mary. Hello there! What's going on? Is any one hurt? What's the matter?" he cried, for, at first, he could see no one in the dim light of the place. The interior was a maze of electrical apparatus.

"Who's here?" demanded Tom, as he advanced.

"Oh, Master! Come quick! Koku 'most dead an' no can let go!" was the cry.

"Yo' jest bet yo' cain't let go!" chimed in the voice of Eradicate. "I done knowed yo' would git into trouble ef yo' come heah, an' I'se glad ob it! So I is!"

"What is it, Rad? What has happened to Koku?" cried Tom, running forward, for though no very powerful current could be turned on in the electrical shop at this period of unuse, there was enough to be very painful. "What is it, Rad?"

"Oh, dat big foolish giant, Koku, done got his se'f into trouble!" chuckled the colored man. "He done got holt ob one ob dem air contraptions, Massa Tom, an' he cain't let go! Ha! Ha! Golly! Look at him squirm!" and Rad laughed shrilly, which accounted for some of the sounds Tom had heard.

Then came yells of rage and pain from the giant, and they were so loud and vigorous, mingling with Eradicate's as they did, that it was no wonder Tom was startled. The sounds were heard in the other shops, and men came running out. But before then Tom had put an end to the trouble.

One look showed him what had happened. Just how or why Koku and Eradicate had entered the electrical shop Tom did not then stop to inquire. But he saw that the giant had grasped the handles of one of the electric machines, designed for charging Leyden jars used in Tom's experiments, and the powerful, though not dangerous, current had so paralyzed, temporarily, the muscles of the giant's hands and arms that he

could not let go, and there he was, squirming, and not knowing how to
turn off the current, and unable to ease himself, while Eradicate stood
and laughed at him, fairly howling with delight.

"Ha! Guess yo' won't do no mo' spadin' in' Massa Tom's garden right
away, big man!" taunted Eradicate.

"Be quiet, Rad!" ordered Tom, as he reached up and pulled out the
switch, thus shutting off the current. "This isn't anything to laugh at."

"But he done look so funny, Massa Tom!" pleaded the colored man. "He
done squirm laik—"

But Eradicate did not finish what he intended to say. Once free from
the powerful current, the giant looked at his numb hands, and then,
seeming to think that Eradicate was the cause of it all, he sprang at the
colored man with a yell. But Eradicate did not stay to see what would
happen. With a howl of terror, he raced out of the door, and, old and
rheumatic as he was, he managed to gain the stable of his mule,
Boomerang, over which he had his humble but comfortable quarters.

"Well, I guess he's safe for a while!" laughed Tom, as he saw the giant
turn away, shaking his fist at the closed door, for Koku, big as he was,
stood in mortal terror of the mule's heels.

Tom locked the door of the electrical shop and Went back to his
interrupted problem. From Jackson he learned that Koku and Eradicate
had merely happened to stroll into the forbidden place, which had been
left open by accident. There, it appeared, Koku had handled some of the
machinery, ending by switching on the current of the machine the handles
of which he later unsuspectingly picked up. Then he received a shock he
long remembered, and for many days he believed Eradicate had been
responsible for it, and there was more than the usual hostile feeling
between the two. But Eradicate was innocent of that trick, at all events.

"Though," said Tom, telling his father about it later, "Rad would have
turned on the current if he had known he could make trouble for Koku by
it. I never saw their like for having disagreements!"

"Yes, but they are both devoted to you, Tom," said the aged inventor.
"But what is this you hinted at—a silent motor you called it, I believe? Are
you really serious in trying to invent one?"

"Yes, Dad, I am. I think there's a big field for an aeroplane that could
travel along over the enemy's lines—particularly at night—and not be
heard from below. Think of the scout work that could be done.

"Well, yes, it could be done if you could get a silent motor, or propellers
that made no noise, Tom. But I don't believe it can be done."

"Well, maybe not, Dad. But I'm going to try!" and Tom, after a further
talk with his father, began work in earnest on the big problem. That it
was a big one Tom was not disposed to deny, and that it would be a
valuable invention even his somewhat skeptical father admitted.

"How are you going to start, Tom?" asked Mr. Swift, several days after
the big idea had come to the young man.

"I'm going to experiment a bit, at first. I've got a lot of old motors, that weren't speedy enough for any of my flying machines, and I'm going to make them over. If I spoil them the loss won't amount to anything, and if I succeed —well, maybe I can help out Uncle Sam a bit more."

As Tom had said he would do, he began at the very foundation, and studied the fundamental principles of sound.

"Sound," the young inventor told Ned Newton, in speaking about the problem, "is a sensation which is peculiar to the ear, though the vibrations caused by sound waves may be felt in many parts of the body. But the ear is the great receiver of sound."

"You aren't going to invent a sort of muffler for the ears, are you, Tom?" asked Ned. "That would be an easy way of solving the problem, but I doubt if you could get the Germans to wear your ear-tabs so they wouldn't hear the sound of the Allied aeroplanes."

"No, I'm not figuring on doing the trick that way," said Tom with a laugh. "I've really got to cut down the sound of the motor and the propeller blades, so a person, listening with all his ears, won't hear any noise, unless he's within a few feet of the plane."

"Well, I can tell you, right off the reel, how to do it," said the bank employee.

"How?" asked Tom eagerly.

"Run your engine and propellers in a vacuum," was the prompt reply.

"Hum!" said Tom, musingly. "Yes, that would be a simple way out, and I'll do it, if you'll tell me how to breathe in a vacuum."

"Oh, I didn't agree to do that," laughed Ned.

But he had spoken the truth, as those who have studied physics well know. There must be an atmosphere for the transmission of sound, which is the reason all is cold and silent and still at the moon. There is no atmosphere there. Sound implies vibration. Something, such as liquid, gas, or solid, must be set in motion to produce sound, and for the purpose of science the air we breathe may be considered a gas, being composed of two.

Not only must the object, either solid, liquid, or gaseous, be in motion to produce sound, but the air surrounding the vibrating body must also be moving in unison with it. And lastly there must be some medium of receiving the sound waves—the ear or some part of the body. Totally deaf persons may be made aware of sound through the vibrations received through their hands or feet. They receive, of course, only the more intense, or largest, sound waves, and can not hear notes of music nor spoken words, though they may feel the vibration when a piano is played. And, as Ned has said, no sound is produced in a vacuum.

"But," said Tom, "since I can't run my aeroplane in a vacume, or even have the propellers revolve in one, it's up to me to solve the problem some other way. The propellers don't really make noise enough to worry about when they're high in the air. It's the exhaust from the motor, and to get rid of that will be my first attempt."

"Can it be done?" asked Ned.

"I don't know," was Tom's frank answer.

"They do it on an automobile to a great extent," went on Ned. "Some of 'em you cant hardly hear."

"Yes, but an aeroplane engine runs many, many times faster than the motor of an auto," said Tom, "and there are more explosions to muffle. I doubt if the muffler of an auto would cut down the sound of an aero engine to any appreciable extent. But, of course, I'll try along those lines."

"They have mufflers or silencers for guns and rifles," went on Ned. "Couldn't you make a big one of those contraptions and put it on an aeroplane?"

"I doubt it," said Tom, shaking his head. "Of course it's the same principle as that in an auto muffler, or on a motor boat—a series of baffle plates arranged within a hollow cylinder. But all such devices cut down power, and I don't want to do that. However, I'm going to solve the problem or—bust!"

And Tom came near "busting," Ned remarked later, when he and his friend talked over the progress of the invention.

Two weeks had passed since the start of his evolution of his new idea, and following the visiting of the representatives of the Universal Flying Machine Company. Since then neither Gale nor Ware had communicated with Tom.

"But I must be on the watch against them," thought the young inventor. "I'm pretty sure Gale heard me mention what I was going to try to invent, and he may get ahead of me, and put a silent motor on the market first. Not that I'm afraid of being done out of any profits, but I simply don't want to be beaten."

The details of Tom's invention cannot be gone into, but, roughly, it was based on the principle of not only a muffler but also of producing less noise when the charges of gasoline exploded in the cylinders. It is, of course, the explosion of gasoline mixed with air that causes an internal combustion engine to operate. And it is the expulsion of the burned gases that causes the exhaust and makes the noise that is heard.

Tom was working along the well-known line of the rate of travel of sound, which progresses at the rate of about 1090 feet a second when air is at the freezing point. And, roughly, with every degree increase in the atmosphere's temperature the velocity of sound increases by one foot. Thus at a temperature of 100 degrees Fahrenheit, or 68 degrees above freezing, there would be added to the 1090 feet the 68 feet, making sound travel at 100 degrees Fahrenheit about 1158 feet a second.

Tom had set up in his shop a powerful, but not very speedy, old aeroplane engine, and had attached to it the device he hoped would help him toward solving his problem of cutting down the noise. He had had some success with it, and, after days and nights of labor, he invited his father and Ned, as well as Mr. Damon, over to see what he hoped would be a final experiment.

His visitors had assembled in the shop, and Eradicate was setting out some refreshments which Tom had provided, the colored man being in his element now.

"What's all this figuring, Tom ?" asked Mr. Damon, as he saw a series of calculations on some sheets of paper lying on Tom's desk.

"That's where I worked out how much faster sound traveled in hydrogen gas than in the ordinary atmosphere," was the answer. "It goes about four times as fast, or nearly four thousand two hundred feet a second. You remember the rule, I suppose. 'The speed of sonorous vibrations through gases varies inversely as the squares of the weights of equal volumes of the gases,' or, in other words—"

"Give it to us chiefly in 'other words,' if you please, Tom!" pleaded Ned, with a laugh. "Let that go and do some tricks. Start the engine and let's see if we can hear it."

"Oh, you can hear it all right," said Tom, as he approached the motor, which was mounted on a testing block. "The thing isn't perfected yet, but I hope to have it soon. Rad! Where is that black rascal? Oh, there you are! Come here, Rad!"

"Yaas sah, Massa Tom! Is I gwine to help yo' all in dish yeah job?"

"Yes. Just take hold of this lever, and when I say so pull it as hard as you can."

"Dat's whut I will, Massa Tom. Golly! ef dat no 'count giant was heah now he'd see he ain't de only one whut's got muscle. I'll pull good an' hard, Massa Tom."

"Yes, that's what I want you to. Now I guess we're all ready. Can you see, Dad—and Ned and Mr. Damon?"

"Yes," they answered. They stood near the side wall of the shop, while Tom and Eradicate were at the testing block, on which the motor, with the noise-eliminating devices attached, had been temporarily mounted.

"All ready," called the young inventor, as he turned on the gas and threw over the electrical switch. "All ready! Pull the starting lever, Rad. and when it's been running a little I'll throw on the silencer and you can see the difference."

The motor began to hum, and there was a deafening roar, just as there always is when the engine of an aeroplane starts. It was as though half a dozen automobile engines were being run with the mufflers cut out.

"Now I'll show you the difference!" yelled Tom, though such was the noise that not a word could be heard. "This shows you what my silencer will do."

Tom pulled another lever. There was at once a cessation of the deafening racket, though it was not altogether ended. Then, after a moment or two, there suddenly came a roar as though a blast had been let off in the shop.

Tom and Eradicate were tossed backward, head over heels, as though by the giant hands of Koku himself, and Mr. Damon, Ned, and Tom's father saw the motor fly from the testing block and shoot through the roof of the building with a rending, crashing, and splintering sound that could be heard for a mile.

After a Spy

Curious as it may seem, Eradicate, the oldest and certainly not the most energetic of the party assembled in the experiment room, was the first to recover himself and arise. Tottering to his feet he gave one look at the testing block, whence the motor had torn itself. Then he looked at the prostrate figures around him, none of them hurt, but all stunned and very much startled. Then the gaze of Eradicate traveled to the hole in the roof. It was a gaping, ragged hole, for the motor was heavy and the roof of flimsy material. And then the colored man exclaimed:

"Good land ob massy! Did I do dat?"

His tone was one of such startled contrition, and so tragic, that Tom Swift, rueful as he felt over the failure of his experiment and the danger they had all been in, could not help laughing.

"I take it, hearing that from you, Tom, that we're all right," said Ned Newton, as he recovered himself and brushed some dirt off his coat. Ned was a natty dresser.

"Yes, we seem to be all right," replied Tom slowly. "I can't say what damage the flying motor has done outside, but—"

"Bless my insurance policy! but what happened?" asked Mr. Damon. "I saw Eradicate pull on that lever as you told him to, Tom, and then things all went topsy-turvy! Did he pull the wrong handle?"

"No, it wasn't Rad's fault at all," said Tom. "The trouble was, as I guess I'll find when I investigate, that I put too much power into the motor, and the muffler didn't give any chance for the accumulated exhaust gases to expand and escape. I didn't allow for that, and they simply backed up, compressed and exploded. I guess that's the whole explanation."

"I'm inclined to agree with you, Son," said Mr. Swift dryly. "Don't try to get rid of all the noise at once. Eliminate it by degrees and it will be safer."

"I guess so," agreed Tom.

By this time a score of workmen from the other shops had congregated around the one though the roof of which the motor had been blown. Tom opened the door to assure Jackson and the others that no one was hurt, and then the young inventor saw the exploded motor had buried in the dirt a short distance away from the experiment building.

"Lucky none of us were standing over it when it went up," said Tom, as he made an inspection of the broken machine. "We'd have gone through the roof with it."

"She certainly went sailing!" commented Ned. "Must have been a lot of power there, Tom."

And this was evidenced by the bent and twisted rods that had held the motor to the testing block, and by the cylinders, some of which were torn apart as though made of paper instead of heavy steel. But for the fact that all the force of the explosion was directly upward, instead of at the sides, none might have been left alive in the shop. All had escaped most fortunately, and they realized this.

"Well," queried Ned, as Tom gave orders to have the damaged machine removed and the roof repaired, "does this end the wonderful silent motor, Tom?"

"End it! What do you mean—"

"I mean are you going to experiment any further?"

"Why, of course! Just because I've had one failure doesn't mean that I'm going to give up. Especially when I know what the matter was—not leaving any vent for the escaping gases. Why this isn't anything. When I was perfecting my giant cannon I was nearly blown up more than once, and you remember how we got stuck in the submarine."

"I should say I did!" exclaimed Ned with a shudder. "I don't want any more of that. But as between being blown through a roof and held at the bottom of the sea, I don't know that there's much choice."

"Well, perhaps not," agreed Tom. "But as for ending my experiments, I wouldn't dream of such a thing! Why, I've only just begun! I'll have a silent motor yet!"

"And a non-explosive one, I hope," added Mr. Damon dryly. "Bless my shoe buttons, Tom, but if my wife knew what danger I'd been in she'd never let me come over to see you any more."

"Well, the next time I invite you to a test I'll be more careful," promised the young inventor.

"There isn't going to be any next time as far as I'm concerned!" laughed Ned. "I think it's safer to sell Liberty Bonds."

And, though they joked about it, they all realized the narrow escape they had had. As for Eradicate, once he knew he had not been the one who caused the damage, he felt rather proud of the part he had taken in the mishap, and for many days he boasted about it to Koku.

True to his determination, Tom Swift did not give up his experimental work on the silent motor. The machine that had been blown through the roof was useless now, and it was sent to the scrap heap, after as much of it as possible had been salvaged. Then Tom got another piece of apparatus out of his store room and began all over again.

He worked along the same lines as at first—providing a chamber for the escaping gases of the exhaust to expend their noise and energy in, at the same time laboring to cut down the concussion of the explosions in the cylinder without reducing their force any. And that it was no easy problem to do either of these, Tom had to admit as he progressed. All previous types of mufflers or silencers had to be discarded and a new one evolved.

"Jackson, I need some one to help me," said Tom to his chief mechanician one day. "Haven't you a good man who is used to experimental work that you can let me take from the works?"

"Why, yes," was the answer. "Let me see. Roberts is busy on the new bomb you got up, but I could take him off that—"

"No, don't!" interposed Tom. "I want that work to go on. Isn't there some one else you can let me have?"

"Well, there's a new man who came to me well recommended. I took him on last week, and he's a wonderful mechanic. Knows a lot about gas engines. I could let you have him—Bower his name is. The only thing about it, though, is that I don't like to give you a man of whom I am not dead certain, when you're working on a new device."

"Oh, that will be all right," said Tom. "There won't be any secrets he can get, if you mean you think he might be up to spy work."

"That's what I did mean, Tom. You never can tell, you know, and you have some bitter enemies."

"Yes, but I'll take care this man doesn't see the plans, or any of my drawings. I only want some one to do the heavy assembling work on the experimental muffler I'm getting up. We can let him think it's for a new kind of automobile."

"Oh, then I guess it will be all right. I'll send Bower to you."

Tom rather liked the new workman, who seemed quiet and efficient. He did not ask questions, either, about the machine on which he was engaged, but did as he was told. As Tom had said, he kept his plans and drawing under lock and key—in a safe to be exact—and he did not think they were in any danger from his new helper.

But Tom Swift held into altogether too slight regard the powers of those who were opposed to him. He did not appreciate the depths to which they would stoop to gain their ends.

He had been working hard on his new device, and had reached a point further along than when the other motor had exploded. He began to see success ahead of him, and he was jubilant. Whether this made him careless does not matter, but the fact was that he left Bower more to himself, and alone in the experimental shop several times.

And it was on one of these occasions, when Tom had been for some time in one of the other shops, where he and Jackson were in consultation over a new machine, that as he came back to the test room unexpectedly, he saw Bower move hastily away from in front of the safe. Moreover, Tom was almost certain he had heard the steel door clang shut as he approached the building.

And then, before he could ask his helper a question, Tom looked from a window and saw a stranger running hastily along the side of the building where his trial motor was being set up.

"Who's that? Who is that man? Did he come in here? Was he tampering with my safe?" cried Tom. He saw Bower hesitate and change color, and Tom knew it was time to act.

The window was open, and with one bound the young inventor was out and running after the stranger he had seen departing in such a hurry. The man was but a short distance ahead of him, and Tom saw he was stuffing some papers into his pocket.

"Here! Come back! Stop!" ordered Tom, but the man ran on the faster.

"That's a spy as sure as guns!" reflected Tom Swift. "And Bower is in with him!" he added. "I've got to catch that fellow!" and he speeded his pace as he ran after the fellow.

A Big Splash

There was no question in the mind of Tom Swift but that the man he was running after was guilty of some wrong-doing. In the first place he was a stranger, and had no right inside the big fence that surrounded the Swift machine plant. Then, too, the very fact that he ran away was suspicious.

And this, coupled with the confusion on the part of Bower, and his proximity to the safe, made Tom fear that some of his plans had been stolen. These he was very anxious to recover if this strange man had them, and so he raced after him with all speed.

"Stop! Stop!" called Tom, but the on-racing stranger did not heed.

The cries of the young inventor soon attracted the attention of his men, and Jackson and some of the others came running from their various shops to give whatever aid was needed. But they were all too far away to give effective chase.

"Bower might have come with me if he had wanted to help," thought Tom. But a backward glance over his shoulder did not show that the new helper was engaging in the pursuit, and he could have started almost on the same terms as Tom himself.

The runaway, looking back to see how near the young inventor was to him, suddenly changed his course, and, noting this, Tom Swift thought:

"I've got him now! He'll be bogged if he runs that way," for the way led to a piece of swampy land that, after the recent rains, was a veritable bog which was dangerous for cattle at least; and more than one man had been caught there.

"He can't run across the swamp, that's sure," reflected Tom with some satisfaction. "I'll get him all right!"

But he wanted to capture the man, if possible, before he reached the bog, and, to this end, Tom increased his speed to such good end that presently, on the firm ground that bordered the swamp, Tom was almost within reaching distance of the stranger.

But the latter kept up running, and dodged and turned so that Tom could not lay hands on him. Suddenly, turning around a clump of trees the fleeing man headed straight for a veritable mud hole that lay directly in his path. It was part of the swamp—the most liquid part of the bog and a home of frogs and lizards.

Too late, the man, who was evidently unaware of the proximity of the swamp, saw his danger. His further flight was cut off by the mud hole, but it was too late to turn back. Tom Swift was at his heels now, and seeing that it was impossible to grab the man, Tom did the next best thing. He stuck out his foot and tripped him, and tripped him right on the edge of the mud hole, so that the man fell in with a big splash, the muddy water flying all around, some even over the young inventor.

For a moment the man disappeared completely beneath the surface, for the mud hole was rather deep just where Tom had thrown him. Then there was another violent agitation of the surface, and a very woebegone and muddy face was raised from the slough, followed by the rest of the figure of the man. Slowly he got to his feet, mud and water dripping from him. He cleared his face by rubbing his hands over it, not that it made his countenance clean, but it removed masses of mud from his eyes, nose, and mouth, so that he could see and speak, though his first operation was to gasp for breath.

"What—what are you doin'?" he demanded of Tom, and as the man opened his mouth to speak Tom was aware of a glitter, which disclosed the 'fact that the man had a large front tooth of gold.

"What am I doing?" repeated Tom. "I think it's up to you to answer that question, not me. What are you doing?"

"You—you tripped me into this mud hole!" declared the man.

"I did, yes; because you were trespassing on my property, and ran away instead of stopping when I told you to," went on Tom. "Who are you and what are you doing? What were you doing with Bower at my shop?"

"Nothin'! I wasn't doin' nothin'!"

"Well, we'll inquire into that. I want to see what you have in your pockets before I believe you. Come on out!"

"You haven't any right to go through my pockets!" blustered the stranger.

"Oh, haven't I? Well, I'm going to take the right. Jackson— Koku—just see that he doesn't get away. We'll take him back and search him," and Tom motioned to his chief machinist and the giant, who had reached the scene, to take charge of the man. But Koku was sufficient for this purpose, and the mud-bespattered stranger seemed to shrink as he saw the big creature approach him. There was no question of running away after that.

"Bring him along," ordered Tom, and Koku, taking a tight grip on the man by the slack of his garments behind, walked him along toward the office, the mud and water splashing and oozing from his shoes at every step.

"Now you look here!" the gold-toothed man cried, as he was forced along, "you ain't got any right to detain me. I ain't done nothin'!" And each time he spoke the bright tooth in his mouth glittered in the sun.

"I don't know whether you've done anything or not," said Tom. "I'm going to take you back and see what you and Bower have to say. He may know something about this."

"If he does I don't believe he'll tell," said Jackson.

"Why not?" asked Tom, quickly.

"Because he's gone."

"Gone! Bower gone?"

"Yes," answered Jackson. "I saw him running out of the experiment shop as we raced along to help you. I didn't think, at the time, that he was doing more than go for aid, perhaps. But I see the game now."

"Oh, you mean—him?" and Tom pointed to the dripping figure.

"Yes," said Jackson in a low voice, as Koku went on ahead with his prisoner. "If, as you say, this man was in league with Bower, the latter has smelled a rat and skipped. He has run away, and I only hope he hasn't done any damage or got hold of any of your plans."

"We'll soon know about that," said Tom. "I wonder who is at the bottom of this?"

"Maybe those men you wouldn't work for," suggested the machinist.

"You mean Gale and Ware of the Universal Flying Machine Company?"

"Yes."

"Oh, I don't believe they'd stoop to any such measures as this—sending spies around," replied Tom. "But I can't be too careful. We'll investigate."

The first result of the investigation was to disclose the fact that Bower was gone. He had taken his few possessions and left the Swift plant while Tom was racing after the stranger. A hasty examination of the safe did not reveal anything missing, as Tom's plans and papers were intact. But they showed evidences of having been looked over, for they were out of the regular order in which the young inventor kept them.

"I begin to see it," said Tom, musingly. "Bower must have managed to open the safe while I was gone, and he must have made a hasty copy of some of the drawings of the silent motor, and passed them out of the window to this gold-tooth man, who tried to make off with them. Did you find anything on him?" he asked, as one of the men who had been instructed to search the stranger came into the office just then.

"Not a thing, Mr. Swift! Not a thing!" was the answer. "We took off every bit of his clothes and wrapped him in a blanket. He's in the engine room getting dry now. But there isn't a thing in any of his pockets."

"But I saw him stuffing some papers in as he ran away from me," said Tom. "We must be sure about this. And don't let the fellow get away until I question him."

"Oh, he's safe enough," answered the man. "Koku is guarding him. He won't get away."

"Then I'll have a look at his clothes," decided Tom. "He may have a secret pocket."

But nothing like this was disclosed, and the most careful search did not reveal anything incriminating in the man's garments.

"He might have thrown away any papers Bower gave him," said Tom. "Maybe they're at the bottom of the mud hole! If they're there they're safe enough. But have a search made of the ground where this man ran."

This was done, but without result. Some of the workmen even dragged the mud hole without finding anything. Then Tom and his father had a talk with the stranger, who refused to give his name. The man was sullen and angry. He talked loudly about his innocence and of "having the law on" Tom for having tripped him into the mud.

"All right, if you want to make a complaint, go ahead," said the young inventor. "I'll make one against you for trespass. Why did you come on my grounds?"

"I was going to ask for work. I'm a. good machinist and I wanted a job."

"How did you get in? Who admitted you at the gate?"

"I—I jest walked in," said the man, but Tom knew this could not be true, as no strangers were admitted without a permit and none had been issued. The man denied knowing anything about Bower, but the latter's flight was evidence enough that something was wrong.

Not wishing to go to the trouble of having the man arrested merely as a trespasser, Tom let him go after his clothes had been dried on a boiler in one of the shops.

"Take him to the gate, and tell him if he comes back he'll get another dose of the same kind of medicine," ordered Tom to one of the guards at the plant, and when the latter had reported that this had been done, he added in an earnest tone:

"He went off talking to himself and saying he'd get even with you, Mr. Swift."

"All right," said Tom easily. "I'll be on the watch."

The young inventor made a thorough examination of his experiment shop and the test motor. No damage seemed to have been done, and Tom began to think he had been too quick for the conspirators, if such they were. His plans and drawings were intact, and though Bower might have given a copy to the stranger with the gold tooth, the latter did not take any away with him. That he had some papers he wished to conceal and escape with, seemed certain, but the splash into the mud hole had ended this.

No trace was found of Bower, and an effort Tom made to ascertain if the man was a spy in the employ of Gale and Ware came to naught. The machinist had come well recommended, and the firm where he was last employed had nothing but good to say of him.

"Well, it's a mystery," decided Tom. "However, I got out of it pretty well. Only if that gold-tooth individual shows up again he won't get off so easily.

A NIGHT TRIP

Taking a lesson from what had happened, Tom was very much more careful in the following experiments on his new, silent motor. He made some changes in his shop, and took Jackson in to help on the new machine, thus insuring perfect secrecy as the apparatus developed.

Tom also changed the safe in which he kept his plans, for the one he had used previous to the episode in which Bower and the stranger who took the mud bath figured, was one the combination of which could easily be ascertained by an expert. The new safe was more complicated, and Tom felt that his plans, specifications, and formulae which he had worked out were in less danger.

"I can just about figure out what happened," said Ned Newton to Tom, when told of the circumstances. "These Universal people were provoked because you wouldn't give them the benefit of your experience on their flying machines, and so they sent a spy to get work with you. They, perhaps, hoped to secure some of your ideas for their own, or they may have had a deeper motive."

"What deeper motive could they have, Ned?" "They might have hoped to disable you, or some of your machines, so that you couldn't compete with them. They're unscrupulous, I hear, and will do anything to succeed and make money. So be on your guard against them."

"I will," Tom promised. "But I don't believe there's any more danger now. Anyhow, I have to take some chances."

"Yes, but be as careful as you can. How is the silent motor coming on?"

"Pretty good. I've had a lot of failures, and the thing isn't so easy as I at first imagined it would be. Noise is a funny thing, and I'm just beginning to understand some of the laws of acoustics we learned at high school. But I think I'm on the right track with the muffler and the cutting down of the noise of the explosions in the cylinders. I'm working both ends, you see— making a motor that doesn't cause as much racket as those now in use, and also providing means to take care of the noise that is made. It isn't possible to make a completely silent motor of an explosive gas type. The only thing that can be done is to kill the noise after it is made."

"What about the propeller blades?"

"Oh, they aren't giving me any trouble. The noise they make can't be heard a hundred feet in the air, but I am also working on improvements to the blades. Take it altogether, I'll have an almost silent aeroplane if my plans come out all right."

"Have you said anything to the government yet?"

"No; I want to have it pretty well perfected before I do. Besides, I don't want any publicity about it until I'm ready. If these Universal people are after me I'll fool 'em."

"That's right, Tom! Well, I must go. Another week of this Liberty Bond campaign!"

"I suppose you'll be glad when it's over."

"Well, I don't know," said Ned slowly. "It's part of my small contribution to Uncle Sam. I'm not like you—I can't invent things."

"But you have an awful smooth line of talk, Ned!" laughed his chum. "I believe you could sell chloride of sodium to some of the fishes in the Great Salt Lake—that is if it has fishes."

"I don't know that it has, Tom. And, anyhow, I'm not posing as a salt salesman," and Ned grinned. "But I must really go. Our bank hasn't reached its quota in the sale of Liberty Bonds yet, and it's up to me to see that it doesn't fall down."

"Go to it, Ned! And I'll get busy on my silent motor."

"Getting busy" was Tom Swift's favorite occupation, and when he was working on a new idea, as was the case now, he was seldom idle, night or day.

"I have hardly seen you for two weeks," Mary Nestor wrote him one day. "Aren't you ever coming to see me any more, or take me for a ride?"

"Yes," Tom wrote back. "I'll be over soon. And perhaps on the next ride we take I won't have to shout at you through a speaking tube because the motor makes so much noise."

From this it may be gathered that Tom was on the verge of success. While not altogether satisfied with his progress, the young inventor felt that he was on the right track. There were certain changes that needed to be made in the apparatus he was building—certain refinements that must be added, and when this should be done Tom was pretty certain that he would have what would prove to be a very quiet aeroplane, if not an absolutely silent one.

The young inventor was engaged one day with some of the last details of the experiment. The new motor, with the silencer and the changed cylinders, had been attached to one of Tom's speedy aeroplanes, and he was making some intricate calculations in relation to a new cylinder block, to be used when he started to make a completely new machine of the improved type.

Tom had set down on paper some computations regarding the cross-section of one of the cylinders, and was working out the amount of stress to which he could subject a shoulder strut, when a shadow was cast across the drawing board he had propped up in his lap.

In an instant Tom pulled a blank sheet over his mass of figures and looked up, a sudden fear coming over him that another spy was at hand. But a hearty voice reassured him.

"Bless my rice pudding!" cried Mr. Damon, "you shut yourself up here, Tom, like a hermit in the mountains. Why don't you come out and enjoy life?"

"Hello! Glad to see you!" cried Tom, joyfully. "You're just in time!"

"Time for what—dinner?" asked the eccentric man, with a chuckle. "If so, my reference to rice pudding was very proper."

"Why, yes, I imagine there must be a dinner in prospect somewhere, Mr. Damon," said Tom with a smile. "We'll have to see Mrs. Baggert about that. But what I meant was that you're just in time to have a ride with me, if you want to go."

"Go where?"

"Oh, up in cloudland. I have just finished my first sample of a silent motor, and I'm going to try it this evening. Would you like to come along?"

"I would!" exclaimed Mr. Damon. "Bless my onion soup, Tom, but I would! But why fly at night? Isn't it safer by daylight?"

"Oh, that doesn't make much difference. It's safe enough at any time. The reason I'm going to make my first flight after dark is that I don't want any spies about."

"Oh, I see! Are they camping on your trail?"

"Not exactly. But I can't tell where they may be. If I should start out in daylight and be forced to make a landing— Well, you know what a crowd always collects to see a stranded airship."

"That's right, Tom."

"That decided me to start off after dark. Then if we have to come down because of some sort of engine trouble or because my new attachment doesn't work right, we sha'n't have any prying eyes."

"I see! Well, Tom, I'll go with you. Fortunately I didn't tell my wife where I was going when I started out this afternoon, so she won't worry until after it's over, and then it won't hurt her. I'm ready any time you are."

"Good! Stay to dinner and I'll show you what I've made. Then we'll take a flight after dark."

This suited the eccentric man, and a little later, after he had eaten one of Mrs. Baggert's best meals, including rice pudding, of which he was very fond, Mr. Damon accompanied Tom to one of the big hangars where the new aeroplane had been set up.

"So that's the Air Scout, is it, Tom?" asked Mr. Damon, as he viewed the machine.

"Yes, that's the girl. 'Air Scout' is as good a name as any, until I see what she'll do."

"It doesn't look different from one of your regular craft of the skies, Tom."

"No, she isn't. The main difference is here," and Tom showed his friend where a peculiar apparatus had been attached to the motor. This was the silencer—the whole secret of the invention, so to speak.

To Mr. Damon it seemed to consist of an amazing collection of pipes, valves, baffle-plates, chambers, cylinders and reducers, which took the hot exhaust gases as they came from the motor and "ate them up," as he expressed it.

"The cylinders, too, and the spark plugs are differently arranged in the motor itself, if you could see them," said Tom to his friend. "But the main work of cutting down the noise is done right here," and he put his hand on the steel case attached to the motor, the case containing the apparatus already briefly described.

"Well, I'm ready when you are, Tom," said Mr. Damon.

"We'll go as soon as it's dark," was the reply. "But first I'll give you a demonstration. Start the motor, Jackson!" Tom called to his chief helper.

Mr. Damon had ridden in aeroplanes before, and had stood near when Tom started them; so he was prepared for a great rush of air as the propellers whirled about, and for deafening explosions from the engine.

The big blades, of new construction, were turned until the gas in the cylinders was sufficiently compressed. Then Jackson stepped back out of danger while Tom threw over the switch.

"Contact!" cried the young inventor.

Jackson gave the blades a quarter pull, and, a moment later, as he leaped back out of the way, they began to revolve with the swiftness of light. There was the familiar rush of air as the wooden wings cut through the atmosphere, but there was scarcely any noise. Mr. Damon could hardly believe his ears.

"I'm not running her at full speed," said Tom. "If I did she'd tear loose from the holding blocks. But you can see what little racket she makes."

"Bless my fountain pen!" cried Mr. Damon. "You are right, Tom Swift! Why, I can hear you talk almost as easily as if no engine were going. And I don't have to shout my head off, either."

This was perfectly true. Tom could converse with Mr. Damon in almost ordinary tones. The exhaust from the motor was nearly completely muffled.

"Out in the air it will seem even more quiet," said Tom. "I'll soon give you a chance to verify that statement."

He ran the engine a little longer, the aeroplane quivering with the vibrations, but remaining almost silent.

"I'm anxious to see what she'll do when in motion," said Tom, as he shut off the gas and spark.

Soon after supper, when the shades of evening were falling, he and Mr. Damon took their places in the first of the Air Scouts, to give it the preliminary test in actual flying.

Would Tom's hopes be justified or would he be disappointed?

THE CRY FOR HELP

"All ready, Mr. Damon?" asked Tom, as he looked to see that all the levers, wheels, valves, and other controls were in working order on his Air Scout.

"As ready as I ever shall be, Tom," was the answer. "I don't know why it is, but somehow I feel that something is going to happen on this trip."

"Nonsense!" laughed Tom. "You're nervous; that's all."

"I suppose so. Don't think I'm going to back out, or anything like that, but I wish it were successfully over with, Tom Swift, I most certainly do."

"It will be in a little while," returned Tom, as he settled himself comfortably in his seat and pulled the safety strap tight. "You've gone up in this same plane before, when it didn't have the silent motor aboard."

"Yes, I know I have. Oh, I dare say it will be all right, Tom. And yet, somehow, I can't help feeling—"

But Tom Swift felt that the best way to set Mr. Damon's premonitions to rest was to start the motor, and this he gave orders to have done, Jackson and some others of the men from the shops congregating about the craft to see the beginning of the night flight. Mr. Swift was there also, and Eradicate. Mary Nestor had been invited, but her Red Cross work engaged her that evening, she said. Ned Newton was away from town on Liberty Bond business, and he could not be present at the test.

However, as Tom expected to have other trials when his motor was in even better shape, he was not exactly sorry for the absence of his friends.

"Contact!" called the young inventor, when Jackson had stepped back, indicating it was time to throw over the switch.

"Let her go!" cried Tom, and the next moment the motor was in operation, but so silently that his voice and that of Mr. Damon's could easily be heard above the machinery.

"Good, Tom! That's good!" cried Mr. Swift, and Tom easily heard his father's voice, though under other, and ordinary, circumstances this would have been impossible.

True, the hearing of Tom and Mr. Damon was muffled to a certain extent by the heavy leather and fur-lined caps they wore. But Tom had several small eyelet holes set into the flaps just over the opening of the ears, and these holes were sufficient to admit sounds, while keeping out most of the cold that obtains in the upper regions.

The aeroplane moved swiftly along the level starting ground, and away from the lighted hangars. Faster and faster it swung along as Tom headed it into the wind, and then, as the speed of the motor increased, the Air Scout suddenly left the earth and went soaring aloft as she had done before.

But there was this difference. She moved almost as silently as a great owl which swoops down out of the darkness—a bit of the velvety blackness itself. Up and up, and onward and onward, went the Air Scout. Tom Swift's improved, silent motor urged it onward, and as the young inventor listened to catch the noise of the machinery, his heart gave a bound of hope. For he could detect only very slight sounds.

"She's a success!" exulted Tom to himself. "She's a success, but she isn't perfect yet," he added. "I've got to make the muffler bigger and put in more baffle-plates. Then I think I can turn the trick."

He swung the machine out over the open country, and then, when they were up at a height and sailing along easily, he called back to Mr. Damon in the seat behind him:

"How do you like it?"

"Great!" exclaimed the eccentric man. "Bless my postage stamp, but it's great! Why, there's hardly a sound, Tom, and I can hear you quite easily."

"And I can hear you," added Tom. "I don't believe, down below there," and he nodded toward the earth, though Mr. Damon could not see this, as the airship, save for a tiny light over the instrument board, was in darkness, "they know that we're flying over their heads."

"I agree with you," was the answer. "Tom, my boy, I believe you've solved the trick! You have produced a silent aeroplane, and now it's up to the government to make use of it."

"I'm not quite ready for that yet," replied the young inventor. "I have several improvements to make. But, when they are finished, I'll let Uncle Sam know what I have. Then it's up to him."

"And you must be careful, Tom, that some of your rivals don't hear of your success and get it away from you," warned Mr. Damon, as Tom guided the Air Scout along the aerial way—an unlighted and limitless path in the silent darkness.

"Oh, they'll have to get up pretty early in the morning to do that!" boasted Tom, and afterward he was to recall those words with a bit of chagrin.

On and on they sailed, and as Tom increased the speed of the motor, and noted how silently it ran, he began to have high hopes that he had builded better than he knew. For even with the motor running at almost full speed there was not noise enough to hinder talk between himself and Mr. Damon.

Of course there was some little sound. Even the most perfect electric motor has a sort of hum which can be detected when one is close to it. But at a little distance a great dynamo in operation appears to be silence itself.

"I can go this one better, though," said Tom as he sailed along in the night. "I see where I've made a few mistakes in the baffle plate of the silencer. I'll correct that and—"

As he spoke the machine gave a lurch, and the motor, instead of remaining silent, began to cough and splutter as in the former days.

"Bless my rubber boots, Tom! what's the matter?" cried Mr. Damon.

"Something's gone wrong," Tom answered, barely able to hear and make himself heard above the sudden noise. "I'll have to shut off the power and glide down. We can make a landing in this big field," for just then the moon came out from behind a cloud, and Tom saw, below them, a great meadow, not far from the home of Mary Nestor. He had often landed in this same place.

"Something has broken in the muffler, I think, letting out some of the exhaust," he said to Mr. Damon, for, now that the motor was shut off, Tom could speak in his ordinary tones. "I'll soon have it fixed, or, if I can't, we can go back in the old style— with the machine making as much racket as it pleases."

So Tom guided the machine down. It went silently now, of course, making, with the motor shut off, no more sound than a falling leaf. Down to the soft, springy turf in the green meadow Tom guided the machine. As it came to a stop, and he and Mr. Damon got out, there was borne to their ears a wild cry:

"Help! Help!"

SOMETHING QUEER

"DiD you hear that?" asked Tom Swift of his companion.

"Hear it? Bless my ear drums, I should say I did hear it! Some one is in trouble, Tom. Caught in a bog, most likely, the same as that spy chap who was at your place. That's it—caught in a bog!"

"There isn't any bog or swamp around here, Mr. Damon. If there was I shouldn't have tried a landing. No, it's something else besides that. Hark!"

Again the cry sounded, seeming to come from a point behind the landing place of the silent airship. It was clear and distinct:

"Help! Help! They are—"

The voice seemed to die away in a gurgle, as though the person's mouth had been covered quickly.

"He's sinking, Tom! He's sinking!" cried Mr. Damon. "I once heard a man who almost drowned cry out, and it sounded exactly like that!"

"But there isn't any water around here for any one to drown in," declared Tom. "It's a big, dry meadow. I know where we are."

"Then what is it?"

"I don't know, but we're going to find out. Some one attacked by some one else—or something, I should say," ventured the young inventor.

"Something! do you mean a wild beast, Tom?"

"No, for there aren't any of those here any more than there is water. Though it may be that some farmer's bull or a savage dog has got loose and has attacked some traveler. But, in that case I think we would hear bellows or barks, and all I heard was a cry for help."

"The same with me, Tom. Let's investigate;"

"That's what I intend doing. Come on. The airship will be all right until we come back."

"Better take a light—hadn't you? It's dark, even if the moon does show now and then," suggested Mr. Damon.

"Guess you are right," agreed Tom. Aboard his airship there were several small but powerful portable electric lights, and after securing one of these Tom and Mr. Damon started for the spot whence the call for help had come. As they walked along, their feet making no noise on the soft turf, they listened intently for a repetition of the call for aid.

"I don't hear anything," said Tom, after a bit.

"Nor I," added Mr. Damon. "We don't know exactly which way to go, Tom."

"That's right. Guess we'd better give him a hail; whoever it is."

Tom came to a halt, and raising his voice to a shout called:

"Hello there! What's the matter? We'll help you if you can tell us which way to come!"

They both listened intently, but no voice answered them. At the same time, however, they were aware of a sound as of hurrying feet, and there seemed to be muttered imprecations not far away. Tom and Mr. Damon looked in the direction of the sound, and the young inventor flashed his light. But there was a clump of bushes and trees at that point and the electrical rays did not penetrate very far.

"Some one's over there!" exclaimed Tom in a whisper. "We'd better go and see what it is."

"All right," agreed Mr. Damon, and he, too, spoke in a low voice.

Why they did this when their previous talk had been in ordinary tones, and when Tom had shouted so loudly, they did not stop to reason about or explain just then. But later they both admitted that they whispered because they thought there was something wrong on foot—because they feared a crime was being committed and they wanted to surprise the perpetrators if they could.

And it was this fact of their whispering that enabled the two to hear something that, otherwise, they might not have heard. And this was the sound of some vehicle hurrying away—an automobile, if Tom was any judge. The cries for help had been succeeded by stifled vocal sounds, and these, in turn, by the noise of wheels on the ground.

"What does it all mean?" asked Mr. Damon in a whisper.

"I don't know," answered Tom, resolutely, "but we've got to find out. Come on

They advanced toward the dark clump of trees and low bushes. There was no need to be especially cautious in regard to being silent, as their feet made little, if any, sound on the deep grass. And, as Tom walked in advance, now and then flashing his light, Mr. Damon suddenly caught him by the coat.

"What is it?" asked the young inventor.

"Look! Just over the top of that hill, where the moon shines. Don't you see an automobile outlined?"

Tom looked quickly.

"I do," he answered. "There's a road from here, just the other side of those trees, to that hill. The auto must have gone that way. Well, there's no use in trying to follow it now. Whoever it was has gotten away."

"But they may have left some one behind, Tom. We'd better look in and around those trees."

"I suppose we had, but I don't believe we'll find anything. I can pretty nearly guess, now, what it was."

"What?" asked Mr. Damon.

"Well, some chauffeur was out for a ride in his employer's car without permission. He got here, had an accident—maybe some friends he took for a ride were hurt and they called for help. The chauffeur knew if there was any publicity he'd be blamed, and so he got away as quickly as he could.

Guess the accident—if that's what it was—didn't amount to much, or they couldn't have run the car off. We've had our trouble for our pains."

"Well, maybe you're right, Tom Swift, butt all the same, I'd like to have a look among those trees," said Mr. Damon.

"Oh. we'll look, all right," assented Tom, "but I doubt if we find anything."

And he was right. They walked in and about the little grove, flashing the light at intervals, but beyond marks of auto wheels in the dust of the road, which was near the clump of maples, there was nothing to indicate what had happened.

"Though there was some sort of fracas," declared Tom. "Look where the dust is trampled down. There were several men here, perhaps skylarking, or perhaps it was a fight."

"Some one must have been hurt, or they wouldn't have cried for help," said Mr. Damon.

"Well, that's so. But perhaps it was some one not used to riding in autos, and he may have imagined the accident was worse than it was, and called for help involuntarily. There is no evidence of any serious accident having happened—no spots of blood, at any rate," and Tom laughed at his own grimness. "It was a new car, too, or at least one with new tires on."

"How do you know?" asked Mr. Damon.

"Tell by the plain marks of the rubber tread in the dust," was the answer. "Look," and Tom pointed to the wheel marks in the focus of his electric lamp. "It's a new tire, too, with square protuberances on the tread instead of the usual diamond or round ones. A new kind of tire, all right."

He and Mr. Damon remained for a few minutes looking about the place whence had come the calls for help, and then the eccentric man remarked:

"Well, as long as we can't do anything here, Tom, we might as well travel on; what do you say?"

"I agree with you. There isn't any use in staying. We'll get the Air Scout fixed up and travel back home. But this was something queer," mused Tom. "I hope it doesn't turn out later that a crime has been committed, and we didn't show enough gumption to prevent it."

"We couldn't prevent it. We heard the cries as soon as we landed."

"Yes, but if we had rushed over at once we might have caught the fellows. But I guess it was only a slight accident, and some one was more frightened than hurt. We'll have to let it go at that."

But the more he thought about it the more Tom Swift thought there was something queer in that weird cry for help on the lonely meadow in the darkness of the night.

The Telephone Call

The defect in the motor which had caused Tom Swift to shut off the power and drift down to earth was soon remedied, once the young inventor began an examination of the craft. One of the oil feeds had become choked and this automatically cut down the gasoline supply, causing one or more cylinders to miss. It was a safety device Tom had installed to prevent the motor running dry, and so being damaged.

Once the clogged oil feed was cleared the motor ran as before, and just as silently, though, as Tom had said, he was not entirely satisfied with the quietness, but intended to do further work toward perfecting it.

"I'll start the propellers now, Mr. Damon," said Tom, when the trouble had been remedied. "You know how to throw the switch, don't you?"

"I guess so," was the answer. Mr. Damon and Tom had traveled so often together in gasoline craft that the young inventor had taught his friend certain fundamentals about them, and in an emergency the eccentric man could help start an aeroplane. This he now did, taking charge of the controls which could be operated from his seat as well as from Tom's. Tom whirled the propellers, and soon the motor was in motion.

Mr. Damon, once the big wooden blades were revolving, slowed down the apparatus until Tom could jump aboard, after which the latter took charge and soon speeded up the machine, sending it aloft.

As the green meadow, dimly seen in the light of the moon, seemed to drop away below them, and the clump of trees vanished from sight, both Tom and Mr. Damon wondered who it was that had called for help, and if the matter were at all serious. They were inclined to think it was not, but Tom could not rid himself of a faint suspicion that there might have been trouble.

However, thoughts of his new silent Air Scout soon drove everything else from his mind, and as he guided the comparatively silent machine on its quiet way toward his own home he was thinking how he could best improve the muffler.

"Well, here we are again, safe and sound," remarked Tom, as he brought the craft to a stop in front of the hangar, and Jackson and his helpers, who were awaiting the return, hurried out to take charge.

"Yes, everything seems to point to success, Tom," agreed Mr. Damon. "That is, unless the slight accident we had means trouble."

"Oh, no, that had nothing to do with the operation of the silencer. But I'm going to do better yet. Some day I'll take you for a ride in a silent machine which will make so little noise that you can hear a pin drop."

"Well," remarked Mr. Damon' with a laugh, "I don't know that listening to falling pins will give me any great amount of pleasure, Tom, but I appreciate your meaning."

"Everything all right?" asked Mr. Swift, as he came out to hear the details from his son. "Do you think you have solved the problem?"

"Not completely, but I'll soon be able to write Q. E. D. after it. Some refinements are all that are needed, Dad."

"Glad to hear it. I was a bit anxious."

Mr. Swift questioned his son about the technical details of the trip, asking how the motor had acted under the pressure caused by so completely muffling the exhaust, and for some minutes the two inventors, young and old, indulged in talk which was not at all interesting to Mr. Damon. They went into the house, and Tom asked to have a little lunch, which Mrs. Baggert set out for him.

"It's rather late to eat," said the young inventor, "but I always feel hungry after I test a new machine and find that it works pretty well. Will you join me in a sandwich or two, Mr. Damon?"

"Why, bless my ketchup bottle, I believe I will."

And so they ate and talked. Tom was on the point of telling his father something of the queer cry for help they had heard on the lonely meadow when Mrs. Baggert produced a letter which she said had come for Tom that afternoon, but had been mislaid by a new maid who had been engaged to help with the housework.

"She took it to the shop after you had left, and only now told me about it," explained Mrs. Baggert. "So I sent Eradicate for it."

"How long ago was that?" asked Tom, as he took the missive.

"Oh, an hour ago," answered Mrs. Baggert, with a smile. "But don't blame poor Rad for that. He wanted to deliver the letter to you personally, and so did Koku. The result was your giant kept after Rad, trying to get the letter from him, and Rad kept hiding and slinking about for a chance to see you himself until I saw what was going on, a little while ago, and took the letter myself. Else you might never have gotten it, so jealous are those two," and Mrs. Baggert laughed.

"Guess it isn't of much importance," Tom said, as he tore open the envelope. "It's from the Universal Flying Machine Company, of New York, and I imagine they're trying to get me to reconsider my refusal to link up with them."

"Yes," he went on, as he read the missive, "that's it. They've raised the amount to thirty thousand a year now, Dad, and they say they feel sure I shall regret it if I do not accept.

"This is a bit queer, though," went on the young inventor. "This letter was written three days ago, but it reached Shopton only today. And it says that unless they hear from me at once they will have to take steps that will cause me great inconvenience. They have nerve, at any rate, and impudence, too! I won't even bother to answer. But I wonder what they mean, and why this letter was delayed?"

"The mails are all late on account of the transportation congestion caused by moving troops to the camps," said Mr. Damon. "Some of my letters are delayed a week. But, as you say, Tom, these fellows are very impudent to threaten that way."

"It's all bluff," declared Tom. "I'm not worrying. And now, Dad, since I've almost reached the top of the hill with my Air Scout, I may be able to help you on that new electric motor you're puzzling over."

"I wish you would, Tom. I am trying to invent a new system of interchangeable brush contacts, but so far I've been unable to make them work. However, there is no great hurry about that. If you are going to offer your silent machine to the government finish that first. We need all the aircraft we can get. The battles on the other side seem to be all in favor of the Germans, so far."

"We haven't got into our stride yet," declared Mr. Damon. "Once Uncle Sam gets the boys over there in force, there'll be a different story to tell. I only wish—"

At that moment the telephone set up an insistent ringing, breaking in on Mr. Damon's remarks.

"I'll answer," said Tom, as Mrs. Baggert moved toward the instrument, which was an extension from the main one.

"Hello!" called the young inventor into the transmitter, and as he received an answer a look of pleasure came over his face.

"Yes, Mary, this is Tom," he said. He remained silent a moment, while it was evident he was listening to the voice at the other end of the wire. Then he suddenly exclaimed:

"What's that? Tell him to come home? Why, he isn't here. I just came in and—what—wait a minute!"

With a rather strange look on his face Tom covered the mouth-piece of the instrument with his hand, and, turning to his father, asked:

"Is Mr. Nestor here?"

"No," replied Mr. Swift slowly, "He was here, though. He came a little while after you and Mr. Damon started off in the Air Scout. But he didn't stay. Said he wanted to see you about something and would call again."

"Oh," remarked the young man. "I didn't know he had been there."

"I meant to tell you," said Mrs. Baggert; "but getting the lunch made me forget it, I guess."

Tom uncovered the transmitter of the telephone again, and spoke to Mary Nestor.

"Hello," he said. "I was wrong, Mary. Your father was here, but he left when he found I wasn't at home. How long ago? Wait a minute and I'll inquire.

"How long ago did Mr. Nestor leave?" asked the young inventor of the housekeeper. "Nearly an hour," he said into the instrument, after he had received the answer. Then, after listening a moment, he added: "Yes, I guess he'll be home soon now. Probably stopped down town to see some of his friends. Yes, Mr. Damon and I tried out the Air Scout. Yes, she worked pretty well, for a starter, but there is something yet to be done. Oh, yes, now I'll have time to come over to see you, and take you for a ride too. We won't have to talk through a speaking tube, either. Tell your father I am sorry I was out when he called. I'll come to see him to-morrow, if he wants me to. Yes—yes. I guess so!" and Tom laughed, it being evident that his remarks at the end of the conversation had to do with personal matters.

"A telegram has come for Mr. Nestor and they were anxious that he should get it," Tom explained to his little audience as he hung up the receiver and put aside the telephone. "I wonder what he wanted to see me about?"

"He didn't say," replied Mrs. Baggert.

Mr. Damon, Tom, and his father remained in conversation a little while longer, and the eccentric man was thinking that it was about time for him to return home, when the telephone rang again.

"Hello," answered Tom, as he was nearest the instrument. "Oh, yes, Mary, this is he. What's that? Your father hasn't reached home yet? And your mother is worried? Oh tell her there is no cause for alarm. As I said, he probably stopped on his way to see some friends."

Tom listened for perhaps half a minute to a talk that was inaudible to the others in the room, and they noticed a grave look come over his face. Then he said:

"I'll be right over, Mary. Yes, I'll come at once. And tell your mother not to worry. I'm sure nothing could have happened. I'll be with you in a jiffy!"

As Tom Swift hung up the receiver he said:

"Mr. Nestor hasn't reached home yet, and as he promised to return at once in case he didn't find me, his wife is much worried. I'll go over and see what I can do."

"I'll come along!" volunteered Mr. Damon. "It isn't late yet."

"Yes, do come," urged Tom. "But I suppose when we get there we'll find our friend has arrived safely. We'll go over in the electric runabout."

A Vain Search

Tom Swift's speedy little electric car was soon at the door in readiness to take him and Mr. Damon to the Nestor home. The electric runabout was a machine Tom had evolved in his early inventive days, and though he had other automobiles, none was quite so fast or so simple to run as this, which well merited the name of the most rapid machine on the road. In it Tom had once won a great race, as has been related in the book bearing the title, "Tom Swift and His Electric Runabout."

"Mary didn't telephone again, did she?" Tom asked his father, as he stopped at the house to get Mr. Damon, having gone out to see about getting the electric runabout in readiness.

"No," was the answer. "The telephone hasn't rung since."

"Then, I guess, Mr. Nestor can't have arrived home," said Tom. "It's a bit queer, his delay, but I'm sure it will be explained naturally. Only Mary and her mother are alone and, very likely, they're nervous. I'll telephone to let you know everything is all right as soon as I get there," Tom promised his father and Mrs. Baggert as he drove off down the road, partly illuminated by the new moon.

Rapidly and almost as silently as his Air Scout Tom Swift drove the speedy car down the highway. It was about three miles from his home to that of Mary Nestor, and though the distance was quickly covered, to Tom, at least, the space seemed interminable. But at length he drove up to the door. There were lights in most of the rooms, which was unusual at this time of night.

The sound of the wheels had not ceased echoing on the gravel of the drive before Mary was out on the porch, which she illuminated by an overhead light.

"Oh, Tom," she cried, "he hasn't come yet, and we are so worried! Did you see anything of father as you came along?"

"No," was Tom's answer. "But we didn't look for him along the road, as we came by the turnpike, and he wouldn't travel that way. But he will be along at any moment now. You must remember it's quite a walk from my house, and—"

"But he was on his bicycle," said Mary. "We wanted him to go in the auto, but he said he wanted some exercise after supper, and he went over on his wheel. He said he'd be right back, but he hasn't come yet."

"Oh, he will!" said Tom reassuringly. "He may have had a puncture, or something like that. Bicyclists are just as liable to them as autoists," he added with a laugh.

"Well, I'm sure I hope it will be all right," sighed Mary. "I wish you could convince mother to that effect. She's as nervous as a cat. Come in and tell us what to do."

"Oh, he'll be all right," declared Mr. Damon, adding his assurances to Tom's.

They found Mrs. Nestor verging on an attack of hysteria. Though Mr. Nestor often went out during the evening, he seldom stayed late.

"And he said he'd be right back if he found you weren't at home, Tom," said Mrs. Nestor. "I'm sure I don't know what can be keeping him!"

"It's too soon to get worried yet," replied the young inventor cheerfully. "I'll wait a little while, and then, if he doesn't come, Mr. Damon and I will go back over the road and look carefully. He may have had a slight fall—sprained his ankle or something like that—and not be able to ride. We came by the turnpike, a road he probably wouldn't take on his wheel. He's all right, you may be sure of that."

Tom tried to speak reassuringly, but somehow, he did not believe himself. He was beginning to think more and more how strange it was that Mr. Nestor did not return home.

"We'll wait just a bit longer before setting out on a search," he told Mary and her mother. "But I'm sure he will be along any minute now."

They went into the library, Mary and her mother, Tom and Mr. Damon. And there they sat waiting. Tom tried to entertain Mary and Mrs. Nestor with an account of his trial trip in the Air Scout, but the two women scarcely heard what he said.

All sat watching the clock, and looking from that to the telephone, which they tried to hope would ring momentarily and transmit to them good news. Then they would listen for the sound of footsteps or bicycle wheels on the gravel walk. But they heard nothing, and as the seconds were ticked off on the clock the nervousness of Mrs. Nestor increased, until she exclaimed:

"I can stand it no longer! We must notify the police—or do something!"

"I wouldn't notify the police just yet," counseled Tom. "Mr. Damon and I will start out and look along the road. If it should happen, as will probably turn out to be the case, that Mr. Nestor has met with only a simple accident, he would not like the notoriety, or publicity, of having the police notified."

"No, I am sure he would not," agreed Mary. "Tom's way is best, Mother."

"All right, just as you say, only find my husband," and Mrs. Nestor sighed, and turned her head away.

"Even if Mr. Nestor had had a fall," reasoned Tom, "he could call for help, and get some one to telephone, unless—"

And as he reasoned thus Tom Swift gave a mental start at his own use of the word "help."

That weird cry on the lonely meadow came back to him with startling distinctness.

"Come on, Mr. Damon!" cried Tom, in a voice he tried to make cheerful. "We'll find that Mr. Nestor is probably walking along, carrying his disabled bicycle instead of having it carry him. We'll soon have him safe back to you," he called to the two women.

"I wish I could go with you, and help search," observed Mary.

"Oh, I couldn't bear to be left alone!" exclaimed her mother.

"We'll telephone as soon as we find him," called Tom to Mrs. Nestor, as he and Mr. Damon again got into the runabout and started away from the place.

"What do you think of it, Tom?" asked the eccentric man, when they were once more on the road.

"Why, nothing much—as yet," Tom said. "That is, I think nothing more than a simple accident has happened, if, indeed, it is anything more than that he has delayed to talk to some friends."

"Would he delay this long?"

"I don't know."

"And then, Tom—bless my spectacles! what of that cry we heard? Could that have been Mr. Nestor?"

There! It was out! The suspicion that Tom had been trying to keep his mind away from came to the fore. Well, he might as well race the issue now as later.

"I've been thinking of that," he told Mr. Damon. "It might have been Mary's father calling for help."

"But we looked, Tom, near the trees, and couldn't discover anything. If he had been calling for help—"

Mr. Damon did not finish.

"He may have fallen from his wheel and been hurt," said Tom, as he turned the electric runabout into the highway that Mr. Nestor would, most likely, have taken on his way from Shopton. "Then be may have called for help, and some autoists, passing, may have heard and taken him away."

"Yes, but where, Tom? Whoever called for help was taken away, that's sure. But where?"

"To some hospital, I suppose."

"Then hadn't we better inquire there? There are only two hospitals of any account around here. The one in Shopton and the one in Waterfield. My wife is on the board of Lady Managers there. We could call that hospital up and—"

"We'll look along the road first," said Tom. "If we begin to make inquiries at the hospitals there will be a lot of questions asked, and a general alarm may be sent out. Mr. Nestor wouldn't like that, if he isn't in any danger. And it may turn out that he has met an old friend, and has been talking with him all this while, forgetting all about the passage of time."

They were now driving along the highway that led from the little suburb where Mr. Nestor lived, to the main part of Shopton, just beyond which was Tom's home. This section was country-like, with very few houses and those placed at rather infrequent intervals. The road was a good one, though not the main-traveled one, and Mr. Nestor, as was known, frequently used it when he rode his bicycle, an exercise of which he was very fond.

As Tom and Mr. Damon drove along, they scanned, as best they could in the light from the young moon and the powerful lamps on the runabout, every part of the highway. They were looking for some dark blot which might indicate where a man had fallen from his wheel and was lying in some huddled heap on the road. But they saw nothing like this, much to their relief.

"Do you know, Tom," said Mr. Damon, when they were nearing the town, and their search, thus far, had been in vain, "I think we're going at this the wrong way."

"Why, so?"

"Because Mr. Nestor may have fallen, and been hurt, and have been carried into any one of a dozen houses along the road. In that case we wouldn't see him. We've passed over the most lonely part of the journey and haven't seen him. If the accident occurred near the houses his cries would have brought some one out to help him. He is well known around here, and, even if he were unconscious and couldn't tell who he was, he could be identified by papers in his pockets. Then his family would be notified by telephone."

"Perhaps you are right, Mr. Damon. We may be wasting time this way. What do you suggest?" asked Tom.

"That we don't delay any longer, but call up the hospitals at once. If he isn't in either of those he must be in some house, and in such condition that his identity cannot be established. In that event it is a case for the police. We haven't found him, and I think we had better give the alarm."

Tom Swift thought it over for a moment. Then he came to a sudden decision.

"You're right!" he told Mr. Damon. "We mustn't waste any more time. He isn't along the road he ought to have traveled in coming from my house to his home—that's sure. But before I call up the hospitals I want to try out one more idea."

"What's that, Tom?"

"I want to go to the place where we heard that cry for help."

"Do you think that could have been Mr. Nestor?"

"It may have been. We'll go and take another look around there. Some man was evidently hurt there, and was taken away. We may get a clue. The lights on the runabout will give us a better chance to look around than we had by the little pocket lamp. We'll try there, and, if we don't find anything, then I'll call up the hospitals."

THE LONG NIGHT

With the speedy runabout it did not take Tom Swift and Mr. Damon long to reach the place where the Air Scout had been grounded a few hours before, and where they had heard the cry for help. All was as dark and as silent as when they had been there before.

But, as Tom had said, the lights from his electric runabout would give a brilliant illumination, and these he now directed toward the clump of trees whence the cry for help had seemed to come.

"Doesn't appear to have been visited by any one since we were here," remarked Torn, as he observed the marks of the new automobile tire in the dust. "Now we'll look about more carefully."

This they did, but they were about to give up in despair and start for the nearest telephone to call up the hospitals, when Mr. Damon gave an exclamation.

"What is it?" asked Tom.

"Something bright and shining!" said his companion. "I saw it gleam in the light of the lamps. You nearly put your foot on it, Tom. Just step back a moment."

Tom did so, and the eccentric man, with another exclamation, this time of satisfaction, reached down and picked something up from the dusty road.

"It's a watch!" he exclaimed. "A gold watch! And it's been stepped on, evidently, or run over by an auto. Not much damaged, but the case is a bit bent and scratched. It's stopped, too!" he added as he held it to his ear.

"What time does it show?" asked Tom.

"Eight forty-seven," answered Mr. Damon, as he consulted the dial. "Why, Tom, that was just about when we heard the cries for help!"

"Yes, it must have been. Let me see that watch."

No sooner had the young inventor taken the timepiece into his hands than he, too, uttered a cry of amazement.

"Do you recognize it?" asked Mr. Damon, in great excitement.

"It's Mr. Nestor's watch!" cried Tom. "He must have fallen here, and been hurt. It was Mr. Nestor who cried for help, and who was taken away by the autoists. They've probably taken him to some hospital. There's been an accident all right."

Tom and Mr. Damon were of one mind now in thinking that Mr. Nestor had met with some mishap on the road—an automobile accident most likely—and that he was the person who had called for help.

"If they had only answered when we hallooed at them," said Tom, "we wouldn't be in all this stew now. We could have told the strangers who came to his aid who he was, and we might even have taken him to the hospital in the airship."

"Well, it's too late to think of that now," returned Mr. Damon. "We had better get into communication with him as soon as we can, and then send word to his wife and daughter. I hope he isn't badly hurt."

Tom hoped so, too, with all his heart.

There was nothing to do but to get back in the runabout and make all speed for the nearest telephone, and Tom Swift lost little time in doing this. They found a drug store which was open a little later than usual, and at once Tom went into the booth and called up the Shopton hospital. He was well known there, as he and his father were liberal supporters of the institution, which was a private affair. Many of Tom's men were treated at the dispensary, and, as accidents were of more or less frequent occurrence at the works, the young inventor had frequent occasions to call up the place.

"Mr. Nestor would ask to be taken there, as it's nearest his home—that is, if he was able to speak," Tom said to Mr. Damon, who agreed with him. There was a little delay in getting the hospital on the wire, but when Tom had it, and was talking to the superintendent, he was rather surprised, to tell the truth, to be told that Mr. Nestor had not been brought in.

"We haven't had any accident cases all day, nor tonight, Mr. Swift," the superintendent reported. "Was this some one special you were inquiring about?"

For Tom, determining not to give Mr. Nestor's name, except as a last resort, had merely inquired whether any recent accident cases had been brought in.

"I'll let you know later, Mr. Millard," he told the superintendent, not exactly answering the question. He hung up the receiver, and, opening the door of the booth, said to Mr. Damon: "He isn't there."

"Then try Waterfield," was the suggestion; and Tom did so, though he could not imagine why an injured man, such as Mr. Nestor might prove to be, should be taken as far as Waterfield, when the hospital at Shopton was nearer.

"Unless," he told Mr. Damon, "the people which ran down Mary's father didn't know about our hospital."

The reply from the institution in Mr. Damon's home town was just as discouraging as had been the answer from Shopton. At first, when Tom inquired, the head nurse had said there was an accident case at that moment being brought in. Tom was all excitement until she went to inquire the name and circumstances, and then he learned that it was the case of a little boy who had fallen downstairs at his home and broken a leg. There was no record of any one answering the description of Mr. Nestor having been brought in that evening.

"Hum! This is getting to be mysterious," mused Tom, as he came out of the booth. "What shall we do—go back and tell Mrs. Nestor and Mary, or communicate with the police?"

"Why not try the Alexian Hospital?" asked Mr. Damon. "That's away over in Center-fiord, to be sure, but it's more likely to be known to passing tourists than either of our institutions around here, especially if the autoists were strangers."

"That's so," agreed Tom. The Alexian Hospital was operated under the direction of the Brothers of that faith, and was well known in that part of the state. Often cases of persons who had been injured by passing automobiles had been taken there for treatment, for, as Mr. Damon had said, it was well known, and Centerford was the nearest large city.

"I can just about see how it happened," said Tom. "They ran Mr. Nestor down, and stopped to pick him up after they heard his cries for help. And the Alexian Hospital was the first one they thought of. We should have called that up first."

But once more disappointment awaited the young inventor and his friend. Word came back over the wire that no accident case, which bore any resemblance to Mary's father, had been brought in.

"Well, I'm stumped!" exclaimed Tom. "What shall we do now, Mr. Damon?"

"Much as I dislike it," said the eccentric man who was too much worried, now, to do any "blessing," which was his favorite expression, "I think we ought to communicate with Mrs. Nestor. She will be very anxious."

"I guess we'll have to," said Tom. "But wait! I'll call up my house first, and see if he has gone back there."

But Mr. Nestor had not done this, and Mrs. Baggert, who answered the telephone, said Mary had been calling frantically for Tom, as her mother was now on the verge of complete collapse.

"No help for it," said Tom, ruefully. "We've got to tell 'em we have no news, and can't find him."

And, hearing this, Mrs. Nestor did collapse, and a doctor was called in.

Thereupon Tom, who with Mr. Damon had gone back to the Nestor home, took charge of matters, sending for Mrs. Nestor's sister to come and stay with her and take charge of the house.

"You'll need some one to stay with you," he told Mary.

"Yes, I shall," she admitted, trying bravely not to give way to her emotion. "Oh, Tom, I wish you could stay, too. I'm sure something dreadful must have happened to poor father. Please stay and help us find him!"

"I will," Tom promised. "As soon as your aunt comes I'll take Mr. Damon home, and then I'll give the rest of my time to you."

And this Tom did, sending word home that he would remain at the Nestor's all night and part of the next day.

Tom got but little sleep that night. He communicated with the police and saw to it that a general alarm was sent out. He called up all hospitals within a radius of fifty miles, but could get no trace of any injured man whose description resembled that of Mr. Nestor.

"What can have happened?" asked Mary tearfully.

"Well, the way I figure it out is this," said Tom. "Your father left my house soon after Mr. Damon and I did in the Air Scout. Mr. Nestor was riding his bicycle, and he must have been run into by an automobile. That is how his watch was damaged and that was when Mr. Damon and I heard the cries for help."

"Oh, do you think he was badly hurt?" asked Mary.

"No, I don't," and Tom answered truthfully. "The voice sounded as though he was in pain, certainly, but it was strong and vigorous, and not at all as though he was dangerously hurt."

"And what do you think happened to him after he was hurt?" asked Mary.

"The autoists took him away," decided Tom. "In fact, we heard the machine go, but of course we never connected the call for help and what followed with your father. The autoists took him away."

"Where?"

"I should say to some hospital. Perhaps a private one of which we know nothing, and which may be near here. I'll get a full list from the Board of Health to-morrow. Or it may be that the autoists, seeing the damage they had done, took your father to the home of one of themselves, and summoned a doctor there."

"Why would they do that?"

"Well, they may have been so frightened they didn't realize what they were doing, or they may have thought he would get better treatment in a private house, if he were not badly injured, than if he should be taken to a hospital. It may have been that one of the persons in the auto was a physician, and wished to try his own skill on the man he had hurt."

"You make me feel more comfortable, Tom," said Mary. "But, even supposing all this, why couldn't they telephone to us that my father was all right? He always carries an identification card with him, and if he were unconscious it could be ascertained who he was."

"That's what I can't understand," said Tom frankly. "It puzzles me. But we'll find him—never fear!"

And so he kept on with his telephone inquiries, while a physician and her sister ministered to Mrs. Nestor. The night was very, very long, and no good news came in.

Silent Sam

Slowly the dawn broke through the mists of darkness, and made the earth light. The sun came straggling in through cracks in the shutters in the home of Mr. Nestor, the gradually increasing gleam paling the electric lights, in the glare of which Tom Swift, Mary, and her aunt sat, waiting for some word of the missing man. But none came.

"What shall we do now?" asked Mary, as she looked at Tom.

"Oh, there's lots to do," he said, trying to make his voice sound cheerful. "We'll be busy all day. I sent word to have one of my touring cars ready to hurry to any part of the country the moment we should get word from your father."

"And do you think we shall get word, Tom?" the girl went on wistfully.

"Of course we shall!" he cried. "Word may come in at any time. Now get ready, eat a good breakfast, and then you can go with me as soon as we hear anything definite. Come, we'll have breakfast!"

"I can't eat a thing!" protested Mary.

"Oh, yes you can," said her aunt, who was a cheerful sort of person. "I'll see about getting something for you and Mr. Swift, and see that your mother is all right."

She left the room to give orders to the servant about the meal, and returned to say that Mrs. Nestor was sleeping quietly. She had been given a sedative. Mary managed to eat a little, and she gave Tom the address of several friends who were called up in the vain hope that, somehow, Mr. Nestor might have gone to see them.

"Tom, what do you really think has happened?" asked Mary again, as they sat facing one another in the library, during a respite from the telephone.

Tom Swift repeated, to the girl his theory of what had happened with an assumption of confidence he did not altogether feel.

His prediction of a speedy end to the suspense did not come true that day, nor for many days. No news was heard of Mr. Nestor. After the first day, when there was no information and when no reports came of any one of his description having been hurt in an automobile accident or having been taken to any hospital, the police started an energetic search.

The authorities in all near-by cities were notified, and all thought of keeping from the public what had happened was given over. Tom's story, of how he and Mr. Damon had heard the cry for help on the lonely meadow, was printed in the papers, though the young inventor did not say that he had been out trying his new aeroplane. That was a detail not needed in the finding of Mr. Nestor.

But Mary's father was not found. The mystery regarding his disappearance deepened, and there was no trace of him after he had left

Tom's house that eventful evening. Persons living along the roads he might have taken in riding his bicycle were questioned, but they had seen nothing of him, nor were they aware of any accident. Tom's testimony and that of Mr. Damon was all the clue there was.

"I don't believe he's dead!" stoutly declared the young inventor, when this dire possibility had been hinted at. "I believe the persons who were responsible for the accident are afraid to reveal his whereabouts until he recovers from possible injuries. You'll see! Mr. Nestor will come back safe!"

And, somehow, though her mother was skeptical, Mary believed what Tom said.

The search was kept up, but without result, and Tom aided all he could. But there was not much he could do. The police and other authorities were at a total loss.

In the intervals of visiting Mary and her mother, and doing what he could for them, Tom worked on his new motor. He knew that he was on the right track and that all that was needed now was to make certain refinements and adjustments in the apparatus he had already constructed, so that it would operate more quietly.

"Absorbing the vibrations from the exhaust, caused by the exploded gases in the cylinders, does the trick," Tom told his father.

"But there is enormous pressure to overcome, Tom. You must be sure your muffler will stand the strain. Otherwise she is going to blow out a gasket some day, when you least expect it. Then the sudden resumption of pressure outside the cylinders is going to cause a change in the equilibrium, and you may turn turtle in the air."

"I've thought of that," said Tom. "At worst it can't be any more than looping the loop. But I'll make the muffler doubly strong."

"Better provide an auxiliary chamber to take care of part of the exhaust in case your main apparatus breaks," advised the older inventor, and Tom said he would. He did, too, for he valued his father's expert advice.

Meanwhile he was busy fitting one of his latest aeroplanes with the new motor. The motor he and Mr. Damon had used in their flight was one patched up from an old one. But now Tom was working on a complete new one, made after his revised model, and in which the silencer was an integral part, instead of being built on.

While giving Mary and her mother all the assistance in his power, Tom still found time to work on his new, pet scheme. He had matters now where he did not fear any tampering with his plans, for he had filed away his papers in a safe place, and was making his new machine from memory.

"But if some one got in and had a look at the inside of your silencer he could see how it is constructed, couldn't he?" asked Ned Newton.

"Yes," assented Tom, "But they're not going to get in very easily. Koku sleeps in the experiment shop now, and my machine is there."

"Oh, well that explains your confidence. I feel sorry for the burglar who makes the attempt, once Koku wakes up. Heard anything more from those Universal people?"

"No, not directly. I understand they are working hard on some new type of plane for army use, but I haven't bothered my head about them. I'm too much occupied with my own affairs and trying to help Mary."

"Very strange about Mr. Nestor, isn't it?"

"Worse than strange," said Tom. "If this keeps on, and he isn't heard from, it will be tragic pretty soon."

"He must be held a prisoner somewhere," declared Ned.

"It begins to look that way," assented Tom. "Though who would have an object in that I can't understand. He had no enemies, as far as is known, and his business affairs were in excellent shape. Unless, as I said, the persons who ran him down are, through fear, keeping him hidden until he recovers, I can't imagine what has become of him."

"Well, it certainly is a puzzle," said Ned. And Tom agreed with his chum.

It was about a week after the disappearance of Mr. Nestor that Mr. Damon came over to see Tom.

"Bless my shoe laces, Tom!" exclaimed the eccentric man, "but you are as busy as ever." For he found the young inventor in the experiment shop, surrounded by a mass of papers and all sorts of mechanical devices.

"Yes, I'm working a little," said Tom. "But you are just in time. Come on out, I want to introduce you to Silent Sam."

"'Silent Sam!'" exclaimed Mr. Damon. "Have you been taking a new trip to the Land of Wonders? Have you brought back some new kind of servant?"

"Not exactly a servant," said Tom with a laugh, "though I hope Silent Sam will serve me well."

"'Silent Sam?' What does it mean? Is that a joke?" asked the puzzled Mr. Damon.

"I hope it doesn't turn out a joke," replied Tom. "But come on, I'll introduce you to him, Mr. Damon."

He led the way to one of the big hangars where his various machines of the air were housed. On the way Mr. Damon asked about news of Mr. Nestor, but was told there was none.

Tom Swift opened the big, swinging doors and pulled aside an enveloping canvas curtain. There stood revealed a big aeroplane, of somewhat new pattern, the wings gleaming like silver from the varnish that had been applied. In shape it was not unlike the machines already in use, except that the propellers were of somewhat different design.

The engine was mounted in front, and even with his slight knowledge of mechanics Mr. Damon could tell that it was exceedingly powerful. But it was certain devices attached to the engine that attracted his attention, for they were totally different from any on any other aeroplane, though they bore some resemblance to apparatus on the plane in which Tom and the eccentric man had made the night flight.

"Is this your new machine, Tom?" asked Mr. Damon.

"Yes."

"Well, I don't see anything of that fellow you spoke of—Silent Sam."

"This is Silent Sam," returned Tom, with a laugh. "I've named my new noiseless aeroplane -Ämy Air Scout—I've named that Silent Sam. Wait until you hear it, or rather, don't hear it, and I think you'll agree with me. Silent Sam for Uncle Sam!"

"Good!" cried Mr. Damon. "Bless my dictionary, but that's a good name! Does it sail silently, Tom?"

"I'll let you judge presently. Silent Sam is all ready for his first trial, and I'll be glad to have you with me. Now, I'll just—"

Tom suddenly ceased speaking and held up a hand to enjoin silence. Then, while Mr. Damon watched, the young inventor began moving noiselessly toward the rear of the big shed, inside which was his new machine.

SUSPICIONS

"Who's there?" suddenly called Tom, and in such a sharp voice that Mr. Damon started, ready as he was for something unusual.

There was no answer and Tom suddenly switched on all the lights in the shed. Up to then there had been only a few glowing—just enough for him to show the new Air Scout to his friend.

"Who's there?" asked Tom again, sharply.

"Bless my opera glasses, Tom!" cried Mr. Damon, "but are you seeing things?"

"No; but I'm hearing them," answered Tom with a short laugh. "Did you think you heard some one moving around near the rudders of Silent Sam, Mr. Damon?"

"No, I can't say that I did. Everything seems to me to be all right."

"Well, it doesn't to me," went on Tom grimly. "I think there is an intruder in this shed, though how any one could get in when the doors have been locked all day, is more than I can figure out. But I'm going to have a look."

"I'll help you," offered Mr. Damon, and, in the bright glare from many electric lights, the two began a search of the big hangar where the new craft was kept.

But though the young inventor and his friend went around to the rear of the aeroplane, walking in opposite directions, they saw no one, nor did any one try to escape past them.

"And yet I was sure I heard some one in here," declared Tom, when a search had revealed nothing. "It sounded as if some one were scuffling softly about in rubber-soled shoes, trying to hide."

"Bless my suspenders!" cried Mr. Damon, "who do you think it could have been, Tom?"

"Who else but some spy trying to get possession of my secrets?" was the answer. "But I guess I was too quick for them. They couldn't learn much from looking at the outside of my muffler, and it hasn't been disturbed, as far as I can see."

"Who would want to gain a knowledge of it in that unlawful way?" asked Mr. Damon.

"Perhaps some of the Universal crowd. They may have been disappointed in perfecting a silent motor themselves, and think stealing my idea would be the easiest way out of it."

"Do they know you are working on such a model as this Silent Sam of yours, Tom?"

"Yes, I imagine they do. One of the firm members, as you recall, overheard something, I think, that gave them a hint as to what my plans were, though, thanks to the time I fooled the spy, they haven't any real data to go by, I believe."

"Let us hope not," said Mr. Damon.

Tom and he made a thorough search of the big shed, but found no one, nor was there any trace of an intruder. Tom notified Jackson, who, in turn, told the guards and watchmen to be on the lookout for any suspicious strangers, but none was seen in the vicinity of the Swift works.

"Well, everything seems to be all right, so we'll have the test," remarked Torn, after a further search of the premises. "Now, Mr. Damon, if all goes as I hope you will see what my new machine can do. Strain your ears for a sound, and let me know how much you hear."

His men helping him, Tom started the new motor which was tried for the first time attached to the new craft. No flight was to be made yet, the motor being tested as though on the block, though, in reality, the craft was ready for instant flight if need be.

Slowly the great propellers began to revolve, and then Tom, taking his place in the cockpit, turned on more power. The new craft—Silent Sam—was made fast so it could not progress even though the propellers revolved at high speed.

"I'm not sending her to the limit," said Tom to his friend, as the young inventor throttled down the motor. "If I did I'd tear her loose from the holding blocks."

"Her!" cried Mr. Damon. "Bless my typewriter, Tom! but I thought Silent Sam was a gentleman aeroplane.

"So he is!" laughed the young man, frankly. "I forgot about 'Silent Sam.' Guess I'll have to say 'him' instead of 'her,' though the latter sounds more natural. Anyhow what do you think?"

"I think it's wonderful!" exclaimed Mr. Damon. "There the motor is, going at almost full speed, and I can hardly hear a thing. You can the easier believe that when I say that I can hear you talk perfectly well. And I guess you hear me, don't you?"

"Yes," replied Tom. "And we don't have to shout, either. This is the best test ever! I think everything is a success."

"Are you going to take her aloft, Tom?" the eccentric man went on.

"Yes, now that I'm sure the engine is all right. Will you go for a flight with me?"

"I certainly will! I only wish we could find him, though. I'd go with a better heart."

"Oh! Mr. Nestor?"

"Yes, I can't imagine what has become of him. It is almost as if the earth had opened and swallowed him. His disappearance is a great mystery."

"It surely is," agreed Tom. "Can't seem to get any trace of him. But if we hear another cry for help, when we have to land, you can make up your mind I'll investigate more quickly than I did at first."

"I agree with you," said Mr. Damon.

It was nearly evening then, and until it was dark enough for his flight Tom spent the time tuning up the engine and seeing that all was in readiness for the latest test. He had decided not to go aloft while it was light enough for curiosity seekers to note the flight.

Tom rather wished Mary Nestor might have a sail with him in his latest improved silent Air Scout, but the girl was too much occupied at home and in trying to find some trace of her father.

Tom, his father, and Mr. Damon had helped all they could, but there were no results. A private detective had been engaged, but he had no more of a clue than the regular police.

At last it was dark enough for the flight, and Tom and Mr. Damon took their places in the machine. Once more the propellers were turned around, and when the compression had been made, and the spark switched on, around spun the big wooden blades, and the great craft moved over the grass.

On and on and up and up sailed Tom and Mr. Damon, and as they left behind them the shops and the Swift homestead, the two passengers were aware of their almost silent flight. The big aeroplane, the exhaust of which, ordinarily, would have nearly deafened them, was now as silent as a bird.

"Silent Sam for Uncle Sam!" cried Tom in delight, as he went on faster. "I'm sure the government ought to be glad to get this plane for air scout work. It's a success! A great success!"

"Yes, so it is!" agreed Mr. Damon. "You do well to speak of it so, Tom."

For, modest as the young inventor was, he felt, in justice to himself, that he must acknowledge the fact that his craft was a success. For it rose and sailed almost as silently as a bat, and a few hundred feet away no one, not seeing it, would have believed a big aeroplane was in motion.

Tom and Mr. Damon flew about twenty miles at a swift pace, and all the fault Tom had to find was that the machine was not as steady in flight as she should have been.

"But I can remedy that with the use of some of dad's gyroscope stabilizers," he told Mr. Damon.

They returned to the hangar safely, and the first trip of the new Silent Sam was an assured success.

It was the following day, when Tom was busy in the machine shop installing the gyroscopes spoken of, that Jackson came to tell him there was a visitor to see him.

"Who is it?" asked the young inventor.

"Mr. Gale of the Universal Company," was the answer.

"I don't want to see him!" declared Tom quickly. "I have nothing to say to him after his clumsy threats."

"He seems very much in earnest," said Jackson. "Better see him, if only for a minute or so."

"All right, I will," assented Tom. "Show him in."

Mr. Gale, as blusteringly bluff as ever, entered the shop. Tom had carefully put away all papers and models, as well as the finished machines, so he had no fear that his visitor might discover some secret.

"Oh, Mr. Swift!" began the president of the Universal Company, when he met the young inventor, "I wish to assure you that what has been done was entirely without our knowledge. And, though this man may have acted as our agent at one time, we repudiate any acts of his that might

"What are you talking about?" asked Tom in surprise. "Have I been so impolite as to sleep during part of your talk? I don't understand what you are driving at."

"Oh, I thought you did," said Gale, and he showed surprise. "I understood that the man who—"

"Do you mean there was some one here in the shed last night?" cried the young inventor suddenly, all his suspicions aroused.

"Some one here last night?" repeated Mr. Gale. "No, I don't refer to last night. But perhaps I am making a mistake. I—er—I—"

"Some one is making a mistake!" said Tom significantly.

ANOTHER FLIGHT

For perhaps a quarter of a minute Tom Swift and the president of the Universal Flying Machine Company of New York sat staring at one another. Mr. Gale's face wore a puzzled expression, and so did Tom's. And, after the last remark of the young inventor, the man who had called to see him said:

"Well, perhaps we are talking at cross purposes. I don't blame you for not feeling very friendly toward us, and if I had had my way that last correspondence with you would never have left our office."

"It wasn't very business-like," said Tom dryly, referring to the veiled threats when he had refused to sell his services to the rival company.

"I realize that," said Mr. Gale. "But we have some peculiar men working for us, and sometimes there is so much to do, so many possibilities of which to take advantage, that we may get a little off our balance. But what I called for was not to renew our offer to you. I understand that is definitely settled."

"As far as I am concerned, it is," said Tom, as his caller seemed to want an answer.

"Yes. Well, then, what I called to say was that if you are thinking of taking any legal action against us because of the action of that man Lydane, I wish to state that he had absolutely no authority to—"

"Excuse me!" broke in Tom, "but by Lydane do you mean the man who also posed as Bower, the spy?"

"No, I do not. Though I regret to say that Bower once worked for us. He, too, had no authority to come here and get a position. He was still in our service when he did that."

"So I have suspected," said Tom. "I realize now that he was a spy, who came here to try to find out for you some of my secrets."

"Not with my permission!" exclaimed Mr. Gale. "I was against that from the first and I came to tell you so. But Bower really did you no harm."

"No, he didn't get the chance!" chuckled Tom. "Nor did that other spy—the one with the gold tooth. I wonder how he liked our mud hole?"

"He was Lydane," said Mr. Gale. "It is about him I came."

"You might have saved yourself the trouble," returned Tom. "I don't wish to discuss him."

"But I wish to make sure," said Mr. Gale, that what he has done will not come back on us. We repudiate him entirely. His methods we can not countenance. He is too daring—"

"Oh, don't worry!" interrupted Tom. "He hasn't done anything to me—he didn't get the chance, as I guess he's told you. You needn't apologize on his account. He did me no harm, and—"

"But I understood from him that—"

"Now I don't want to seem impolite!" broke in Tom, "nor do I want to take pattern after some of your company's acts, if not your own. But I am very busy. I have an important test to make for the government, and my time is fully occupied. I am afraid I shall have to bid you good-morning and—"

"But won't you give me a chance to—" began the president.

"Now, the less we discuss this matter the better!" interrupted Tom. "Lydane, as you call the man with the gold tooth didn't really do anything to me nor any great harm to any of my possessions, as far as I can learn. His career is a closed book— a book with muddy covers!" and the young inventor laughed.

"Oh, well, if you look at it that way, there is nothing further for me to say" said Mr. Gale stiffly. "I understood— But hasn't my partner, Mr. Ware, seen you?" he asked Tom quickly.

"No. And I don't care to see him."

"Oh, then that accounts for it," was the quick answer. "Well, if you regard the matter as closed I suppose we should also. We are not to blame for what Lydane does when he is no longer in our employ, and we repudiate anything he may do, or may have done."

This struck Tom, afterward, as being rather a queer remark, but he did not think so at the time.

The truth was that the young inventor wished very much to try out a new device on his noiseless aeroplane and wanted to get rid of Mr. Gale before doing so. So he did not pay as much attention to the remarks of the president as, otherwise, he might have done.

It was not until after Mr. Gale had taken his leave and Tom had finished the particular work on which he was engaged when the president of the rival company came in, that the young man did some hard thinking. And this thinking was done after he had received a telephone call from Mary Nestor, asking, if by any chance, he had beard anything like a clue as to the whereabouts of her father.

Tom had been obliged to tell her that he had not. Everything possible was being done to find the missing man but he had disappeared as completely as though he had ridden on his bicycle into the crater of some extinct volcano on the meadow, and had fallen to the bottom.

An effort was made to trace him through an automobile association which had a large membership. That is, the members were asked to make inquiries to ascertain, if possible, whether any one had heard of an unreported accident—one in which Mr. Nestor might have been carried away by persons who accidently ran him down.

But this came to naught, and the police and other authorities were at a loss how farther to proceed. It was a theory in some quarters that Mr. Nestor was perfectly safe, but that he was out of his mind, and was either wandering around, not knowing who he was, or was, in this condition, detained somewhere, the persons having him in charge not realizing that he was the missing man so widely sought.

This belief was a relief to Mrs. Nestor and Mary in many ways for it prevented them from giving way to the fear that Mr. Nestor was dead. That he was alive was Tom Swift's firm opinion, and he was doing all he could to prove it.

It was not until the day after the visit of Mr. Gale that Tom, having concluded some intricate calculations about the strength of cylinder valves, uttered an exclamation.

"I wonder if he could have meant that?" cried the young inventor. "I wonder if he could have meant that? I must find out at once! Queer I didn't think of that before!"

He put in a long distance call to New York, asking to speak to Mr. Gale. But when, eventually, he was connected with the office of the Universal Flying Machine Company he was told that Mr. Gale and Mr. Ware had sailed for France that day, going over as government representatives to investigate aeroplane motors. Gale's visit to Tom had been just previous to taking the boat, it was said.

"This is tough luck!" mused Tom, his suspicions doubly aroused now. "I can't let this rest here! I've got to get after it! As soon as I make this final test, and invite Uncle Sam's experts out to see how my noiseless motor works, I'll get after Gale and Ware if I have to follow them to the battlefields of France! I wonder if it was that he was hinting at all the while! I begin to believe it was!"

Tom Swift had decided on another flight for his new craft before he would let the government experts see it.

"Silent Sam must do his very best work for Uncle Sam before I turn him over," said the young inventor.

"And after this flight I'll offer the machine to the government, and then devote all my time to finding Mr. Nestor," said Tom. "I'd do it now, but private matters, however deeply they affect us, must be put aside to help win the war. But this will end my inventive work until after Mr. Nestor is found—if he's alive."

Preparations for the test flight went on apace, and one afternoon Tom and Jackson took their places in the big, new aeroplane. He no longer feared daylight crowds in case of an accident. They made a good start, and the motor was so quiet that as Tom passed over his own plant the men working in the yard, who did not know of the flight, did not look up to see what was going on. They could not hear the engine.

"I think we've got everything just as we want it, Jackson," said Tom, much pleased.

"I believe you," answered the mechanician. "It couldn't be better. Now if—"

And at that moment there came a loud explosion, and Silent Sam began drifting rapidly toward the earth, as falls a bird with a broken wing.

Queer Marks

"What happened?" cried Jackson to Tom, as he leaned forward in his seat which was in the rear of the young inventor's.

"Don't know, exactly," was the answer, as Tom quickly shifted the rudders to correct the slanting fall of his craft. "Sounded as though there was a tremendous back-fire, or else the muffler blew up. The engine is dead."

"Can you take her down safely?"

"Oh, yes, I guess so. She's a bit out of control, but the stabilizer will keep her on a level keel. Good thing we installed it."

"You're right!" said Jackson.

Now they were falling earthward with great rapidity, but, thanks to the gyroscope stabilizer, the "side-slipping," than which there is no motion more dreaded by an aviator, had nearly ceased. The craft was volplaning down as it ought, and Tom had it under as perfect control as was possible under the circumstances.

"We'll get down all right if something else doesn't happen," he said to Jackson, with grim humor.

"Well, let's hope that it won't," said the mechanic. "We're a good distance up yet."

They were, as a matter of fact, for the explosion, or whatever had happened to the craft, had occurred at a height of over two miles, and they at once began falling. As yet Tom Swift was unaware of the exact nature of the accident or its cause. All he knew was that there had been a big noise and that the engine had stopped working. He could not see the silencer from where he sat, as it was constructed on the underside of the motor, but he had an idea that the same sort of mishap had occurred as on the occasion when the test machine had sailed through the roof of his workshop.

"But, luckily, this wasn't as bad," mused Tom. "Anyhow the motor is out of business."

And this was very evident. The young inventor had tried to start the apparatus after its stoppage by the explosion, but it had not responded to his efforts, and then he had desisted, fearing to cause some further damage, or, perhaps, endanger his own life and that of Jackson.

Down, down swept Silent Sam—doubly silent now, and Tom began looking about for a good place to make a landing. This was nothing new for either him or his mechanician, and they accepted the outcome as a matter of course.

"Not a very lively place down there," remarked Jackson, as he looked over the side of the cockpit.

"If we have to depend for help on any one down there, I guess we'll be a long time waiting," agreed Tom. They were about to land in a very lonely spot. It was one he had never before visited, though he knew it could not be much more than twenty miles from his own home, as they had not flown much farther than that distance.

But, somehow or other, Tom had not visited this particular section, and knew nothing of it. He saw below him, as Jackson had seen, a lonely stretch of country—a big field, once a wood-lot, evidently, as scattered about were some stumps and some second growth trees. There were also a number of evergreens—Christmas trees Jackson called them. And this was the only open place for miles, the surrounding country being a densely wooded one. There did not appear to be a house or other building in sight where they might seek help.

"But maybe we can make the repairs ourselves and keep on," the lad thought.

With practiced eye he picked out a smooth, grassy, level spot, in the midst of scattered evergreen trees, and there Tom Swift skillfully brought his Air Scout to rest. With a gentle thud the rubber-tired wheels struck the Earth, rolled along a little distance, and then called to a stop.

Hardly had the aeroplane ceased moving when Tom and his companion jumped out and began eagerly to examine the machinery to see the extent of damage.

"I thought so!" Tom exclaimed. "The silencer cracked under the strain. Those exhaust gases have more pressure that I believed possible. I increased the margin of safety on this muffler, too. But she's cracked, and I can't use the machine until I put on a new one. Good thing I didn't ask for a government inspection until after this trial flight."

"That's so," agreed Jackson. "But can't you patch it up, or go on without a muffler, so we can get back home?"

"I'm afraid not," Tom answered. "You see I removed all the old exhaust pipe fittings when I put on my new silencer. Now if I took off my attachment there wouldn't be anything to carry off the discharged gases, and they'd form a regular cloud about us. We couldn't stand it without gas masks, such as they use in the trenches, and we haven't any of those with us."

"That's right," agreed Jackson. "Well, what do you want to do? Have me stay here and guard the machine while you go for help? Or shall I go?"

"I don't know why we both can't go," said Tom. "There is no use trying to patch up this machine here. I'll have to send a truck after it, and dismantle it before I can get it home.

"As for either of us staying here on guard, I don't quite see the need of that. This looks like the jumping-off place to me. I don't believe there's a native within miles. I didn't see any houses as we came down, and I think Silent Sam will be perfectly safe here. No one can run off with him, anyhow. He'd be as hard to start as an automobile with all four wheels gone. Let's leave it here and both walk back."

"All right," agreed Jackson. "That suits me. Might as well leave our togs here, too. It will be easier walking without them," and he began taking off the fur-lined suit, his cap, and his goggles, such as he and Tom wore against the piercing cold of the upper regions.

"We can stuff them in the cockpit and leave them," went on the mechanician, as he divested himself of his garments. As he stowed them away in his seat he gave one more look at the broken muffler. As Tom Swift said, his new silencer had literally blown up, a large piece having been torn from the gas chamber.

Something that Jackson saw caused him to utter an exclamation that brought Tom Swift to his side.

"What is it?" asked the young inventor.

"Look!" was the answer. "See! Just at the edge of that break! It's been filed to make the metal thinner there than anywhere else. You didn't do that, did you?"

"I should say not!" cried Tom. "Why, to file there would mean to weaken the whole structure."

"And that's exactly what's happened!" declared Jackson, as he gave another look. "Some one has filed this nearly throughÄleaving only a thin metal skin, and when the gas pressure became too much it blew out. That's what happened!"

Tom Swift made a quick but thorough examination.

"You're right, Jackson!" he exclaimed. "That was filed deliberately to cause the accident. And it must have been done lately, for I carefully inspected the silencer when I put it on, and it was in perfect order. There's been spy work here. Some one got into the hangar and filed that casing. Then the accumulated pressure of the gases did the rest."

"As sure as you're alive!" agreed Jackson. "Maybe that's what Gale did when he called."

"No," returned Tom, shaking his head, "he didn't get a chance to do anything like that. I watched him all the while. But perhaps this is what he referred to when he said he and his company would repudiate any act of that spy with the gold tooth—Lydane, so Gale said his name was. Maybe that's what Lydane did."

"He was capable of it," agreed the mechanic, "but he couldn't have done it that time you tripped him into the mud puddle. This silencer wasn't built then."

"No, you're right," assented Tom. "Then he must have been around since, doing some of his tricky work!"

"I don't see how that could have been," said Jackson slowly. "We've kept a very careful watch, and your shop has been specially guarded."

"I know it has," said Tom. "There couldn't much get past Koku; but some one seems to have done it, or else how could that filing have been done?"

Jackson shook his head. The problem was too much for him. He looked carefully at the exploded and broken silencer, and Tom, too, gave it a critical eye. There was no doubt but that it had been filed in several places to weaken the structure of the metal.

"When did you last see that it was in perfect condition?" asked Jackson. Tom named a certain date.

"That was just before Gale called," observed the mechanician. "He might have known of it."

"I wish I'd known of it at the time," said Tom savagely. "He wouldn't have gotten away as easily as he did. Well, there's no use standing here talking about it. Let's get back to civilization and we'll send back one of the trucks. Luckily I have another silencer I can put on for the government test. This one will never be of any more use, though I may be able to save some of the valves and baffle plates."

Slowly they turned from the disabled aeroplane and started to look for a path that would lead them out of the lonely place. Tom as the first to strike what seemed to be a cow path, or perhaps what had been a road into the wood lot in the early days.

As he tramped along it, followed by Jackson, the young inventor suddenly stopped, as he came to a sandy place, and, stooping over, looked intently at some queer marks in the soil.

"What is it?" asked the mechanician.

"Looks like the marks of an automobile," said Tom slowly. "And I was just trying to remember where I'd seen marks like these before."

THE DESERTED CABIN

For several seconds the young inventor remained bending over the queer marks in that little sandy path of the lonely field in the midst of the silent woods. Jackson watched him curiously, and then Tom straightened up, exclaiming as he did so:

"I have it! Now I know where it was! I saw marks like these the night Mr. Nestor disappeared. Mr. Damon and I noticed the marks in the dust on the road the time we made the forced landing the first night we tried out the silent motor. That's it! They are the same marks! I'm sure of it!"

"I wouldn't go so far as to say that," said Jackson slowly. He was more deliberate than Tom Swift, a fact for which the young inventor was often glad, as it saved him from impulsive mistakes.

"This may not be the same auto," went on the mechanician. "I'll admit I never saw square tire marks like those before. Most of the usual ones are circular, diamond-shape or oblong. Some tire manufacturer must have tried a new stunt. But as for saying these marks were made by the same machine you saw evidences of the night Mr. Nestor disappeared, why, that's going a little too far, Tom."

"Yes, I suppose it is," admitted the young inventor. "But it's a clue worth following. Maybe Mr. Nestor has been brought to some lonely place like this, and is being held."

"Why would any one want to do that?" asked Jackson. "He had no enemies.

"Well, perhaps those who ran him down and injured him are afraid to let him go for fear he will prosecute them and ask for heavy damages," suggested Tom. "They may be holding him a captive until he gets well, and aim on treating him so nicely that he won't bring suit."

"That's a pretty far-fetched theory," said the mechanician as he carefully looked at the tracks. "But of course it may be true. Anyhow, these tire marks are rather recent, I should say, and they are made by a new tire. Do you think we can follow them?"

"I'm going to try !" declared Tom. "The only trouble is we can't tell whether it was going or coming—that is we don't know which way to go."

"That's so," agreed his companion. "And so the only thing to do is to travel a bit both ways. The path, or road, or whatever you call it, is plainly enough marked here, though you can't always pick out the tire marks. They show only on bare ground. The grass doesn't leave any tracks that we can see, though doubtless they are there.

"But as for thinking this car is the same one the marks of which you saw on the lonely moor, the night you heard the call for help—that's going too far, Tom Swift."

"Yes, I realize that. Of course there must be more than one car with tires which have square protuberances. But it's worth taking a chance on—following this clue."

"Oh, sure!" agreed Jackson.

"The only question is, then, which way to go," returned Tom.

They settled that, arbitrarily enough, by going on in the direction they had started after leaving the stranded airship. They followed a half-defined path, and were rewarded by getting occasional glimpses on bare ground of the odd tire marks.

Through a devious winding way, now hidden amid a lane of trees, and again cutting across an open space, the path led. They saw the marks often enough to make sure they were on the right trail, and in one place they saw several different patches of the odd marks.

They went on perhaps half a mile more. when they came to a lonely road and saw where the car had turned from that into the wood-lot, as Tom called the place where his craft had settled down.

"Look!" cried the young inventor to Jackson. "They've been here more than once, and have gone along the road in both directions. They seem to have used this turning into the lot as a sort of stopping place."

This was plain enough from an examination of the marks in the sandy soil of the road, which was one not often used. The automobile with the queer, square marks on the tires had turned into the lot, coming and going in both directions.

"This settles it!" cried Tom, when he finished making an examination. "There's something farther back in this lot that we've got to see. This auto has been coming and going, and we should have followed the tracks the other way from the point where we first saw them, instead of coming this way."

"Except that we've learned the place of departure," suggested Jackson. "Evidently the wood-lot is a blind alley. The car goes in, but it can come out only just at this point, or, at least, it does."

"That's right!" agreed Tom. "Now the thing to do is to follow our track back to where we started. There must be some place where the car went to—some headquarters, or meeting place with some one, farther back in the lot. If we can only follow the trail back as well as we did coming, we may find out something."

"Well, let's try, anyhow," suggested Jackson.

They had no difficulty in making their way back to the spot where they had first seen the queer marks. But from then on their task was not so easy. For sandy or bare patches of earth were not frequent, and they had to depend on these to give them direction, for the road was overgrown and not well defined.

Often they would search about for some time after leaving one patch of the marks before they found another that would justify them in keeping on.

"They have headquarters, or a rendezvous, somewhere back in this lot!" declared Tom, as they hurried on. "I think we're on the track of a mystery."

"Unless it turns out that some farmer has treated himself to an auto with new tires of square tread, and is hauling wood," said Jackson. "It may turn out that way."

"Yes, it may," agreed Tom. "But, taking everything into consideration, I think we're on the verge of finding out something. Even if we do discover that the owner of this auto is only hauling wood, he may be able to help us to a clue as to the whereabouts of Mr. Nestor."

"How?"

"Well, maybe he was in his machine on the moor the night the call for help came. He may even have aided to carry Mr. Nestor away. And if he doesn't know a thing about it—which, of course, is possible—the man who bought these queer tires can tell us who makes them, or who deals in them, and we can find out what autoists around here have their cars equipped with this odd tread."

"Yes," agreed Jackson, "that can be done."

And so they kept on, scouting here and there to either side of the half-defined path, until they were far back from the spot where they had left the Air Scout.

"We don't appear to be getting any warmer, as the children say," remarked Jackson, as he straightened up and looked about, for his back ached from so much stooping over to look for the odd marks.

"We haven't seen anything yet, I'll admit," said Tom. "But it won't be dark for another hour or so, and I vote that we keep on."

"Oh, I wasn't thinking of giving up!" exclaimed Jackson. "If there's anything here—at the end of the route, as you might say —we'll find it. Only I hope it doesn't turn out to be just a wood pile, from which some farmer has been hauling logs."

"That would be a disappointment," assented Tom.

The day was waning, and they realized that they ought not to spend too much time on what might turn out to be a wild goose chase. They were in a lonely neighborhood, and while they were not at all apprehensive of danger, they felt it would be best to get to shelter before dark.

"We'll want to send word to Mr. Swift that we're all right."

"Yes," said Tom, "I'd like to get to a place where I can telephone to him or Mrs. Baggert. Well, if we don't find something pretty soon we'll have to turn back. I must complete work on the new motor, for if I'm to offer it to Uncle Sam for air scout purposes, the sooner I can do so the better. Things are getting pretty hot over in Europe, and if ever the United States needed aircraft on the western front they need them now. I want to help all I can, and I also want to help Mary—you understand— Miss Nestor."

"I understand," said Jackson simply. "I only hope you can help her. But I'm afraid—this may turn out to be nothing—following these marks, you know."

"And yet," said Tom slowly, "it would be strange if it was only a coincidence—the two tire marks being the same—the night Mr. Nestor disappeared and now."

And so they kept on, hoping.

The half-defined path through the wood-lot led them in a series of turns and twists, and it extended through a dense patch of woods, growing thickly, where it was so dark that it seemed as if night had fallen.

"We can't spend much more time here," said Tom. "If we don't find something in the next half mile we'll go back and take up the search to-morrow. I'm going to find out what's at the end of this road—even if it's only a wood pile."

For ten minutes more the two went on, making sure, by occasional glimpses at the marks, that they were on the right track. Then, suddenly, they saw something which made them feel sure they had reached their goal.

In a clearing among the trees was a little cabin —a shack of logs—and from the appearance it was deserted. There was not a sign of life around

Clues at Last

For a moment, at sight of the deserted cabin, staring at Tom and his friend, as it were, from its hiding place amid the trees, the young inventor and his companion did not move. They just stood looking at the place.

"Well," said Tom,. at length, "we found it, didn't we

"We found something anyhow," agreed Jackson. "Whether it amounts to anything or not, we've got to see."

"Come on!" cried Tom, impulsively. "I'm going to see what's there."

"There doesn't appear to be much of anything," said Jackson, as he looked toward the lonely cabin with critical eyes. "I should say that place hadn't been used, even as a chicken coop, in a long while."

"We can soon tell!" exclaimed Tom, striding forward.

"Wait just a minute!" cried his companion, catching him by the coat. "Don't be in such a hurry."

"Why not?" asked Tom. "There isn't any danger, is there?"

"I don't know about that. There's no telling who may be hidden in that cabin, in spite of its deserted appearance. And though there aren't any 'No Trespass' signs up, it may be that we wouldn't be welcome. If there are some tramps there, which is possible, they might take a notion to shoot at us first and ask questions as to our peaceable intentions afterward—when it would be too late."

"Nonsense!" exclaimed Tom. "There aren't any tramps there and, if there were, they wouldn't dare shoot. I'm going to see what the mystery is—if there is one."

But there was no sign of life, and, taking this as an indication that their advance would not be disputed, Jackson followed Tom. The latter advanced until he could take in all the details of the shack. It was made of logs, and once had been chinked with mud or clay. Some of this had fallen out, leaving spaces between the tree trunks.

"It wasn't a bad little shack at one time," decided Tom. "Maybe it was a place where some one camped out during the summer. But it hasn't been used of late. I never knew there was such a place around here, and I thought I knew this locality pretty well."

"I never heard of it, either," said Jackson. "Let's give a shout and see if there's any one around. They may be asleep. Hello, there !" he called in sufficiently vigorous tones to have awakened an ordinary sleeper.

Put there was no answer, and as the shadows of the night began to fall, the place took on a most lonely aspect.

"Let's go up and knock—or go in if the door's open," suggested Tom. "We can't lose any more time, if we're to get out of here before night."

"Go ahead," said Jackson, and together they went to the cabin door.

"Locked!" exclaimed Tom, as he saw a padlock attached to a chain. It appeared to be fastened through two staples, driven one into the door and the other into the jamb, at right angles to one another and overlapping.

"Knock!" suggested Jackson. But when Tom had done so, and there was no answer, the machinist took hold of the lock. To his own surprise and that of Tom, one of the staples pulled out and the door swung open. The place had evidently been forced before, and the lock had not been opened by a key. The staple had been pulled out and replaced loosely in the holes.

For a moment nothing could be made out in the dark interior of the shack. But as their eyes became used to the gloom, Tom and his companion were able to see that the shack consisted of two rooms.

In the first one there was a rusty stove, a table, and some chairs, and it was evident, from pans and skillets hanging on the wall, as well as from a small cupboard built on one side, that this was the kitchen and living room combined.

"Anybody here?" cried Tom, as he stepped inside.

Only a dull echo answered.

The two could now see where a door gave entrance to an inner room, and this, a quick glance showed, was the sleeping apartment, two bunks being built on the side walls.

"Well, somebody had it pretty comfortable here," decided Tom, as he looked around. "They've been cooking and sleeping here, and not so very long ago, either. It wouldn't be such a bad place if it was cleaned out."

"That's right," agreed Jackson. "Wouldn't mind camping here myself, if there was any fishing near."

"The river can't be far away," suggested Tom. "And now let's see what we can find, and see if we can get a line on who has been here. But first we'll let in a little light."

He opened a window in the sleeping room, and pushed back the heavy plank shutter that had been closed. When the light entered it was seen that both bunks bore evidence of having been lately slept in. The blankets were tossed back, as if the occupants had risen, and in the outer room, on the stove, were signs that indicated a meal had been served not many days gone by.

"Now," observed Tom musingly, as he wandered about the place, "if we could only find out who owns this, and who has been here lately—"

Jackson stooped over, and, thrusting aside an end of the blankets that trailed on the floor from one of the bunks, picked up something.

"What is it?" asked Tom.

"Looks like a leather pocketbook," was the answer. "That's what it is," the mechanic went on, as he held the object to the light. "It's a wallet."

"Let me see it!" exclaimed Tom quickly. He took the wallet from the hands of Jackson. Then the young inventor uttered a cry. "A clue at last!" he exclaimed. "A clue at last! Mr. Nestor has been in this cabin!"

"How do you know?" asked Jackson quickly.

"This is his wallet," said Tom excitedly. "I've often seen him have it. In fact he had it with him on Earthquake Island, the time I sent the wireless message for help. I saw it several times then. He kept in it what few papers he had saved from the wreck. And I've seen it often enough since. That's Mr. Nestor's wallet all right. Besides, if you want any other evidence—look!" He opened the leather flaps and showed Jackson on one, stamped in gold letters, the name of Mary's father.

"Well, what do you make of it, Tom?" asked the mechanician, as he finished his examination of the wallet. "What does it mean? The pocket-book is empty and that—"

"Might mean almost anything," completed Tom. "But it's a clue all right! He's been here, and I'm pretty certain he was brought here in the auto with the odd tires—the one Mr. Damon and I saw traces of the night we heard the cries for help."

"But that doesn't help us now," said Jackson. "The point is to find out how lately Mr. Nestor was here, and what has happened to him since. There isn't anything in the wallet, is there?"

"Nothing," answered Tom, making a careful examination so as to be sure. "It's as empty as a last year's bird nest. He's been robbed—that's what has happened to Mr. Nestor. He was waylaid that night, instead of being run down as I thought—waylaid and robbed and then his body was brought here."

"There you go again, Tom! Jumping to conclusions!" said Jackson, with a friendly smile, and with the familiarity of an old and valued helper. "Maybe he's in perfectly good health. Just because you found his empty wallet doesn't argue that your friend is in serious trouble. He may have dropped this on the road and some one picked it up. I'll admit they may have taken whatever was in it, but that doesn't prove anything. The thing for us to do is to find out who knows about this shack; who owns it, on whose land it is, and whether any one has been seen here lately."

"They've been here lately whether they've been seen or not," said Tom positively. "There are the auto tracks. It rained two days ago, and the tracks were made since. Mr. Nestor must have been here within two days."

"He may or may not," said Jackson. "Say, rather, that some one was here and left his wallet after him. Now see if we can find other clues!"

They looked about in the fast fading light, but at first could discover nothing more than evidences that three or four persons had been living in the shack and at some recent date—probably within a day or two.

They had had their meals there and had slept there. But this seemed to be all that could be established, other than that Mr. Nestor's wallet was there, stripped of its contents.

Tom was looking through the closet, from which a frightened chipmunk sprang as he opened the door. There were the remains of some food, which accounted for the presence of the little striped animal. And, as Tom poked about, his hand came in contact with something wrapped in paper on an upper shelf. It was something that clinked metallicly.

"What's that?" asked Jackson. "Knives, or some other weapons?"

"Neither," answered Tom. "It's a couple of files, and they've been used lately. I can see something in the grooves yet and—"

Suddenly Tom ceased speaking and drew from his pocket a small but powerful magnifying glass. Through this he looked at one of the files, taking it out in front of the shack where the light was better.

"I thought so!" he cried. "Look here, Jackson!"

"What is it?"

"Another clue!" answered Tom.

THE GOVERNMENT TEST

For a moment Jackson thought Tom had discovered a clue to, or evidences of, some crime. He had an unpleasant suspicion, for an instant, that there was blood on the files, and that it might prove to be the blood of Mr. Nestor.

But the satisfaction that showed on Tom's face did not seem to indicate such dire possibilities as these.

"What is it?" asked Jackson, unable to guess at what Tom was looking through the powerful glass. "What do you see?"

"Metal filings on the grooves of these files," said the young inventor. "And, unless I'm greatly mistaken, the particles of filings are from the case of my aircraft silencer!"

"What!" cried the machinist. "Do you mean those are the files used in weakening the outer case of your new machine, so that it burst a little while ago?"

"That what I think," answered Tom. "I know it sounds pretty far-fetched," he went on. "But take a look for yourself. If those particles on, the files aren't exactly of the same color and texture as the material of which the silencer case is made, I'll never build another machine."

Jackson peered through the powerful glass moving out a little farther from the shack, so as to get the best light possible on the subject of his examination. It was fast getting dark, but there was enough glow in the western sky for his purpose.

"Am I right?" asked Tom.

"You're right!" declared his helper. "This is exactly the same metal as that of which your silencer case is made. It's a peculiar mixture of aluminum and vanadium steel. I never knew it used in any shop but yours, and these filings are certainly of that metal. It would seem, Tom, that these were the files used to cut a crease in the case of your silencer to weaken it so it would burst."

"My idea exactly!" cried Tom. "The spy, who got into my shop in some undiscovered manner, did his work and then fled here to hide. He left his files behind. Mr. Nestor must have been here, either before or after. No, I'll not say that, either. Finding his wallet here doesn't prove that he was here. It might have been brought here by one of the spies and dropped. But I'm sure we're on the track of the men who damaged my airship, as well as those who know something of the mystery of Mr. Nestor."

"I agree with you," said Jackson. "Of course there's a possibility that the same peculiar metal you used in your silencer case may have been used in some other machine shop, and these files may have come from there, and have been employed in perfectly regular work. But the chances are—"

"There's only one way to make sure," said Tom. "Let's take the files with us and see if they fit in the grooves where the break came. We'll take these back to where we left the Air Scout," and he clinked the files he held.

"We can just about make it before it gets black dark," returned Jackson. "But that won't give us any more time to look around here," and he indicated the hut.

"I fancy we've seen all there is to see here," said Tom. "Mr. Nestor isn't here, and whether he was or not is a question. Anyhow, some one was here who had something to do with him after his disappearance, I'm positive of that. And I'm sure some one was here who damaged my airship. Now we'll run down both those clues, find out who owns this place, who has been using it, and all we can along that line. So, if you're ready, let's travel."

The two set out to make their way back to where they had left the stranded airship. It was fast becoming dark, but they could hurry along with more speed now, as they did not have to stop to look for the marks of the peculiar automobile tires. They had noticed the path along which they had traveled, and in half the time they had spent coming they were back where the Air Scout rested undisturbed in the meadow amid the trees.

Making sure that, as far as they could tell, no one had visited the craft since they had left it, Tom and Jackson compared the file marks on what was left of the broken silencer case with the files they had found in the hut. They used a small, but powerful electric lamp to aid them in this examination, as it was too dark to see otherwise, and what they saw caused the young inventor to exclaim:

"That settles it! These were the files used!"

"That's right!" agreed his assistant. "You've called the turn, Tom. The next thing to do is to find who connects with the files."

"Yes. To do that and find Mr. Nestor," said Tom. "We have plenty of work ahead of us. But let's get nearer civilization and send some word to the folks at home. They'll be getting worried."

"It doesn't seem as if there was a way out of here without using an airship," remarked Jackson.

But he and Tom finally reached the seldom-used road which ran along the field that contained the lonely shack, and, following this, they reached a farmhouse about a mile farther on. Greatly to their relief, there was a telephone in the place. True it was only a party line, set up by some neighboring farmers for their own private use, but one of the subscribers, to whose home the private line ran, had a long distance instrument, and after a talk with him, this man promised Tom to call up Mr. Swift and acquaint him with the fact that his son and Jackson were all right, and would be home later.

"And now," said Tom, after thanking their temporary host, a farmer named Bloise, "can you tell us anything about an old cabin that stands back there?" and he indicated the location of the mysterious shack.

"Well, yes, I can tell you a little about it, but not very much," said Mr. Bloise. "It was built, some years ago, by a rich New Yorker, who bought up a lot of land around here for a game preserve. But it didn't pan out. This cabin was only the start of what he was going to call a 'hunting lodge,' I believe it was. There was to be a big building on the same order, but it never was built.

"Some say the fellow lost all his money in Wall Street, and others say the state wouldn't let him make a game preserve here. However it was, the thing petered out, and the old shack hasn't been used since."

"Oh, yes, it has!" exclaimed Tom. "We just came from there, and there are signs which show some one has been sleeping there and eating there."

"There has!" exclaimed the farmer. "Well, I didn't know that."

"I did," said his son, a young man about Tom's age. "I meant to speak of it the other day. I saw an automobile turn into the old road that the men used when they built the shack. I thought it was kind of queer to see a touring car turn in there, and I meant to speak of it, but I forgot. Yes, some one has been at the old cabin lately."

"Do you know who they are?" asked Tom eagerly. "We are looking for a Mr. Nestor, who disappeared mysteriously about two weeks ago, and I just found his wallet there in the shack!"

"You did!" exclaimed Mr. Bloise. "That's queer! You relatives of this Mr. Nestor?" he asked.

"Not exactly," Tom answered. "Just very close friends."

"Well, it's too bad about his being missing in that way," went on the farmer. "I read about it in the paper, but I never suspected he was around here."

"Oh, we're not sure that he was," said Tom quickly. "Finding his wallet doesn't prove that," and he told the story of his own and Jackson's appearance on the scene, to the no small wonder of the farmer and his family. Tom said nothing about the finding of the files, nor the evidence he deduced from them. That was another matter to be taken up later.

"Who were in the auto you saw?" asked Tom of the farmer's son. "Was Mr. Nestor in the car?"

"I couldn't be sure of that. There were two men in the machine, and they were both strangers to me. They were talking together, pretty earnestly, it seemed to me."

"One did not appear as if he was being taken away against his will, did he?" asked Tom.

"No, I can't say that he did," was the answers "They looked to me, and acted like, business men looking over land, or something like that. They just turned in on the road that leads to the old hunting cabin, as we call it around here, and didn't pay any attention to me. Then I forgot all about them."

"Neither of them could have been Mr. Nestor," decided Tom. "At least it doesn't seem as if he'd talk at all companionably to a man who had treated him as we think Mr. Nestor has been treated. I guess that clue isn't going to amount to much."

"It may!" insisted Jackson. "They may have had Mr. Nestor in the car all the while—concealed in the back you know. We've got to find out more about these men and their auto, Tom."

"Well, yes, perhaps we have. But how?"

"Station some one at the shack, or at the beginning of the private road. The men may come back."

"That's so—they may. We'll do that!" cried the young inventor. "We must tell the police and Mr. Nestor's folks what we have learned. How can we get back to Shopton in a hurry?" he asked the farmer.

"Well, I can drive you to the railroad station" was the answer.

"Thank you," remarked Tom. "We'll accept your offer. And as soon as we get back we must send some one from the shop to stand guard over the airship," he added in an aside to Jackson. "Those file fellows may come back."

"That's so, we can't take any chances."

The farmer soon had his team at the door, and, after they had had a hasty but satisfying supper at the farmhouse, the son drove Tom and Jackson several miles to a railroad station, where they could catch a train for Shopton.

In due season Tom's home was reached. He intended to stop but a minute, to assure his father that everything was all right, and then get out his speedy runabout to go to see Mary, to tell her the news.

But when Tom sought his father in the library, he was told that there was a visitor in the house.

"Tom," said his father, "this gentleman is from Washington. He wants to arrange for a government test of your silent airship. I told him I thought you were about ready for it."

"A government test !" cried Tom. "Why, I didn't think the government even knew I was working on such an idea!" Tom was greatly surprised.

In the Moonlight

With a reassuring smile the visitor from Washington looked at Tom Swift.

"The government officials," he said, "know more than some people give them credit for—especially in these war times. Our intelligence bureau and secret service has been much enlarged of late. But don't be alarmed, Mr. Swift," went on the caller, whose name was Mr. Blair Terrill. "Your secret is safe with the government, but I think the time is ripe to use it now—that is, if you have perfected it to a point where we can use it."

"Yes," answered Tom slowly, "the invention is practically finished and it is a success, except for a few minor matters that will not take long to complete.

"Our accident this afternoon had nothing to do with the efficiency of the silencer," Tom went on. "It was deliberately damaged by some spy. I'll take that up later. That I am interested to know how you heard of my Air Scout, as I call it."

"Well, we have agents, you know, watching all the inventors who have helped us in times past, and we haven't forgotten your giant cannon or big searchlight. I might say, to end your curiosity and lull your suspicions, that your friend, Ned Newton, who has been doing such good Liberty Bond work, informed us of your progress on the silent motor."

"Oh, so it was Ned!" exclaimed Tom.

"Yes. He told us the time was about ripe for us to make you an offer for your machine. I think we can use it to great advantage in scout work on the western front," went on the agent, and he soon convinced Tom that when it came to a knowledge of airships, he had some very pertinent facts at his disposal.

"When can you give me a test?" Mr. Terrill asked Tom.

"As soon as I can get my craft back to the shop and fit on a new outer case. That won't take long, as I have some spare ones. But I must help the Nestors," he went on, speaking to his father. "I didn't mention it over the wire," he added, "but we've found in the cabin a clue to the missing man. I must tell Mary and her mother, and help them all I can."

"And allow me to help, too," begged Mr. Terrill. "Since this affects you, Mr. Swift, and since you are, in a way, working for Uncle Sam, you must let him help you. This is the first I have heard of the missing gentleman, of whom your father just told me something, but you must allow me to help search for him. I will get the United States Secret Service at work."

"That will be fine!" cried Tom. "I wanted to get their aid, but I didn't see how I could, as I knew they were too busy with army matters and tracing seditious alien enemies, to bother with private cases. I'm sure the Secret

Service men can get trace of the persons responsible for the detention of Mr. Nestor, wherever he is."

"They'll do their best," said Mr. Terrill. "I'm a member of that body," he went on, "and I'll give my personal attention to the matter."

Then followed a busy time. Tom did not get to bed until nearly morning. For he had to arrange to send some of his men to guard the stranded airship, and then he went to see Mary and her mother, taking them the good news that the search for Mr. Nestor would be prosecuted with unprecedented vigor.

"If it isn't too late!" sadly said the missing man's wife.

"Oh, I'm sure it isn't !" declared Tom.

In addition to sending a guard to the airship, other men, some of them hastily summoned from the nearest federal agency, were sent to keep watch in the vicinity of the lonely cabin. They had orders to arrest whoever approached, and a relay of the men was provided, so that watch could be kept up night and day. Besides this, other men from the Secret Service began scouring the country around the locality of the cabin, seeking a trace of the two persons the farmer's son had seen in the automobile.

"If Mr. Nestor is to be found, they'll find him!" declared Tom Swift.

Mr. Damon, as might be expected, was very much excited and wrought up over all these happenings.

"Bless my watch chain, Tom Swift!" cried the eccentric man, "but something is always happening to you. And to think I wasn't along when this latest happened!"

"Well, you can be in at the finish," promised Tom, and it was strange how his promise was fulfilled.

Meanwhile there was much to do. During the time the Secret Service men were busy looking up clues which might lead to the finding of Mr. Nestor and keeping watch in the vicinity of the hut, Tom had his airship brought back to the hangar, and a new silencer was attached. While this work was going on the place was guarded night and day by responsible men, so there was no chance for an enemy spy to get in and do further damage.

An investigation was made of the Universal Flying Machine Company, but nothing could be proved to link them with the outrage. Gale and Ware were in Europe—ostensibly on government business, but it was said that if anything could be proved connecting them with the attempt made on Tom Swift's craft, they would be deprived of all official contracts and punished.

All this took time, and the waits were wearisome, particularly in the case of Mr. Nestor. No further trace of him was found, though every effort was made. Tom began to feel that his boast of his enemies having to get up early in the morning to get ahead of him, had been premature, to say the least.

Tom Swift worked hard on his new Air Scout. He determined there would be nothing lacking when it came to the government test, and not only did he make sure that no enemy could tamper with his machine, but he took pains to see that no inherent defect would mar the test.

Jackson and the other men helped to the best of their ability, and Mr. Swift suggested some improvements which were incorporated in the new machine.

One of the puzzles the Secret Service men had to solve was that of the connection, if any, between the men who had to do with the missing Mr. Nestor and those who had damaged Tom's airship by filing the muffler case so it was weakened and burst. That there was some connection Tom was certain, but he could not work it out, nor, so far, had the government men.

At last the day came when the big government test was to be made. Tom had completed his Air Scout and had refined it to a point where even his critical judgment was satisfied. All that remained now was to give Mr. Terrill a chance to see how silently the big craft could fly, and to this end a flight was arranged.

Tom had put the silencer on a larger machine than the one he and Jackson had used. It held three easily, and, on a pinch, four could be carried. Tom's plan was to take Mr. Damon and Mr. Terrill, fly with them for some time in the air, and demonstrate how quiet his new craft was. Then, by contrast, a machine without the muffler and the new motor with its improved propellers would be flown, making as much noise as the usual craft did.

"I only wish," said Tom, as the time arrived for the official government test, "that Mary could be here to see it. She was the one who really started me on this idea, so to speak, as it was because I couldn't talk to her that I decided to get up a silent motor."

But Mary Nestor was too grief-stricken over her missing father to come to the test, which was to take place late one afternoon, starting from the aerodrome of the Swift plant.

"First," said Tom, to Mr. Terrill, "I'll show you how the machine works on the ground. I'll run the motor while the plane is held down by means of ropes and blocks. Then we'll go up in it."

"That suits me," said the agent. "If it does all you say it will do, and as much as I believe it will do, Uncle Sam will be your debtor, Mr. Swift."

"Well, we'll see," said Tom with a smile.

Preparations were made with the greatest care, and Tom went over every detail of the machine twice to make certain that, in spite of the precautions, no spy had done any hidden damage, that might be manifested at an inopportune moment. But everything seemed all right, and, finally, the motor was started, while Mr. Terrill, and some of his colleagues from the Army Aviation department looked on.

"Contact!" cried Tom, as Jackson indicated that the compression had been made.

The mechanic nodded, gave the big propeller blades a quarter turn and jumped back. In an instant the motor was operating, and the craft would have leaped forward and cleaved the air but for the holding ropes and blocks. Tom speeded the machinery up to almost the last notch, but those in the aerodrome hardly heard a sound. It was as though some great, silent dynamo were working.

"Fine!"

"Wonderful!"

"Wouldn't have believed it possible!"

These were some of the comments of the government inspectors.

"And now for the final test—that in the air," said Mr. Terrill.

Previous to this he and his colleagues had made a minute examination of the machinery, and had been shown the interior construction of the silencer by means of one built so that a sectional view could be had. Tom's principles were pronounced fundamental and simple.

"So simple, in fact, that it is a wonder no one thought of it before," said a navy aviation expert. "It is the last word in aircraft construction—a silent motor that will not apprise the enemy of its approach! You have done wonders, Mr. Swift!"

"I'd rather hear you say that after the air test," replied Tom, with a laugh. "Are you ready, Mr. Terrill?"

"Whenever you are."

"How about you, Mr. Damon?"

"Oh, I'm always ready to go with you, Tom Swift. Bless my trench helmet, but you can't sail any too soon for me!"

There was a genial laugh at his impetuosity, and the three took their seats in the big craft. Once more the engine was started. It operated as silently as before, and the first good impressions were confirmed. Even as the machine moved along the ground, just previous to taking flight into the air, there was no noise, save the slight crunch made by the wheels. This, of course, would be obviated when Silent Sam was aloft.

Up and up soared the great craft, with Tom at the engine and guide controls, while Mr. Terrill and Mr. Damon sat behind him, both eagerly watching. Mr. Terrill was there to find fault if he could, but he was glad he did not have to.

"The machine works perfectly, Mr. Swift," he said. "My report cannot be otherwise than favorable."

"We mustn't be in too much of a hurry," said Tom, who had learned caution some time ago. "I want to sail around for several hours. Sometimes a machine will work well at first, but defects will develop when it is overheated. I'm going to do my best to make a noise with this new motor."

But it seemed impossible. The machinery worked perfectly, and though Silent Sam took his passengers high and low, in big circles and small ones, there was no appreciable noise from the motor. The passengers could converse as easily, and with as little effort, as in a balloon.

"Of course that isn't the prime requisite," said Mr. Terrill, "but it is a good one. What we want is a machine that can sail over the enemy's lines at night without being heard, and I think this one will do it—in fact, I'm sure it will. Of course the ability of the passengers to converse and not have to use the uncertain tube is a great advantage."

As Tom Swift sailed on and on, it became evident that the test was going to be a success. The afternoon passed, and it began to grow dark, but a glorious full moon came up.

"Shall I take you down?" the young inventor asked Mr. Terrill.

"Not quite yet. I thoroughly enjoy this, and it isn't often I get a chance for a moonlight airship ride. Go a little lower, if you please, and we'll see if we attract any attention from the inhabitants of the earth. We'll see if they can possibly hear the machine, though I don't see how they can."

And they did not. Tom piloted the machine over Shopton, sailing directly over the center of the town, where there was a big crowd walking about. Though the airship sailed only a few hundred feet above their heads, not a person was aware of it, since the craft's lights were put out for this test.

"That settles it," said Mr. Terrill. "You have succeeded, Tom Swift!"

But Tom was not yet satisfied. He wanted a longer test. Hardly knowing why he did it he sent the craft in the direction of Mary Nestor's home. As he sailed across her lawn he saw, in the moonlight, that she and her mother were walking in the garden. They did not look up as the aircraft passed over their heads, and were totally unaware of its presence, unless they caught a glimpse of it as it flitted silently along, like some great bird of the night.

"It is perfectly wonderful!" declared Mr. Terrill, and he spoke in ordinary tones, that carried perfectly to the ears of Tom and Mr. Damon.

"Wonderful!" cried the eccentric man. "Bless my chimney, but it's the greatest invention in the world! Yes, it is! Don't tell me it 'isn't!'"

And no one did.

Passing the Nestor home, the saddened occupants of which were unaware of the passage, Tom sent the Air Scout about in a circle, intending to proceed to the hangar. And then, some whim, perhaps, caused him to guide Silent Sam out toward the lonely hut. Mr. Damon and Mr. Tenrill seemed perfectly content to sail on and on indefinitely in the moonlight. Tom thought he would take them over a lonely neighborhood, and then bring them back.

In a little while the craft was directly over the stretch of country where the aeroplane accident bad occurred, and where Tom and Jackson had found the deserted hut.

Rather idly Tom looked down, wondering if the Secret Service men were on the watch and if they had discovered anything.

Suddenly Tom was aware of an automobile moving along the field path toward the cabin. There were two men in the car, both on the front seat, and as Tom looked down the brilliant moonlight showed him the figure of another man, behind, and huddled in the tonneau of the car. The aeroplane was low enough for all these details to be seen by the moon's gleam, but the men in the car, not hearing any noise, did not look up, so they were unconscious of this aerial espionage.

"Look! Look!" exclaimed Tom in a low voice to his companions. "Doesn't that seem suspicious?"

THE GOLD TOOTH

Eagerly Mr. Damon and the government agent leaned over and looked down. In the moonlight they saw the same sight that had attracted Tom Swift. The touring car, the two men in front, and the huddled, bound figure in the back.

"Can you go down, Tom, without letting them hear you?" asked Mr. Damon, using a low voice, as if fearful the men in the automobile would hear him.

"I guess so," answered the young inventor. "I can land nearer to the cabin than Jackson and I did, and then we can see what these fellows are up to. It looks suspicious to me. That is, unless they're some of the Secret Service men, and have made a capture," he added to Mr. Terrill.

"Those aren't any of Uncle Sam's men," declared the agent. "That is, unless the bound one is. I can't see him very well. Better go down, and we'll see if we can surprise them."

"My plan," voiced Tom.

Quickly he shifted the rudder, and then, shutting off the motor, as he wanted to volplane down, he headed his craft for an open spot that showed in the bright moonlight. By this time the automobile and its occupants were out of sight behind a clump of trees, but Tom and his companions felt sure of the destination of the men—the deserted cabin in the wood.

As silently as a wisp of grass falling, the big craft came down on a level spot, and then, leaping out, the young inventor and his two companions crept along the path toward the cabin. Mr. Terrill was armed, Tom carried a flashlight, while Mr. Damon picked up a heavy club.

As soon as he came near a place where he thought the marks of the automobile wheels would show, Tom flashed his light.

"I thought so!" he exclaimed, as he saw the square, knobby tread marks left by the tires. "It's the same gang, or some of them in the same car. If we can only capture them!"

"The Secret Service men ought to do that," returned Mr. Terrill, but, as it developed later, they were not on hand, though through no fault of theirs.

On and on crept Tom and the two men, until they came within sight of the cabin. They saw a light gleaming in it, and Tom whispered:

"Now we have them! Work our way up quietly and make them surrender, if we find they're what we think."

"Is there a rear door?" asked Mr. Terrill in a whisper.

Tom answered in the negative, and then all three, in fan shape, crept up to the front portal. It was open, and silently reaching a place where they could make an observation, Tom and his companions looked in.

What they saw filled them with wild and righteous rage, and brought to an end the mystery of the disappearance of Mr. Nestor. For there he sat, bound in a chair, and at a table in front of him were two forbidding-looking men.

"What do you intend to do now?" asked Mr. Nestor in a faint voice. "I cannot stand this captivity much longer. You admit that you don't want me—that you never wanted me—so why do you keep me a prisoner? It cannot do the least good."

"There's no use going over that again !" exclaimed the harsh voice of one of the men. told you that if you will promise to keep still about what happened to you, and not to give the police any information about us, we'll let you go gladly. We don't want you. It was all a mistake, capturing you. You were the wrong man. But we re not going to let you go and have you set the police on us as soon as you get a chance. Give us your promise to say nothing, and we'll let you join your friends. If you don't—"

"Make no promises, Mr. Nestor!" cried Tom Swift in a ringing voice, as he leaped from his hiding place, followed by his companions. "Your friends are here, and you can tell them everything!"

"Up with 'em!" called Mr. Terrill to the two conspirators as he confronted them with his automatic pistol ready for firing. He had no need to mention hands—they knew what he meant and took the characteristic attitude.

"Tom! Tom Swift!" cried Mr. Nestor, struggling ineffectually at his bonds. "Is it really you?"

"Well, I hope it isn't any imitation," was the grim answer. "We'll tell you all about it later. Jove, but I'm glad we found you! If it hadn't been for Silent Sam we might never have been able to."

"Well, I don't know who Silent Sam is," said Mr. Nestor faintly. "But I'm sure I'm much obliged to him and your other friends. It has been very hard. Tell me, are my wife and Mary all right?"

"In good health, yes, but, of course, worrying," said Tom. "We saw them in the garden a little while ago. Now don't talk until I set you free."

And as Tom cut the ropes from Mr. Nestor, Mr. Damon used them to bind the two conspirators, while Mr. Terrill stood guard over them. And when they were safely bound, and Mr. Nestor had somewhat recovered from the shock, Tom had a chance to examine the prisoners.

"What does it all mean? Who are you fellows, anyhow, and what's your game?" he demanded.

"Guess it—since you're so smart!" snapped one.

And no sooner had he opened his mouth and Tom had a glance of something gleaming brightly yellow, than the young inventor cried:

"The gold tooth! So it's you again, is it, you spy?"

The man shrugged his shoulders with an assumption of indifference. And, as Tom took a closer look, he became aware that the man was surely none other than Lydane, the spy he had chased into the mud puddle some weeks before. His companion was a stranger to Tom.

"What does it all mean, Mr. Nestor?" asked Tom. "Have these men held you a prisoner ever since you called for help on the moor that night?"

"Yes, Tom, they have. And I did call for help after they attacked me as I was riding my wheel, but I didn't know any one heard me. I began to be afraid no one would ever help me."

"We've been trying to, a long time," said Mr. Damon, "but we couldn't find you. Where did they keep you?"

"Here, part of the time," was Mr. Nestor's answer. "And in other lonely houses. They bound and gagged me when they took me from place to place."

"But what was their object?" asked Tom, concluding it was useless to question the two captives. "Why did they make you a prisoner, Mr. Nestor?"

"Because they took me for you, Tom."

"For me?"

"Yes. The night I called at your house, and found you were not at home, I put back in my pocket a bundle of papers I had brought over to show you. They were plans of a little kitchen appliance a friend of mine had invented, and I wanted to ask your opinion of it."

"These scoundrels must have followed me, or have seen the bundle of papers, and, mistaking me for you, they followed, attacked me in a lonely spot and, bundling me and my wrecked wheel into an auto, carried me off. They first demanded that I gave up the 'plans,' and when I wouldn't they choked off my cries for help and knocked me into unconsciousness. Then they brought me here, and kept me here for several days.

"They soon learned that the plans I had weren't those they wanted, though what they were thin after I couldn't imagine. Only, from what I laser overheard, I knew they mistook me for you and that they were bitterly disappointed in not getting plans of some new airship you were working on. They have kept me a prisoner ever since, and though they offered to let me go if I would keep silent, I refused. I did not think, to secure my own comfort, I should let such men go unpunished if I could bring about their arrest."

"I should say not!" cried Tom.

"Did they treat you brutally, Mr. Nestor?" asked Mr. Damon.

"Not after they found out who I was, by looking through my wallet. Of course they didn't behave very decently, but they weren't actually cruel, except that they bound and gagged me. Oh, but I'm glad you came, Tom! How did it happen?"

Then they told Mr. Nestor their story, and how the test of the new Air Scout had led to his rescue.

"But where are the Secret Service men?" asked Mr. Terrill, when it became evident that none them was on guard at the cabin.

Later it developed that, by following a false clue, the Secret Service men had been drawn miles away from the cabin. And only that Tom and his companions in the silent airship saw the men. Mr. Nestor might not have been rescued for some further time.

His version of what had happened was correct. He had been mistaken for Tom, and the spy with the gold tooth and his accomplice had waylaid Mary's father, under the belief that it was Tom Swift with the plans of the new silent motor. Mr. Nestor had been attacked while riding his wheel in a lonely place, and had been carried off and kept in hiding, a prisoner even after his identity became known.

"Well, this is a good night's work!" exclaimed Tom, when the two rogues had been sent to jail and Mr. Nestor taken to the Bloise farmhouse, to be refreshed before he went home. Word of his rescue was telephoned to Mary and her mother, and it can be imagined how they regarded Tom Swift for his part in the affair.

Little the worse for his experience, save that he was very nervous, Mr. Nestor was taken home. He gave the details of his being waylaid, and told how the men, for many days, were at their wits' ends to keep him concealed when they found what a stir his disappearance had created. The conspirators were well supplied with money, and in the automobile they took their prisoner from one place to another. They had usurped the use of the cabin and had lived there nearly a week in hiding, leaving just before the first visit of Tom and Jackson. The rifled wallet had been dropped by accident.

And it did not take much delving to disclose the fact that, Lydane, "Gold Tooth," as he was called, and his crony, were spies in the pay of the Universal Flying Machine Company. As the men went under several aliases there is no need of giving their names. It is to be doubted if they ever used their real ones—or if they had any.

Of course, there was quite a sensation when Mr. Nestor was found, and a greater one when it became known the part the Universal Flying Machine people had in his disappearance in mistake for Tom. The officials of the company were indicted, and several of the minor ones sent to jail but Gale and Ware escaped by remaining abroad.

It came out that they both knew of the acts of Lydane and his companion in crime, and that the two officials realized the mistake that had been made by their clumsy operatives. It was believed that this knowledge led to the visit of Gale to Tom, the time the latter's suspicions were first aroused. Gale made a clumsy attempt to clear his own skirts of the conspiracy, but in vain, though he did escape his just punishment.

What had happened, in brief, was this. Gale and Ware, unable to secure Tom's services, even by the offer of a large sum of money, had stooped to the sending of spies to his shop, to get possession of information about his silent motor. This was after Gale had, by accident, heard Tom speaking of it to Mr. Damon.

But, thanks to Tom's vigilance, Bower was discovered. The man tripped into the mud hole lost in the muck the plans Bower passed to him. They were never recovered. Then Lydane tried again. He managed, through bribery, to gain access to the hangar where the new silent machine was kept, and, unable to get the silencer apart, tried to file it. In doing so he weakened it so that it burst.

The attempt to waylay Tom, and so get the plans from him, had been tried before this, only a mistake had been made, and Mr. Nestor was caught instead. Finding out their error, Lydane and his companions did not tell the Universal people of their mistake, though Gale and Ware knew the attempt was to be made against Tom Swift.

Later, hearing that the young inventor was still at work on his invention, Gale was much surprised, and paid his queer visit, in an attempt to repudiate the actions of Lydane. At this time it was assumed that Gale and his partner did not know that it was Mr. Nestor who had been kidnapped by mistake or they might have insisted on his release. As it was, Lydane had Mary's father, and was afraid to let him go, though really their prisoner became a white elephant on the hands of the conspirators and kidnappers.

And it was after all this was cleared up, and Mr. Nestor restored to his family and friends, that one day, Tom Swift received another visit from Mr. Terrill, the government agent.

"Well, Mr. Swift," was the genial greeting, "I have come to tell you that the favorable report made by my friends and myself as to the performance of your noiseless motor, has been accepted by the War Department, and I have come to ask what your terms are. For how much will you sell your patent to the United States?"

Tom Swift arose.

"The United States hasn't money enough to buy my patent of a noiseless motor," he said.

"Wha—what!" faltered Mr. Terrill. "Why, I understood—you don't mean—they told me you were rather patriotic, and—"

"I hope I am patriotic!" interrupted Tom with a smile. "And when I say that the United States hasn't money enough to buy my latest invention I mean just that."

"My Air Scout is not for sale!"

"You mean," faltered the government agent. "You say—"

"I mean," went on Tom, "that Silent Sam is for Uncle Sam without one cent of cost! My father and I take great pleasure in presenting such machines as are already manufactured, those in process of making, and the entire patents, and all other rights, to the government for the winning of the war!"

"Oh!" said Mr. Terrill in rather a strange voice. "Oh!"

And that was all he could say for a little while.

But Tom Swift reckoned without a knowledge of a peculiar law which prohibits the United States from accepting gifts totally without compensation, and so, in due season, the young inventor received a check for the sum of one dollar in full payment for his silent motor, and the patent rights thereto. And Tom has that check framed, and hanging over his desk.

And so the silent motor became an accomplished fact and a great success. Those of you who have read of its work against the Boches, and how it helped Uncle Sam to gain the mastery of the sky, need not be reminded of this. By it many surprise attacks were made, and much valuable information was obtained that otherwise could not have been brought in.

One day, after the rogues had been sent to prison for long terms, and Tom had turned over to his government his silent aircraft—except one which he was induced to keep for his own personal use—the young inventor went to call on Mary Nestor. The object of his call, as I believe he stated it, was to see how Mr. Nestor was, but that, of course, was camouflage.

"Would you like to come for a ride, Mary, in the silent airship?" asked Tom, after he had paid his respects to Mr. Nestor and his wife. "We can talk very easily on board Silent Sam without the use of a speaking tube. Come on—we'll go for a moonlight sky ride."

"It sounds enticing," said Mary, with a shy look at Tom. "But wouldn't you just as soon sit on a bench in the garden? It's moonlight there, and we can talk, and—and—"

"I'd just as soon!" said Tom quickly.

And out they went into the beautiful moonlight; and here we will leave them and say good-bye.

Tom Swift and His Undersea Search
Or The Treasure on the Floor of the Atlantic

TABLE OF CONTENTS:

UNTOLD MILLIONS

"Tom, this is certainly wonderful reading! Over a hundred million dollars' worth of silver at the bottom of the ocean! More than two hundred million dollars in gold! To say nothing of fifty millions in copper, ten millions in—"

"Say, hold on there, Ned! Hold on! Where do you get that stuff; as the boys say? Has something gone wrong with one of the adding machines, or is it just on account of the heat? What's the big idea, anyhow? How many millions did you say?" and Tom Swift, the talented young inventor, looked at Ned Newton, his financial manager, with a quizzical smile.

"It's all right, Tom! It's all right!" declared Ned, and it needed but a glance to show that he was more serious than was his companion. "I'm not suffering from the heat, though the thermometer is getting close to ninety-five in the shade. And if you want to know where I get 'that stuff' read this!"

He tossed over to his chum, employer, and friend—for Tom Swift assumed all three relations toward Ned Newton—part of a Sunday newspaper. It was turned to a page containing a big illustration of a diver attired in the usual rubber suit and big helmet, moving about on the floor of the ocean and digging out boxes of what was supposed to be gold from a sunken wreck.

"Oh, that stuff!" exclaimed Tom, with a smile of disbelief as he saw the source of Ned's information. "Seems to me I've read something like that before, Ned!"

"Of course you have!" agreed the young financial manager of the newly organized Swift Construction Company. "It isn't anything new. This wealth of untold millions has been at the bottom of the sea for many years—always increasing with nobody ever spending a cent of it. And since the Great War this wealth has been enormously added to because of the sinking of so many ships by German submarines."

"Well, what's that got to do with us, Ned?" asked Tom, as he looked over some blue prints and other papers on his desk, for the talk was taking place in his office. "You and I did our part in the war, but I don't see what all this undersea wealth has to do with us. We've got our work cut out for us if we take care of all the new contracts that came in this week."

"Yes, I know," admitted Ned. "But I couldn't help calling your attention to this article, Tom. It's authentic!"

"Authentic? What do you mean

"Well, the man who wrote it went to the trouble of getting from the ship insurance companies a list of all the wrecks and lost vessels carrying gold and silver coin, bullion, and other valuables. He has gone back a hundred years, and he brings it right down to just before the war. Hasn't had time to compile that list, the article says. But without counting the vessels the

Germans sank, there is, in various places on the bottom of the ocean today, wrecks of ships that carried, when they went down, gold, silver, copper and other metals to the value of at least ten billions of dollars!"

Tom Swift did not seem to be at all surprised by the explosive emphasis with which Ned Newton conveyed this information. He gazed calmly at his friend and manager, and then handed the paper back.

"I haven't time to look at it now," said Tom. "But is there anything new in the story? I mean has any of the wealth been recovered lately—or is it in a way to be?"

"Yes!" exclaimed Ned. "It is! A company has been formed in Japan for the purpose of using a new kind of diving bell, invented by an American, it seems. The inventor claims that in his machine he can go down deeper than ever man went before, and bring up a lot of this lost ocean wealth."

"Well, every so often an inventor, or some one who calls himself that, crops up with a new proposal for cleaning up the untold millions on the floor of the Atlantic or the Pacific," replied Tom. "Mind you, I'm not saying it isn't there. Everybody knows that hundreds of ships carrying gold and silver have gone down in storms or been sunk in war. And some of the gold and silver has been recovered by divers—I admit that. In fact, if you recall, my father and I perfected a new style diving dress a few years ago that was successfully used in getting down to a wreck off the Cuban coast. A treasure ship went down there, and I believe they recovered a large part of the gold bullion—or perhaps it was silver.

"But this diving bell stunt isn't new, and it hasn't been successful. Of course a man can go down to a greater depth in a thick iron diving bell than he can in a diving suit. That's common knowledge. But the trouble with a diving bell is that it can't be moved about as a man can move about in a diving suit. The man in the bell can't get inside the wreck, and it's there where the gold or silver is usually to be found."

"Can't they blow the wreck apart with dynamite, and scatter the gold on the bottom of the ocean?" asked Ned.

"Yes, they could do that, but usually they scatter it so far, and the ocean currents so cover it with sand, that it is impossible ever to get it again. I admit that if a wreck is blown apart a man in a diving bell can perhaps get a small part of it. But the limitations of a diving bell are so well recognized that several inventors have tried adjusting movable arms to the bell, to be operated by the man inside."

"Did they work?" asked Ned.

"After a fashion, yes. But I never heard of any case where the gold and silver recovered paid for the expenses of making the bell and sending men down in it. For it takes the same sort of outfit to aid the man in the diving bell as it does the diver in his usual rubber or steel suit. Air has to be pumped to him, and he has to be lowered and raised."

"Well, isn't there any way of getting at this gold on the floor of the ocean?" asked Ned, his enthusiasm a little cooled by the practical "cold water" Tom had thrown.

"Oh, yes, of course there is, in a way," was the answer of the young inventor. "Don't you remember how my father and I, with Mr. Damon and Captain Weston, went in our submarine, the Advance, and discovered the wreck of the Boldero?"

"I do recall that," admitted Ned.

"Well," resumed Tom, "there was a case of showing how much trouble we had. An ordinary diving outfit never would have answered. We had to locate the wreck, and a hard time we had doing it. Then, when we found it, we had to ram the old ship and blow it apart before we could get inside. Even after that we just happened to discover the gold, as it were. I'm only mentioning this to show you it isn't so easy to get at the wealth under the sea as writers in Sunday newspaper supplements think it is."

"I believe you, Tom. And yet it seems a shame to have all those millions going to waste, doesn't it?" And Ned spoke as a banker and financial man, who is not happy unless money is earning interest all the while.

"Well, a billion of dollars is a lot," Tom admitted. "And when you think of all that have been sunk, say even in the last hundred years, it amazes one. But still, all the gold and silver was hidden in the earth before it was dug out, and now it's only gone back where it came from, in a way. We got along before men dug it out and coined it into money, and I guess we'll get along when it's under water. No use worrying over the ocean treasures, as far as I'm concerned."

"You're a hopeless proposition!" laughed Ned. "You'd never make a banker, or a Napoleon of finance."

"That's why my father and I got you to look after our financial affairs," and Tom smiled. "You're just the one—with your interest-bearing mind—to keep us off the shoals of business trouble."

"Yes, I suppose I can do that, while you and your father go on inventing giant cannons, great searchlights, submarines, and airships," conceded Ned. "But this, to me, did look like an easy way of making money."

"How's that, Ned?" asked Tom, a new note coming into his voice. "Were you thinking of going to Japan and taking a hand in the undersea search?"

"No. But stock in this company is being sold, and shareholders stand to win big returns—if the wrecks are come upon."

"That's just it!" exclaimed Tom. "If they find the wrecks! And let me tell you, Ned, that there's a mighty big 'if' in it all. Do you realize how hard it is to find anything on the ocean, to say nothing of something under it?"

"I hadn't thought of it."

"Well, you'd better think of it. You know on the ocean sailors have to locate a certain imaginary position by calculation, using the sun and stars as guides. Of course, they have navigation down pretty fine, and a good pilot can get to a place on the surface of the ocean and meet another craft there almost as well as you and I can make an appointment to meet at Main and Broad streets at a certain hour.

"But lots of times there are errors in calculations or a storm comes up hiding the sun and stars, and, instead of a captain getting to where he wants to, he's anywhere from one to a hundred miles out. Now the location of Broad and Main Streets doesn't change even in a storm.

"And I'm not saying that a location on an ocean changes. I'm only saying that the least disturbance or error in calculation makes it almost impossible to find the exact spot. And if it's that hard on the surface, where you can see what you're doing, how much harder is it in regard to something on the bottom of the sea? So don't take any stock in these ocean treasure recovering companies. They may not be fakes, but they're mighty uncertain."

"Oh, I don't know that I was really going to buy any stock in this Japanese concern, Tom. I only thought it would be interesting to think about. And perhaps you might sell them a submarine or some of your diving apparatus."

"Nothing doing, Ned. We've got other plans, my father and I. There's that new tractor for use in the big wheat-growing belt, to say nothing of—"

Tom's remarks were interrupted by voices outside his office door. One voice, in particular, rose above the others. It said:

"No can go in! The Master he am busily! No can go in!"

"Nonsense, Koku!" exclaimed a man, and at the sound of his voice Tom and Ned smiled. "Nonsense! Of course I can go in! Why, bless my watch fob, I must go in! I've got the greatest proposition to lay before Tom Swift that he ever heard of! There's at least a million in it! Let me pass, Koku!"

"Mr. Damon!" murmured Tom Swift. "I wonder what he has on his mind now

As he spoke the door opened rather violently and a short, stout man, evidently much excited, fairly burst into the room, followed, more sedately, by a stranger.

A STRANGE OFFER

"Hello, Tom Swift! Hello, Ned! Glad to see you both! Busy, as usual, I'll wager. Bless my check book! I never saw you when you weren't busy at some scheme or other, Tom, my boy. But I won't take up much of your time. Tom Swift, let me introduce my friend, Mr. Dixwell Hardley. Mr. Hardley, shake hands with Tom Swift, one of the youngest, and yet one of the greatest, inventors in the world! I've told you a little about him, but it would take me all day to tell you what he really has done and—"

"Hold on, Mr. Damon!" laughed Tom, as he shook hands with the man whom Mr. Damon had named Dixwell Hardley. "Hold on, if you please. There's a limit to it, you know, and already you've said enough about me to—"

"Bless my ink bottle, Tom, I haven't said half enough!" interrupted the little, eccentric man. "Wait until you hear what he has done, Mr. Hardley. Then, if you don't say he's the very chap for your wonderful scheme, I'm mighty much mistaken! And shake hands with Ned Newton, too. He's Tom's financial manager, and of course he'll have something to say. Though when he hears how you are going to turn over a couple of million dollars or more, why, I know he'll be on our side."

Ned's eyes sparkled at the mention of the money. In truth he dealt in dollars and cents for the benefit of Tom Swift. Ned shook hands with Mr. Hardley and Tom motioned Mr. Damon and his friend to chairs.

"Now, Tom," went on the strange little man, "I know you're busy. Bless my adding machine, I never saw you when—"

At that moment there arose in the corridor outside Tom's private office a discord of voices, in which one could be heard exclaiming:

"Now yo' clear out oh heah! Massa Tom done tole me to sweep dish yeah place, an' ef yo' doan let me alone, why—why—"

"Huh! Radicate him big stiff—dat's what! Big stiff! Too stiff for sweep Master's floor. Koku sweep one hand!"

"Oh, yo' t'ink 'case yo' is sich a big giant, yo' kin git de best ob ole black Rad! But I'll show yo' dat—"

"Excuse me a moment," said Tom, with a smile to his guests as he arose. "Eradicate and Koku are at it again, I'm sorry to say. I'll have to go out and arbitrate the strike," and he left the room.

While he is settling the differences between his faithful old black servant and Koku, the giant, I will take the opportunity of telling my new readers something about Tom Swift.

Those who are familiar with the previous books of this series may skip this part. But it will give my new audience a better insight into this story if they will bear with me a moment and peruse these few lines.

As related in the first book, "Tom Swift and His Motor Cycle," the hero seemed born an inventive genius. It was this inventive faculty which enabled him to take the motor cycle that tried to climb a tree with Mr. Wakefield Damon on it and make the wreck into a serviceable bit of mechanism. Thus Tom became acquainted with Mr. Damon, who among other eccentricities, was always "blessing" something personal.

Tom Swift lived in the city of Shopton with his father and their faithful housekeeper, Mrs. Baggert. It was so named because the Swift shops were an important industry there. Tom's father, as well as Tom himself, was an inventor of note, and employed many men in building machines of various kinds. During the Great War the services of Tom and his father had been dedicated to the government.

There are a number of books dealing with Tom's activities, the list of titles of which may be found at the beginning of this volume.

Sufficient to say here, that Tom invented and operated motor boats, airships, and submarines. In addition he traveled on many expeditions with Mr. Damon, Ned, and others. He went among the diamond makers and it was when he escaped from captivity that he managed to bring away Koku, the giant, with him. Since then Koku and Eradicate Sampson, the faithful colored man, had periodic quarrels as to who should serve the young inventor.

Besides inventing and using many machines of motive power, Tom Swift engaged in other industries. He helped dig a big tunnel, he constructed a photo-telephone, a great searchlight and a monster cannon. Occasionally he had searched for treasure, once under the sea, with considerable success.

Of late his and his father's industries had become so important that a number of new buildings had been constructed and the plant greatly enlarged. Ned Newton, who had once worked in a Shopton bank, became financial manager for Tom and his father, and plenty of work he found with which to occupy himself.

Just prior to the opening of this story Tom had perfected a noiseless aeroplane—or one so nearly silent as to justify the name. The details of it will be found in the book called "Tom Swift and His Air Scout." In this mechanism of the air Tom had had some wonderful experiences, and they had not been at home more than a few weeks when New Newton broached the subject of undersea wealth.

The talk of Tom and his financial manager was interrupted by the arrival of Mr. Damon and the stranger he had introduced as Mr. Hardley.

Eradicate, or "Rad," and Koku, have been mentioned. Rad was an ancient colored man who once owned a mule named Boomerang. Sampson was the colored servant's last name, and he declared he had chosen the one "Eradicate" because in his younger days he was a great cleaner and whitewasher, "eradicating" the dirt, so to speak.

Boomerang had, some time since, gone where all good mules go, though Eradicate declared he would get another and call him Boomerang II. But, so far, he had not done so.

Rad, though too old to do heavy work, still believed he was indispensable to the welfare of Tom and his father; and as the giant Koku, who was physically an immense man, held the same view, it followed there were frequent clashes between the two, as on the occasion just mentioned.

"What was the matter, Tom?" asked Ned, when the young inventor came back into the room.

"Oh, the same old story," replied Tom. "Rad wanted to sweep the hall, and Koku insisted he was to do it."

"What'd you do, Tom?" asked Mr. Damon.

"I settled it by having Rad sweep this hall and sending Koku to do another—a bigger one I told him. He likes hard work, so he was pleased. Now we'll have it quiet for a little while. Did I understand you to say, Mr. Damon, that—er—Mr. Hardley I believe the name is—had a proposition to make to me

"That's exactly it, my dear Mr. Swift!" broke in the man in question. "I have a wonderful offer to make you, and I'm sure you will admit that it will be well worth your while to consider and accept it. There will be at least a million in it—"

"Bless my check book, I thought you said several millions!" exclaimed Mr. Damon.

"So I did," was the rather nettled answer. "I was about to say, Mr. Damon, that there will be at least a million in it for Mr. Swift, and another million for myself. There may be more, but I want to be conservative."

"Talking in millions, and calling himself conservative," mused Ned Newton. "Somehow or other I don't just cotton to this fellow!"

"When our mutual friend, Mr. Damon, told me about you, my dear Mr. Swift," went on Mr. Hardley, "I at once came to the conclusion that you were the very man I wanted to do business with. I'm sure it will be to our mutual advantage."

Tom Swift said nothing. He was willing to let the other talk, while he waited to see how far he would go. And, as Tom said afterward, he, as had Ned, took an instinctive dislike to Mr. Hardley. He could not say definitely what it was, but that was his feeling. That he might be mistaken, he admitted frankly. Time alone could tell.

"Have you a half hour to give me while it explain matters?" asked Mr. Hardley. "I may go farther and say I need considerable time to go into all the details. May I speak now?"

To tell the truth Tom Swift had many important matters to consider, and, in addition, Ned Newton was prepared to go over some financial ends of the business with Tom. But the young inventor felt that, in justice to his friend Mr. Damon, who had brought Mr. Hardley, he could do no less than give the stranger a hearing. But only the introduction by Mr. Damon brought this about.

"I shall be glad to hear what you have to say, Mr. Hardley," said Tom, as courteously as he could. "I will not go so far as to say that my time is unlimited, but I will listen to you now if you care to go into details."

"That's good!" exclaimed the visitor. "I'm sure that when you have listened you will agree with me."

"He's a little bit too sure!" mused Ned.

"Bless my pocketbook, Tom, but there are millions in it!" exclaimed Mr. Damon. "Literally millions, Tom!"

Mr. Hardley settled himself comfortably in his chair and looked from Tom to Ned.

"May I speak freely here?" he asked, with obvious intent.

"You may," the young inventor answered. "Mr. Newton is my financial manager, and I do nothing of importance without consulting him. You may regard him as a member of the firm, in fact, as he does own some stock. My father is practically retired, and I do not trouble him with unimportant details. So Mr. Newton and I are prepared to listen to you."

"Very well, Mr. Swift, I'm going to ask you a question. Have you all the money you want?"

Tom laughed.

"I suppose any man would answer that question in the negative," he replied. "Frankly, I could use more money, though I am not poor."

"So I have heard. Well, would a million dollars clear profit appeal to you?"

"It certainly would," was the answer.

"Then I am prepared to offer you that sum," went on Mr. Hardley. "But there are certain conditions, and I may say that this vast wealth is not easy to come at. However, with your inventive genius, I am sure you will be able to solve the mystery of the sea. Now then as to details. There lies, on the floor of the ocean—"

"Hark!" exclaimed Tom, raising a hand to enjoin silence. "I think I hear some one coming." At that moment there was a knock at the door.

THINKING IT OVER

"Father, is that you?" asked Tom. "Father hasn't been feeling well, of late," he said to the assembled company, "and I told him to go to lie down. But he's hard to manage, and he won't rest more than ten minutes at a time. My father, I might explain, Mr. Hardley," Tom went on, "is actively associated with me in business."

"So I have understood," said the man who had been introduced by Mr. Damon.

"Dis Koku!" came the guttural voice of the giant from the other side of the door. "Koku want more work. Hall, him all clean. Maybe I help dat no-good Rad now."

"No you don't, Koku!" exclaimed the young inventor, with a laugh. "You keep away from Rad. You'll get to disputing again and interrupt me, and I have business on hand. Here, wait a minute. I'll find something for you to do," he went on, opening the door to disclose the immense man standing outside, a broom in his hand seeming like a toy.

"Excuse me one moment," went on Tom to his friends. Taking up his desk telephone he called one of the shops, asking: "Have you any heavy work on hand this morning; lifting big castings, or anything like that? You have? Good! I'll send Koku right over."

Turning to the giant who apparently had not paid much attention to the talk over the wire, Tom said:

"Koku, go over to shop number ten, ask for the foreman, and he'll keep you busy. There are some five-hundred-pound castings that need assembling, and you can help him."

"Good!" exclaimed the giant, with a cheerful grin. "Koku like big work—no like sweep. Good for women and Rad, but not for Koku!"

"He spoke the truth there," remarked Ned Newton, as the giant stalked down the hall. "I never saw such a strong man. I'm afraid to shake hands with him, for fear I'll be minus a couple of fingers in the operation."

"Well, he's disposed of," remarked Tom, as he closed the door. "And now, Mr. Hardley, I'm at your service, as far as listening to your proposition is concerned."

"Thank you. I shall endeavor to be brief," remarked the visitor. "Am I correct in assuming that you have had some experience in submarine work? I believe Mr. Damon mentioned something of that sort."

"Submarine work? Bless my hydrometer, I should say so!" exclaimed the eccentric man. "And not only in submarine, but in aeroplane! but you don't need any aeroplanes, my dear Mr. Hardley. It's the submarine end of it that you are interested in, as far as Tom Swift is concerned. Now go ahead and tell him what you told me, and how many millions there are in it."

"Very well," assented the visitor. "Have you ever had any experience in recovering treasure from sunken wrecks?" he asked Tom.

"Yes," was the answer. "And it is curious that you should ask me that, for my friend here, Ned Newton, and I were just talking about that very matter. Here's what brought it up," and Tom showed the page from the Sunday paper.

"Hum! Yes!" musingly remarked Mr. Hardley. "That's all very well. Part of it is true; but I imagine most of it is the work of imagination of some enterprising reporter. Of course there is no question but that there are untold millions on the bottom of the ocean. The only trouble, as I think you will agree with me, Mr. Swift, is in coming at the money."

"Exactly," said Tom.

"And will you bear me out when I say that if the wreck of a treasure ship could be exactly located in water that is not too deep, half the trouble would be solved?" asked Mr. Hardley.

"A good share of it would," answered Tom. "That is usually the chief difficulty—locating the wreck. Nearly always they are anywhere from one to five miles from where the persons seeking them think they are. And five miles, or even half a mile, is a good distance on the bottom of the ocean."

"Exactly," echoed Mr. Hardley. "Then if I could give you the exact location of a sunken treasure ship, and prove to you that the owners had given up the search for it, leaving it open to salvage on the part of whoever wished to try—would that be any inducement to you to make an attempt, Mr. Swift?"

"I should want to hear more about it before I gave an answer," replied Tom. "As perhaps Mr. Damon has told you, I once went on a hunt for treasure in my submarine. We found it, but only after considerable trouble, and then I declared I'd never again engage in such a search. There wasn't enough net profit in it."

"But there are millions in this, Tom! Bless my gold tooth, but there are millions!" cried the excitable Mr. Damon. "Hurry up and tell him!" he urged his friend.

"I will," assented Mr. Hardley. "I can readily believe," he went on, "that the cost of hunting for undersea treasure is great. I have taken that into consideration. Now, in brief, my plan is this. I will join forces with you, and bear half the expense if I am allowed to share half the proceeds. That's fair, isn't it?" he asked Tom.

"So far, yes," replied the young inventor.

"Now then, to business!" exclaimed the visitor. "Will you join with me in searching for some of the wealth-laden wrecks that are rotting at the bottom of the sea, Mr. Swift?"

"Do you mean make an indiscriminate search for any one of a number of wrecks?" Tom wanted to know.

"I should want the understanding broad enough to include all wrecks we might discover," was the answer, "but I have in mind one in particular now. It is the wreck of the steamer Pandora which was sunk off the coast of one of the West Indian Islands about a year ago."

Ned Newton quickly caught up the page of the Sunday supplement and scanned the list of wrecks given there.

"No mention of the Pandora here," he said.

"No," agreed Mr. Hardley, "the story of this wreck is not generally known, and the story of the treasure she carried is hardly known at all. As a matter of fact, this money, mostly in gold, was to finance a South American revolution, and such matters are generally kept quiet. That is why nothing much appeared in the papers about the Pandora. But I happen to know that she carried over two million dollars in gold, and I know—"

"Think of that, Tom! Think of that!" cried Mr. Damon. "Two million dollars in gold! Why bless my—bless my—"

But the eccentric man could think of nothing adequate to bless under the circumstances, and he subsided with a murmur.

"Excuse me for interrupting you," he said to his new friend. "But I just couldn't help it."

"That's all right," Mr. Hardley remarked, with a smile that showed two rows of very even, white teeth. "I don't blame you for getting excited. Does that interest you?" he asked Tom. "Two million dollars in gold, besides a quantity of silver —just how much I don't know."

"It certainly sounds interesting," replied Tom, with a smile. "But are you sure of your facts?"

"Absolutely," was the answer. "I was a passenger on the Pandora when she was wrecked in a storm. I saw the gold put on board. It was not taken off, and is on her now as she lies at the bottom of the sea."

"And the location?" queried Tom.

"I know that, too!" said Mr. Hardley eagerly. "I was with the captain just before we had to abandon ship, and I heard the exact nautical location given him by an officer who made the calculation. I have it written down to the second—latitude and longitude. That will be a help in locating the wreck, won't it?"

"Why, yes," Tom had to agree, "it will be. but if you know it, then the captain and others must know it. And what is to prevent them from making a search for the Pandora if they have not already done so

"The best reason in the world," was the answer. "The boat containing the captain and the officer who gave him the ship's position was sunk, and all on board lost. The boat I was in was the only one picked up, and I believe I am the only one who knows exactly where the Pandora lies.

"Now, here is my offer, Mr. Swift," went on the seeker after the ocean's hidden wealth. "I will bear half the expense of fitting out a submarine, or for any other kind of expedition to go in search of the wreck of the

Pandora. I will furnish you with the exact nautical location, as I have it. And when the wealth is found and brought to the surface, I will give you half—in other words at least a million dollars! Does that appeal to you?"

"I must say it is a fair, though perhaps strange, offer," conceded Tom. "And a million dollars is not made every day nor every year. But what about the title to this money? After we have recovered it—provided we are successful—will not some person or some government lay claim to it?"

"None can successfully," declared Mr. Hardley. "As I told you, the money was to finance a revolution. It was raised for an unlawful purpose, so to speak, and no one has a valid claim to it under the circumstances, so lawyers whom I have consulted have told me. But if that is not enough, I have papers to prove that those who might be called the owners have given up the search for it. More than a year has elapsed, and though I don't know just how long it takes to outlaw an under-ocean claim, I feel sure that we would have a legal and moral right to take this gold if we could find it."

"I should want to be satisfied on that point before I undertook the search," said Tom.

"Then you will undertake it?" eagerly exclaimed Mr. Hardley.

"I will think it over," Tom answered quietly—so quietly that distinct disappointment showed on the face of the visitor.

AGAINST HIS WILL

For a moment it seemed that Mr. Damon, as well as Mr. Hardley, felt disappointment at Tom's answer, for the eccentric man exclaimed:

"Bless my leather belt, Tom, but you aren't very keen on making a million dollars!"

"Oh, yes, I like to make money," the young inventor answered. "I guess you know that, as well as any one, for you've been with me on several trips. And I don't mind hard work, nor danger."

"I'll say you don't!" added Ned, as he thought of some of Tom's perilous voyages, among the diamond makers and in the caves of ice.

"Well, if you are anxious to make money, as I admit I am," said Mr. Hardley, "why can't you give me an answer now?"

"Because," answered Tom, "there are many things to be considered. Hunting for a treasure on the floor of the Atlantic isn't like going to some location on land, however wild or inaccessible it might be. Do you realize, Mr. Hardley, what a large difference in miles a small error in nautical calculations makes? We might go to the exact spot where you thought the wreck of the Pandora lies, only to find that we would have to hunt around a long time.

"I must think of that, and also think of my other business affairs. Then, too, there is my father. He is getting old, and while he is still active in the affairs of the company, particularly when it comes to taking up new lines of work, I do not like to think of leaving him, as I should have to, in case I went on this trip."

"Take him along!" exclaimed Mr. Damon. "He's gone with us before, Tom."

"He's too old now," said the young inventor a bit sadly. "Father will never make another extended trip. But I will let you have my answer as soon as I can, Mr. Hardley, and I will give the matter considerable thought."

"I'm sure I hope you will, and also that you will consent to go," was the answer. "A million is not easily to be come at in these days after the Great War."

"I realize that," agreed Tom with a smile. "And you shall have my answer as soon as possible."

With this the visitor was forced to be content, and a little later he withdrew with Mr. Damon, the latter telling Tom that he would see him again soon.

"Well, that was queer, wasn't it?" remarked Ned, when he and Tom were alone again.

"What was?" asked Tom, as though his mind was far away, as indeed it was.

"That this man should come in with his project to search for a sunken treasure wreck just as we were talking about how many millions were on the bottom of the ocean."

"Yes, it was quite a coincidence," Tom admitted.

"What do you think of it—and him?" asked Ned.

"Well, to tell you the truth, I didn't take a great fancy to Mr. Hardley," Tom said. "I think he's altogether too cocksure, and takes too much for granted. Still I may misjudge him. Certainly he doesn't have a chance at a million dollars every day."

"Do you think you could get the treasure out of this wreck, Tom, if you could locate her?"

"Why, it's possible; yes. We proved that with the Boldero."

"Would you use the same submarine?"

"No, I think I'd have to rebuild it, or make an altogether new one. Possibly I might get one of Uncle Sam's and add some improvements of my own."

"Yes, you could do that," agreed Ned. "You've done so much for the government that it couldn't refuse you something reasonable, now that the war is over. Then do you think you'll go?"

"Really, Ned, I can't make up my mind yet. Now let's forget the Pandora and all the millions and get down to business. This Criterion company seems to me to want altogether too much, We'll have to trim their request down a bit. They owe the money and ought to pay it."

"Yes, I'll get after them," said Ned, and then he and his chum, as well as employer, plunged into a mass of business details.

It was the next afternoon, when Tom, following a strenuous morning of work, leaned back in his chair at his desk, that Mr. Damon was announced.

"Tell him to come in," ordered Tom, always glad to see his friend. "Wait a minute, though!" he called to the messenger. "Is any one with him?"

"No, sir; he is alone."

"Good! Then show him right in. I was afraid," said Tom to Ned, who was also in the office, "that he had Hardley with him. I'm not quite ready to see him yet."

"Then you haven't made up your mind about going for the treasure?"

"Not exactly. I shall, perhaps, this week."

"Bless my matchbox, Tom, but I'm glad to see you!" cried Mr. Damon, as he hastened forward with outstretched hand. "I was afraid you might be out. Now look here! What about my friend Hardley? He's very anxious to know your decision about going for that treasure, and I said I'd come over and sound you. I don't mind saying, Tom, that if you go I'm going too; if you'll take me, of course."

"Well, Mr. Damon, you know you'll always be welcome, as far as I am concerned," said the young inventor; "but, as a matter of fact, I don't believe I'm going."

"What? Not going to pick up a million dollars off the floor of the ocean, Tom? Bless my bank balance! but that's foolish, it seems to me."

"Perhaps it is, but I can't help it."

"What's your principal objection?" asked the eccentric man. "It isn't that you don't want the money, is it?"

"Not exactly."

"Then it must be that you object to Mr. Hardley personally." went on Mr. Damon. "I began to suspect that, Tom, and I want to say that you are wrong. Mr. Hardley is a friend of mine—a good friend. I have not known him long, but he strikes me as being all right. He had some good letters of introduction, and I believe he has money."

"Where'd he get it?" asked Tom.

"I don't know, exactly. Seems to me I heard him mention silver mines, or it may have been gold. Anyhow, it had something to do with getting wealth out of the ground. Now, Tom, I don't mind saying that I stand to make a little money in case this thing goes through."

"How's that, Mr. Damon?" asked the young scientist in surprise.

"Why, I agreed to bear part of the expense," was the answer. "I thought this was a pretty good scheme, and when Mr. Hardley came to me and told me of the possibilities I agreed to help him finance the expenses. That is, I have taken shares in the company he formed to raise his half of the expense money.

"Of course I thought of you at once when he spoke of having to search out a sunken wreck, and I proposed your name. He'd heard of you, he said, but didn't know you. So I brought you together and now—bless my apple pie, Tom! I hope you aren't going to turn down a chance to make a million and, incidentally, help an old friend."

"Well," remarked Tom, slowly, "I must admit, Mr. Damon, that I didn't think you'd go into a thing like this. Not that it is more risky than other schemes, but I thought you didn't care for speculation."

"Well, this sort of appealed to me Tom. You know—sunken wreck under the ocean, down in a diving bell perhaps, and all that! There's romance to it."

"Yes, there is romance," agreed Tom. "And hard work, too. If I undertook this it would mean an extra lot of work getting ready. I suppose I could use my own submarine. I could get her in commission, and make improvements more quickly than on any other."

"Then you'll go?" quickly cried the eccentric man.

"Well, since you tell me you are interested financially, I believe I will," assented Tom, but he spoke reluctantly. "As a matter of fact, I am going against my better judgment. Not that I fear we shall be in danger," he hastened to add; "but I think it will prove a failure. However, as Mr. Hardley will bear half the expense, and as by using my own submarine that will not be much, I'll go!"

"Then I'll tell him!" exclaimed Mr. Damon. "Hurray! This is great! I haven't had an exciting trip for a long while! Don't tell my wife about it," he begged Tom and Ned. "At least not until just before we start. Then she can't object in time. I'll have a wonderful experience, I know. This will be good news to Dixwell Hardley!"

And as Mr. Damon hastened away to acquaint his new friend with Tom's decision, the young inventor remarked to Ned:

"I'll go; but, somehow, I have a feeling that something will happen."

"Something bad?" asked the financial manager. "No, I wouldn't go so far as to say that. But I believe we'll have trouble. I'll start on the search for the sunken millions, but rather against my better judgment. However, maybe Mr. Damon's luck and good nature will pull us through!"

BUSY DAYS

Once Tom Swift had made up his mind to do a thing he did it— even though it was against his better judgment. His word, passed, was his bond.

In conformity then with his decision to take Mr. Damon and the latter's friend, Mr. Hardley, on an undersea search for treasure, Tom at once proceeded to make his preparations. Ned, too, had his work to do, since the decision to make what might be a long trip would necessitate a change in Tom's plans. But, as in everything he did, he threw himself into this whole-heartedly and with enthusiasm.

Not once did Tom Swift admit to himself that he was going into this scheme because he thought well of it. It was all for Mr. Damon, after Tom had learned that his friend had invested considerable money in a company Mr. Hardley had formed to pay half the expenses of the trip.

Tom even tried to buy Mr. Damon off, by offering the latter back all the money the eccentric man had invested with his new friend. But Mr. Damon exclaimed:

"Bless my gasolene tank, Tom! I'm in this thing as much for the love of adventure, as I am for the money. Now let's go on with it. You will like Hardley better when you know him better."

"Perhaps," said Tom dryly, but he did not think so.

The young inventor insisted, before making any preparations for the trip, that all the cards be laid on the table. That is, he wanted to be sure there had been such a ship as the Pandora, that she was laden with gold, and that she had sunk where Mr. Hardley said she had. The latter was perfectly willing to supply all needful proofs, even though some were difficult, because of the nature of the voyage of the treasure craft. As a filibuster she was not trading openly.

"Here are all the records," said Mr. Hardley to Tom one day, when the young inventor, Ned, and Mr. Damon were gathered in Tom's office. "You may satisfy yourself."

And, with Ned's help, Tom did.

There was no question but what the Pandora had sailed from a certain port on a certain date. The official reports proved that. And that she did carry a considerable treasure in gold was also established to the satisfaction of Tom Swift. Because the gold was to be used for furthering ends against one of the South American governments, the gold shipment was not insured and, in consequence, no recovery could be made.

"Then you are satisfied, are you, Mr. Swift, that the ship, set out with over two millions in gold on board?" asked Mr. Hardley. "Yes, that seems to be proved," Tom admitted, and Ned nodded. "The next thing to prove is that she foundered in a storm about the position I am going to tell you," went on Mr. Damon's friend.

"He doesn't tell you the exact location now, Tom," explained Mr. Damon, "because it might leak out. He'll disclose it to us as soon as we are out of sight of land in the submarine."

"I'm willing to agree to that proposition," Tom said. "But I want to be sure she really did sink."

This was proved to him by official records. There was no question but that the Pandora had gone down in a big storm. And Mr. Hardley was on board. He proved that, too, a not very difficult task, since the official passenger list was open to inspection.

Mr. Hardley repeated his story about having overheard the exact location of the ship a few minutes before she sank, and he also told of the captain and several members of the ship's company having been drowned. This, too, was confirmed.

"Then," went on Mr. Hardley, "all that remains for me to do is to deposit at some bank my half of the expenses and await your word to go aboard the submarine."

"I believe that is all," returned Tom. "But, on my part, it will take some little time to fit the submarine out as I want to have her. There are some special appliances I want to take along which will aid us in the search for the gold, if we find the place where the Pandora is sunk."

"Oh, we'll find that all right," declared Mr. Hardley, "if you will only follow my directions."

Tom looked slightly incredulous, but said nothing.

Then followed busy days. The submarine Advance, which had made several successful trips, as related in the book bearing the title, "Tom Swift and His Submarine Boat," was hauled into dry dock and the work of overhauling her begun. Tom put his best men to work, and, after a consultation with his father, decided on some radical changes in the craft.

"Tom, my boy," said the aged Mr. Swift, "I wish you weren't going on this trip."

"Why, Dad?" asked the young inventor.

"Because I fear something will happen. We don't really need this money, and suppose—suppose—"

"Oh, I'm not worrying, Dad," was the answer. "I've taken worse risks than this, many a time. I'm really doing it as a favor to Mr. Damon. He's got too much money invested to let him lose it. And we can use a million dollars ourselves. It will enable me to put in operation a plan to pension our workmen. I've long had that in mind, but I've never had enough capital to carry it out."

"Well, of course, Tom, that's a worthy object, and I won't make any further objections. But take my advice, and strengthen the submarine."

"Why, Dad?" asked Tom in some surprise. "Because you'll find the water there of a greater depth than you think," was the answer. "I know you have the official hydrographic charts, but there's a mistake, I'm sure. I once made a study of that part of the ocean, and there are currents there at certain seasons of the year that no one suspects, and deep caverns that aren't charted. If the Pandora lies in one of these you'll need a great strength of walls to your submarine to withstand the pressure of deep water."

The craft Tom Swift proposed to use in searching for the treasure ship Pandora was of the regular cigar-shape, but inside it had many special features. It was more comfortable than the usual submarine, not being intended for fighting, though it did carry guns and a torpedo tube. Tom intended renaming the craft, which had been called Advance, and one day, when there had been some discussion as to what the undersea craft ought to be called, Ned explained:

"Why don't you name it after her?"

"After whom?" inquired Tom, in some surprise, looking up from a letter he was writing.

"Your friend and future wife, Mary Nestor," answered Ned. "I'm sure she'd appreciate it."

"That isn't such a bad idea," conceded Tom musingly. "The only thing about it is that I don't want Mary's name bandied about that way."

"Use her initials, then," suggested Ned.

"How do you mean

"Why not call it the M. N. 1.? Isn't that a good name?"

"The M. N. 1." mused Tom. "Not so bad. If the N. C. 4 flew over the ocean the M. N. 1 ought to be able to navigate under it. I think I'll do that, Ned."

So the Advance, rebuilt and refitted in many ways, was christened the M. N. 1, and a wonderful craft she proved to be. Mary Nestor was quite pleased when Tom told her what he had done. She appreciated the delicate compliment he had paid her.

Busy and more busy were the days that passed. As the M. N. 1 had to be refitted some miles from Tom's home, where it was feasible to launch her for the trip, he had to make the journey between the drydock and his shop either by automobile or aeroplane. Often he choose the latter, since he had a number of small, speedy craft in his hangars. Sometimes Ned or Mr. Damon went with him, but Mr. Hardley could never be induced to ride in an airship.

"I'll travel on the ocean or under it," he said, "but I'm not going to take a chance in the air. I'm too afraid of falling."

"Tom, what's this?" asked Ned one day, when he and Tom had come to see how the work of remodeling the submarine was getting along. "It looks like something you used when you dug your big tunnel."

"That's a new kind of diving bell," Tom answered. "You know it isn't easy to get treasure out of a sunken ship. It isn't like picking it off the bottom of the ocean. We've got to get it out from inside—perhaps from inside a strong box or a safe. This bell may come in useful."

"Can't you use the special diving suits that you always used to carry?" the financial manager wanted to know.

"We might, if the water isn't too deep," replied Tom. "But you know there is a limit to how far down a man in even my kind of diving dress can go. With this diving bell a much greater depth can be reached. And this diving bell is not like any you have ever seen or read about. My father gave me the idea for it. I'll demonstrate it to you some day."

A diving bell is shaped like its name. A common glass tumbler thrust down into a pail of water, with the open side down, will show exactly the principle on which a diving bell works. It illustrates the fact that two things cannot occupy the same place at the same time.

Pushing the tumbler, open end down, into the pail of water, leaves a space in the upper end of the tumbler which the water cannot fill, because it is already occupied with air. Imagine a big tumbler, made of thick steel, lowered into the water. Air pumped into the upper part not only keeps the water from entering, but also enables a man inside to breathe and to move about inside the bell which may be lowered to the floor of the ocean. But, as Tom told Ned, his diving bell was a big improvement over those commonly used.

The two young men inspected the progress made in refitting the submarine, and Tom expressed himself as satisfied.

"How soon do you think you can start?" asked Ned.

"In about two weeks," was the answer. "I'll want to get to the West Indies before the fall storms start. Not only will it be impossible to make a search then, but the very location of the sunken wreck may be changed."

"How so?" asked Ned.

"Because of undersea currents. They are strong enough, not only to sweep a wreck away from the place where it may have settled, but they may cover it with sand, and then it is hopeless to try to dig it out. So We've got to go soon, if we go at all."

"Well, I'm with you!" exclaimed Ned. "Hello! here's some one looking for you, I guess," he added, as a boy came hurrying down to the dock from the temporary office Tom had set up there.

"You're wanted on the telephone, Mr. Swift," said the messenger. "It's important, too."

"All right. I'll come at once," was the answer. "Hope it isn't bad news," mused Ned, as his chum hurried on in advance. "Maybe Hardley has found out he hasn't a right to search for that sunken gold after all. That would be too bad for Mr. Damon!"

Mary's Odd Story

"Hello! Hello! Yes, this is Tom Swift. What's that? You've had an accident? Great Scott, Mary! I hope you aren't hurt."

Ned overheard these words as he stood outside the temporary office, from inside which Tom Swift was telephoning.

"There's been an accident!" thought the financial manager. "I wonder if I can help?"

He was about to hurry in to offer his services when he heard Tom laugh, and then he knew it was all right. He heard his chum say:

"I'll be right over and get you. Just where are you?"

Then followed a period of listening on the part of Tom, to be broken by the words:

"All right, I'll be right with you. Lucky I have my Air Scout with me. You aren't afraid to ride in that, are you? No, that's good! I'll be right over. Ned is here with me, and I'll have him telephone to your father and mother."

With that Tom hung up the receiver and joined his chum.

"Mary had a slight automobile accident about five miles from here," Tom told his chum. "Some green driver ran into her and dished one of her wheels. No one hurt, but she hasn't a spare wheel and can't navigate. She called me up at the house, not wishing to alarm her father, and Mrs. Baggert told her you and I had come down to the dock, so she reached me here. I'll go in the small aeroplane and get her. Luckily I left it here the last time I made a trip. Will you call up Mary's home and let them know she's all right and that I'll soon be home with her? They might hear an exaggerated account of the accident."

Ned promised to do this, and at once put in a call for the home of his chum's fiancee, while Tom had one of his men run out the Air Scout. This was an aeroplane recently perfected by the young inventor which slipped through space with scarcely a sound. So silent was it that the craft had been dubbed "Silent Sam," and it stood Tom in good stead as those of you know who have read the volume just before the present book. This sky glider Tom would now use in going to the rescue of Mary Nestor was not, however, the same large craft that figured in the previous story. That airship had been given to the United States government for war purposes. But Tom had built himself a smaller one for his own use. It had the advantage of enabling him to carry on a conversation with his passenger when he took one aloft.

About a week before Tom and Ned had flown from Shopton to the dry dock where the submarine was being reconstructed in this small airship. Engine trouble had developed after they had landed, and they had gone back by automobile, leaving the Air Scout to be repaired. This had been done, and now Tom intended to use it in going to Mary's rescue.

Now, when the Air Scout had been run out of the hangar, Tom climbed into it.

"Sorry I can't take you along," he called to Ned, who had finished telephoning to Mary's home, "but, under the circumstances—"

"Two's company and three's a crowd!" laughed Ned. "I know!"

"No, I didn't mean that," Tom said. "You know Mary likes you, but this will carry only two."

"I know!" answered his chum. "On your way!"

And with an almost noiseless throb of her engine and a whirr of her propeller, the aeroplane rolled swiftly over the level starting ground and took the air like a swan leaving its lake.

Tom did not rise to a great height, as he would need only a few minutes to reach the place where Mary was stalled by the accident to her machine. Soon he was hovering over a level field, one of several that lined the country highways in that section. A small crowd on the turnpike gathered about an evidently disabled automobile gave Tom the clue he needed, and presently he made a landing. Instantly the throng of country people who had gathered to look at the automobile crash deserted that for a view of something more sensational—an airship.

Cautioning the boys who gathered about not to "monkey" with any of the mechanism, Tom hastened over to where Mary was standing near her car.

"Are you sure you aren't hurt?" he asked her anxiously.

"Oh, yes, very sure," she replied, smiling at him. "It isn't much of an accident—only one wheel smashed. We were both going slowly."

"But it was all my fault!" insisted a young fellow who had been driving the car that crashed into Mary's. "I'm all kinds of sorry, and of course I'll pay all damages. I wanted this young lady to let me drive her home and then send a garage man to tow her car, but she said she had other plans. I don't blame her for not wanting to ride in my jitney bus when I see what kind of car you have," and he looked over toward Tom's aeroplane.

"Thank you, just the same," murmured Mary. "I'm not quite sure that it was all your fault. But if you will be so good as to send a man after my machine I'll go back with Mr. Swift. Wait until I get my bag," she added, and she extracted it from the seat in her automobile. "There'll be room for this, won't there?" she asked. "I've been shopping."

"You must have made some large purchases," laughed Tom, looking critically at the small bag. "Yes, there'll be room for that, all right."

He made a brief examination of Mary's machine, ascertaining that the dished wheel was the main damage, and then, having given the young man who caused the accident directions for the garage attendant, Tom led his pretty companion across the field to the waiting airship.

Of course a crowd gathered to see them start off, and this was not long delayed, as Tom was not fond of curiosity seekers. In a few minutes he and Mary were soaring aloft.

"Well, how are you?" he asked Mary, when they were alone well above the earth.

"Fine and dandy," she answered, smiling at him, for they were riding side by side and could converse with little difficulty owing to the silent running of Tom's latest invention. "I'm sorry to have called you away from your work," she added, "but when Mrs. Baggert told me you were at the submarine dock I thought perhaps you could run out and get me in your machine. I didn't expect you to fly to me."

"I'm always ready to do that!" exclaimed Tom, as he shot upward to avoid a bank of low-lying clouds. "Were you frightened at the crash in the machine?"

"Not greatly. I saw it coming, and knew it was unavoidable. That chap hasn't been running autos very long, I imagine, and he lost his head in the emergency. But I had my brakes on and he just coasted into me. I was lucky in that it wasn't worse."

"I should say so! Do you want to get right home?"

"I think I'd better. Mother and father may be a little worried about me. And they've had trouble enough of late."

"Trouble!" exclaimed Tom, in a questioning voice. "Anything serious?"

"No, just family financial matters. Not ours she hastened to add, as she saw Tom look quickly at her. "A relative. I shouldn't have mentioned it, but father and mother are a little worried, and I don't want to add to it."

"Of course not," agreed Tom. "If there's anything I can do?"

"Oh, I expected you to say that!" laughed Mary. "Thanks. If there is we'll call on you. But it may all be straightened out. Father was expecting a message from Uncle Barton today. So, though I'd like to take a cloud-ride with you, I think I'd better get home."

"All right," agreed Tom. "I told Ned to telephone that you were all right, so they won't worry. And now try to enjoy yourself."

"I'll try," promised Mary, but it was obvious, even from the quick glances Tom gave her, that she was worried about something. Mary was not her usual, spontaneous, jolly self, and Tom realized it.

"Well, here we are!" he announced a little later, as they soared above a level field not far from her home. "Sorry I can't let you down right on your roof, but it isn't flat enough nor big enough."

"Oh, I don't mind a little walk, especially as I didn't have to hike it all the way in from Bailey Corners," she said, referring to the place of the automobile accident. "I suppose the time will come when everybody who now has an auto will have an airship and a landing place, or a starting place, for it at his own door," she added.

"Either that, or else we'll have airships so compact that they can set off and land in as small a space as an auto now requires," said Tom. "The latter would be the best solution, as one great disadvantage of airships now is the manner of starting and stopping. It's too big."

Tom left his Air Scout in a field owned by Mr. Nestor, where he had often landed before, and walked up to the house with Mary.

"Oh, I'm glad you're back!" exclaimed Mrs. Nestor, when she saw the two coming up the steps.

"You weren't worried, were you, after Ned telephoned?" asked Tom.

"Not exactly worried, but I thought perhaps he was making light of it. Do tell me what happened, Mary!"

Thereupon the girl related all the circumstances of the smash, and Tom added his share of the story.

"Did father hear anything from Uncle Barton?" asked Mary, after her mother's curiosity had been satisfied.

"Yes," was the answer, in rather despondent tones, "he did, but the news was not encouraging. The papers cannot be found."

"It's mother's brother we're talking about," Mary explained to Tom. "Barton Keith in his name. Perhaps you remember him?"

"I've heard you speak of him," Tom admitted.

"Well," resumed Mary, "Uncle Barton is in a. peck of trouble. He was once very rich, and he invested heavily in oil lands, in Oklahoma, I believe."

"No, in Texas," corrected Mrs. Nestor.

"Yes, it was Texas," agreed Mary. "Well he bought, or got, somehow, shares in some valuable oil lands in Texas, and expected to double his fortune. Now, instead, he's probably lost it all."

"That's too bad!" exclaimed Tom. "How did it happen?"

"In rather an odd way," went on Mary. "He really owns the lands, or at least half of them, but he cannot prove his title because the papers he needs were taken from him, and, he thinks, by a man he trusted. He's been trying to get the documents back, and every day we've been expecting to hear that he has them, but mother says there has been no result."

"No," said Mrs. Nestor. "My brother thought sure he had a trace of the man he believes has the papers, or who had them, but he lost track of him. If we could only find him—"

At that moment a maid came into the room to announce that Tom Swift was wanted at the telephone.

THE TRIAL TRIP

"This is my busy day!" announced the young inventor as he went into the Nestor sitting room, where the telephone was installed.

"Perhaps it is some one else who wants you to come to their rescue," suggested Mary.

But it was not, as Tom related a little later when he had finished his talk over the wire.

"Just a business matter," he announced to Mary and her mother, when he rejoined them. "A gentleman with whom I expect to make a submarine trip is at the house, and wants to consult with me about details. He is getting anxious to start. Mr. Damon is there, too."

"Blessing every thing he lays eyes on, I suppose," remarked Mrs. Nestor, with a smile.

"Yes, and some things he doesn't see," agreed Tom. "He is going with us on this submarine trip."

"Oh, Tom, are you going to undertake another of those dangerous voyages?" asked Mary, in some alarm.

"Well, I don't know that they are particularly dangerous," replied Tom, with a smile. "But we expect to make a search for a sunken treasure ship in a submarine. That's the vessel I'm working on now," he added. "We're rebuilding the Advance, you know, making her more up-to-date, and adding some new features, including her name—M. N. 1."

"I suppose Mr. Damon's friend is getting anxious to make a start, particularly as he has already invested several thousand dollars in the project," went on the young inventor. "He formed a company to pay half the expenses of the search, and they will share in the~ treasure—if we find it," Tom said. "I wish Mr. Damon, who holds most of the shares the promoter let out of his own hands, had not gone into it, but, since he has, I'm going to do the best I can for him."

"Then aren't you friendly with the other man?" asked Mary.

"I don't especially care for him," the young inventor admitted. "He isn't just my style—too fond of himself, and all that. Still I may be misjudging him. However, I'm in the game now, and I'm going to stick. I'll have to be traveling on," he said. "Mr. Damon and his friend are at my house, and they've been telephoning all over to find me. I guess this was one of the first places they tried," he said with a smile, referring to the fact that he spent considerable time at Mary's home.

"Well, I'm glad they found you, but I'm sorry you have to go," Mary said with a smile.

A little later Tom Swift, with Ned, for whom he called, was on his way back home in his Air Scout, having said goodbye to Mary and her mother and expressing the hope that Mr. Keith would soon be over his business troubles.

"Oil wells are queer, anyhow," mused Tom.

Then Tom got to thinking about Dixwell Hardley: "I don't like the man, and the more I see of him the less I like him. But I'm in for it now, and I'll stick to the finish. I only wish I could locate the treasure ship, give him his share, and get back to my work. I'm going to try to turn out an airship that a man can use as handily as he does a flivver now."

Musing on the possibilities in this field, Tom, having left Ned at the latter's home, soared down from aloft, and a little later, having told Koku to look after the Air Scout, much to the delight of the giant and the discomfiture of Rad, the young inventor was closeted with Mr. Damon and Dixwell Hardley.

"Bless my straw hat, Tom!" exclaimed the eccentric man, "but we just couldn't wait any longer. How are you coming on, and when can we start on this treasure-hunting trip? I declare it makes me feel young again to think about it!"

"Well, it won't be long now," was the answer. "The men are working hard to get the submarine in shape, and I should say that in another week, or two weeks at the most, we could set off!"

"Good!" exclaimed Mr. Hardley. "I have received additional information," he went on, "to the effect that the amount of gold on board the Pandora was even greater than we at first thought."

"That sounds encouraging," replied Tom. "It only remains to find the sunken ship now. But what interests me greatly is whether, after we have gotten this gold, supposing we are successful, we shall be allowed to keep it."

"Bless my bank book! why not?" asked Mr. Damon. "Isn't it wealth abandoned at the bottom of the sea, and isn't finding keeping?"

"Not always," answered Tom. "There are certain rules and laws about treasure, and it might happen that after we got this—if we do—it could be taken away from us."

"I think there will be no difficulty on this score," said Mr. Hardley. "In the first place, two attempts were made to get this wealth, and were unsuccessful. Then it was practically abandoned, and I believe under the law the persons who now find it will be entitled to keep it. Besides the persons who gathered it together did so for an unlawful purpose—that of starting a revolution in a friendly country—and they would not dare claim it for fear of giving their secret away."

"Well, perhaps you are right," assented Tom. "We'll make a try for it, anyhow."

"You say the submarine is nearly ready?" asked Mr. Hardley.

"She will be ready for a trial trip at the end of this week," said Tom, "and be fitted up for the voyage within another seven days, I hope. Then for the great adventure!" and he laughed, though, truth to tell, he had no real liking for his task. The more he saw of Mr. Hardley the less he liked him.

"I shall begin getting my affairs in shape," said the latter, as he gathered up some papers he had brought to attempt to prove to Tom that the wealth of the Pandora was greater than had been supposed. "I have many large interests," he went on, rather pompously, "and they need looking after; especially if I undertake anything so extra hazardous as a submarine trip."

"Yes, there always is some danger," admitted Tom. "But then there is danger walking along the street."

"Oh, there's no danger with Tom Swift!" exclaimed Mr. Damon. "I've been under the sea and above the clouds with him, and, bless my rainbow! he always brought us safe home."

"And I'll try to do the same this time," said the young inventor.

Busy days followed for Tom Swift and his friends. The force at work on the submarine turned night into day to rush her completion, and in due season she was set afloat in the dry dock basin and formally rechristened the M. N. 1.

Mary blushed as she gave the boat her new name, and there was a little cheer from the group of workmen gathered at the dock. There was no launching in the real sense of the word, since as the Advance that ceremony had been gone through with for the undersea craft.

She had been greatly changed interiorly and outwardly. Her skin, or plates, having been doubled and strengthened. For Tom proposed to go to a much greater depth than ever before.

In addition to using the submarine herself in a search for the gold on the Pandora, Tom had installed on board some new kinds of diving apparatus and also a diving bell. If one would not serve, the other might, he reasoned.

"Well, Tom," remarked his aged father the night before they were to start on the trial trip, "I understand you have practically rebuilt the Advance."

"Yes; and I think she's a much better craft, too, Father."

"Glad to hear that, Tom. Of course you kept the gyroscope rudder feature?"

"No, I didn't," replied Tom. "If I had left that installed it would have meant carrying a smaller diving bell, and I think that last will be more useful than the gyroscope. I put in a set of double-acting depth rudders instead."

Mr. Swift shook his head.

"I'm sorry for that, Tom," he remarked. "There's nothing like the gyroscope rudder in a tight pinch—say when there's a storm. And for holding the boat steady, if you have to make a sudden turn under water, to avoid an obstruction you come upon unexpectedly, a gyroscope can't be improved on. It holds you steady and prevents your turning turtle."

"I've put side fin-keels to correct that," Tom explained.

But still his father was not satisfied.

"I'd rather you had kept the gyroscope," he said, and the time was to come when Tom Swift wished that himself.

But it was too late to make the change now, and so, with more than usual confidence in his own designing abilities, the next day the young inventor and his friends went aboard the M. N. 1 for the trial trip.

"You don't easily get seasick, do you?" Tom asked Mr. Hardley, as they descended the hatchway into the interior of the craft.

"No, I'm considered a good sailor."

"Well, you'll need to be," went on Tom, with a smile. "Not that we are likely to strike any rough water now, though the reports say a stiff breeze is blowing in the bay. But when we once start for the West Indies you are likely to experience a new sensation. I've known sailors who never had any qualms, even in terrible storms, to get ill in a submarine when she went through only a small blow. The motion is different from that on a surface boat."

"I can imagine so," returned Mr. Hardley. "But I'll be thinking of the millions in gold on the Pandora, and that will keep my mind off being seasick."

"Let us hope so," murmured Tom.

He gave the word, they all descended, the hatch covers were closed down, and the M. N. 1 was ready to start on a trial trip.

THE MUD BANK

"What's that noise?" asked Mr. Hardley.

Mr. Hardley, Tom Swift, Mr. Damon, Ned Newton, Koku, and one or two navigating officers of the craft, were gathered in the operating cabin of the M. N. 1.

"That's water being pumped into the tanks," explained Tom. "We are now going down. If you'll watch the depth gauge you can note our progress."

"Going down, are we?" remarked Mr. Hardley. "Well, it's interesting to say the least," and he observed the gauge, which showed them to be twenty feet under the surface.

"Bless my hydrometer, but he's got nerve for a first trip in a submarine! He's all right, isn't he?" whispered Mr. Damon to Tom.

"Well, I'm glad to see he isn't nervous," remarked Tom, honest enough to give his visitor credit for what was due him. And indeed many a person is nervous going down in a submarine for the first time. "Still we can't go more than thirty feet down in this water," went on Tom. "A better test will be when we get about five hundred feet below the surface. That's a real test, though as far as knowing it is concerned, a person can't tell ten feet from ten hundred in a submarine under water, unless he watches the gauge."

"Well, I think you'll find Mr. Hardley all right," said Mr. Damon, who seemed to have taken a strong liking to his new friend.

Certainly the latter showed no signs of nervousness as the craft slowly settled to the proper depth. He asked numberless questions, showing his interest in the operation of the M. N. 1, but he showed not the least sign of fear. However, as Tom said, that might come later.

"We are going down now," Tom explained, as he pointed out to Mr. Hardley the various controlling wheels and levers, "by filling our ballast tanks with water. We can rise, when needful, by forcing out this water by means of compressed air. When we are on the ocean we can go down by using our diving rudders, and in much quicker time than by filling our tanks."

"How is that?" asked the seeker after the Pandora's gold.

"Filling the tanks is slow work in itself," replied Tom, "and they have to be filled very carefully and evenly, so we don't stand on our stern or bow in going down. We want to sink on an even keel, and sometimes this is hard to accomplish. But we are doing it now," and he called attention to an indicator which told how much the M. N. 1 might be listing to one side or to one end or the other.

"A submarine, as everyone knows, is essentially a water-tight tank, shaped like a cigar, with a propeller on one end. It can sink below the surface and move along under water. It sinks because rudders force it down, and water taken into tanks in its interior hold it to a certain depth. It can rise by ejecting this extra water and by setting the rudders in the proper position.

A submarine moves under water by means of electric motors, the current of which is supplied by storage batteries. On the surface when the hatches can be opened, oil or gasolene engines are used. These engines cannot be used under water because they depend on a supply of air, or oxygen, and when the submarine is tightly sealed all the air possible is needed for her crew to breathe. While cruising on the surface a submarine recharges her storage batteries to give her motive power when she is submerged.

There are many types of submarines, some comparatively simple and small, and others large and complex. In some it is possible for the crew to live many days without coming to the surface.

Tom Swift's reconstructed craft compared favorably with the best and largest ever made, though she was not of exceptional size. She was very strong, however, to allow her to go to a great depth, for the farther down one goes below the surface of the sea, the greater the pressure until, at, say, six miles, the greatest known depth of the ocean, the pressure is beyond belief. And yet is possible that marine monsters may live in that pressure which would flatten out a block of solid steel into a sheet as thin as paper.

"Well, we are as deep down as it is safe to go in the river," announced Tom, as the gauge showed a distance below the surface of a little less than twenty-nine feet. "Now we'll move into the bay. How do you like it, Mr. Hardley?"

"Very well, so far. But it isn't very exciting yet."

"Bless my accident policy!" exclaimed Mr. Damon, "I hope you aren't looking for excitement."

"I'm used to it," was the answer. "The more there is the better I like it."

"Well, you may get your wish," said Tom.

He turned a lever, and those on board the submarine became conscious of a forward motion. She was no longer sinking.

She trembled and vibrated as the powerful electric motors turned her propellers, and Tom, having seen that all was running smoothly in the main engine room, called Mr. Damon, Ned, and Mr. Hardley to him.

"We'll go into the forward pilot house and give Mr. Hardley a view under water," he announced. "Of course, you'll see nothing like what you'll view when we're in the ocean," added the young inventor, "but it may interest you."

The four were soon in the forward compartment of the craft. She could be directed and steered from here when occasion arose, but now Tom was letting his navigator direct the craft from the controls in the main engine room. A conning tower, rising just above the deck of the craft, gave the pilot the necessary view.

"Here you are!" exclaimed Tom, as he switched out the lights in the cabin. For a moment they were in darkness, and then, with a click, steel plates, guarding heavy plate glass bull's-eyes, moved back, and Mr. Hardley for the first time looked out on an underwater scene. He saw the murky waters of river down which they were proceeding to the bay moving past the glass windows. Now and then a fish swam up, looking in, and, with a swirl of its tail, shot away again, apparently frightened well-nigh to death.

"Bless my shoe laces, Tom!" exclaimed Mr. Damon, "this isn't a marker compared to some of the sights we've seen, is it?"

"I can imagine not," said Mr. Hardley. "But it is interesting. I shall be anticipating more wonderful sights."

"And you'll get them!" exclaimed Ned. "Do you remember, Tom, the time the big octopus tried to hold us back?"

"Yes, indeed," answered the young inventor. "That gave us a scare for the time being."

Steadily the M. N. 1 kept on her way under water. Her path was illuminated to a considerable degree by a broad, diffused beam of light from a powerful searchlight that was fixed just back of the conning tower, giving the helmsman a certain degree of vision. This light also served to illuminate the water, so that those in the forward cabin could see what was going on around them.

"There isn't much of interest in the river," said Tom. "No big fish, or anything else of moment. Even in the bay we won't see much to attract our attention. But I want to make sure everything is working smoothly before we start for the West Indies."

"That's right!" agreed Mr. Hardley. "We want to make a success of this trip."

He remained at the glass bull's-eyes, now and then exclaiming as some shad or other fair-sized fish came into view. Suddenly, however, his exclamation was sharper than usual.

"Look!" he exclaimed. "There's part of a wreck!"

Ned, Mr. Damon, and Tom looked out and saw, sweeping past them, the ribs and worm-eaten timbers of some craft, lying on the bottom of the river.

"Yes, that's the remains of an old brick scow," the young inventor explained. "That's one of our water-marks, so to speak. It is at the bend of the river. We turn now, and head for the bay."

As he spoke they all became aware of a sudden swerve in the course of the submarine. The helmsman had, doubtless, noted the "water-mark," as Tom termed it, and as an automobilist on land might swing at the cross-roads, the steersman was changing the course of his craft.

"We'll go deeper," said Tom a moment later, as the wreck passed out of view. "We can go about fifty feet down now. Yes, he's sinking her," he added, as a gauge showed the craft to be descending. "Nelson knows his business all right."

"He is your captain?" asked Mr. Hardley.

"One of the best, yes. He'll go with us on the search for the Pandora."

They talked of various matters, Tom relating to Mr. Hardley how a tug had rammed the brick scow some years ago, and sunk it in the river.

The submarine was now about forty-eight feet below the surface, and suddenly they all became aware that her speed had increased.

"Guess he's going to give the motors a good try-out," observed Tom. "I think I'll go back to the engine room. You may remain here, if you like, and you'll probably see—"

A cry from Mr. Damon interrupted him.

"Bless my rubber boots, Tom! Look!" cried the eccentric man. "We're going to ram a mud bank!"

As he spoke they all became aware of a solid black mass looming in front of the bull's-eye window. An instant later the submarine came to a jarring stop, as if she had struck some soft, yielding substance. There was a confused shouting throughout the craft, the noise of machinery, a trembling and vibration, and then ominous quiet.

Ready to Start

Characteristic it was of Tom Swift to act calmly in times of stress and danger, and he ran true to form now. Only for an instant did he show any sign of perturbation. Then with calmness and deliberation the young inventor quickly did a number of things to the controls within his reach.

First of all he signaled to the engine room that he was going to take charge of the boat. This meant that the navigator in the conning tower was to keep his hands off the various levers and wheel-valves. It was possible to operate the M. N. 1 from three positions, but Tom wanted no triplicate handling of his craft now.

Almost the instant Tom signaled that he would take charge back came flashing the electrical signal from the conning tower that his orders were understood. The next thing that those aboard the craft became aware of was a tremor that seemed to run through the whole under-sea ship. The quiet had changed to a subdued humming, and the ominous lack of motion was succeeded by violent vibration.

"Backing her up, Tom?" asked Ned, in a low voice.

"Trying to," was the answer. "But I'm afraid her nose has gone in pretty deep. I've reversed the propellers."

For perhaps a minute this vibration continued, showing that the powerful electric motors were turning over the twin propellers at the blunt stern of the craft. But she did not change her position.

With a touch of his hand, and still almost as cool as the proverbial cucumber (though why they should be cool it is hard to say), Tom stopped the motors. Once again the craft was quiet, but now, instead of the occupants being able to see clearly from the thick, glass windows in the forward cabin, the water showed muddy and murky in the glare of the underwater searchlight.

"Bless my postage stamps, Tom! what has happened?" exclaimed Mr. Damon. "Has a giant squid attacked us, as one did some time ago, and is he roiling up the water?"

"No, it isn't a squid, Mr. Damon," replied the young inventor easily; "though the water does look as if a squid had spilled a lot of his ink in it. This is just the effect of mud stirred up by our propellers. There may be more of it."

Ned looked toward Mr. Hardley to see how he was taking it. The seeker after gold apparently had good control of his nerves, or else he was ignorant of what was going on. For he asked, casually enough:

"Have we stopped?"

"We have," answered Tom. "I thought I'd give you a view of the scenery."

Perhaps he spoke sarcastically, but, if he did, Mr. Damon's friend did not seem to be aware of it. Coolly enough he replied:

"Well, if this is a fair sample of underwater scenery I prefer something up above, though I appreciate that this may be needful."

"We'll soon be traveling along," announced Tom. "Koku," he added to the giant, who had been calmly sitting during the excitement, "go to the engine room and help with the big levers."

"Yes, Master," was the answer. Koku had implicit faith in Tom.

Waiting a moment for his faithful servant to reach the post assigned to him, Tom again signaled to his helpers and then quickly turned a wheel which produced startling results. For all within the submarine suddenly slid forward across the cabin floor.

"Bless my hammock hooks, Tom! are you standing her on her head?" cried Mr. Damon.

"That's exactly what I'm doing," was the answer. "I've started to empty one of the after ballast tanks, and that, naturally, raises the stern while the nose is held down."

The submarine was indeed in a peculiar position. She was on a slant in the water, her nose held fast in the soft mud bank, and it was Tom's idea that by making the stern buoyant it might help to pull her free.

To this end he also gave what assistance the propellers were capable of adding by starting the motors again, so that the craft once more trembled and vibrated.

But it all seemed to no purpose. Aside from the slanting position, there was no change in the M. N. 1. Ned, looking out into the murky water, which had cleared slightly, saw that the craft was still held fast. And then, for the first time, Mr. Hardley seemed to become aware that something serious was the matter. Up to now he seemed to think that all that had occurred was done for the purpose of testing the newly outfitted underseas boat.

"Is there anything wrong?" he asked sharply of Tom. "Why are we in this position, and why don't we go on out to the open ocean and make a test at considerable depth? We'll have to go down deeper than this if we find the Pandora!"

"I suppose so," agreed Tom. "But we have had an accident, and—"

"An accident!" interrupted the gold-seeker, and then Ned saw him turn pale. "Do you mean to say this is not part of the test?"

"We have run into a mud bank," said Tom. "The steersman must have become confused, or else, since we last used the submarine, there has been a shift of the mud banks in this river and one exists where there was none before. At any rate, we ran our nose deep into it, and here we are—stuck!"

"Can't we get loose—go up to the surface?" demanded Mr. Hardley.

"I'm trying to bring that about," announced Tom calmly. "So far her engines haven't been able to pull her loose."

"But Great Scott, man, we can't stay here!" cried the now excited adventurer. "We'll be drowned like rats in a trap! Let me out! Isn't there some way? I'll be shot through a torpedo tube, if necessary! I must get out! I can't stay here to be drowned! I have too much at stake!"

"Now wait a minute!" calmly advised Tom Swift. "You haven't any more at stake than the rest of us. None of us wants to be drowned, and there is only a remote possibility that we shall be. I haven't played all my cards yet. We can live on this boat for a week, if need be."

"You mean under water as we are now?" asked Mr. Hardley.

"Yes. I always keep the boat provisioned and with plenty of air and water for a long stay, if need be," replied Tom. "And I did not overlook the fact that we might have an accident on the trial trip."

"I don't see how you let an accident happen before we even got started," complained the gold-seeker. "I should think your steersman would have been more careful."

"He is very careful," explained Tom. "But we have not used the craft for some time, and, meanwhile, there have been changes in the river, due, I suppose, to heavy tides. But we may get out of the grip of the mud bank soon."

"And if we don't, what then?" asked Mr. Hardley.

"Then there is always the torpedo tube," said Tom calmly. "And we are not very deep down. I think I can save you all."

"I certainly hope so!" was the fretful comment of the adventurer. "I have too much at stake to be drowned like a rat in a trap! You must send me up first if it becomes necessary to use the tube."

Tom did not answer. But as he looked out of the observation windows to see if possible the conformation of the mud bank, the young inventor whispered to Ned one word. And that word was:

"Yellow!"

"You said it!" was Ned's whispered rejoinder.

Tom Swift arrived at a sudden determination. Once again the motors were stopped, and the boat gradually assumed an even keel.

"What are you going to try, Tom?" asked Ned.

"I'm going to shove her farther into the mud bank," announced the young inventor. "I think that's the only way to get her loose."

"Bless my apple pie, Tom!" cried Mr. Damon, "doesn't that seem a foolish thing to do?"

"It's the only thing to do, I believe," was the answer. "This mud is of a peculiar sticky and holding kind. The sub's nose is in it like a peg in a hole. What I propose to do now is to enlarge the hole, and then our nose will come loose—I hope."

"But you haven't any right to shove our nose further in!" cried Mr. Hardley. "I won't allow it! I demand to be put on the surface! I won't be drowned down here before I get the gold that's coming to me—the gold and—"

"Now look here!" suddenly cried Tom. "I'm in command of this boat, and you'll do as I say. I'll gladly set you on the surface if I can, and this is the only way it can be brought about—it's the only way to save all of us. I'm going to enlarge the mud hole so we can pull out. Please keep still!"

Mr. Hardley stared at the young inventor a moment, seemed about to say something, and then changed his mind.

"Hold fast, everybody!" suddenly called Tom. The next moment the M. N. 1 began behaving in a most peculiar manner.

She appeared to be acting like a corkscrew. While her bow was comparatively steady, her stern described a circle in the water which was churned to mud by the two propellers, each being revolved in a different direction.

"I'm trying to make the hole bigger just as an amateur carpenter makes a nail hole bigger, so he can pull out the nail, by twisting it around," explained Tom. "The motion may be a bit unpleasant, but it is needful."

And indeed the motion was unpleasant. Tom, veteran airman and sailor that he was, began to feel a trifle seasick, and Hr. Hardley was in very evident distress.

Suddenly, however, something happened. The M. N. 1 gave a lurch to one side and then shot upward so quickly that Ned and Mr. Damon lost their balance and slumped over on the bench that ran around three sides of the room.

"Are we free?" cried Mr. Hardley.

"We have come loose from the mud bank," said Tom quietly. "By boring into it the hole was enlarged sufficiently to enable us to pull loose. There is no more danger!"

His announcement was received in momentary silence, and then Ned exclaimed:

"Hurray!"

"Bless my accident policy!" voiced Mr. Damon.

Mr. Hardley appeared dazed, and then, as the submarine was again moving through the water, seemingly none the worse for the accident, the gold seeker approached Tom Swift.

"I want to apologize, Mr. Swift, for my actions and words," said Mr. Hardley frankly. "I admit that I lost my head. But it's my first trip in a submarine."

"I realize that," said Tom, equally frank, "and we'll forget all about it. It was a strain on you—on all of us—though there really was no very great danger. Now, are you game enough to continue the trip?"

"Try me!" exclaimed the adventurer. "You won't find me acting so like a baby again."

Nor did he, even when the craft reached the open ocean and went down to a considerable depth, where, had any accident occurred, there would have been grave danger to all. But Mr. Hardley seemed to enjoy it.

"Maybe I've misjudged him," Tom said to Ned, when they were getting ready to go back.

"It's possible," agreed the financial manager. This trial, which so nearly ended disastrously, was only one of several. No damage resulted from the collision with the river mud bank, and that trip and the ones following gave Tom some new ideas in interior construction which he followed out.

About a month later all was ready for the trip to the West Indies to look for the ill-fated Pandora. Tom's affairs were put in shape, the submarine was laden with stores and provisions, the new diving bell and other wonderful apparatus were put aboard, and the crew and officers picked. Ned, Mr. Damon, Koku, and Tom were, of course, together, and though Mr. Hardley was a stranger, he seemed to become more friendly as the days passed.

"Well, we start in the morning," said Tom to Ned one evening. "I'm going over to tell Mary goodbye."

"Give her my regards," requested Ned, and Tom said he would.

STARTLING REVELATIONS

"Oh, Tom! And so you are really ready to start on that perilous trip!" exclaimed Mary Nestor, a little later that same evening, when Tom called at Mary's house in his speedy electric runabout, a car in which he had once made a sensational ride.

"Perilous? I don't know why you call it that!" exclaimed the young inventor.

"Didn't you tell me you were stuck in a mud bank away down under the river and had hard work to get loose?" asked the young lady, as she made a place for Tom on the sofa beside her.

"Oh, that! Why, that wasn't anything!" he declared.

"It would have been if you hadn't come up."

"Ah, but we did come up, Mary."

"Suppose you get in a similar position when you find the wreck of the Pandora? You won't get up so easily, will you?"

"No. But there aren't any mud banks in that part of the Atlantic, so I can't be stuck in one," answered Tom.

For some time Tom Swift and Mary talked of mutual friends and happenings in which they were both interested. Mr. and Mrs. Nestor stepped into the room for a minute, to wish the young inventor good luck on his voyage, and when they had gone out, promising to see Tom before he left for the night, the latter remarked to Mary:

"Did your uncle ever find the oil-well papers and get his affairs straightened out?"

"No," was the answer, "he never did. And we feel very sorry for him. Just think, he had a fortune in his grasp, and now it is slipping away."

"Just what happened?" asked Tom, hoping there might be some way in which he could aid Mary's uncle. Of course, Tom wanted to help Mary, and this was one of the ways.

"Well, I don't exactly understand it all," she replied. "Father says I'll never have a head for business. But as nearly as I can tell, my uncle, Barton Keith, went into partnership with a man to prospect for oil in Texas. My uncle has been in that business before, and he was very successful. He supplied the working knowledge about oil wells, I believe, and the other man put up the money. My uncle was to have a half share in whatever oil wells he located, and his partner supplied the cash for putting down the pipe, or whatever is done."

"I believe putting down a pipe is the proper term," said Tom.

"Well, anyhow," went on Mary, "my uncle spent many weary months prospecting in Texas. In fact, he made himself ill, being out in all sorts of weather, looking after the drilling. At last they struck oil, as I believe they call it. They drilled down until they brought in what my uncle called a 'gusher,' and there was a chance of him and his partner getting rich."

"Why didn't he?" asked Tom. "A gusher, I believe, is one of the best sort of oil wells. Why didn't your uncle clean up a fortune, to use a slang term?"

"Because he lost the papers showing that he had a right to half the oil well," answered Mary. "At least my uncle thinks he lost them, but he was so ill, directly after the well proved a success, that he says he isn't sure what happened. At any rate, his partner claims everything and my uncle can do nothing. He has been hoping he might find the papers somewhere, or that something would happen to prove the rights of his claim."

"And nothing has?" inquired Tom.

"Not yet. My father and mother have been trying to help him, and dad engaged a lawyer, but he says nothing can be done unless my uncle recovers the partnership and other papers. As it stands now, it is my uncle's word against the word of his partner, and both are equally good in a court of law. But if Uncle Barton could find the documents everything would come out all right. He could claim his half of the oil well then."

"Is it still producing?" Tom questioned.

"Yes, better than ever. But that's all the good it does my uncle. He is ill, discouraged, and despondent. All his fortune was eaten up in prospecting, and he depended on the gusher to make him rich again. And now, because of a rascally partner, he may be doomed to die a poor man. Of course we will always help him, but you know what it is to be dependent on relatives."

"I can imagine," conceded Tom. "It is tough luck! I wish I could help, and perhaps I can after I get back from this trip."

"The only way you or any one could help, would be to get back my uncle's missing papers," said Mary. "And as he himself isn't sure what became of them, it seem hopeless."

"It does," Tom agreed. "But wait until I get back."

"I wish you weren't going," sighed Mary.

"So do I—more than a little," was Tom's remark. "I'm sorry I ever let Mr. Damon persuade me to go into this deal with Dixwell Hardley!"

Mary sat bolt upright on the couch.

"What name did you say?" she cried.

"Dixwell Hardley," repeated Tom. "That's he name of the man who claims to know where the wreck of the Pandora lies. He says she has two millions or more in gold on board, and I'm to get half."

"Well!" exclaimed Mary, with spirit, "if you don't get any bigger share out of the wreck than my uncle got out of the oil well, you won't be doing so very nicely, Tom."

"What do you mean?" asked the young inventor. "What has the oil well to do with recovering gold from the wreck?"

"A good deal, I should say," answered the girl, "seeing that the same man is mixed up in both."

"What same man?"

"Dixwell Hardley!"

"Is he the man who cheated your uncle?" cried Tom.

"I won't say that he cheated him," said Mary. "But Dixwell Hardley is the man who furnished the money when my uncle went into partnership with him to locate oil wells in Texas. The oil wells were located, Mr. Hardley got his share, and my uncle got nothing. And just because he can't prove there was a legal partnership! I hope you won't have the same experience with Mr. Hardley, Tom."

"Whew!" whistled the young inventor. "This is news to me! I can say one thing, though. Mr. Hardley doesn't take a dollar out of that wreck unless I get one to match it. I think I hold the best cards on this deal. But, Mary, are you sure it's the same man?"

"Pretty sure. Wait, I'll call my father and make certain," she answered, and as she went from the room to summon Mr. Nestor, Tom felt a vague sense of uneasiness.

BARTON KEITH'S STORY

"What's this Mary tells me, Tom?" asked Mr. Nestor, as he followed his daughter back into the room.

"You mean about Dixwell Hardley?"

"Yes. Do you suppose he can be the same man who has so meanly treated my brother-in-law?"

"I wouldn't want to say, Mr. Nestor, until you describe to me the Mr. Hardley you know. Then I can better tell. But from what little I have seen of the man to whom I was introduced by my friend Mr. Damon, I'd say, off hand, that he was capable of such action."

"Does Mr. Damon know this Mr. Hardley well?" asked Mrs. Nestor, who accompanied her husband.

"I wouldn't say that he did," Tom replied. "I don't know just how Mr. Damon met this chap—I think it was in a financial way, though."

"Well, if it's the same Mr. Hardley, I'll say he has some queer financial ways," said Mr. Nestor. "Now let's see if we can make the two jibe. Describe him, Tom."

This the young inventor did, and when this description had been compared with one given of the Mr. Hardley with whom Mr. Keith once was associated, Mrs. Nestor said:

"It surely is the same man! The Mr. Hardley who wants you to get wealth from the bottom of the ocean, Tom, is the same fellow who is keeping my brother out of the oil well property! I'm sure of it!"

"It does seem so," Tom agreed. "Dixwell Hardley is not a usual name; but we must be careful In spite of its unusualness there may be two very different men who have that name. I think the only way to find out for certain is to see Mr. Keith. He'd know a picture of the Dixwell Hardley who, he claims, cheated him, wouldn't he?"

"Indeed he would!" exclaimed Mrs. Nestor. "But where could we get a picture of your Mr. Hardley? I call him that, though I don't suppose you own him, Tom," and she smiled at her future son-in-law.

"No, I don't own him, and I don't want to," was Tom's answer. "But I happen to have a picture of him. I made him furnish me with proofs that he was on the Pandora at the time she foundered in a gale, and among the documents he gave was his passport. It has his picture on. I have it here."

Tom drew the paper from his pocket. In one corner was pasted a photograph of the man who had been introduced to Tom by Mr. Damon.

"It looks like the same man my brother described," said Mrs. Nestor, "but of course I couldn't be sure."

"There is only one way to be," Tom stated, "and that is to show this picture to Mr. Keith. Where is he?"

"Ill at his home in Bedford," answered Mrs. Nestor.

"Then we'll go there and see him!" declared Tom.

"But it's a hundred miles from here!" exclaimed Mary. "And you are leaving on your submarine trip the first thing in the morning, Tom!"

"No, I'm not leaving until I settle this matter," declared the young inventor. "I'm not going on an undersea voyage with a man who may be a cheater. I want this matter settled. I'll postpone this trip until I find out. A day's delay won't matter."

"But it will take longer than that," said Mr. Nestor. "Bedford is a small place, and there's only one train a day there. You'll lose at least three days Tom, if you go there."

"Not necessarily," was the quick answer. "I can go by airship, and make the trip in a little over an hour. I can be back the same day, perhaps not in time to start our submarine trip, as Mr. Keith may be too ill to see me. But I won't lose much time in my Air Scout.

"Mary, will you go with me to see your uncle? We'll start the first thing in the morning and I'll show him this picture. Will you go?"

"I will!" exclaimed the girl.

"Good!" cried Tom. "Then I'll make preparations. I don't want to form any rash judgment, so we'll make certain; but it wouldn't surprise me a bit to have it turn out that the Dixwell Hardley who wants me to help him recover the Pandora treasure is the same one who is trying to cheat Mr. Keith."

Early the next morning, when Tom arose in his own home, he met Mr. Damon and Mr. Hardley, both of whom were guests at the Swift house, pending the beginning of the undersea trip.

"Well, Tom," began the eccentric man, "we have good weather for the start. Bless my rubber boots! Not that it much matters, though, what sort of weather we have when we're in the submarine. But I always like to start in the sunshine."

"So do I," agreed Mr. Hardley. "I suppose we'll get off early this morning," he added.

"We'll go to the dock in the auto, as usual, shall we not?" he asked.

"We aren't going to start this morning," said Tom, as he sat down to breakfast.

"Not going to start this morning!" exclaimed Mr. Hardley. "Why —why—"

"Bless my alarm clock!" voiced Mr. Damon, "has anything happened, Tom? No accident to the M. N. 1 is there? You aren't backing out now, at the last minute, are you?"

"Oh, no," was the easy answer. "We'll go, as arranged, but not today. I had some unexpected news last night which necessitates making a trip this morning. I expect to be back tonight, if all goes well, and we'll start tomorrow morning instead of this. It's a matter of important business."

"Well, I don't know that we can find fault with Mr. Swift for attending to business," said Mr. Hardley, with a short laugh. "Business is what keeps the world moving. And we are a little ahead of our schedule, as a matter of fact. May I ask where you are going, Mr. Swift?"

"To Bedford, to call on a Mr. Barton Keith," answered Tom quickly, looking the adventurer straight in the eyes.

Mr. Hardley was a good actor, or else he was a perfectly innocent man, for he showed not the least sign of perturbation.

"Oh, Bedford," he remarked. "Don't know that I ever heard of the place."

"Or Mr. Keith, either?" asked Tom, a bit sharply.

"No, certainly not. Why should I?" he asked, boldly.

"I didn't know," Tom replied. "I'm sorry to postpone our trip, but it's necessary," he added. "I'll be back as soon as I can. Everything is in readiness, so there will be no delay."

Tom made a hurried meal, and then, giving Ned a hint of what was in the wind, but cautioning him to say nothing about it, Tom had the small Air Scout brought out, and in that he flew over to Mary's home.

He found her waiting for him, and, after being duly cautioned by her mother to "be careful," though whether that was of any value or not is possibly debatable, the small, speedy craft again took the air.

"You haven't heard anything from your uncle since last night, have you?" asked Tom, as they flew along.

"Yes," answered Mary, "mother had a letter. He is worse, if anything, and the doctor says the only thing that will save him is the knowledge that the oil-well matter has turned out right and that my uncle will get his share of the wealth."

"That's too bad!" sympathized Tom. "I hope we can make it turn out that way. If the two Dixwell Hardley chaps are the same it may be that I can do something for your uncle. If not—we'll have to wait and see."

It was not difficult for Tom and Mary to talk while in the aeroplane, as it was almost noiseless. In due time, Bedford was reached without mishap, and Tom and Mary were soon at the home of her uncle.

An explanation to the housekeeper and an inspection on the part of the nurse, brought forth permission for Tom to see the patient. Though he had never known Mr. Keith he could see that the man's health was indeed fast waning.

Wasting little time in preliminaries, the object of the visit was told and Tom showed the passport photograph of Dixwell Hardley.

"Is that the man who cheated you on the oil-well deal?" asked the young inventor.

"I won't admit he has yet cheated me, but he is trying to!" exclaimed Mr. Keith, with something of a return of his former spirit. "If I ever get off my back I'm going to fight him tooth and nail. But that's the same scoundrel! He got me to locate the wells, and when they panned out big—bigger than either of us dreamed—he turned me out cold. He denied he had ever offered to share with me, and said I was only working for monthly wages! Why, sometimes I didn't get even that!"

"How did he get the best of you?" asked Tom.

"By making away with or hiding the papers by which I could prove our partnership and my right to half a share in all the wells," answered Mary's uncle. "Yes, that's the same man all right. I'd know his face anywhere, and he ha& the same name."

"He isn't going under a false name, that's sure," agreed Tom. "He must be a bold chap."

"He is—bold and unscrupulous! That's what makes him so successful in his own way!" declared Mr. Keith. "And so you are working with him! Well, I'm sorry for you."

"I'm not exactly working with him," replied Tom. "As a matter of fact, I'm sorry I ever agreed to look for this wreck."

He told the details of the pending treasure-trove expedition, and mentioned it as his belief that Mr. Damon had been mistaken in his estimate of Mr. Hardley.

"But, so far, Mr. Damon is quite taken with him," Tom went on. "Now, Mr. Keith, if it isn't too much for you, I should like to hear all the particulars."

Thereupon Mary's uncle told his story. It was a long one. After many hardships in life, which Mr. Keith related in some detail to Tom. the oil-well prospector at last fell in with Dixwell Hardley. Then followed the combination of interests.

"We are actually partners," declared Mr. Keith. "I agreed to do the work, and he agreed to furnish the money. I must say this for him, that he kept to that end of the bargain. He supplied the money to locate and drill the wells, but I got very little of it personally. And I fulfilled my end of it. I discovered the wells. Then, when the break came, and I wanted to be rid of the man—for I caught him in some crooked transactions—he surprised me by telling me to get out. I asked for my share of the oil-well stock, and was told I was not entitled to any.

"I put up a fight, naturally, and took the matter to court. But when it came to trial Dixwell Hardley did not appear, and, though I won a technical victory over him, I never got any money."

"Where was he during the trial?" asked Tom.

"At sea, I believe."

"At sea?"

"Yes, he was mixed up in some South American revolution, I heard."

"A South American revolution!" exclaimed Tom, and a great light came to him.

"Yes," went on Mary's uncle. "He was always that kind—mixing up in anything he thought would produce money. He didn't make out very well in the revolution business, so I understood. The revolutionary party was beaten, or they lost their shipment of arms, or something like that. At any rate, Dixwell Hardley had a narrow escape with his life when a ship went down, and from then on I've been trying to get him to restore my rights to me."

"Did he have the papers that would prove you were entitled to a half share in the oil wells?" asked Tom.

"He certainly did!" said the sick man, who was obviously being weakened by this long and exhausting talk. "At first I was not sure of what happened, but now I am positive he stole the papers and took them to sea with him. What happened to them after that I don't know. But if I had Dixwell Hardley here—now—I—I'd—"

Mr. Keith fell back in a faint on the bed, and, in great alarm, Tom summoned the nurse.

In Deep Waters

Mary Nestor, as well as Tom Swift, felt great alarm over the condition of Mr. Keith. But the nurse, after reviving him, said:

"He is in no special immediate danger. Talking about his trouble overstrained him, but in the end it may do him good."

"Then will he get well?" asked Mary.

"He may," was the noncommittal answer. "His recovery would be hastened, however, if his mind could be relieved. He keeps worrying about the loss of his papers that proved his share in the Texas oil wells. Until they can be given back to him he is bound to suffer mentally, and of course that effects him physically."

"Oh, if we only could do something!" murmured Mary.

"Perhaps we can," said Tom in a low voice. "I've learned something these last few hours. I don't want to promise too much, but I think I begin to see how matters lie. There, he's rousing. Speak to him, Mary."

Mr. Keith opened his eyes, and smiled at his niece.

"Did I dream it," he asked in a low voice, "or was there some young man with you, Mary, my dear, to whom I was telling my troubles about the oil-well papers?"

"You didn't dream it, Uncle," Mary answered. "You were talking to Tom Swift. Here he is," and Tom came forward.

"Oh, yes, I remember now," said Mr. Keith passing his hand wearily over his eyes. "I thought, for a moment, that he had recovered my papers for me. But that was a dream, I'm sure."

"It may not be, Mr. Keith!" exclaimed Tom.

"May not be? What do you mean?"

"I mean," replied the young inventor, "that I am much interested in what you have told me. Now that I have proved that the Dixwell Hardley who is to sail with me is the same one who has treated you so shabbily, I think I understand the truth. I don't want to make a promise that I may not be able to carry out, but I am going to watch this man while he's on the submarine with me."

"Then you are going on with the voyage, Tom?" asked Mary.

"I shall have to," he said. "I have entered into an agreement with this man and I'm not going to break my contract, no matter what he does. But I think I know what his game is. Mr. Keith, I'm going to ask you to keep quiet about this matter until I come back from the treasure search. I may then have some news for you."

"I hope you do, young man, I hope you do!" exclaimed the oil contractor, with more energy than he had previously shown. "It means a lot, at my age, to lose a small fortune. If I were well and strong I'd tackle this

Dixwell Hardley myself, and make him give up the papers I'm sure he has hidden away. He has them, I'm positive."

"Well, he may not have them, but perhaps he knows where they are," said Tom. "And I'm going to make it my business to watch him and see if I can find out his secret. I won't let him know I've heard from you. I'll apply the old saying of giving him plenty of rope, and I'll watch what happens.

"Now, Mr. Keith, take care of yourself. Mary and I must be getting back. Try not to worry, and I'll do my best for you," Tom concluded.

Mary added a few words of comfort and encouragement to her uncle, and then she and Tom took leave of him, flying back to Shopton in the speedy Air Scout.

"What are you going to do, Tom?" asked Mary, as he left her at her home, having told Mr. and Mrs. Nestor his part in the visit to Barton Keith.

"I'm going to start on the submarine voyage tomorrow," was the answer of the young inventor.

"Do you really believe there is a treasure ship?"

"Well, I've satisfied myself that a ship named the Pandora sunk about where Hardley says it did, and she had some treasure on board. Whether it's just the kind he has told me it was I don't know. But I'm going to find out."

"Then you'll be saying goodbye for a long time," observed Mary, rather wistfully.

"Oh, it may not be for so very long," and Tom tried to speak cheerfully. "I'll bring you back some souvenirs from the bottom of the sea," he added with a laugh.

"Bring me back—yourself!" said Mary in a low voice, and then she hurried away.

By appointment Tom met Mr. Damon and Mr. Hardley at the submarine dock the next morning. Everything had been made ready for the start, postponed from the day before. Mr. Hardley's estimated share of the expenses had been deposited in a bank, to be paid over later.

"Well, are we really going this time, or are you going to delay again?" asked the gold seeker, and his voice lacked a pleasant tone.

"Oh, were going this time!" exclaimed Tom. "And I hope everything turns out the way I want it to," he added meaningly.

"We'll find the treasure on the ship all right, if we can find the ship," said Mr. Hardley. "That part is your job, Mr. Swift."

"And I'll find her if she's where you say she went down," answered Tom. "Now then, as soon as Ned comes we'll start."

Ned Newton had been intrusted with some last-moment messages, but he arrived a little later, and hurried on board the M. N. 1 which lay at her dock, just afloat.

"All aboard!" called Tom, when he saw his financial manager coming down the pier. "We're ready to start now."

"Bless my fountain pen!" exclaimed Mr. Damon, "but we ought to do something, Tom—sing a song, make a speech or something, oughtn't we

"We'll sing a song of victory when we come back," replied Tom, with a laugh. "Everything all right at home, Ned?" he asked, for his chum had just come on from Shopton.

"Yes; your father sent his regards, but he told me to make a last appeal to you to install a gyro-scope rudder."

"It's too late for that now," said Tom. "He attaches, I think, too much importance to that device. I shan't need it with the improvements I have made to the craft. Get aboard!"

Ned climbed down the hatchway, which, however, was not closed, as it was decided to navigate the craft on the surface until it was necessary to submerge her because of too rough water, or when the vicinity of the wreck was reached.

"Though we will go down to the bottom when we get to the Atlantic for the purpose of testing her in deep water," decided Tom. "Most of the time we'll steam on the surface, for we'll save our batteries that way, and it's more comfortable breathing natural air."

So, with part of her deck above the surface, the M. N. 1 began her voyage, sent on her way by the cheers of the small force of Tom's workmen at the submarine plant. The general public was not admitted, for the object of the quest was kept secret from all save those immediately interested.

"Rad, him be plenty mad he not come," said Koku to Tom, as the giant moved about the cabin, putting things to rights.

"Well, don't start crowing over him until we get back," warned the young inventor. "He may have the laugh on us."

"Rad no laugh," declared Koku. "Rad him too mad dat I come on trip."

"A submarine voyage is no place for old, faithful Eradicate," murmured Tom. "He's better off looking after my father."

The first part of the trip was without incident of moment. No mishap attended the voyage of the M. N. 1 down the river, out into the bay, and so on to the great Atlantic.

Fairly good time was made, as there was no particular object in speeding, and on the second day after leaving the dock Tom gave orders for the hatch to be closed, the deck cleared, and everything made tight and fast.

"What's up?" asked Ned, hearing the instructions passed around.

"We're approaching deep water," was the answer. "I'm going to submerge."

A little later, by means of her diving rudders, aided also by the tanks, the M. N. 1 began to sink. Down, down, down she went.

"Now I'll be able to show you some pretty sights, Mr. Hardley," said Tom, as he and his friends entered the forward compartment, while the steel shutters were rolled back from the heavy glass windows. "We'll be in deep waters presently."

Ten minutes later the depth gauge showed that they were down about three hundred feet, and that is pretty deep for a submarine. But Tom's boat was capable of even greater depths than that.

At first there was nothing much to observe save the opal-tinted water illuminated by the powerful lights of the submarine. Small, and evidently frightened, fish darted to and fro, but there was nothing especially to attract the attention of Tom and his friends, who had made much more sensational trips than this under water.

Mr. Hardley, however, was fascinated, and kept close to the observation windows.

"Are there any wrecks around here?" he asked Tom.

"Possibly," was the answer. "Though they do not contain any treasure, I imagine—brick schooners or cargo boats would be about all."

The submarine went deeper, plowing her way through the Atlantic at a depth of more than three hundred and fifty feet, for Tom wanted to subject her to a good test.

Suddenly Mr. Hardley, who was now alone at the window on the port side, uttered a cry of alarm.

"Look! Look!" he fairly shouted. "We're surrounded by a school of sharks! What monsters! Are we in danger?"

THE SEA MONSTER

Tom Swift, who had been making readings of the various gauges, taking notes for future use, and otherwise busying himself about the navigation of his reconstructed craft, turned quickly from the instrument board at the cry from Mr. Hardley. The gold-seeker, with a look of terror on his face, had recoiled from the observation windows.

"Bless my hat band!" cried Mr. Damon. "Look, Tom!"

They all turned their attention to the glass, and through the plates could be seen a school of giant fishes that seemed to be swimming in front of the submarine, keeping pace with it as though waiting for a chance to enter.

"Are we well protected against sharks, Mr. Swift?" demanded the adventurer. "Are these sea monsters likely to break, the glass and get in at us?"

"Indeed not!" laughed Tom. "There is absolutely no danger from these fish—they aren't sharks, either."

"Not sharks?" cried Mr. Hardley. "What are they, then?"

"Horse mackerel," Tom answered. "At least that is the common name for the big fish. But they are far from being sharks, and we are in no danger from them."

"Oh!" exclaimed Mr. Hardley, and he seemed a little ashamed of the exhibition of fear he had manifested. "Well, they certainly seem determined to follow us," he added.

The big fish were, indeed, following the submarine, and it required no exertion on their part to maintain their speed, since below the surface the M. N. 1 could not move very fast, as indeed no submarine can, due to the resistance of the water.

"They do look as though they'd like to take a bite or two out of us," observed Ned. "Are they dangerous, Tom?"

"Not as a rule," was the answer. "I don't doubt, though, but if a lone swimmer got in a school of horse mackerel he'd be badly bitten. In fact, some years ago, when there was a shark scare along the New Jersey coast, some fishermen declared that it was horse mackerel that were responsible for the death and injury of several bathers. A number of horse mackerel were caught and exhibited as sharks, but, as you can easily see, their mouths lack the under-shot arrangement of the shark, and they are not built at all as are the man-eaters."

"Bless my toothbrush!" exclaimed Mr. Damon. "Still, between a horse mackerel and a shark there isn't much choice!"

Mr. Hardley, with a shudder, turned away from the glass windows, and Tom glanced significantly at Ned. It was another exhibition of the man's lack of nerve.

"We'll have trouble with him before this voyage is over," declared the young inventor to his chum, a little later.

"What makes you think so?" asked Ned.

"Because he's yellow; that's why. I thought him that once before, and then I revised my opinion. Now I'm back where I started. You watch—we'll have trouble."

"Well, I guess we can handle him," observed the financial manager.

"I'm going a little deeper," announced Tom, toward evening on the first day of the voyage on the open ocean. "I want to see how she stands the pressure at five hundred feet. I feel certain she will, and even at a greater depth. But if there's anything wrong we want to correct it before we get too far away from home. We're going down again, deeper than before."

A little later the submarine began the descent into the lower ocean depths. From three hundred and fifty feet she went to four hundred, and when the hand on the gauge showed four hundred and fifty there was a tense moment. If anything went wrong now there would be serious trouble.

But Tom Swift and his men had done their work well. The M. N. 1 stood the strain, and when the gauge showed four hundred and ninety feet Mr. Damon gave a faint cheer.

"Bless my apple dumpling, Tom!" he replied, "this is wonderful."

"Oh, we've been deeper than this," replied the young inventor, "but under different conditions. I'm glad to see how well she is standing it, though."

Suddenly, as the needle pointer on the depth gauge showed five hundred and two feet, there came a slight jar and vibration that was felt throughout the craft.

"What's that?" suddenly and nervously cried Mr. Hardley. "Have we struck something?"

"Yes, the bottom of the ocean," answered Tom quietly. "We are now on the floor of the Atlantic, though several hundred miles, and perhaps a thousand, from the treasure ship. We bumped the bottom, that's all," and as he spoke he brought the submarine to a stop by a signal to the engine room.

And there, as calmly and easily as some of the masses of seaweed growing on the ocean floor around her, rested the M. N. 1. It was a test of her powers, and well had she stood the test, though harder ones were in store for her.

And inside the submarine Tom and his party were under scarcely greater discomfort than they would have been on the surface. True, they were confined to a restricted space, and the air they breathed came from compression tanks, and not from the open sky. The lights had to be kept aglow, of course, for it was pitch dark at that depth. The sunlight cannot penetrate to more than a hundred feet. But sunlight was not needed, for the craft carried powerful electric lights that could illuminate the sea in the immediate vicinity of the submarine.

"Are you going to stay here long?" asked Mr. Hardley, when Tom had spent some time making accurate readings of the various instruments of the boat. "Of course, I realize that you are the commander, but if we don't get to the treasure ship soon some one else may loot her before we have a chance. She's been given up as a hopeless task more than once, but the lure of the millions may attract another gang."

"I want to stay here until I make sure that nothing is leaking and that everything is all right," answered the young inventor. "This is a test I have not given her since the rebuilding. But I think she is coming through it all right, and we can soon start off again. Before we do, though, I want to try the new diving outfit. Ned, are you game for it now? This is a little deeper than you have gone out in for some time, but—"

"Oh, I'm game!" exclaimed the young financial manager. "Get out the suit, Tom, and I'll put it on. I'll go for a stroll on the bottom of the sea. Who knows? Perhaps I may pick up a pearl."

"Pearls aren't found in these northern waters, any more than are sharks," said Tom with a laugh. "However, I'll have the suits made ready. I'll send Koku with you, and I'll stay in this time. Mr. Damon, do you want to go out?"

"Not this time, Tom," answered the eccentric man. "My heart action isn't what it used to be. The doctor said I mustn't strain it. At a depth not quite so great I may take a chance."

"How about you, Mr. Hardley?" asked Tom. "Do you want to put on one of my portable diving suits and walk around on the bottom of the sea?"

"I—I don't believe I've had enough experience," was the hesitating answer. "I'll watch the others first."

Tom felt that it would be this way, but he said nothing. He ordered the diving suits made ready, a special size having been built for the giant, and soon preparations were under way for the two to step outside the craft.

Those who have read of Tom Swift's submarine boat know how his special diving outfit was operated. Instead of the diver being supplied with the air through a hose connected with a pump on the surface, there was attached to the suit a tank of compressed air, which was supplied as needed through special reducing valves.

The diving dress, too, was exceptionally strong, to withstand the awful pressure of water at more than five hundred feet below the surface. The usual rubber was supplemented by thin, reinforced sheets of steel, and this feature, together with an auxiliary air pressure, kept the wearer safe.

Thus Ned and Koku could leave the submarine, walk about on the floor of the ocean as they pleased, and return, unhampered by an air hose or life line. In dangerous waters, infested by sea monsters, weapons could be carried that were effective under water. The diving suit was also provided with a powerful electric light operated by a new form of storage current, compact and lasting.

"Well, I think we're all ready," announced Ned, as he and Koku were helped into their suits and they waited for the glass-windowed helmets to be put on. Once these were fastened in place talk would have to be carried on with the outside world by means of small telephones or by signals.

"Give me axe!" exclaimed Koku, as some of the sailors were about to put his helmet in place.

"What do you want of an axe?" Tom asked.

"Maybe so one them cow fish come along," explained the giant. "Koku whack him with axe."

"He means horse mackerel," laughed Ned. "Give him the axe, Tom. I don't like the looks of those fish, either. I'll take a weapon myself."

Two keen axes were handed to the divers, their helmets were screwed on, and they immediately began breathing the compressed air carried in a tank on their shoulders.

Slowly and laboriously they walked to the diving chamber. Their progress would be easier in the water, which would buoy them up in a measure. Now they were heavily weighted.

To leave the submarine the divers had to enter a steel chamber in the side of the craft. This craft contained double doors. Once the divers were inside the door leading to the interior of the submarine was hermetically closed. Water from outside was then admitted until the pressure was equalized. Then the outer door was opened and Ned and Koku could step forth.

They entered the chamber, the door was closed tightly and then Tom Swift turned the valve that admitted the sea water. With a hiss the Atlantic began rushing in, and in a short time the outer door would be opened.

"If you'll come around to the observation windows you can see them," said Tom, when a look at the indicators told him Ned and Koku had stepped forth.

To the front cabin he and the others betook themselves, and when the interior lights were turned out and the exterior ones turned on they waited for a sight of the two divers.

"Bless my pickle bottle!" cried Mr. Damon, "there they are, Tom."

As he spoke there came into view, moving slowly, Ned and Koku. Their portable lights were glowing, and then, in order to see them better, Tom turned out the exterior searchlights. This made the two forms, in their rather grotesque dress, stand out in bold relief amid the swirling green waters of the Atlantic.

Ned and the giant moved slowly, for it was impossible to progress with any speed wader that terrific pressure. They looked toward the submarine and waved their hands in greeting. They had no special object on the ocean floor, except to try the new diving dress, and it seemed to operate successfully. Ned made a pretense of looking for treasure amid the sand and seaweed, and once he caught and held up by its tail a queer turtle. Koku stalked about behind Ned, looking to right and left, possibly for a sight of some monster "cow fish."

"They're coming back in, I think," remarked Tom, when he saw Ned turn and start back for the side of the craft, where, amidships, was located the diving chamber. "They're satisfied with the test."

Suddenly Koku was seen to glide to the side of Ned, and point at something which none of the observers in the M. N. 1 could see. The giant was evidently perturbed, and Ned, too, showed some agitation.

"Bless my rubber shoes! what's the matter?" cried Mr. Damon.

"I don't know," answered Tom. "Perhaps they have sighted a wreck, or something like that."

"Look! It's a sea monster!" cried Mr. Hardley. "I can see the form of some great fish, or something. Look! It's coming right at them!"

As he spoke all in the observation chamber saw a great, black form, as if of some monster, move close to the two divers.

In Strange Peril

"What is it, Tom? What is it?" cried Mr. Damon, not stopping in this moment of excitement to bless anything. "What is going to attack Ned and Koku?"

"I don't know," answered the young inventor. "It's some big fish evidently. I must get to the diving chamber!"

He gave a quick glance through the observation windows. Ned and the giant were moving as fast as they could toward the side of the craft where they could enter. The black, shadowy form was nearer now, but its nature could not be made out.

Calling to his force of assistants, Tom stood ready to let his chum and Koku out of the diving chamber as soon as the water should have been pumped from it.

A little later, as they all stood waiting in tense eagerness, there came a signal that the two divers had entered the side chamber. Quickly Tom turned the lever that closed the outer door.

"They're safe!" he exclaimed, as he started the pumps to working. But even as he spoke they felt a jar, and the submarine rolled partly over as if she had collided with some object. Yet this could not be, as she was stationary on the floor of the ocean.

"Bless my cake of soap, Tom!" cried Mr. Damon, "what in the world is that?"

"If it's an accident!" exclaimed Mr. Hardley, "I think it ought to be prevented. There have been too many happenings on this trip already. I thought you said your submarine was safe for underwater trips!" he fairly snapped at Tom.

The young inventor gave one look at the irate man who was coming out in his true colors. But it was no time to rebuke him. Too much yet remained to be done. Ned and Koku were still in the chamber and protected from some unknown sea monster by only a comparatively thin door. They must be inside to be perfectly safe.

Tom speeded up the pumps that were forcing the water from the chamber so the inner door could be opened. Eagerly he and his men watched the gauges to note when the last gallon should have been forced out by the compressed air. Not until then would it be safe to let Ned and Koku step into the interior of the craft.

The submarine had not ceased rolling from the force of the blow she had received when there came another, and this time on the opposite side. Once more she rolled to a dangerous angle.

"Bless my tea biscuit!" cried Mr. Damon, "what is it all about, Tom Swift?"

"I don't know," was the low-voiced answer, "unless a pair of monsters are attacking us on both sides alternately. But we'll soon learn. There goes the last of the water!"

The gauge showed that the diving chamber was empty. Quickly the inner doors were opened, stud, with their suits still dripping from their immersion in the salty sea, Ned and Koku stepped forth. In another moment their helmets were loosed from the bayonet catches, and they could speak.

"What was it, Ned?" cried Tom.

"Big fish!" answered Koku.

"Two monster whales!" gasped Ned. "We barely got away from them! They're ramming the sub, Tom!"

As he spoke there came a blow on the port side, greater than either of the two preceding ones. Those in the M. N. 1 staggered about, and had to hold on to objects to preserve their footing.

"Both at the same time!" cried Ned. "The two whales are coming at us both at once!"

This was evidently the case. Tom Swift quickly hurried to the engine room.

"What are you going to do?" asked Mr. Hardley. "You ought to do something! I'm not going to be killed down here by a whale. You've got to do something, Swift! I've had enough of this!"

Tom did not deign an answer, but hurried on. Mr. Damon followed him, having seen that some of the sailors were helping Ned and Koku out of the diving suits.

"Are we in any danger, Tom?" asked the eccentric man.

"Yes; but I think it is easily remedied," was the answer. "We'll go up to the surface. I don't believe the whales will follow us. Or, if they do, they can't do much damage when we are in motion. It's because we are stationary and they are moving that the blows seem so violent. Unless they collide head on with us, in the opposite direction to ours, we ought to be able to get clear of them. If they persist in following us—"

He paused as he pulled over the lever that would send the M. N. 1 to the surface.

"Well, what then?" asked Mr. Damon.

"Then we'll have to use some weapon, and I have several," finished the young inventor.

A few moments later the craft was in motion, not before, however, she was struck another blow, but only a glancing one.

"We're puzzling them!" cried Tom.

Having done all that was possible for the time being, Tom hurried to the observation chamber, followed by the ethers. There Tom switched on the powerful lights. For a moment nothing was to be seen but the swirling, green water. Then, suddenly, a great shape came into view of the glass windows, followed by another.

"Whales!" cried Tom Swift. "And the largest I've ever seen

It was true. Two immense specimens of the cetacean species were in front of the submarine, one on either bow, evidently much puzzled over the glaring lights. They were bow-heads, and immense creatures, and it would not take many blows from them to disable even a stouter craft than was the submarine.

But the motion of the undersea ship, the bright lights, and possibly the feel of her steel skin was evidently not to the liking of the sea monsters. One, indeed, came so close to the glass that he seemed about to try to break it, but, to the relief of all, he veered off, evidently not liking the look of what he saw.

Just once again, before the craft reached the surface, was there another blow, this time at the stern. But it was a parting tap, and none others followed.

"They've gone!" exclaimed Mr. Damon, as the whales vanished from the sight of those in the forward cabin.

"Have you any adequate protection against these monsters of the deep?" asked Mr. Hardley in a fault-finding voice. "I should think you would have taken precautions, Swift!"

He had dropped the formal "Mr." and seemed to treat Tom as an inferior.

"We have other protection than running away," said the young inventor quietly. "There are guns we can use, and, if the whales had been far enough away, I could have sent a small torpedo at them. Close by it would be dangerous to use that, as it would operate on us just as the depth bombs operated on the German submarines. However, I fancy we have nothing more to fear."

And Tom was right. When the surface was reached and the main hatch opened, the sea was calm and there was no sight of the whales. They evidently had had enough of their encounter with a steel fish, larger even than themselves.

"But they surely were monsters," said Ned, as he told of how he and Koku had sighted the animals; for a whale is an animal, and not a fish, though often mistakenly called one.

"Koku was for attacking them with his axe," went on Ned, "but I motioned to him to beat it. We wouldn't have stood a show against such creatures. They were on us before we noticed their coming, but I presume the big submarine attracted them away from us."

"It might have been the lights you carried that drew them," suggested Tom. "I am glad you came out of it so well."

Mr. Hardley seemed to recover some of his former manners, once the peril was passed, but his conduct had been a revelation to Mr. Damon.

"Tom," said the eccentric man in private to the young inventor, "I'm disgusted with that fellow. I don't see how I was ever bamboozled into taking up his offer."

"I don't, either," replied Tom frankly. "But we're in for it now. We've agreed to do certain things, and I'll carry out my end of the bargain. However, I won't put up with any of his nonsense. He's got to obey orders on this ship! I know more than he thinks I do!"

The next two days the M.N.1 progressed along on the surface, and nothing of moment occurred. Then, as they neared southern waters, and Tom desired to make some observations of the character of the bottom, it was decided to submerge. Accordingly, one day the order was given.

Not until the gauge showed a hundred fathoms, or six hundred feet, did the craft cease descending, and then she came to rest on the bottom of the sea—a greater depth than she had yet attained on this voyage.

"How beautiful!" exclaimed Mr. Damon, when Tom turned on the lights and they looked out of the forward cabin windows. "How wonderful and beautiful!"

Well might he say that, for they were resting on pure white sand, and about them, growing on the bottom of this warm, tropical sea were great corals, purple and white, of wondrous shapes, waving plants like ferns and palms, and, amid it all, swam fish of queer shapes and beautiful colors.

"This is worth waiting for!" murmured Ned. "If only moving pictures of this could be taken in colors, it would create a sensation."

"Perhaps I may try that some day," said Tom with a smile. "But just now I have something else to do. Ned, are you game for another try in the diving dress? I want to see how it operates with a new air tank I've fitted on. Want to try?"

"Sure I'll go out," was the ready answer. "It's nicer walking around on this white sand than on the black mud where we saw the whales. You can see better, too."

A little later he and one of the sailors were outside the submarine, walking around in the diving dress, while Tom and the others watched through the glass windows. The new air tank seemed to be working well, for Ned, coming close to the window, signaled that he was very comfortable.

He walked around with the sailor, breaking off bits of odd-shaped coral to bring back to Tom. Suddenly, as those inside the craft looked out, they saw the sailor turn from Ned's side, and with a warning hand, point to something evidently approaching. The next instant a queer shape seemed to envelope Ned Newton, coming out from behind a ledge of weed-draped coral. And a cry went up from those in the submarine as Ned was seen to be enveloped in long, waving arms.

"An octopus!" cried Mr. Damon. "Bless my soul, Tom, an octopus has Ned!"

"No, it isn't that!" cried the young inventor hoarsely. "It's some other monster. It has only five arms—an octopus has eight! I've got to save Ned!"

And he hurried toward the diving chamber, while the others, in fascinated horror, looked at the diver who was in such strange peril.

TOM TO THE RESCUE

Mr. Damon came to a pause in the compartment from which the diving chamber gave access to the ocean outside. Tom, standing before the sliding steel door, had summoned to him several of his men and was rapidly giving them directions.

"What are you going to do, Tom Swift?" asked the eccentric man.

"I'm going out there to save Ned!" was the quick answer. "He's in the grip of some strange monster of the sea. What it is I don't know, but I'm going to find out. Koku, you come with me!"

"Yes, Master, me come!" said the giant simply, as if Tom had told him to go for a pail of water instead of risking his life.

"Barnes, the electric gun!" cried the young inventor to one of his helpers, while others were getting out the diving suits.

"The electric gun!" exclaimed the man. "Do you mean the small one?"

"No, the largest. The improved one."

"Right, sir! Here you are!"

"Do you mean to say you are going out there, where that monster is, and attack it with a gun?" asked Mr. Hardley.

"That's what I'm going to do!" answered Tom, as he began to put on the suit of steel and rubber, an example followed by Koku.

"But you may be attacked by the monster! You may be killed! You are risking your life!" cried the gold seeker.

"I know it." Tom spoke simply. "Ned would do the same for me!"

"But hold on!" cried Mr. Hardley. "If you are killed there will be no one to navigate this boat to the place of the wreck! You can't desert this way!"

Tom gave the man one look of contempt. "You need have, no fears," he said. "This submarine is under international maritime laws. If I die, Captain Nelson, the next in command, takes charge, and the original orders will be carried out. If it is possible to get the gold for you it will be done. Now let me alone. I've got work to do!"

"Bless my apple cart, Tom, that's the way to talk!" exclaimed Mr. Damon, and he, too, for the first time, seemed ready to break with Hardley. "If I were a bit younger I'd go out with you myself and help save Ned."

"Koku and I can do it—if he's still alive!" murmured the young inventor. "Lively now, boys! Is that gun ready?"

"Yes, and doubly charged," was the answer. "Good! I may need it. Koku, take a gun also!"

"Me take axe, Master," replied the giant.

"Well, perhaps that will be better," Tom agreed. "If two of us get to shooting under the water we may hit one another. Quick, now! The helmets. And, Nash, you work the big searchlight!"

"Aye, aye, sir!" answered the sailor.

The helmets were now put on, and any further orders Tom had to give must come through the telephone, and it was by that same medium that he must listen to the talk of his friends. It was possible for the divers to talk and listen to one another while in the water by means of these peculiarly constructed telephones.

"All ready, Koku?" asked Tom.

"All ready, Master," answered the giant, as he grasped his keen axe.

The inner door of the diving chamber was now opened, and, the water having been pumped out of the chamber since Ned and the sailor had emerged, it was ready for Tom and Koku. They entered, the door was closed, and presently they felt the pressure of water all about them, the sea being admitted through valves in the outer door.

While this was going on Mr. Damon, the gold-seeker, and some of the crew and officers went into the forward chamber to observe the undersea fight against the monster that had attacked Ned.

Suddenly the waters glowed with a greatly increased light, and in this illumination it was seen that the monster, whatever it was, had almost completely enveloped Tom's chum with its five arms.

"What makes it possible to see better?" asked Mr. Damon.

"I've turned on the big searchlight," was the answer. "Mr. Swift had it installed at the last moment. It's the same kind he invented and gave to the government, but he retained the right to use it himself."

"It's a good thing he did!" exclaimed the eccentric man. "Now he can see what he's doing! Poor Ned! I'm afraid he's done for!"

"Look!" exclaimed one of the crew. "Norton, the sailor who went out with Mr. Newton, is trying to kill the monster with his spear!"

This was so. Ned's companion, armed with a lone pole to which he had lashed a knife, was stabbing and jabbing at the black form which almost completely hid Ned from sight. But the efforts of the sailor seemed to produce little effect.

"What in the world can it be?" asked Mr. Damon. "Tom says it isn't an octopus, and it can't be, unless it has lost three of its arms. But what sort of monster is it?"

No one answered him. The powerful searchlight continued to glow, and in the gleam Ned could be seen trying to break away from the grip of the Atlantic beast. But his efforts were unavailing. It was as if he was enveloped in a sort of sack, made in segments, so that they opened and closed over his head. About all that could be seen of him was his feet, encased in the heavy lead-laden boots. The form of the other sailor, who had gone out of the submarine with him, could be seen moving here and there, stabbing at the huge creature.

"Here comes Tom!" suddenly exclaimed Mr. Damon, and the young inventor, followed by the giant Koku, came into view. They had emerged from the diving chamber, walked around the submarine as it rested on the ocean floor, and were now advancing to the rescue. Tom carried his electric rifle, and Koku an axe.

So desperately was Norton engaged in trying to kill the sea beast that had attacked Ned, that for the moment he was unaware of the approach of Tom and Koku. Then, as a swirl of the water apprised him of this, he turned and, seeing them, hastened toward them.

"What is it?" Tom asked through the telephone, this information being given to the watchers in the submarine later, as all they could gather then was by what they saw. "What sort of monster is it?"

"A giant starfish!" answered Norton, speaking into his mouthpiece and the water serving as a transmitting medium instead of wires. "I never knew they grew so big! This one has its five arms all around Mr. Newton!"

"A starfish!" murmured Tom. This accounted for it, and, as he looked at the monster from closer quarters, he saw that Norton had spoken the truth.

Small starfish, or even large ones, two feet or more in diameter, may be seen at the seashore almost any time. Nearly always the specimens cast up on the beach are in extended form, either limp, or dead and dried. In almost every instance they are spread out just as their name indicates, in the conventional form of a star.

But a starfish alive, and at its business of eating oysters or other shell animals in the sea, is not at all this shape. Instead, it assumes the form of a sack, spreading its five radiating arms around the object of its meal. It then proceeds to suck the oyster out of its shell, and so powerful a suction organ has the starfish that he can pull an oyster through its shell, by forcing the bivalve to open.

And it was a gigantic starfish, a hundred times as large as any Tom had ever seen, that had Ned in its grip. The creature had doubtless taken the diver for a new kind of oyster, and was trying to open it. An octopus has suckers on the inner sides of its eight arms. A starfish has little feelers, or "fingers," arranged parallel rows on the inner side of its armsÄthousands of little feelers, and these exert a sort of sucking action.

The gigantic starfish had attacked Ned from above, settling down on him so that the head of the diver was at the middle of the creature's body, the five arms, dropping over Ned in a sort of living canopy. And the arms held tightly.

"Come on, Koku, and you, too, Norton!" called Tom through his headpiece telephone. "We'll all attack it at once. I'll fire, and then you begin to hack it. The electric charge ought to stun it, if it doesn't kill the beast!"

Tom's new electric gun, unlike one kind he had first invented, did not fire an electrically charged bullet. Instead it sent a powerful charge of electricity, like a flash of lightning, in a straight line toward the object aimed at. And the current was powerful enough to kill an elephant.

Bracing his feet on the white sand, which gleamed and sparkled in the glare of the searchlight, Tom aimed at the gigantic starfish which had enveloped Ned. Standing on either side of him, ready to rush in and attack with axe and lance, were Koku and Norton.

For an instant Tom hesitated. He was wondering whether the powerful electric charge might not penetrate the body of the starfish and kill his chum.

"But the rubber suit ought to insulate and protect him," mused the young inventor. "Here goes!"

Taking quick aim, Tom pulled the switch, and the deadly charge shot out of the rifle toward the sea monster.

GASPING FOR AIR

For an instant after the electrical charge had been fired nothing seem to happen. The giant starfish still enveloped Ned Newton in its grip, while Tom and his two companions stood tensely waiting and those in the submarine looked anxiously out through the thick glass windows.

Then, as the powerful current made itself felt, those watching saw one of the arms slowly loosen its grip. Another floated upward, as a strand of rope idly drifts in the current. Tom saw this, and called through his telephone:

"He's feeling it! Go to him, boys! Koku, you with the axe!"

They needed no second urging.

Springing toward the monster, Koku with upraised axe and Norton with the lance, they attacked the starfish. Hacking and stabbing, they completed the work begun by Tom's electric gun. With one powerful stroke, even hampered as he was by the heavy medium in which he operated, Koku lopped off one of the legs. Norton thrust his lance deep into the body of the monster, but this was hardly needed, for the starfish was now dead, and gradually the remaining arms relaxed their hold.

Pushing with their weapons, the giant and the sailor now freed Ned from the bulk of the creature, which floated away. It was almost immediately attacked by a school of fish that seemed to have been waiting for just this chance. Ned Newton was freed, but for a moment he staggered about on the floor of the sea, hardly able to stand.

"Are you all right, Ned? Did he pierce your suit?" asked Tom, anxiously through the telephone.

"Yes, I'm all right," came back the reassuring answer. "I'm a bit cramped from the way he held me, but that's all. Guess he found this suit of rubber and steel too much for his digestion."

Slowly, for Ned was indeed a bit stiff and cramped, they made their way back to the submarine, passing through a vast horde of small fishes which had been attracted by the dismemberment of the monster that had been killed.

"There'll be sharks along soon," said Tom to Ned through the telephone. "They're not going to miss such a gathering of food as these small fry present. And sharks will present a different emergency from starfish."

Tom spoke truly, for a little later, when they were all once more safely within the submarine, looking through the windows, they saw a school of hungry sharks feeding on the millions of small fish that gathered to eat the creature that had attacked Ned.

"What did you think was happening to you out there?" asked Tom, when the diving suits had been put away.

"I didn't know what to think," was the answer. "I was prospecting around, and I leaned over to pick up a particularly beautiful bit of coral. All at once I felt something over me, as a cloud sometimes hides the sun. I looked up, saw a big black shape settling down, and then I felt my arms pinned to my sides. At first I thought it was an octopus, but in a moment I realized what it was. Though I never thought before that starfish grew so large."

"Nor I," added Tom. "Well, you've had an experience, to say the least."

They remained a little longer in the vicinity, Tom and his officers making observations they thought would be useful to them later, and then the submarine went up to the surface.

They cruised in the open the rest of that day, recharging the storage batteries and getting ready for the search which, Tom calculated, would take them some time. As he had explained, it would not be easy to locate the Pandora in the fathomless depths of the sea.

Ned and Mr. Damon did some fishing while they were on the surface, and, as their luck was good, there was a welcome change from the usual food of the M.N.1. Though, as Tom had installed a refrigerating plant, fresh meat could be kept for some time, and this, in addition to the tinned and preserved foods, gave them an ample larder.

"When are we going to begin the real search for the gold?" asked Mr. Hardley that evening.

"I should say in another day or two," Tom answered, after he had consulted the charts and made calculations of their progress since leaving their dock. "We shall then be in the vicinity of the place where you say the Pandora went down, and, if you are sure of your location, we ought to be able to come approximately near to the location of the gold wreck."

"Of course I am sure of my figures," declared Mr. Hardley. "I had them directly from the first mate, who gave them to the captain."

"Well, it remains to be seen," replied Tom Swift. "We'll know in a few days."

"And I hope there will be no more taking chances," went on the gold-seeker. "I don't see any sense in you people going out in diving suits to fight starfish. We need those suits to recover the gold with, and it's foolish to take needless risks."

His tone and manner were dictatorial, but Tom said nothing. Only when he and Mr. Damon were alone a little later the eccentric man said:

"Tom will you ever forgive me for introducing you to such a pest?"

"Oh, well, you didn't know what he was," said Tom good-naturedly. "You're as badly taken in as I am. Once we get the gold and give him his share, he can get off my boat. I'll have nothing more to do with him!"

Not wishing to navigate in the darkness, for fear of not being able to keep an accurate record of the course and the distance made Tom submerged the craft when night came and let her come to rest on the bottom of the sea. He calculated that two days later they would be in the vicinity of the Pandora.

The night passed without incident, situated, as they were, on the sand about three hundred feet below the surface; and after breakfast Tom announced that they would go up and head directly for the place where the Pandora had foundered.

The ballast tanks were emptied, the rising rudder set, and the M.N.1 began to ascend. She was still several fathoms from the surface when all on board became aware of a violent pitching and tossing motion.

"Bless my postage stamp, Tom!" exclaimed Mr. Damon, "what's the matter now?"

"Has anything gone wrong?" demanded Mr. Hardley.

"Nothing, except that we are coming up into a storm," answered the young inventor. "The wind is blowing hard up above and the waves are high. The swell makes itself felt even down here."

Tom's explanation of the cause of the pitching and rolling of the submarine proved correct. When they reached the surface and an observation was taken from the conning tower, it was seen that a terrific storm was raging. It was out of the question to open the hatches, or the M.N.1 would have been swamped. The waves were high, it was raining hard and the wind blowing a hurricane.

"Well, here's where we demonstrate the advantage of traveling in a submarine," announced Tom, when it was seen that journeying on the surface was out of the question. "The disturbance does not go far below the top. We'll submerge and be in quiet waters."

He gave the orders, and soon the craft was sinking again. The deeper she went the more untroubled the sea became, until, when half way to the bottom, there was no vestige of the storm.

"Are we going to lie here on the bottom all day, or make some progress toward our destination?" asked the gold-seeker, when Tom came into the main cabin after a visit to the engine room. "It seems to me," went on Mr. Hardley, "that we've wasted enough time! I'd like to get to the wreck, and begin taking out the gold."

"That is my plan," said Tom quietly. "We will proceed presently—just as soon as navigating calculations can be made and checked up. If we travel under water we want to go in the right direction."

His manner toward the gold-seeker was cool and distant. It was easy to see that relations were strained. But Tom would fulfill his part of the contract.

A little later, after having floated quietly for half an hour or so, the craft was put in motion, traveling under water by means of her electric motors. All that day she surged on through the salty sea, no more disturbed by the storm above than was some mollusk on the sandy bottom.

It was toward evening, as they could tell by the clocks and not by any change in daylight or darkness, that, as the submarine traveled on, there came a sudden violent concussion.

"What's that?" cried Mr. Damon.

"We've struck something!" replied Tom, who was with the others in the cabin, the navigation of the craft having been entrusted to one of the officers. "Keep cool, there's no danger!"

"Perhaps we have struck the wreck!" exclaimed Mr. Hardley.

"We aren't near her," answered the young inventor. "But it may be some other half-submerged derelict. I'll go to see, and—"

Tom's words were choked off by a sudden swirl of the craft. She seemed about to turn completely over, and then, twisted to an uncomfortable angle, so that those within her slid to the side walls of the cabin, the M.N.1 came to an abrupt stop. At the same time she seemed to vibrate and tremble as if in terror of some unknown fate.

"Something has gone wrong!" exclaimed Tom, and he hurried to the engine room, walking, as best he could with the craft at that grotesque angle. The others followed him.

"What's the matter, Earle?" asked Tom of his chief assistant.

"One of the rudders has broken, sir," was the answer. "It's thrown us off our even keel. I'll start the gyroscope, and that ought to stabilize us."

"The gyroscope!" cried Tom. "I didn't bring it. I didn't think we'd need it!"

For a moment Earle looked at his commander. Then he said:

"Well, perhaps we can make a shift if we can repair the broken rudder. We must have struck a powerful cross current, or maybe a whirlpool, that tore the main rudder loose. We've rammed a sand bank, or stuck her nose into the bottom in some shallow place, I'm afraid. We can't go ahead or back up."

"Do you mean we're stuck, as we were in the mud bank?" asked Mr. Hardley.

"Yes," answered Tom, and Earle nodded to confirm that version of it.

"But we'll get out!" declared Tom. "This is only a slight accident. It doesn't amount to anything, though I'm sorry now I didn't take my father's advice and bring the gyroscope rudder along. It would have acted automatically to have prevented this. Now, Mr. Earle, we'll see what's to be done."

All night long they worked, but when morning came, as told by the clocks, they were still in jeopardy.

And then a new peril confronted them!

Earle, coming from the crew's quarters, spoke to Tom quietly in the main cabin.

"We'll have to turn on one of the auxiliary air tanks," he said. "We've consumed more than the usual amount on account of the men working so hard, and we used one of the compressed air motors to aid the electrics. We'll have to open up the reserve tank."

"Very well, do so," ordered Tom.

But a grim look came to his face when Earle, returning a little later, reported with blanched cheeks:

"The extra tank hasn't an atom of air in it, sir!"

"What do you mean?" asked Tom, in fear and alarm.

"I mean that the valve has been opened in some way—broken perhaps by accident—and all the air we have is what's in the submarine now. Not an atom in reserve, sir!"

"Whew!" whistled Tom, and then he stood up and began breathing quickly.

Already the atmosphere was beginning to be tainted, as it always becomes in a closed place when no fresh oxygen can enter. Without more fresh air the lives of all in the submarine were in imminent peril. And even as Tom listened to the report of his officer, he and the others began gasping for breath.

WHERE IS IT?

"Down on your faces!" called Tom to those with him in the cabin. "Lie down, every one! The freshest air is near the floor; the bad air rises, being lighter with carbonic acid. Lie down!"

All obeyed, Tom following the advice he himself gave. It was a little easier to breathe, lying on the tilted cabin floor, but how long could this be kept up? That was a question each one asked himself.

"Is every bit of our reserve air used?" asked Tom, speaking to Earle.

"As far as I can learn, yes, sir. If I had known that the auxiliary tank was empty I wouldn't have ordered the compressed air motor used. But I didn't know."

"No one is to blame," said Tom in a low voice. "It is one of the accidents that could not be foreseen. If there is any blame it attaches to me for not installing the gyroscope rudder. If we had had that when we were caught in the cross current, or the whirlpool swirl, our equilibrium would have been automatically maintained. As it is—"

He did not finish, but they all knew what he meant.

"Bless my soda fountain, Tom!" murmured Mr. Damon, "but isn't there any way of getting fresh air?"

"None without rising to the top," Tom answered. "We'll have to try that. Come with me to the engine room, Mr. Earle. It may be possible we can pull her loose."

They started to crawl on their hands and knees, to take advantage of the purer air at the floor level. The situation of the M.N.1 was exactly the same as it had been when she ran into the mud bank in the river, with the exception that now she was in graver danger, for the supply of air for breathing was almost exhausted.

Reaching the engine room, where he found the crew lying down to take advantage of the better air near the floor, Tom made a hasty examination of the apparatus. There was still plenty of power left in the storage batteries, but, so far, the motors they operated had not been able to pull the craft loose from where her nose was stuck fast.

"Are the tanks completely emptied?" asked Tom.

"As nearly so as we could manage with the pumps not acting to their full capacity," answered Earle. "If we could turn the craft on a more level keel we might empty them further, and then her natural buoyancy would send her up."

"Then that's the thing to try to do!" exclaimed Tom, his head beginning to feel the heaviness due to the impure air. "We'll move every stationary object over to the port side, and we'll all stand there, or lie there, ourselves. That may heel her over, and help loosen the grip of the sand."

"It's worth trying," said Earle. "Get ready, men!" he called to the crew.

Tom crawled back to the main cabin and told Mr. Damon and the others what was to be attempted.

"Koku, you come and help move things," requested Tom.

"Me move anything!" boasted the giant, who, because of his great strength and reserve power did not seem as greatly affected as were the others.

Going back to the engine room with Koku, Tom assisted, as well as he could, in the shifting of pieces of apparatus, stores and other things that were movable. They all worked at a great disadvantage except Koku, and he did not seem to feel the lack of vitalizing air.

One thing after another was shifted, and still the M.N.1 maintained the dangerous angle.

"It isn't going to work!" gasped Tom, as he noticed the indicator which told to what angle the craft was still off an even keel. "We'll have to try something else."

"Is there anything to try?" asked Earle, in a faint voice. He was on the point of fainting for lack of air.

Tom looked desperately around. There was one piece of heavy machinery that might be moved to the other side of the engine room. It was bolted to the floor, but its added weight, with that of the crew and passengers, together with what had already been shifted, might turn the trick.

"Let's try to move that!" said Tom faintly, pointing to it.

"It will take an hour to unbolt it," said one of the men.

"Koku!" gasped Tom, pointing to the heavy apparatus. "See if— see if you—"

Tom's breath failed him, and he sank down in a heap. But he had managed to make the giant understand what was wanted.

"Koku do!" murmured the big man. Striding to the piece of machinery, the legs of which were bolted to the floor, Koku got his arms under it. Bending over, and arching his back, so as to take full advantage of his enormous muscles, the giant strained upward.

There was a cracking of bone and sinew, a rasping sound, but the machinery did not leave the floor.

"Him must come!" gasped the giant. "One more go!"

He took a hold lower down. Tom's eyes were dim now, and he could not see well. Some of the men were unconscious.

Then, suddenly, there was a loud, breaking sound, and something tinkled on the steel floor of the submarine engine room. It was the heads of the bolts which Koku had torn loose. Like hail they fell about the giant, and in another instant the big man had pulled loose the machine, weighing several hundreds of pounds. In another moment he shoved it across the floor, toward the elevated side of the craft.

For a second or two nothing happened. Then slowly, very slowly, the M.N.1 began to heel over.

"She's turning!" some one gasped.

An instant later, freed by this turning motion from the grip of the sand bank, the submarine shot to the surface. Up and up she went, breaking out on the open sea as a great fish darts upward from the hidden depths.

It was the work of only a few seconds for the man nearest it to open the hatch, and then in rushed the life-giving air. Tom and his companions were saved, and by Koku's strength.

"Me say him machine got to come up—him come up!" said the giant, smiling in happy fashion, when, after they had all gulped down great mouthfuls of the precious oxygen, they were talking of their experience.

"Yes, you certainly did it," said Tom, and due credit was given to Koku.

"Never again will I travel without a gyroscope," declared Tom. "I'm almost ready to go back and have one installed now."

"No, don't!" exclaimed the gold-seeker. "We are almost at the place of the wreck."

"Well, I suppose we can travel more slowly and not run a risk like that again," decided Tom. "I'll put double valves on the emergency air tank, so no accident will release our supply again."

This was done, after the broken valves had been repaired, and then, when the machine Koku had torn loose was fastened down again, and the submarine restored to her former condition, a consultation was held as to what the next step should be.

They were in the neighborhood of the West Indies, and another day, or perhaps less, of travel would bring them approximately to the place where the Pandora had foundered. The latitude and longitude had been computed, and then, with air tanks filled, with batteries fully charged, and everything possible done to insure success, the craft was sent on the last leg of her journey.

For two days they made progress, sometimes on the surface, and again submerged, and, finally, on the second noon, when the sun had been "shot," Tom said:

"Well, we're here!"

"You mean at the place of the wreck?" asked Mr. Hardley.

"At the place where you say it was," corrected Tom.

"Well, if this is the place of which I gave you the longitude and latitude, then it's down below here, somewhere," and the gold-seeker pointed to the surface of the sea. It was a calm day and the ocean was the proverbial mill pond.

"Let's go down and try our luck," suggested Tom.

The orders were given, the tanks filled, the rudders set, and, with hatches closed, the M.N.1 submerged. Then, with the powerful searchlight aglow, the search was begun. Moving along only a few feet above the floor of the ocean, those in the submarine peered from the glass windows for a sight of the sunken Pandora.

All the rest of that day they cruised about below the surface. Then they moved in ever widening circles. Evening came, and the wreck had not been found. The search was kept up all night, since darkness and daylight were alike to those in the undersea craft.

But when three days had passed and the Pandora had not been seen, nor any signs of her, there was a feeling of something like dismay.

"Where is it?" demanded Mr. Hardley. "I don't see why we haven't found it! Where is that wreck?" and he looked sharply at Tom Swift.

A Separation

"Mr. Hardley," began Tom calmly, as he took a seat in the main cabin, "when we started this search I told you that hunting for something on the bottom of the sea was not like locating a building at the intersection of two streets."

"Well, what if you did?" snapped the gold-seeker. "You're supposed to do the navigating, not I! You said if I gave you the latitude and longitude, down to seconds, as well as degrees and minutes, which I have done, that you could bring your submarine to that exact point."

"I said that, and I have done it," declared Tom. "When we computed our position the other day we were at the exact location you gave me as being the spot where the Pandora foundered."

"Then why isn't she here?" demanded the unpleasant adventurer. "We went down to the bottom at the exact spot, and we've been cruising around it ever since, but there isn't a sign of the wreck. Why is it?"

"I'm trying to explain," replied Tom, endeavoring to keep his temper. "As I said, finding a place on the open sea is not like going to the intersection of two streets. There everything is in plain sight. But here our vision is limited, even with my big searchlight. And being a few feet out of the way, as one is bound to be in making nautical calculations, makes a lot of difference. We may have been close to the wreck, but may have missed it by a few yards."

"Then what's to be done?" asked Mr. Hardley.

"Keep on searching," Tom answered. "We have plenty of food and supplies. I came out equipped for a long voyage, and I'm not discouraged yet. Another thing. The ship may have moved on several fathoms, or even a mile or two, after her last position was taken before she went down. In that case she'd be all the harder to find. And even granting that she sank where you think she did, the ocean currents since then may have shifted her. Or she may be covered by sand."

"Covered by sand!" exclaimed the gold-seeker.

"Yes," replied Tom. "The bottom of the ocean is always changing and shifting. Storms produce changes in currents, and currents wash the sand on the bottom in different directions. So that a wreck which may have been exposed at one time may be covered a day or so later. We'll have to keep on searching. I'm not ready to give up."

"Maybe not. But I am!" snapped out Mr. Hardley.

"What do you mean?" asked the young inventor.

"Just what I said," was the quick answer. "I'm not going to stay down here, cruising about without knowing where I'm going. It looks to me as if you were hunting for a needle in a haystack."

"That's just about what we are doing," and Tom tried to speak good-naturedly.

"Then do you know what I think?" the gold-seeker fairly shot forth.

"Not exactly," Tom replied.

"I think that you don't understand your business, Swift!" was the instant retort. "You pretend to be a navigator, or have men who are, and yet when I give you simple and explicit directions for finding a sunken wreck you can't do it, and you cruise all around looking for it like a dog that has lost the scent! You don't know your business, in my estimation!"

"Well, you are entitled to your opinion, of course," agreed Tom, and both Mr. Damon and Ned were surprised to see him so calm. "I admit we haven't found the wreck, and may not, for some time."

"Then why don't you admit you're incompetent?" cried Mr. Hardley.

"I don't see why I should," said Tom, still keeping calm. "But since you feel that way about it, I think the best thing for us to do is to separate."

"What do you mean?" stormed the other.

"I mean that I will set you ashore at the nearest place, and that all arrangements between us are at an end."

"All right then! Do it! Do it!" cried Mr. Hardley, shaking his fist, but at no one in particular. "I'm through with you! But this is your own decision. You broke the contract—I didn't, and I'll not pay a cent toward the expenses of this trip, Swift! Mark my words! I won't pay a cent! I'll claim the money I deposited in the bank, and I won't pay a cent!"

"I'm not asking you to!" returned Tom. with a smile that showed how he had himself in command. "You put up a bond, secured by a deposit, to insure your share of the expenses—yours and Mr. Damon's. Very well, we'll consider that bond canceled. I won't charge you a cent for this trip. But, mark this, Hardley: What I find from now on, is my own! You don't share in it!"

"You mean that—"

"I mean that if I discover the wreck of the Pandora and take the gold from her, that it is all my own. I will share it with Mr. Damon, provided he remains with me—"

"Bless my silk hat, Tom, of course I'll stay with you!" broke in the eccentric man.

"But you don't share with me," went on the young inventor, looking sternly at the gold-seeker. "What I find is my own!"

"All right—have it that way!" snapped the adventurer. "Set me ashore as soon as you can—the sooner the better. I'm sick of the way you do business!"

"Nothing like being honest!" murmured Ned. But, as a matter of fact, he was glad the separation had come. There had been a strain ever since Hardley came aboard. Mr. Damon, too, looked relieved, though a trifle worried. He had considerable at stake, and he stood to lose the money he had invested with Dixwell Hardley.

"This is final," announced Tom. "If we separate we separate for good, and I'm on my own. And I warn you I'll do my best to discover that wreck, and I'll keep what I find."

"Much good may it do you!" sneered the other. "Perhaps two can play that game."

No one paid much attention to his words then, but later they were recalled with significance.

"Get ready to go up!" Tom called the order to the engine room.

"Where are you going to land me?" asked Mr. Hardley. "I have a right to know that?"

"Yes," conceded Tom, "you have. I'll tell you in a moment."

He consulted a chart, made a few calculations and then spoke.

"I shall land you at St. Thomas," answered the young inventor. "I do not wish to bring my submarine to a place that is too public, as too many questions may be asked. From St. Thomas you can easily reach Porto Rico, and from there you can go anywhere you wish."

"Very well," murmured the malcontent. "But I don't consider that I owe you a cent, and I'm not going to pay you."

"I wouldn't take your money," Tom answered. "And don't forget what I said—that what I find is my own."

The other answered nothing. Nor from then on did he hold much conversation with Tom or any others in the party. He kept to himself, and a day later he was landed, at night, at a dock, and if he said "good-bye" or wished Tom and his friends a safe voyage, they did not hear him.

They were steaming along on the surface the next day, and at noon the submarine suddenly halted.

"What's on now, Tom?" asked Ned, as he saw his chum prepare to go up on deck with some of the craft's officers.

"We're going to 'shoot the sun' again," was the answer. "I want to make sure that we were right in our former calculations as to the position of the Pandora. The least error would throw us off."

Using the sextant and other apparatus, some of which Tom had invented himself, the exact position of the submarine was calculated. As the last figure was set down and compared with their previous location, one of the men who had been doing the computing gave an exclamation.

"What's the matter?" asked Tom.

"Look!" was the answer, and he pointed to the paper. "There's where a mistake was made before. We were at least two miles off our course

"You don't say so!" exclaimed Tom, and, taking the sheet, he went rapidly over the results.

THE SERPENT WEED

All waited eagerly for Tom Swift to verify the statement of the other mathematician, and the young inventor was not long in doing this, for he had what is commonly known as a "good head for figures."

"Yes, I see the mistake," said Tom. "The wrong logarithm was taken, and of course that threw out all the calculations. I should say we were nearer three miles off our supposed location than two miles."

"Does that mean," asked Mr. Damon, "that we began a search for the wreck of the Pandora three miles from the place Hardley told us she was

"That's about it," Tom said. "No wonder we couldn't find her."

"What are you going to do?" Ned wanted to know.

"Get to the right spot as soon as possible and begin the search there," Tom answered. "You see, before we submerged as nearly as possible at the place where we thought the Pandora might be on the ocean bottom. From there we began making circles under the sea, enlarging the diameter each circuit.

"That didn't bring us anywhere, as you all know. Now we will start our series of circles with a different point as the center. It will bring us over an entirely different territory of the ocean floor."

"Just a moment," said Ned, as the conference was about to break up. "Is it possible, Tom, that in our first circling that we covered any of the ground which we may cover now? I mean will the new circles we propose making coincide at any place with the previous ones

"They won't exactly coincide," answered the young inventor. "You can't make circles coincide unless you use the same center and the same radius each time. But the two series of circles will intersect at certain places."

"I guess intersect is the word I wanted," admitted Ned.

"What's the idea?" Tom wanted to know.

"I'm thinking of Hardley," answered his chum. "He might assert that we purposely went to the wrong location with him to begin the search, and if we afterward find the wreck and the gold, he may claim a share."

"Not much he won't!" cried Tom.

"Bless my check book, I should say not!" exclaimed Mr. Damon.

"Hardley broke off relations with us of his own volition," said Tom. "He 'breached the contract,' as the lawyers say. It was his own doing.

"He has put me to considerable expense and trouble, not to say danger. He was aware of that, and yet he refused to pay his share. He accused me of incompetence. Very well. That presuggested that I must have made an error, and it was on that assumption that he said I did not know my business. Instead of giving me a chance to correct the error, which he declared I had made, he quit—cold. Now he is entitled to no further consideration.

"An error was made—there's no question of that. We are going to correct it, and we may find the gold. If we do I shall feel I have a legal and moral right to take all of it I can get. Mr. Hardley, to use a comprehensive, but perhaps not very elegant expression, may go fish for his share."

"That's right!" asserted Mr. Damon.

"I guess you're right, Tom," declared Ned. "There's only one more thing to be considered."

"What's that?" asked the young inventor.

"Why, Hardley himself may find out in some way that we were barking up the wrong tree, so to speak. That is, learn we started at the wrong nautical point. He may get up another expedition to come and search for the gold and—"

"Well, he has that right and privilege," said Tom coolly. "But I don't believe he will. Anyhow, if he does, we have the same chance, and a better one than he has. We're right here, almost on the ground, you might say, or we shall be in half an hour. Then we'll begin our search. If he beats us to it, that can't be helped, and we'll be as fair to him as he was to us. This treasure, as I understand it, is available to whoever first finds it, now that the real owners, whoever they were, have given it up."

"I guess you're right there," said Mr. Damon. "I'm no sea lawyer, but I believe that in this case finding is keeping."

"And there isn't one chance in a hundred that Hardley can get another submarine here to start the search," went on Tom. "Of course it's possible, but not very probable."

"He might get an ordinary diving outfit and try," Ned suggested.

"Not many ordinary divers would take a chance going down in the open sea to the depth the Pandora is supposed to lie," Tom said. "But, with all that, we have the advantage of being on the ground, and I'm going to make use of that advantage right away."

He gave orders at once for the M.N.1 to proceed, and this she did on the surface. It was decided to steam along on the open sea until the exact nautical position desired was reached. This position was the same Mr. Hardley had indicated, but that position was not before attained, owing to an error in the calculations.

As all know, to get to a certain point on the surface of the ocean, where there is no land to give location, a navigator has to depend on mathematical calculations. The earth's surface is divided by imaginary lines. The lines drawn from the north to the south poles are called meridians of longitude. They are marked in degrees, and indicate distance east or west of the meridian of, say, Greenwich, England, which is taken as one of the centers. The degrees are further divided into minutes and seconds, each minute being a sixtieth of a degree and each second, naturally, the sixtieth of a minute.

Now, if a navigator had to depend only on the meridian lines indicating distance east and west, he might be almost any distance north or south of where he wanted to go. So the earth is further divided into sections by other imaginary lines called parallels of latitude. As all know, these indicate the distance north or south of the middle line, or the equator. The equator goes around the earth at the middle, so to speak, running from east to west, or from west to east, according as it is looked at. The meridian of Greenwich may be regarded as a sort of half equator, running half way around the earth in exactly the opposite direction, or from north to south.

The place where any two of these imaginary lines, crossing at right angles, meet may be exactly determined by the science of navigation. It is a complicated and difficult science, but by calculating the distance of the sun above the horizon, sometimes by views of stars, by knowing the speed of the ship, and by having the exact astronomical time at hand, shown on an accurate chronometer, the exact position of a ship at any hour may be determined.

By this means, if a navigator wants to get to a place where two certain lines cross, indicating an exact spot in the ocean, he is able to do so. He can tell for instance when he has reached the place where the seventy-second degree of longitude, west from Greenwich, meets and crossed the twentieth parallel of latitude. This spot is just off the northern coast of Haiti. Other positions are likewise determined.

It was after about an hour of rather slow progress on the surface of the calm sea, no excess speed being used for fear of over-running the mark, that Tom and his associates gathered on deck again to make another calculation.

Long and carefully they worked out their position, and when, at last, the figures had been checked and checked again, to obviate the chance of another error, the young inventor exclaimed:

"Well, we're here!"

"Really?" cried Ned.

"No doubt of it," said his chum.

"Bless my doormat!" cried Mr. Damon. "And do you mean to say, Tom Swift, that if we submerge now we'll be exactly where the Pandora lies, a wreck on the floor of the ocean

"I mean to say that we're at exactly the spot Where Hardley said she went down," corrected Tom, "and we weren't there before —that is not so that we actually knew it. Now we are, and we're going down. But that doesn't guarantee that we'll find the wreck. She may have shifted, or be covered with sand. All that I said before in reference to the difficulty in locating something under the surface of the sea still holds good."

Once more, to make very certain there was no error, the figures were gone over, Then, as one result checked the other, Tom put away the papers, the nautical almanac, and said:

"Let's go!"

Slowly the tanks of the M.N.1 began to fill. It was decided to let her sink straight down, instead of descending by means of the vertical rudders. In that way it was hoped to land her as nearly as possible on the exact spot where the Pandora was supposed to be.

"How deep will it be, Tom?" asked Ned, as he stood beside his chum in the forward observation cabin and watched the needle of the gauge move higher and higher.

"About six hundred feet, I judge, going by the character of the sea bottom around here. Certainly not more than eight hundred I should say." And Tom was right. At seven hundred and eighty-six feet the gauge stopped moving, and a slight jar told all on board that the submarine was again on the ocean floor.

"Now to look for the wreck!" exclaimed Tom. "And it will be a real search this time. We know we are starting right."

"Are you going to put on diving suits and walk around looking for her?" asked Ned.

"No, that would take too long," answered Tom. "We'll just cruise about, beginning with small circles and gradually enlarging them, spiral fashion. We'll have to go up a few feet to get off the bottom."

As Tom was about to give this order Ned looked from the glass windows. The powerful searchlight had been switched on and its gleams illuminated the ocean in the immediate vicinity of the craft.

As was generally the case, the light attracted hundreds of fish of various shapes, sizes, and, since the waters were tropical, beautiful colors. They swarmed in front of the glass windows, and Ned was glad to note that there were no large sea creatures, like horse mackerel or big sharks. Somehow or other, Ned had a horror of big fish. There were sharks in the warm waters, he well knew, but he hoped they would keep away, even though he did not have to encounter any in the diving suit.

Slowly the submarine began to move. And as she was being elevated slightly above the ocean bed, to enable her to proceed, Ned uttered an exclamation and pointed to the windows.

"Look, Tom!" he cried.

"What is it?" the young inventor asked.

"Snakes!" whispered his chum. "Millions of 'em! Out there in the water! Look how they're writhing about!"

Tom Swift laughed.

"Those aren't snakes!" he said. "That's serpent grass—a form of very long seaweed which grows on certain bottoms. It attains a length of fifty feet sometimes, and the serpent weed looks a good deal like a nest of snakes. That's how it got its name. I didn't know there was any here. But we must have dropped down into a bed of it."

"Any danger?" asked Ned.

"Not that I know of, only it may make it more difficult for us to see the wreck of the Pandora."

As Tom turned to leave the cabin the submarine suddenly ceased moving. And she came to a gradual stop as though she had been "snubbed" by a mooring line.

"I wonder what's the matter!" exclaimed Tom. "We can't have come upon the wreck so soon."

At that moment a man entered the cabin.

"Trouble, Mr. Swift!" he reported.

"What kind?" asked Tom.

"Our propellers are tangled with a mass of serpent weed," was the answer. "They're both fouled, and we can't budge."

"Bless my anchor chain!" ejaculated Mr. Damon. "Stuck again!"

The Devil Fish

It was true. The long sinuous strands of ocean grass, known under the name of "serpent weed," had caught around the whirling propellers and there had been wound and twisted very tightly. Just as sometimes the stern line gets so tightly twisted around a motor boat propeller as to require hours of work with an axe to free it, the seaweed was twisted around the blades of the M.N.1.

Slowly the undersea craft came to a stop, and there she remained, floating freely enough, but a few feet above the bottom of the ocean. There was a look of alarm on the faces of Ned and Mr. Damon, but Tom Swift smiled.

"This is annoying, and may cause us delay," he announced, "but there is no danger."

"How are we to get free from the weed?" asked Mr. Damon. "We can't move if it's wound around our propellers, can we?"

"Not very well," Tom answered. "But all that will have to be done will be for some of us to put on diving suits, go out and chop the strands of weed away. We can do it more easily than could an ordinary vessel, for they would have to go into dry dock for the purpose. I think I'll go out myself. I want to look around a little."

"I'll go with you," said Ned. "As long as we haven't seen any sharks I don't mind."

"Nor gigantic starfish, either," added Tom with a smile, and Ned nodded in agreement.

"We might try reversing the propellers," suggested the man from the engine room, who had come in with the information about the serpent weed. "The chief didn't like to try that. We saw the weed from our observation windows and stopped as soon as we felt we had fouled it."

"That was right," commended Tom. "Well, try reversing. It can't do any harm, and it may make it easier for us to free the propellers when we go out."

He went to the engine room himself to see that everything was properly attended to. Slowly the motors were reversed, and only a slight current was given them, as, with the resistance of the tightly wound weed, too powerful a force might burn out the insulation.

Slowly the starting lever was thrown over. There was a low humming and whining as the current jumped from the batteries, and a slight vibration of the craft. Tom looked at the movable pointer which showed the speed and direction of the propellers. The hand oscillated slightly and then stopped.

"Shut off the current!" cried Tom. "It's of no use. The propellers are held as tight as a drum! We've got to go out and cut loose the serpent weed!"

The experiment of reversing the propellers had failed. But still Tom did not believe his craft was in danger. He gave orders for the engine room force to stand by and then arranged for himself, Ned, and Koku to go outside in diving dress and cut the weed off the shafts. There were twin propellers on the submarine, each revolving independently by separate motors, and each capable of being sent in forward or reverse direction.

"Start the engines as soon as we give the signal," Tom told the machinist. "Two knocks on the hull with an axe will mean go ahead, and three will mean reverse."

"I understand," said Weyth, the machinist. "But stand away from the propellers after you give the signal. I'll give you three minutes to move clear."

"That will be enough," Tom said. "But better make it half speed in either case. My idea is that if we can partly cut the weed off, starting the propellers, either forward or in reverse, will finish the trick."

"It may," agreed Weyth.

Armed with axes and sharp steel bars, Tom, Ned, and Koku were soon ready to step outside the submarine.

They entered the diving chamber. In the usual manner water was admitted, and, when the pressure was equalized, the outer door was opened and they walked out on the floor of the ocean, the submarine having been allowed to settle down again on the bottom of the Atlantic.

The powerful searchlight had been turned so that the beams were diffused toward the stern. In addition to this Tom and his two companions carried, attached to their suits, small, but brilliant, electric torches. Of course they had their air tanks with them, and also the telephones, by means of which they could communicate with one another.

As they emerged into the warm waters surrounding the submarine they disturbed thousands of small fish which were feeding all about. Like ocean swallows, the creatures scattered in all directions, some even brushing the divers as they slowly made their way toward the stern of the craft.

"Nice place here," said Ned to Tom, as they walked along, Koku coming just behind them.

"Yes. If we could take this up above and exhibit it in some city park it would make a hit all right," answered the young inventor.

They were walking on the pure, white, sandy floor of the ocean, some seven hundred feet below the surface, protected from the awful pressure of the water by means of the specially constructed suits which Tom had invented. About them, growing as if in a garden, were great masses of coral, some so thin and sinuous that it waved as do palms and ferns in the open air. Other coral was in great rock masses.

Then, too, there was the unpleasant serpent weed. It did not grow all over, but in patches here and there, as rank grass springs up in a meadow.

And it had been the misfortune of the M.N.1 that she poked her tail into a mass of this long, tough grass, which was now wound about her propellers.

In addition to the many wonderful vegetable forms that grew on the ocean floor, some rivalling in beauty the orchids of the tropics, and almost as delicate, there were the fishes, which darted to and fro, now swiftly swimming beneath some coral arch, and again poising around some mass of waving sea fronds.

"Well, let's get busy," called Tom to Ned through the telephone. "We want to free the propellers and find the wreck of the Pandora. She may be a hundred feet from us, or a mile away, and in that case it's going to take longer to locate her."

Together they walked to the stern of the disabled craft. One look at the propeller shafts, the examination being made by the diffused glow from the searchlight, as well as from the electric torches carried, showed that the diagnosis of the trouble was correct.

Wound around both propellers was a mass of the serpent weed, tightly bound because the machinery had whirled it around and around after the grass had once been caught. It was almost as bad as though manila cable had been thus accidentally fastened.

"Well, might as well begin to cut it loose," said Tom to his companions. "Koku, you take the port propeller, and Ned and I will work on the other. You ought to be able to beat us at this game."

"Me do," said the giant, as he got his axe ready for work.

Blows struck in water lose much of their force. This can easily be proved by filling a bathtub full of water, rolling up the sleeves, and then taking a hammer in the hand, immersing it fully, and trying to strike some object held in the other hand. The water hampers the blows.

It was this way with Tom and his friends. Nearly half of Koku's great strength was wasted. But they knew they could take their time, though they did not want to waste many hours.

The streamers of weed were like strands of tightly wound rope, and this, under certain circumstances, acquires almost the density of wood. Tom and Ned, working together, had managed to chop a little off their propeller shaft, and Koku had done somewhat better with his task, when Ned became aware of a shadow passing above him.

Instinctively he looked up, and as he did so he could not repress a start of horror. Tom, too, as well as Koku, saw the menacing shadow. Ned grasped more tightly his sharp, steel bar and spoke through the telephone to his companions.

"Devil fish!" he said. "The devil fish are after us."

A WAR REMINDER

To a large number of people the name devil fish brings to mind a conception of an octopus, squid, cuttle fish, or a member of that species. This is, however, a mistake.

The true devil fish of the tropics is a member of the sting ray family, and the common name it bears is given to it because of two prongs, or horns, which project just in front of its mouth. His Satanic Majesty is popularly supposed to have horns, together with a tail, hoofs and other appendages, and the horns of this sting ray fish are what give it the name it bears.

The devil fish, some specimens of which grow to the weight of a ton and measure fifteen feet from wing tip to wing tip, are armed with a long tail, terminating in a tough, horny substance, like many of the ray family members. This horn-tipped tail, lashing about in the water, becomes a terrible weapon of defense. Possibly it is used for offense, as the devil fish feeds on small sea animals, sweeping them into its mouth by movements of the horns mentioned. These horns, swirled about in the water, create a sort of suction current, and on that the food fishes are borne into the maw of the gigantic creature.

A whale rushes through a school of small sea animals with open mouth, takes in a great quantity of water, and the fringe of whalebone acts as a strainer, letting out the water and retaining the food. In like manner the devil fish feeds, except that it has no whalebone. Its "horns" help it to get a meal.

The "wing tips" of the devil fish have been spoken of. They are not really wings, though when one of these fish breaks water and shoots through the air, it appears to be flying. The wings are merely fins, enormously enlarged, and these give the fish its great size, rather than does the body itself. It is the whipping spike-armed tail of the devil fish that is to be feared, aside from the fact that the rush of a monster might swamp a small boat.

It was two or three of these devil fish that were now floating in the water above Tom and his companions, who were grouped about the stern of the disabled submarine.

"They won't attack us unless we disturb them," said Tom through his telephone, speaking to Ned and Koku. "Keep still and they'll swim away. I guess they're trying to find out what new kind of fish our boat is."

All might have gone well had not Koku acted precipitately. One of the devil fish, the smallest of the trio, measuring about ten feet across, swam down near the giant. It was an uncanny looking creature, with its horns swirling about in the water and its bone-tipped tail lashing to and fro like a venomous serpent.

"Look out!" cried Tom. But he was too late. Koku raised his axe and struck with all his force at the sea beast. He hit it a glancing blow, not enough to kill it, but to wound it, and immediately the sea was crimsoned with blood.

The devil fish was able to observe under water better than its human enemies, and it was in no doubt as to its assailant. In an instant it attacked the giant, seeking to pierce him with the deadly tail.

These tails are not only armed with a tip of horn-like hardness, they are also poisonous, and their penetrating power is great. Fishermen have sometimes caught small sting rays, which are a sort of devil fish. Lashing about in the bottom of a boat a sting ray can send its tail tip through the sole of a heavy boot and inflict a painful wound which may cause serious results.

The beast Koku had wounded was trying to sting the giant, and the latter, aware of his peril, was striking out with the axe.

"Look out, Tom!" called Ned through his telephone, as he saw one of the two unwounded devil fish swirl down toward the young inventor. Tom looked up, saw the big, horrible shape above him, and jabbed it with the sharp, steel bar. He inflicted a wound which added further to the crimson tinge in the sea, and that fish now attacked Tom Swift.

In another instant all three divers were fighting the terrible creatures, that, knowing by instinct they were in danger, were using the weapon with which nature had provided them. They lashed about with their sharp-pointed tails, and more than one blow fell on the suits of the divers.

Had there been the least penetration, of course almost instant death would have followed. For the sea, at that depth and pressure, entering the suits would have ended life suddenly. But Tom had seen to it that the suits were well made and strong, with a lining of steel. And however great a thickness of leather the devil fish could send his sting through, it could not overcome steel.

There was danger, though, that the slender tip might slip through the steel bars across the windows in the helmets and shatter the glass. And that would be as great a danger as if the suits themselves were penetrated.

"We've got to fight 'em!" gasped Tom through his instrument, and, seeing his chance, he gave another jab to the devil fish attacking him. Koku, too, was standing up well under the attack of the monster he had first wounded. Ned, watching his chance, got in several blows, first at one and then at the other of the huge creatures. The third devil fish, which had not been wounded, had disappeared. Finally Koku, with a desperate blow, succeeded in severing the tail from the beast attacking him, and that battle was over.

As if realizing that it had lost its power to harm, the devil fish at once swam off, grievously wounded. Then Koku turned his attention to Tom's enemy. Ned, too, lent his aid, and they succeeded in wounding the creature in several places, so that it sank to the bottom of the sea and lay there gasping.

Slowly the red waters cleared and the three divers, exhausted by the fight, could view the remaining creature—the one wounded to death. It was the largest of the three, and truly it was a monster. But it was past the power to harm, and in a few minutes an under sea current carried it slowly away. Later it would float, doubtless, or be devoured by sharks or other ocean pirates before reaching the surface.

"Thank goodness that's over!" said Ned to Tom. "I don't want to see any more of them."

"There may be more about," Tom said. "We'd better keep watch. Ned, you lay off and Koku and I will work on the propellers. Then you can take your turn."

This plan was followed. Koku, not being tired, did not need to stop working, and he was the first to free his shaft partially of the entangling weeds. Tom rapped a signal, the blades were slowly revolved and then came free. A little later the second was in like condition.

"Now we can move!" said Tom, as they started back toward the diving chamber. "I hope we don't run into another patch of that serpent grass."

"Nor see any more devil fish," added Ned.

"Same here!" echoed the young inventor.

Luck seemed to be with the gold-seekers after that, for as the submarine was sent ahead, no more of the long, entangling grass was encountered.

The search for the sunken Pandora was now begun in earnest, since they were positive that they were at the right spot.

No immediate sign of her was found. But Tom and his friends hardly expected to be as lucky as that. They were willing to make a search. For, as Tom had said, a current might have shifted the position of the wreck.

They followed the plan of moving about in ever-widening circles. Only in this way could they successfully cover the ground. It was the third day after the encounter with the devil fish that Tom, Ned and Mr. Damon were in the forward observation cabin. The eccentric man suddenly pointed to something visible from the starboard window.

"There's a wreck, Tom!" he cried. "Maybe it's the Pandora!"

Tom and the others hurried to Mr. Damon's side and peered out into the sea, illuminated by the great searchlight.

"That isn't the Pandora!" said the young inventor.

"But it's a wreck, isn't it?" asked Ned.

"Yes, it's a sunken vessel, all right," Tom assented. "But it's a reminder of the Great War. Look! She has been blown up by a torpedo!"

STUDYING CURRENTS

There was no question about Tom's statement. They had approached close to the side of a small, sunken and wrecked steamer, and in her side was torn a great hole. In the light from the submarine it could be seen that the plates bent inward, indicating that the explosion was from outside.

"What are you going to do, Tom?" asked Ned, as he saw his chum move the engine room telegraph signal to the stop position.

"Going to investigate," was the answer. "We might as well take the time. We may learn something of value."

"Do you think there is any treasure in her?" asked Mr. Damon.

"There might be," answered Tom. "We'll put on the diving suits and go outside."

"I hope there aren't any devil fish," remarked Ned.

"Same here," Tom agreed. "But I don't believe we'll meet with any. Will you take a chance, Ned?"

"I surely will! I'd like to find out what sort of ship that is —or rather, was, for there isn't much left of her."

He spoke truly, for indeed the torpedo had created fearful havoc. The full extent of it was not observed until Tom, Ned, Koku and two of the crew had put on diving suits and approached the hulk. She lay on her side on the sandy bottom, heeled over somewhat, and when the investigators had walked around her, as they were able to do, they saw a second, and even larger hole in the opposite side.

"Two submarines must have attacked her," said Ned, speaking through his telephone to Tom.

"Either that, or else one sent a torpedo into her, dived, came up on the other side and sent another."

"Well, let's see if she has any treasure aboard," Ned proposed. "Wouldn't it be queer if we should discover two treasure ships?"

"More queer than likely," Tom answered. "We've got to be careful going inside her."

"Why?" asked Ned. "Do you think we'll set off a hidden mine?"

"No, but part of the wreckage might be loosened if we climbed over it, and we might fall and be pinned down. I've read of divers being caught that way. We must be careful."

"Do you suppose a German sub did this?" Ned asked.

"I think very likely," Tom answered. "Maybe we can tell if we can discover the nationality of this craft."

They made their way to a position just outside the gaping hole in the starboard side of the craft. Evidently; it was, or had been, a tramp steamer, and the torpedo hole on her starboard side was about amidships.

She must have filled and sunk quickly with two such great holes torn in her.

Standing near the wound in the steel skin, Tom and his companions tried to see what was inside. Their portable torches did not give light enough to make out clearly the character of the cargo carried, and it was too risky to venture into the mass of wreckage that must be the result of the explosion of the torpedo.

"Let's try the other side," suggested Tom, and they moved around the stern of the craft. When they reached the place where the name was visible Tom raised his electric torch and, in the glow of it, they all read the painted inscription, Blakesly, New York.

"That's the vessel that disappeared so mysteriously!" exclaimed Ned, speaking through his instrument. "I remember reading about her. She sailed from New York for Brest, but was never heard of. At last we have solved the mystery!"

"Yes," agreed Tom, "but without much avail. We are too late to do any good."

"Not one of her crew or passengers was ever heard of," went on Ned. "It was surmised that a German sub attacked her, and that she was either sunk 'without a trace' or else her survivors were taken aboard the submarine and carried to Germany."

"Perhaps we may learn something to that end," said Tom, as they got around to the other side. The hole there was not quite so big, and as it seemed safe to enter Tom and Ned prepared to do so, the others remaining outside to give them aid in case of necessity.

It was comparatively easy to enter by this wound in the side of the Blakesly, and, proceeding cautiously, Tom and Ned made the attempt. They found they could not penetrate far, however, because of the mass of wreckage scattered about by the explosion. They could see through into the engine room, and there the machinery was in every stage of destruction, while below the boilers were disrupted.

"She must have gone down in a hurry," remarked Tom.

"Yes, and with part of her crew," added Ned, as he pointed to where a heap of white bones lay—grim reminders of the Great War. The engine room forces had been trapped and carried down to death.

"I wonder if, by any chance, she did carry gold," suggested Ned.

"It wouldn't be down here if she did," asserted Tom. "And if she was a treasure ship, and the huns knew it, they wouldn't leave any on board."

"That's just it," went on his chum. "They may not have known it, and have ripped a couple of torpedoes at her without any warning. It would be just like them."

"Granted," assented the young inventor. "Well, we can take another look around outside. Maybe there's a way of getting on deck, and so going below from there. I wouldn't chance it from here."

"Me, either," Ned answered.

They looked around a little more, a further view showing how dangerous it would be to attempt to enter the shattered engine room, where a misstep or a sudden change of equilibrium might cause disaster.

"Nothing there," Tom reported to Koku and the others waiting for him outside.

"Rope by up go him stern," said Koku, motioning toward the after part of the wreck.

"What does he mean?" Tom asked one of his crew.

"Oh, he went walking around outside while you were inside, sir," was the answer, "and he seems to have found a rope ladder or a chain, or something hanging from the stern."

"Let's go and see it," proposed Tom. "I've been wondering if we could get on deck."

"Are we going to spend much time here?" Ned wanted to know.

"Not much longer," Tom replied. "Why?"

"Well, I was thinking we'd better keep on looking for the Pandora. I don't want that fellow Hardley to get the bulge on us."

"Oh," laughed Tom, "he isn't likely to. But we won't take any chances. As soon as I see if we can learn anything that may be useful from this hulk, we'll go back and start on our way again."

The party of divers, led by Koku, who wanted to point out his discovery, walked slowly along on the bottom of the sea, around to the stern of the Blakesly.

"See!" said the giant through his telephone, and, as the instruments were interchanging, all heard him.

Koku pointed to several ropes and chains that were dangling from the stern of the sunken craft. Evidently they had been used by those who sought to escape from the sinking ship after she had been torpedoed.

"Wait a minute!" Tom telephoned, as he saw Koku grasp a chain, evidently with the object of hoisting himself up on deck by the simple method of going up hand over hand. He could easily do this by adjusting the air pressure inside his diving suit to make himself more buoyant.

"Koku go up!" said the giant.

"Better make sure that chain will hold you," cautioned Tom. The giant proved it by several powerful tugs, and then began to raise himself from the sandy bed of the ocean.

"Well, if it will hold him it will hold us," asserted Tom. "Ned, we'll go up. You two stay here," he said to the members of his crew. "We can't take any chances of all getting in the same accident if there should be one."

A little later Tom, Ned, and Koku stood on the deck of the sunken craft. Much of what she had carried had been swept off, either in the explosions or by reason of currents generated by storms since the fatality. But what seemed to be the cabin of the captain, or of some of the officers, was in plain view and easy of access from this level.

"Let's take a look!" said Tom.

Ned followed him to the door. It had been torn off, and inside was a table made fast to the floor. From the appearance of the room it was evidently the compartment where the charts were kept, and where the captain or his officers worked out the reckoning. But it was tenantless now, and if any maps or papers had been out they were dissolved in sea water some time since.

"Let's see if we can find the log book," proposed Ned.

"Good idea," assented Tom.

Using the iron bars they carried, they forced open some of the lockers, but aside from pulp, which might have been charts or almost anything in the way of documents, nothing was come upon that would tell anything.

Unless the log book was kept in a water-tight case the ink would all run, once it was wet," Tom said, when they were about ready to give up their search.

"I suppose so," agreed Ned. "But I would like to know whether she carried treasure."

However, it was impossible to discover this, and dangerous to look too far into the interior. So Tom and his party were forced to leave without discovering the secret of the Blakesly, if she possessed one.

Later, however, when they had returned home, Tom and Ned made a report of what they had seen, and so cleared up the fate of the vessel. They learned that she carried no treasure, and they were glad they had not risked their lives looking for it. What had happened to her crew was never learned.

They returned to the submarine and told what they had viewed. And then, with a last look at the wreck, they passed on in their search for the Pandora.

Several fruitless days followed, and though a careful search was made in the vicinity of the true location given by Mr. Hardley, nothing was discovered.

"How long will you keep at it before you give up?" asked Ned one evening, as they went aloft to replenish the air tanks and charge the batteries.

"Oh, another week, anyhow. I have a new theory, Ned."

"What's that?"

"Ocean currents. I believe there are powerful currents in these waters, and that they may have shifted the position of the Pandora considerably. I'm going to study the currents."

"Good idea!" cried his chum.

And the next day they began observations which were destined to have surprising results.

AN UNDERSEA COLLISION

Under the warm, tropical sun the submarine floated idly on the surface of the calm sea. She had risen from the depths, her hatches had been opened, and now the crew, the owner, and his guests were breathing free air. The men were taking advantage of the period above water to wash out some of their garments, hanging them on improvised lines stretched along the deck. For Tom Swift had said he would remain above the surface all day.

Some slight repairs were necessary to the electric motors, and they could be made only when the craft was on the open sea. This, too, would afford a chance to recharge the batteries and repair one of them.

For the time being the search under the sea for the treasure ship Pandora had been abandoned. But it was not given up entirely. As Tom had announced to Ned, a new theory would be worked out. So far, cruising about in the place where the fillibuster ship was supposed to have gone down had resulted in nothing.

Mr. Damon, who had been below, shaving, came up on deck to see Tom and Ned tossing into the water large pieces of cork taken from spare life preservers. Tom tossed his in from one side of the deck, and Ned from the other. Then, as the eccentric man listened, he heard Tom say:

"I think mine is going to beat yours, Ned!"

"Then you've got another guess coming," declared the young financial man. "Mine's going twice as fast as yours is now, though yours did start off better."

"Bless my beefsteak!" exclaimed Mr. Damon, "what's this, Tom Swift? I thought we came on a treasure-hunting expedition, and here I find you and Ned playing some childish game! I hope you aren't laying any wagers on it!" Mr. Damon did not approve of gambling in any form.

"No, we aren't doing that," laughed Tom, as he dropped another bit of cork into the ocean.

"We are trying to arrive at some valuable scientific facts, Mr. Damon."

"Scientific facts—that childish play?"

"It isn't play," said Tom, turning to remark to Ned: "I think we've settled it. The current has a decided twist to the north."

"Yes," agreed his chum. "You were right, Tom."

"If you don't mind explaining," began Mr. Damon, "I should like to know—"

"We're trying to determine the drift of the ocean currents in this locality," Tom said.

"So we'll know better where to look for the Pandora," added Ned.

"Oh, so you haven't given up the hunt, then?" asked the eccentric man.

"By no means!" exclaimed Tom. "It's this way, Mr. Damon. We went down at as nearly the exact spot where the treasure-ship was sunk as we could determine by means of calculations. She wasn't there, nor could we find her by going around in circles. Then it occurred to me, and to some of the others also, including Ned, that the ocean currents might have shifted the position of the craft after she had sunk. There are powerful currents in the ocean, as you know, the Gulf Stream being one and the Japan Current another. Now there may be smaller ones in these waters that would produce a local effect.

"So Ned and I have been dropping bits of cork of different shapes into the water and watching which way they drifted. Our conclusion is that the currents here have a decided set toward the north."

"And what does that indicate?" asked Mr. Damon.

"That we should have begun our search some distance north of the point where we actually did begin," answered Tom.

"How far north?" the eccentric man wanted to know.

"That's just what we have yet to ascertain," the young inventor replied. "So far our conclusions have been arrived at merely from surface data. Now we've got to go below."

"And play with bits of cork there?" asked Mr. Damon.

"No, we'll have to use something heavier than cork," Tom said. "We'll probably use weights, and see how far they move along the bottom in a given time. But we have established one thing, and I begin to have hopes now that we may locate the Pandora."

The remainder of the day was spent in various ways aboard the submarine, which continued to float idly on the waves.

It was toward evening, when the red, setting sun gave promise of a fair day on the morrow that the submarine's deck lookout approached Tom, and, waiting until he had the attention of the young inventor, reported:

"There is a smudge of smoke dead astern, sir."

"Is there?" exclaimed Tom. "Let me have the glasses."

He took them from the lookout and made a long and careful study of the slight, black smudge which was low down on the horizon.

"A steamer," decided Tom, "and coming on fast. We'll go below!" he added. "Please make ready," he said to the officer in charge.

"What's up, Tom?" asked Ned, as his chum gathered up the papers on which he had been figuring on an improvised table set under an awning on deck.

"Some craft is coming, and I'd just as soon she wouldn't sight us," was the answer.

"You mean she might interfere with our search for the treasure-ship?"

"Not exactly. But she might want to start a search on her own account, and there's no use of giving our presence away, or letting them guess at what might be right conclusions as to the location of the Pandora."

"But, Tom, no one knows of the wreck! At least, no one is supposed to but our party and—"

"Hardley. Exactly!" exclaimed Tom, as he saw his chum about to utter the name.

"And you think he is coming?"

"I shouldn't be a bit surprised. Anyhow, it's just as easy for us to submerge and let them do their own guessing. I was going down soon, anyhow, and another hour won't make any difference. Here, take a look, if you like."

Ned peered through the glasses, but his eyes not being trained in sea interpretation, as were Tom's, he could make out nothing but a black smudge, now larger and darker.

"It might be a cloud for all I can tell," he said, as he handed the binoculars back to Tom.

"Well, it's a steamer all right, and she's under forced draft, too, if I'm any judge. We'll go below before she sights us."

"Perhaps she has already," suggested Ned, as the crew began clearing the submarine's deck.

"No, we lie too low in the water for that. Well, now we can start our underwater observations of current trends."

It did not take long, once she started, for the M.N.1 to go down. Just as the sun sank below the horizon, and while the smudge of smoke was becoming more distinct, the waves closed over the steel deck of the submarine. Half an hour later she was nearly a quarter of a mile below the surface, resting on the bottom of the sea again.

On this trip Tom did not go to any such depths as he did on his former voyage in the Advance. Not that the reconstructed submarine was not capable of it, for she was even stronger than when first built. But the wreck they were seeking did not lie in so great a depth of water, and there was no need of running useless risks.

"Well," remarked Ned, when they came to a stop, "I don't believe any one will find us here."

"Not an ordinary diver, at any rate," Tom agreed. "And after supper I'm going to have another go at the currents."

The meal was served as usual, and a very good one it was, considering the fact that not as many supplies could be carried in the rather limited space of a submarine as may be transported in an ocean liner. Then, as it was still early, Tom and Ned, with the help of some of the officers, got ready for a new series of experiments.

The big searchlight was set aglow, and, going out on the ocean bed in diving suits, Tom and his friends dropped on the sand various weighted objects.

These were made in the shape of the hull of a steamer, and in proportion. Once they were on the sand, an iron rod was thrust into the ocean bed near each object.

"Now," remarked Tom, as they all went into the submarine again, "we'll let them drift until morning. Then we'll make new calculations. I think we'll arrive at some results, too."

"Just what are you aiming to do?" asked Mr. Damon.

"See how far each one of those weighted objects drifts," Tom replied. "We have planted them in different spots on the ocean bed. Some will drift farther than others. Some are large and some are small. By striking an average we may be able to tell about how far from the supposed location of the Pandora we ought to look for her."

The night passed without incident and as calmly and peacefully as though they were all in some deep cave beneath a great mountain. In the morning after breakfast Tom and his friends went outside the submarine again and noted the weighted objects. Some had drifted farther than others. Measurements were carefully taken, and then began a series of intricate calculations.

The distance each object had drifted from the iron bar marker was considered in reference to its size and shape. Also the elapsed time was computed. The results were then compared, an average struck, and then the size and weight of the Pandora, as nearly as they could be ascertained, were figured. The resultant figures were compared, and Tom announced:

"If we are anywhere near right in our conclusions we ought to begin to search for the treasure-ship about four miles from here, in a general northerly direction."

"Do you think she has drifted that far?" asked Ned.

"Fully that," Tom answered. "That is only our starting point— the center of a new series of circles."

A moment later Tom gave the order to rise to the surface.

"Going up?" exclaimed Ned.

"Yes, I want to make some observations to determine our exact nautical position."

"But suppose that other steam—"

"We'll have to take a chance. We can submerge quickly if we have to, and I don't believe she's able to do that."

An observation was taken through the conning tower, however, before the M.N.1 went all the way up, and there was not a sail nor a smudge of smoke on the horizon.

"So far so good," murmured Tom. "Now we'll 'shoot the sun,' and after we submerge we'll begin our search in earnest. I think we are on the right track now."

The observation was made at noon, and then, as nearly as possible, the submarine was moved to a position approximately four miles north of the place where the Pandora was supposed to have foundered.

"Down we go!" exclaimed Tom, and down they went.

The depth gauge showed more than a thousand feet below the surface when the M.N.1 came to rest. This was deeper than Tom had thought to find the wreck, but his craft was able to withstand the pressure. A brief wait, to make sure that everything was in readiness, was followed by the beginning of the new search. In gradually widening circles the craft moved about under water.

If the voyagers had expected to locate at once the treasure-ship, they would have been disappointed. For the first day gave no signs. But Tom had not promised immediate results, and no one gave up hope.

It was shortly after noon on the second day of the search at the new location that, as they were proceeding at rather greater speed than usual, something happened.

Ned had just suggested that he and Tom might go out and try the current-setting experiments again, when suddenly they were both thrown off their feet by a terrific jar and concussion. The M.N.1 seemed to reel back, as if from a great blow.

"Bless my safety razor!" cried Mr. Damon, "what's the matter, Tom?"

"I think we've had a collision!" was the answer. "I must see how badly we are damaged!"

THE TREASURE SHIP

Sudden and forceful had been the underwater collision in which the M.N.1 had participated. Either the lookout, aided though he was by the focused rays of the great searchlight, had failed to notice some obstruction in time to signal to avoid it, or there was an error somewhere else. At any rate the submarine had rammed something—what it was remained to be discovered.

"Bless my shotgun," cried Mr. Damon, "perhaps it was one of those big whales, Ned!"

"It didn't feel like a whale," answered the young financial man.

"And it wasn't!" declared Tom, who was hastening to the engine room. "It was too solid for that."

Following the collision there had been considerable confusion aboard the vessel. But discipline prevailed, and now it was necessary to determine the extent of the damage. This, Tom and his officers and crew proceeded to do.

There were automatic devices in the various control cabins, as well as in the main engine room, which told instantly if a leak had been sprung in any part of the craft. In that serious difficulty automatic pumps, controlled by an electrical device, at once began forcing out the water. Other apparatus rushed a supply of compressed air to the flooded compartment in order to hold out the water if possible. For further security the submarine was divided into different compartments, as are most ships in these days. The puncturing or flooding of one did not necessarily mean the foundering of the craft, or, in the case of a submarine, prevent her rising.

But Tom had sensed that the collision was almost a head-on one, and in that case it was likely that the plates might have started in several sections at once. This he wanted to discover, and take means of safety accordingly.

"How do you make it, Mr. Nelson?" cried the young inventor to the captain in the engine room.

"Only a slight leak in compartment B 2," he answered, as Tom's eyes rapidly scanned the tell-tale gauges. "The pumps and air are taking care of that."

"Good!" cried Tom. "It doesn't seem possible that there isn't more than that, though. We struck a terrible blow."

"Yes, but a glancing one, I think, sir."

"Send for the lookout," ordered Tom. "I can't understand why he didn't see whatever we've hit in time to avoid it."

The lookout came in, very much frightened, it must be admitted. Only by a narrow margin had all escaped death.

"It was impossible to see it, Mr. Swift," he said. "We had a clear course, not a thing in sight. The bottom was white sand, and I could almost count the fishes. All at once there was a big swirl of water that threw our nose around, and before I could signal to slow down or reverse we were right into her."

"Into what?" asked Tom.

"Some sort of wreck, I took it to be. I shoved the wheel hard over as quickly as I could, and we struck only a glancing blow."

"That's good," murmured Tom. "I thought that must have been the explanation. But what's that about a sudden swirl of water?"

"It seemed to me like a change in the current," the lookout answered. "It threw us right over against the wreck."

"I can very easily imagine something like that happening," admitted Tom. "Well, as long as we're not badly damaged I think we'll go outside and take a look. If we hit a wreck—"

"Bless my looking glass!" cried Mr. Damon, "it may be the Pandora, Tom."

"That's too good to be true!" cried Ned. "Anyhow, let's get out and take a look."

Tom first made sure that the slight leak was not likely to increase, and then arrangements were made for himself, Ned, Koku, and some of the others to go outside in the diving suits. Mr. Damon wanted to be of the party, but Tom was afraid to permit him in that depth of water. Mr. Damon, in spite of his jollity, was not as young as he had been.

Shortly after the collision, which had missed being a disaster by a narrow margin, Tom and his companions were outside the submarine, walking on the white, sandy bottom of the sea. Around them was a myriad of fishes, some of large size, but seemingly harmless, as they scudded rapidly away after a glance at the strange creatures who appeared to have come to dispute with them for possession of Father Neptune's element.

Moving more slowly than usual, because of the greater pressure of water at that depth, Tom and the others made their way around the nose of the submarine. And then, in the glow of the big searchlight, they saw the dim outlines of a steamer, partly imbedded in the sand. Her stern was toward the undersea craft that had rammed her, and the name was not so obliterated but what the young inventor could read it.

"The Pandora!" exclaimed Tom, speaking into his helmet telephone transmitter, the others all hearing him. "We've found the treasure-ship at last!"

And so they had. An accident had brought them to the end of their quest, though it is probable they would have found the Pandora anyhow, since they were making careful circles in her vicinity.

"Yes, that's the Pandora," said Ned. "And now the thing to do is to find out if she really has any treasure on board."

"That's what I'm going to do," declared Tom. "But first I want to investigate this queer current. We can't feel it here, but we may if we get out beyond the wreck. We don't want to be swept off our feet."

"Yes, we had better be careful," said one of the officers.

Accordingly they proceeded with caution along the length of the sunken Pandora. And as they neared her bow they all began to feel some powerful force in the current.

"This is far enough!" said Tom. "Don't get out beyond the protection of the hull. I see what it is. The steamer has drifted here from where she was originally sunk. And here two currents meet, forming a very strong one. It was that which threw us off our course. As long as we remain behind the wreck we'll be safe. But beyond her we may be in danger. She's firmly held in the sand, or, at best, is drifting only slightly. She'll be a sort of undersea breakwater for us. And now to see if we can get on board!"

This proved comparatively easy. Several lengths of chain and one iron ladder were over the stern, evidently having been used when the crew abandoned the ship in the storm that destroyed her. By means of these Tom and his companions gained the main deck near the stern.

The Pandora was a typical tramp steamer. She was high in the bows and stern and low amidships, and it was evident that the quarters of the officers and passengers, if any of the latter were carried, were in the stern. Tom was glad to find the vessel thus comparatively easy of access.

She lay on an almost even keel, and all he and his companions had to do was to walk along the deck and enter the cabins. As they did not have to look out for life lines or air hose they could enter, and even go below decks, in comparative safety.

"Well, here's for it," said Tom to the others. "Let's go in.

"Where would the treasure be, if she had any?" asked Ned.

"Captain's cabin or the purser's strong room, I imagine," Tom answered. "Hardley didn't actually see it, but he said those two places were constantly guarded. I'm inclined to think the purser would have charge of the gold. But we'll try both places."

It was easy to learn which had been the commander's cabin. It had the name "Captain" on a brass plate over the door. Tom and Ned entered. The place was in confusion, and confusion not all caused by the ocean currents. A small safe in the room stood with rusted door open, and the contents of the strong box were gone. Drawers and lockers, too, were opened and empty.

"I guess the captain took as much with him as he could when he got into his boat," commented Tom.

"And the gold, too," added Ned, pointing to the empty safe.

"That wouldn't have held two million dollars in gold," Tom retorted. "I believe the purser's cabin is the place to look."

Making sure they were not missing anything in the captain's room, they came out, to find Koku and the others waiting for them on deck.

"Nothing there," Tom reported. "Did any of you locate the purser's strong room?" One of the men pointed to an open door to the left.

"That's it!" exclaimed Tom. "Yes, and there's a safe here big enough to hold gold for all the revolutions in South America," he added. "I guess we're on the right track at last."

It needed but a look to show them that they had at last reached the place of the treasure. The great safe stood open, and piled inside were a number of small boxes, such as are generally used to ship gold in. Ned, from his bank experience, recognized them at once.

"There's the gold!" he exclaimed. "We've found the treasure!"

"They tried to take some of it with them," said one of the submarine officers, pointing to some opened boxes which were floating near the cabin ceiling. They were caught on some projections which had prevented them from being washed out.

"Maybe they looted the whole safe," suggested Tom. "We'd better have a look."

He tried to pull out one of the many boxes set in tiers in the safe, but it was beyond his strength.

"Me do!" murmured Koku.

It was easy for the giant to pry out one of the boxes with his iron bar, and with another blow from his bar he opened the cover.

"Gold!" cried Ned, as he saw a gleam of yellow showing in the glow from his torch. "There's the gold!"

There was a table in the purser's cabin, made fast to the floor so it had not floated away. At a sign from Tom, the giant turned the box bottom side up on this table.

And then a murmur of wonder came from all who saw the result. For aside from the top layer of gold pieces, the box was filled with iron disks cut to the size of twenty-dollar gold pieces. In an instant it was borne to all what this meant.

"A fake!" exclaimed Tom Swift. "If all the boxes are like this there isn't enough gold on the treasure ship to pay the expenses of this trip! Somebody has been fooled! Open another box, Koku!"

THE STEEL BOX

Perhaps the least of all affected by what had taken place was the giant. Gold meant nothing to him. To serve Tom Swift was his whole aim in life. Born in a savage country, he had not acquired an overwhelming desire for wealth.

Consequently he was cool enough as he tore another box from the many that were fitted into the safe. The water had swelled the wood, and it was not easy to get them out.

A pressure of the giant's iron bar broke the sealed lid. On top was the same layer of gold pieces, but when the box was emptied the same trick was discovered. Iron disks made up the remainder of the contents.

"Bilked! That's what I call it! Regularly bilked!" exclaimed one of the divers, an Englishman who had been in Tom's service several years. "Somebody's got the cream of this pudding before we did!"

"I'm inclined to agree with you," said Tom. "Unless it transpires that not all the boxes have been thus camouflaged. We must take time to examine."

Then began a period of hard work. Laboring in relays of divers, every box that had been locked in the purser's safe was brought out on the submerged cabin table, broken open, and the contents examined. The hoax was even worse than indicated at first. For after the front section of boxes had been taken out none of the others remaining contained any gold at all. There were only iron disks.

"Well, Tom, what do you think of it?" asked Ned of his chum, when they had returned to the cabin of the submarine, leaving some members of the crew to complete the examination. For this the diving bell was used, as well as the suits.

"I don't think very much," was the answer. "It looks as though we had been sold."

"Do you think Hardley knew that the gold had been changed to iron—that is, all but a small part of it?"

"No, I don't believe he did," Tom answered. "If he were here I'd warrant he would be as much surprised as we are. He certainly believed the Pandora was a regular treasure-ship."

"Just how much did she really have in gold?" asked Mr. Damon, looking at the double eagles on the table of the M.N.1.

"Well, at a rough guess I'd say ten thousand dollars," Tom answered. "We haven't brought it all out yet, and it's possible they may find a full box in the safe. But, unless there is one, I guess ten or fifteen thousand dollars will cover it."

"And Hardley said two millions!" exclaimed Ned. "Whew, what a difference!"

"Do you think he was in on the change?" asked one of the officers.

"No," replied Tom. "I guess it was like a good many of these filibustering plots. Somebody put up good money to be used to gain control of a country—perhaps for the country's good. But somebody else made the substitution, and the patriots were left. I don't believe Hardley knew this."

"Well, you'll get a little out of it, Tom," Ned remarked.

"Nothing worth while," was the answer. "But I'm not disappointed; that is, very much. Of course I could use the money, but I don't really need it. The trip has been a wonderful experience, and I have learned something I didn't know before. I'm sorry for you, though, Mr. Damon. You invested considerable with Hardley, didn't you?"

"About twenty thousand dollars, Tom. It will be hard to lose it, but I guess I can stand it."

Tom privately made up his mind to see that his old friend did not suffer financially, for the gold discovered on the Pandora, while it was far from the amount hoped for, would almost reimburse Mr. Damon. But the young inventor did not say anything about that just then.

They were looking at the recovered gold and getting ready to store it in some of the boxes that had been brought from the wreck when the divers that had remained on the Pandora to bring the last of the treasure returned through the chamber. Two of them carried a small steel box.

"What's that?" asked Tom, when they had their helmets off.

"Don't know," was the answer. "It was in the purser's safe. Stuck away in the far corner."

"Maybe it has jewels in it!" exclaimed Ned. "If it has—"

At that moment the lookout who had maintained his position in the conning tower called for Tom on the telephone.

"What is it?" asked the young inventor.

"There's some sort of grappling iron, or cable with a hook on it, being lowered from the surface, and it's near the wreck," was the answer. "If it isn't any of your apparatus it may be some other ship having a try for the gold."

"It must be Hardley!" cried Tom. "He's come back with another ship, as he half threatened to do, and, instead of diving for the wreck, which he can't get ordinary men to do in this depth, he's trying to grapple for it. Come on, we'll have a look!"

Ned and Mr. Damon followed Tom to the conning tower. Looking out through the heavy glass windows, while the searchlight illuminated the waters, the young inventor and his friends saw a great grappling iron swaying this way and that through the sea not far from the wreck, and once, indeed, uncomfortably close to their own craft.

"He's struck it uncommonly near," remarked Tom. "I guess it's time for us to be leaving."

"Suppose it's Hardley up above there?" suggested Ned.

"I don't doubt but it is."

"Well, are we going off and leave the wreck—and possibly other gold that may be hidden on her?"

"I wouldn't give ten dollars for the chance of searching for any more gold!" Tom exclaimed. "We'll take this steel box—it may contain something of value. The rest we'll leave to Hardley."

Preparations for rising to the surface were quickly made. Up and up went the M.N.1, leaving the ill-starred Pandora to whatever else fate had in store for her.

Tom's craft broke water with gentle undulations of the waves. The top of the hatch was thrown back, admitting the bright sunshine on those who had been long in the shadow of the underseas. And, as the young inventor and his friends went out on deck, they saw a small steamer riding on the ocean not far away.

One look was enough to tell them it was from this craft that the grappling iron had been let down, and as the submarine drifted nearer the form of Hardley was seen on deck. He was directing operations.

Some one must have called his attention to the M.N.1, for he hurried to the rail of the craft which he had evidently chartered to seek the Pandora, and he exclaimed:

"What are you doing here, Swift?"

"The same thing you are, I believe," coolly answered Tom. "Cleaning up the treasure ship. You might as well save your money though, for we have all the gold there is!"

"Impossible!" cried the now irate man. "You cannot have found the Pandora!"

"That's just what we did, though," answered Tom. "And, for your information, I'll say that we took all the gold we found, though it was considerably less than you stated."

"How dare you?" stormed the adventurer. "I'll have the law on you for this!"

"I guess you forget," replied Tom, "that we parted company at your request and that I told you I was on my own. Finding is keeping. I didn't find what I expected to, and, on the other hand, I got something I didn't look for."

"What do you mean

"The Pandora was rightly named," went on Tom. "If you recall the old story, Pandora had a box of treasures. They all flew out except Hope, which remained in the bottom. Well, most of the gold seems to have flown away, but we found a box on the Pandora. What's in it I don't know yet, as I haven't opened it. Still, if it doesn't contain more than Hope I shall be disappointed."

The face of Hardley showed the rage felt.

"Give me that box! Give me that box!" he cried, shaking his fist at Tom.

"Not today," was the cool answer of the young inventor. "I may let you know what I find in it if you leave your address. Goodbye!"

Tom waved his hand, gave orders to close the hatches and submerge the M.N.1, and a few moments later the sea closed over her, leaving the other vessel to grapple uselessly for the treasure-ship.

"What are you going to do, Tom?" asked Ned of his chum, as they were all gathered in the main cabin half an hour later.

"Head for home as soon as we can. I've had enough of this, and I want to get at something else I have in mind. But first I'm going to see what's in this box."

It required the strength of Koku to open the small steel box, but when it was torn apart, for the combination was impossible to guess at, all that was seen were bundles of papers. The case having been hermetically closed, no water had penetrated it, though it had been submerged a long time.

"What are they?" asked Ned of his chum.

Tom did not answer for a moment. Then having quickly examined the papers, he cried:

"We've struck it!"

"What?" they all wanted to know.

"The very thing Hardley was after. These are the missing papers in the oil-well deal—the papers that prove Barton Keith has a half share in property worth many millions of dollars. It was these papers that Hardley was after. He may have thought he could get the gold, too, but he wanted most these oil shares. Boys, we've found the fortune anyhow, in spite of the fellows who looted the gold boxes!"

There was no doubt about it. There were all the papers—the certificates of shares, the partnership agreement and other documents—to show that Mary's uncle was a rich man. The wreck of the Pandora held a fortune after all.

"How do you account for Hardleys acts?" asked Ned of his chum.

"Well, there are several explanations. I think we may be certain that he knew these papers were aboard the Pandora, for he must have intrusted them to the purser himself when he made a trip on the ship. When she sank he had not time to get them to take with him."

"He either knew then, or found out later, that the vessel carried, or was supposed to carry, a large amount of gold. He may have been honestly mistaken in thinking it was two millions. In any case he was playing safe, for he only promised me half if the treasure was found. He could have claimed this box as his property, and that is probably what he was after from the beginning. He was using me as a cat's paw, so to speak."

"Well, you beat him to it," observed Ned.

"Bless my necktie, I should say so!" agreed Mr. Damon. "Do you think he really expected to find the gold?"

"Either that or the papers," was Tom's answer. "He must have engaged the vessel and the grappling apparatus, and, possibly, a diver, after we set him ashore at St. Thomas. Well, we'll leave him to his own fun."

The M.N.1 made good time back to her home port, nothing except a terrific storm occurring to mark the voyage. And as she submerged when that was on she did not feel it. After greeting his father, Tom lost little time in going to Mary's house with the box of securities and other papers.

"I want you to hand these to your uncle with my compliments," he said. "I've got the Air Scout out in the meadow. We'll go over in that. How is Mr. Keith?"

"Not very well," Mary answered, after she had got over her surprise at seeing Tom. "But this good news will restore him, I think."

And it certainly was a great tonic. Mr. Keith could hardly believe the story that Mary and Tom jointly told him. But at length he grasped the idea that he was a wealthy man again, and he exclaimed:

"Tom Swift, I'm going to share half with you!"

"Oh, no," retorted the young inventor. "I couldn't think of that. If you want to pay part of the expenses of the trip I shan't object to that, as I intend giving the gold I recovered to Mr. Damon. But as for taking any of the oil shares—"

"Then, Mary, you shall take half!" exclaimed Mr. Keith. "I have more money now than I'll ever spend. Mary, half of it is yours, and if you don't let Tom Swift have a say in the spending of it— Say, Mary, have you thanked him yet?" he asked with a twinkle of his eyes. "Well, Uncle Barton, I—I don't know—"

"Then do it now!" cried her uncle. "Tom, if you could have any reward you wanted, what would it be?"

Tom took Mary in his arms and—But I refuse to betray any secrets. Anyhow, some time later when Ned asked his chum if he felt entirely satisfied with the result of his undersea search, the young inventor replied: "I certainly do!"

Tom admitted to his father that a mistake had been made in not installing the gyroscope rudder. There was no excuse for not taking it. Tom declared, as it was small and took up little room, and it might have saved them from what was a close call at one time.

"I'll take it on my next submarine trip," the young inventor promised.

Ned wanted to bring suit against Hardley to recover half the expenses of the trip, but Tom would not consent to it. After all, the value of the oil well property was more than the gold the Pandora was reputed to have carried. No attempt was made to take from Tom the comparatively small amount he had salvaged. Perhaps whoever had put it on board did not want to admit the trick that had been played in filling the boxes with iron disks.

Dixwell Hardley made no further trouble. He could not, for he was so entirely in the wrong. He sold out his shares in the oil property, and a company took possession which gave fair treatment to Mary's uncle.

And this is the end of the story. But the future holds further adventures for Tom Swift which, let it be hoped, he will see fit to order recorded.

Tom Swift among the Fire Fighters
Or Battling with Flames from the Air

TABLE OF CONTENTS:

A Bad Place for a Fire

"Impossible, Ned! It can't be as much as that!"

"Well, you can prove the additions yourself, Tom, on one of the adding machines. I've been over 'em twice, and get the same result each time. There are the figures. They say figures don't lie, though it doesn't follow that the opposite is true, for those who do not stick closely to the truth do, sometimes, figure. But there you have it; your financial statement for the year," and Ned Newton, business manager for Tom Swift, the talented young inventor, shoved a mass of papers across the table to his friend and chum, as well as employer.

"It doesn't seem possible, Ned, that we have made as much as that this past year. And this, as I understand it, doesn't include what was taken from the wreck of the Pandora?"

Tom Swift looked questioningly at Ned Newton, who shook his head in answer.

"You really didn't get anything to speak of out of your undersea search, Tom," replied the young financial manager, "so I didn't include it. But there's enough without that."

"I should say so!" exclaimed Tom. "Whew!" he whistled, "I didn't think I was worth that much."

"Well, you've earned it, every cent, with the inventions of yourself and your father."

"And I might add that we wouldn't have half we earn if it wasn't for the shrewd way you look after us, Ned," said Tom, with a warm smile at his friend. "I appreciate the way you manage our affairs; for, though I have had some pretty good luck with my searchlight, wizard camera, war tank and other contraptions, I never would have been able to save any of the money they brought in if it hadn't been for you."

"Well, that's what I'm here for," remarked Ned modestly.

"I appreciate that," began Tom Swift. "And I want to say, Ned—"

But Tom did not say what he had started to. He broke off suddenly, and seemed to be listening to some sound outside the room of his home where he and his financial and business manager were going over the year's statement and accounting.

Ned, too, in spite of the fact that he had been busy going over figures, adding up long columns, checking statements, and giving the results to Tom, had been aware, in the last five minutes, of an ever-growing tumult in the street. At first it had been no more than the passage along the thoroughfare of an unusual number of pedestrians. Ned had accounted for it at first by the theory that some moving picture theater had finished the first performance and the people were hurrying home.

But after he had finished his financial labors and had handed Tom the first of a series of statements to look over, the young financial expert began to realize that there was no moving picture house near Tom's home. Consequently the passing throngs could not be accounted for in that way.

Yet the tumult of feet grew in the highway outside. Ned had begun to wonder if there had been an attempted burglary, a fight, or something like that, calling for police action, which had gathered an unusual throng that warm, spring evening.

And then had come Tom's interruption of himself when he broke off in the middle of a sentence to listen intently.

"What is it?" asked Ned.

"I thought I heard Rad or Koku moving around out there," murmured Tom. "It may be that my father is not feeling well and wants to speak to me or that some one may have telephoned. I told them not to disturb me while you and I were going over the accounts. But if it is something of importance—"

Again Tom paused, for distinctly now in addition to the ever-increasing sounds in the streets could be heard a shuffling and talking in the hall just outside the door.

"G'wan 'way from heah now!" cried the voice of a colored man.

"It is Rad!" exclaimed Tom, meaning thereby Eradicate Sampson, an aged but faithful colored servant. And then the voice of Rad, as he was most often called, went on with:

"G'wan 'way! I'll tell Massa Tom!"

"Me tell! Big thing! Best for big man tell!" broke in another voice; a deep, booming voice that could only proceed from a powerfully built man.

"Koku!" exclaimed Tom, with a half comical look at Ned. "He and Rad are at it again!"

Koku was a giant, literally, and he had attached himself to Tom when the latter had made one of many perilous trips. So eager were Eradicate and Koku to serve the young inventor that frequently there were more or less good-natured clashes between them to see who would have the honor.

The discussion and scuffle in the hall at length grew so insistent that Tom, fearing the aged colored man might accidentally be hurt by the giant Koku, opened the door. There stood the two, each endeavoring to push away the other that the victor might, it appeared, knock on the door. Of course Rad was no match for Koku, but the giant, mindful of his great strength, was not using all of it.

"Here! what does this mean?" cried Tom, rather more sternly than he really meant. He had to pretend to be stern at times with his old colored helper and the impulsive and powerful giant. "What are you cutting up for outside my door when I told you I must be quiet with Mr. Newton?"

"No can be quiet!" declared the giant. "Too much noise in street—big crowds—much big!"

He spoke an English of his own, did Koku.

"What are the crowds doing?" asked Ned. "I thought we'd been hearing an ever increasing tumult, Tom," he said to the young inventor.

"Big crowds—'um go to see big—"

"Heah! Let me tell Massa Tom!" pleaded Rad. Poor Rad! He was getting old and could not perform the services that once he had so readily and efficiently done. Now he was eager to help Tom in such small measure as carrying him a message. So it was with a feeling of sadness that Tom heard the old man say again, pleadingly:

"Let me tell him, Koku! I know all 'bout it! Let me tell Massa Tom whut it am, an'—"

"Well, go ahead and tell me!" burst out Tom, with a good-natured laugh. "Don't keep me in suspense. If there's anything going on—"

He did not finish the sentence. It was evident that something of moment was going on, for the crowds in the street were now running instead of walking, and voices could be heard calling back and forth such exclamations as:

"Where is it?"

"Must be a big one

"And with this wind it'll be worse!"

Tom glanced at Ned and then at the two servants.

"Has anything happened?" asked the young inventor.

"Dey's a big fire, Massa Tom!" exploded Rad.

"Heap big blaze!" added Koku.

At the same time, out in the street high and clear, the cry rang out: "Fire! Fire!"

"Is it any of our buildings?" exclaimed Tom, in his excitement catching hold of the giant's arm.

"No, it's quite a way off, on de odder side of town," answered the colored man. "But we t'ought we'd better come an' tell yo', an'—"

"Yes! Yes! I'm glad you did, Rad. It was perfectly right for you to tell me! I wish you'd done it sooner, though! Come on, Ned! Let's go to the blaze! We can finish looking over the figures another time. Is my father all right, Rad?"

"Yes, suh, Massa Tom, he's done sleepin' good."

"Then don't disturb him. Mr. Newton and I will go to the fire. I'm glad it isn't here," and Tom looked from a side window out on many shops that were not a great distance from the house; shops where he and his father had perfected many inventions.

The buildings had grown up around the old Swift homestead, which, now that so much industry surrounded it, was not the most pleasant place to live in. Tom and his father only made this their stopping place in winter. In the summer they dwelt in a quiet cottage far removed from the scenes of their industry.

"We'll take the electric runabout, Ned," remarked Tom, as he caught up a hat from the rack, an example followed by his friend. Together the young inventor and the financial manager hurried out to the garage, where Tom soon had in operation a small electric automobile, that, more than once, had proved its claim to being the "speediest car on the road."

As they turned out of the driveway into the street they became aware of great crowds making their way toward a glow of sinister red light showing in the eastern sky.

"Some blaze!" exclaimed Tom, as he turned on more power.

"You said it!" ejaculated Ned. "Must be a general alarm," he added, as they caught the sound from the next street of additional apparatus hurrying to the fire.

"Well, I'm glad it isn't on our side of town," remarked Tom, as he looked back at the peaceful gloom surrounding and covering his own home and work buildings.

"Where do you reckon it is?" asked Ned, as they sped onward.

"Hard to say," remarked the young inventor, as he steered to one side to pass a powerful imported automobile which, however, did not have the speed of the electric runabout. "A fire at night is always deceiving as to direction. But we can locate it when we get to the top of the hill."

Shopton, the suburb of the town where Tom lived, was named so because of the many shops that had been erected by the industry of the young inventor and his father. In fact the town was named Shopton though of late there had been an effort to change the name of the strictly residential section, which lay over the hill toward the river.

Tom's car shot up the slope with scarcely any slackening of speed, and, as he passed a group of men and boys running onward, Tom shouted:

"Where is it?"

"The fireworks factory!" was the answer.

"Fireworks factory!" cried Ned. "Bad place for a fire!"

"I should say so!" exclaimed Tom.

The chums had become gradually aware of the gale that was blowing, and, as they reached the summit of the hill and caught sight of the burning factory, they saw the flames being swept far out from it and toward a collection of houses on the other side of a vacant lot that separated the fireworks industrial plant from the dwellings. As Tom Swift glimpsed the fire, noted its proportions and the fierceness of the flames, and saw which way the wind was blowing them, he turned on the power to the utmost.

"What are you doing, Tom?" yelled Ned.

"I'm going down there!" cried Tom. "That place is likely to explode any minute!"

"Then why go closer?" gasped Ned, for his breath was almost taken away by the speed of the car, and he had to hold his hat to keep it from blowing away. "Why don't you play safe?"

"Don't you understand?" shouted Tom in his chum's ear. "The wind is blowing the fire right toward those houses! Mary Nestor lives in one of them!"

"Oh—Mary Nestor!" exclaimed Ned. Then he understood—Mary and Tom were engaged to be married.

"They may be all right," Tom went on. "I can't be sure from this distance. Or they may be in danger. It's a bad fire and—"

His voice was blotted out in the roar of an explosion which seemed to hurl back the electric runabout and bring it to a momentary stop.

No Use of Living!

Only momentarily was Tom Swift halted in his progress toward the scene of the blaze in the fireworks factory. To him, and to the chum who sat beside him on the seat of the electric runabout, it appeared that the blast had actually stopped the progress of the car. But perhaps that was more their imagination than anything else, for the machine swept on down the hill, at the foot of which was the conflagration.

"That was a bad one, Ned!" gasped Tom, as he turned to one side to pass an engine on its way to the scene of excitement.

"I should say so! Must have been somebody hurt in that blow-up!"

"I only hope it wasn't Mary or her folks!" murmured Tom. "The wind is sweeping the fire right that way!"

"What are you going to do, Tom?" yelled his chum, as the business manager saw the young inventor heading directly for the blaze. "What's the idea?"

"To rescue Mary, if she's in danger!"

"I'm with you!" was Ned's quick response. "But you can't go any closer. The police are stretching the fire lines!"

"I guess they'll let me through!" said Tom grimly.

He slowed his car as he approached a place where an officer was driving back the throng that sought to come closer to the blaze.

"Git back! Git back, I tell you!" stormed the policeman, pushing against the packed bodies of men and boys. "There'll be another blow-up in a minute or two, and a lot more of you killed!"

"Are there any killed?" asked Tom, stopping the car near the officer.

"I guess so—yes. And some of the houses are catching. Git back now! You, too, with that car! You'll have to back up!"

"I've got to go through!" replied Tom, with tightening lips. "I've got to go through, Cassidy!" He knew the officer, and the latter now seemed, for the first time, to recognize the young inventor.

"Oh, it's you, is it, Mr. Swift?" he exclaimed. "Well, go ahead. But be careful. 'Tis dangerous there—very dangerous, an'—"

His voice was lost in the roar of another explosion, not as loud or severe as the first, but more plainly felt by Tom and Ned, for they were nearer to it.

"Now will you git back!" cried Policeman Cassidy, and the crowd did, without further urging.

Tom started the runabout forward again.

"We've got to rescue Mary!" he said to Ned, who nodded.

In another moment the two young men were lost to sight in a swirl of smoke that swept across the street. And while they are thus temporarily hidden may not this opportunity be taken of telling new readers something of the hero of this story?

The young inventor was introduced in the first volume of this series, called "Tom Swift and his Motor Cycle." It was Tom's first venture into the realms of invention, after he had purchased from Mr. Wakefield Damon a speedy machine that tried to climb a tree with that excitable gentleman.

Tom, with the help of his father, an inventor of note, rebuilt the motor cycle adding many improvements, and it served Tom in good stead more than once.

From then on the career of Tom Swift was steadily onward and upward. One new invention led to another from his second venture, a motor boat, through an airship and other marvels, and eventually to a submarine. In each of these vehicles of motion and travel Tom and his friends, Ned Newton and Mr. Damon, had many adventures, detailed in the respective volumes.

His venture in proceeding to save Mary Nestor from possible danger in the blaze of the fireworks factory was not the first time Tom had rendered service to the Nestor family. There was that occasion on which he had sent his wireless message from Earthquake Island, as related in an earlier volume.

Space forbids the detailing of all that had happened to the young inventor up to the time of the opening of this story. Sufficient to say that Tom's latest achievement had been the recovery of treasure from the depths of the ocean.

Tom Swift's activities in connection with his inventions had become so numerous that the Swift Construction Company, of which Ned Newton was financial manager and Mr. Damon one of the directors, had been formed. And when the rumor came that there was a chance to salvage some of the untold wealth at the bottom of the sea, Tom was interested, as were his friends.

It was decided to search for the wreck of the Pandora, sunk in the West Indies, and one of Tom's latest submarine craft was utilized for this purpose.

Not to go into all the details, which are given in the last volume of this series, entitled "Tom Swift and His Undersea Search," suffice it to say that the venture was begun. Matters were complicated owing to the fact that Mary Nestor's uncle, Barton Keith, was in trouble over the loss of valuable papers proving his title to some oil lands. Mary mentioned that a person, Dixwell Hardley, was the man who, it was supposed, was trying to defraud her relative. And the complications may be imagined when it is said that this same Hardley was the man who had interested Tom in the undersea search for the riches of the Pandora.

Tom had been at home some time now, and it was while going over his accounts with Ned, and, incidentally, planning new activities, that the cry of fire broke in on them.

"Whew, Tom, some heat there!" gasped Ned, lowering his arm from his face, an action which had been necessitated by Tom's daring in driving the car close to the blazing fireworks factory.

"I should say so!" agreed Tom. "I can almost smell the rubber of my tires burning. But we're out of the worst of it."

"Lucky she didn't take the notion to blow up as we were passing," grimly commented Ned. "Where are you aiming for now?"

"Mary's house. It's just beyond here. But we can't see it on account of the smoke."

A few seconds later they had passed through the black pall that was slashed here and there with red slivers of flame, and, coming to a more open space, Ned and Tom cleared their eyes of smoke.

"I guess there's no immediate danger," remarked Tom, as he saw that the home of Mary Nestor and the houses near her residence were, for the time being, out of the path of the flames. The explosion had blown down part of the blazing factory nearest the residential section, and the flames had less to feed on.

But the conflagration was still a fierce one. Not half the big factory was yet consumed, and every now and then there would sound dull, booming reports, causing nervous screams from the women who were out in front of their homes, while the men would crouch down as though fearing a shower of fiery embers.

"Oh, Tom, I'm so glad you're here!" cried Mary, as the runabout drew up in front of her home. "Do you think it will be much worse?" and she clutched his arm, as he got down to speak to her.

"I think the worst is over, as far as you people here are concerned," the young inventor replied. "The wind has shifted a bit."

"And there are several engines near us, Tom," said Mr. Nestor, coming forward. "The firemen tell me they will play streams of water on the roofs and outsides of our houses if the flames start this way again."

"That ought to do the trick," said Tom, with a show of confidence. "Anybody hurt around here?" he asked. "One of the policeman said he heard several were killed."

"They may have been—in the factory," said Mr. Nestor. "Of course if the fire and explosions had taken place in the daytime the loss of life would have been great. But most of the workers had left some time before the blaze was discovered. There are a few men on a night shift, though, and I shouldn't be surprised but what some of them had suffered."

"Too bad!" murmured the young inventor. "You're not worried about your home, are you, Mrs. Nestor?" he asked of Mary's mother.

"Oh, Tom, I certainly am!" she exclaimed. "I wanted to bring out our things, but Mr. Nestor said it wouldn't be of any use."

"Neither it would, if we've got to burn, but I don't believe we have—now," said her husband. "That last explosion and the shift of the wind saved us. I appreciate your coming over, Tom," he went on. "We might have needed your help. It's queer there isn't some better, or more effective, way of fighting a fire than just pouring on a comparatively insignificant bit of water," he added, as, from what was now a safe distance, they watched the firemen using many lines of hose.

"They do have chemical extinguishers," said Ned.

"Yes, for little baby blazes that have just started," went on Mr. Nestor. "But in all the progress of science there has not been much advance in fighting fires. We still do as they did a hundred years ago—squirt water on it, and mighty little of it compared to the blaze. It would take a week to put this fire out by the water they are using if it were not for the fact that the blaze eats itself up and has nothing more to feed on."

"We'll have to get Tom to invent a new way of fighting fire," remarked Ned.

The young inventor was about to reply when several firemen, equipped with smoke helmets which they adjusted as they ran, came running down the street.

"What's the matter?" asked Tom of one whom he knew.

"Some men are trapped in a small shed back of the factory," was the answer. "We just heard of it, and we're going in after them. Oh! Oh—my—my heart!" he gasped, and he sank to the sidewalk. Evidently he was either overcome by the smoke and poisonous gases or by his exertions.

Tom grasped the situation instantly. Taking the smoke helmet from the exhausted fire-fighter, the young inventor shouted:

"I'll fill your place! See if you can grab a hat, Ned, and come on!"

One of the other firemen had two helmets, and he offered Ned one. Pausing only long enough to see that Mr. Nestor and some others were looking after the exhausted "smoke-eater," Ned raced on after Tom. The two young men, following the firemen, made their way around the end of the factory to the smoke-filled yard in the rear. But for the helmets, which were like the gas masks of the Great War, they would not have been able to live.

One of the firemen pointed through the luridly-lighted smoke to a small structure near the main building. This was beginning to burn. With quick blows of an axe the door was hewed down, and the rescue party, including Tom and Ned, made its way inside. In the light from the blaze, as it filtered through the windows, it could be seen that a man lay in a huddled heap on the floor.

By motions the leader of the rescue squad made it clear that the man was to be carried out, and Tom helped with this while Ned, using an axe, cleared away some debris to enable the door to be opened fully so the men could pass out carrying their burden.

The man was taken to the Nestor yard and stretched out on the grass. Word was relayed to one of the ambulance doctors who were on the scene attending to several injured firemen, and in a short time the man, who, it appeared, had been overcome by smoke, was revived.

"Well, that was a narrow squeak for you," said one of the firemen, glad to breathe without a mask on.

"Yes, it was touch and go," remarked the young doctor, who had used heroic measures to bring the man back from the brink of the grave. "But you'll live now, all right."

The revived man looked dully about him. He seemed somewhat bewildered.

"Of what use to live?" he murmured. "You might as well have let me die in there. Life isn't worth living now," and he sank into a stupor, while Tom and the others looked wonderingly at one another.

Tom's New Idea

"What's the matter with him, Doctor?" asked Tom in a low voice of the young physician who had been working over the man. "Do you think he is worse hurt than appears? Is he dying, and is his mind wandering?"

"I don't believe so," answered the doctor. "At least I don't believe that he is dying, though his mind may be wandering. He isn't injured—at least not outwardly. Just temporarily overcome by smoke is what it looks like to me. But of course I haven't made a thorough examination."

"Hadn't we better get him into the house, Doctor?" asked Mr. Nestor, who stood with Tom, Ned and a group of men and boys about the inert form of the man lying on the grass. The rescued one was again seemingly unconscious.

"The best medicine he can have is fresh air, the doctor replied. "He's better off out here than in the house. Though if he doesn't revive presently I will send him to the hospital."

The man did not appear to be so badly off but what he could hear, and at these words he opened his eyes again.

"I don't want to go to the hospital," he murmured. "I'll be all right presently, and can go home, though—Oh, well, what's the use?" he asked wearily, as though he had given up some fight. "I've lost everything."

"Well, you've got a deal of life left in you yet; and that's more than you could say of some who have come out of smaller fires than this," said one of the firemen who, with Tom, had carried the man out of the shed. "Come on, we'd better be getting back," he said to his companion. "The worst of it is over, but there'll be plenty to do yet."

"You said it!" commented the other grimly.

They went out of the Nestor yard, many of the crowd that had gathered during the rescue following. The doctor administered some more stimulant in the shape of aromatic spirits of ammonia to the man, who, after his momentary revival, had again lapsed into a state of stupor.

"Who is he?" asked Tom, as the physician knelt down beside the silent form.

"I don't know," said Mr. Nestor. "I know quite a number connected with the fireworks factory, but this man is a stranger to me."

"I've seen him going into the main offices several times," remarked Mary, who was standing beside Tom. "He seemed to be one of the company officers."

"I don't believe so, Mary," stated her father. "I know most of the fireworks company officials, and I'm sure this man is not one of them. Poor fellow! He seems to be in a bad way."

"Mentally, as well as physically," put in Ned. "He acted as if sorry that we had saved his life."

"Too bad," murmured Mary, and then a policeman, who had just come into the yard to get the facts for his report, looked at the figure lying on the grass, and said:

"I know him."

"You do?" cried Tom. "Who is he?"

"Name's Baxter, Josephus Baxter. He's a chemist, and he works in the fireworks factory here. Not as one of the hands, but in the experiment laboratory. I've seen him there late at night lots of times. That's how I got acquainted with him. He was going in around two o'clock one morning, and I stopped him, thinking he was a thief. He proved his identity, and I've passed the time of day with him many a time since"

"Where does he live?" asked Mr. Nestor.

"Down on Clay Street," and the officer mentioned the number. "He lives all alone, so he told me. He's some sort of an inventor, I guess. At least I judged so by his talk. Do you want an ambulance, Doctor?" he asked the physician.

"No, I think he's coming around all right," was the answer. "If we had an auto we could send him home."

"I'll take him in the runabout," eagerly offered Tom. "But if he lives all alone will it be safe to leave him in his house?"

"He ought to be looked after, I suppose," the doctor stated. "He'll be all right in a day or so if no complications set in, but he'll be weak for a while and need attention."

"Then I'll take him home with me!" announced Tom. "We have plenty of room, and Mrs. Baggert will feel right at home with some one to nurse. Bring the runabout here, will you please, Ned?"

As Ned darted off to run up the machine, the man opened his eyes again. For a moment he did not seem to know where he was or what had happened. Then, as he saw the lurid light of the flames which were now dying away and realized his position, he sighed heavily and murmured:

"It's all over!"

"Oh, no, it isn't!" cheerfully exclaimed the doctor. "You will be all right in a few days."

"Myself, yes, maybe," said the man bitterly, and he managed to rise to his feet. "But what of my future? It is all gone! The work of years is lost."

"Burned in the fire?" asked Tom, wondering whether the man was a major stockholder in the company. "Didn't you have any insurance? Though I suppose you couldn't get much on a fireworks plant," he added, for he knew something of insurance matters in connection with his own business.

"Oh, it isn't the fire—that is directly," said the man, in the same bitter tones. "I've lost everything! The scoundrels stole them! And I—Oh, never mind!" he cried. "What's the use of talking? I'm down and out! I might just as well have died in the fire!"

Tom was about to make some remark, but the doctor motioned to him to refrain, and then Ned came up with the runabout. At first Josephus Baxter, which was the name of the man who had been rescued, made some objections to going to Tom's home. But when it was pointed out that he might lapse into a stupor again from the effects of the smoke poisons, in which event he would have no one to minister to him at his lonely home, he consented to go to the residence of the young inventor.

"Though if I do lapse into unconsciousness you might as well let me keep on sleeping until the end," said Mr. Baxter bitterly to Tom and Ned, as they drove away from the scene of the fire with him.

"Oh, you'll feel better in the morning," cheerfully declared Ned.

The man did not answer, and the two chums did not feel much like talking, for they were worn out and weary from their exertions at the fire. The factory had been pretty well consumed, though by strenuous labors the blaze had not extended to adjoining structures. The home of Mary Nestor was saved, and for this Tom Swift was thankful.

Mrs. Baggert, the Swift's housekeeper, was indeed glad to have some one to "fuss over," as Tom put it. She prepared a bed for Mr. Baxter, and in this the weary and ill man sank with a sigh of relief.

"Can I do anything for you?" asked Tom, as he was about to go out and close the door.

"No—thank you," was the halting reply. "I guess nothing can be done. Field and Melling have me where they want me now—down and out."

"Do you mean Amos Field and Jason Melling of the fireworks firm?" asked Tom, for the names were familiar to him in a business way.

"Yes, the—the scoundrels!" exclaimed Mr. Baxter, and from his voice Tom judged that he was growing stronger. "They pretended to be my friends, giving me a shop in which to work and experiment, and when the time came they took my secret formulae. I believe that is what they started the fire for—to conceal their crime!"

"You don't mean that!" cried Tom. "Deliberately to start a fire in a factory where there was powder and other explosives! That would be a terrible crime!"

"Field and Melling are capable of just such crimes as that!" said Josephus Baxter, bitterly. "If they took my formulae they wouldn't stop at arson."

"Were your formulae for the manufacture of fireworks?" asked Tom.

"Not altogether," was the reply. "I had several formulae for valuable chemical combinations. They could be used in fireworks, and that is why I could use the laboratory here. But the main use of my discoveries is in the dye industry. I would have been a millionaire soon, with the rise of the American dye industry following the shutting out of the Germans after the war. But now, with my secret formulae gone, I am no better than a beggar!"

"Perhaps it will not be as bad as you think," said Tom, recognizing the fact that Mr. Baxter was in a nervous and excited state. "Matters may look brighter in the morning."

"I don't see how they can," was the grim answer. "However, I appreciate all that you have done for me. But I fear my case is hopeless."

"I'll see you again in the morning," Tom said, trying to infuse some cheerfulness into his voice.

He found Ned waiting for him when he came downstairs.

"How is he?" asked the young business manager.

"In rather a bad way—mentally, at least," and Tom told of the lost formulae. "Do you know, Ned," he went on, "I have an idea!"

"You generally do have—lots of 'em!" Ned rejoined.

"But this is a new one," went on Tom. "You saw what trouble they had this evening to get a stream of water to the top stories of that factory, didn't you?"

"Yes, the pressure here isn't what it ought to be," Ned agreed. "And some of our engines are old-timers."

"Why is it necessary always to fight a fire with water?" Tom continued. "There are plenty of chemicals that will put out a fire much quicker than water."

"Of course," Ned answered. "There are plenty of chemical fire extinguishers on the market, too, Tom. If your idea is to invent a new hand grenade, stay off it! A lot of money has been lost that way."

"I wasn't thinking of a hand grenade," said Tom, as he drew some sheets of paper across the table to him. "My idea is on a bigger scale. There's no reason, Ned, why a big fire in a tall building, like a sky-scraper, shouldn't be fought from above, as well as from below. Now if I had the right sort of chemicals I could—"

Tom paused in a listening attitude. There was the rush of feet and a voice cried:

"I'll get them! I'll get the scoundrels!"

AN EXPERIMENT

"That can't be Koku and Rad in one of their periodic squabbles, can it?" asked Ned.

"No. It's probably Mr. Baxter," Tom answered. "The doctor said he might get violent once or twice, until the effects of his shock wore off. There is some quieting medicine I can give him. I'll run up."

"Guess I'd better go along," remarked Ned. "Sounds as if you'd need help."

And it did appear so, for again the frenzied shouts sounded:

"I'll get 'em! I'll get the scoundrels who stole my secret formulae that I worked over so many years! Come back now! Don't put the match near the powder!"

Tom and Ned hurried to the room where the unfortunate chemist had been put to bed, to find him out in the hall, wrapped in a bedquilt, and with Mrs. Baggert vainly trying to quiet him. Mr. Baxter stared at Tom and Ned without seeing them, for he was in a delirium of fever.

"Have you my formulae?" he asked. "I want them back!"

"You shall have them in the morning," replied Tom soothingly. "Lie down, and I'll bring them to you in the morning. And drink this," he added, holding out a glass of soothing mixture which the doctor had ordered in case the patient should become violent.

Josephus Baxter glared about with wild eyes, but between them Tom and Mrs. Baggert managed to get him to drink the mixture.

"Bah! It's as bad as some of my chemicals!" spluttered the chemist, as he handed back the glass. "You are sure you'll have my formulae in the morning?" he asked, as he turned to go back to his room.

"I'll do my best," declared Tom cheerfully. "Now please lie down."

Which, after some urging, Mr. Baxter consented to do. Eradicate wanted to lie down in the hall outside the excited chemist's door to guard against his emerging again, but Tom decided on Koku. The giant, though not as intelligent as the colored man, was more efficient in an emergency because of his great strength. Eradicate was getting old, and there was a pathetic droop to his figure as he shuffled off when Koku superseded him.

"Ah done guess Ah ain't wanted much mo'," muttered Rad sadly.

"Oh, yes, you are!" cried Tom, as, the excitement over, he walked downstairs with Ned. "I'm going to start something new, Rad, and I'll need your help."

"Will yo', really, Massa Tom?" exclaimed faithful Rad, his face lighting up. "Dat's good! Is yo' goin' off after mo' diamonds, or up to de caves of ice?"

"Not quite that," answered the young inventor, recalling the stirring experiences that had fallen to him when on those voyages. "I'm going to work around home, Rad, and I'll need your help."

"Anyt'ing yo' wants, Massa Tom! Anyt'ing yo' wants!" offered the now delighted Rad, and he went to bed much happier.

"Well, to resume where we left off," began Ned, when he and Tom were once more by themselves, "what's the game?"

"Oh, I don't know that it's much of a game," was the answer. "But I just have an idea that a big fire in a towering building can be fought from above with chemicals, as well as from the ground with streams of water."

"Well, I guess it could be," Ned agreed. "But how are you going to get your chemicals in at the top? Shoot 'em up through a hose? If you do that you'll need a special kind of hose, for the chemicals will rot anything like rubber or canvas."

"I wasn't thinking of a hose," returned Tom. "What then?" asked the young financial manager.

"An airship!" Tom exclaimed with such sudden energy that Ned started. "It just came to me!" explained the youthful inventor. "I was wondering how we could get the chemicals in from the top, and an airship is the solution. I can sail over the burning building and drop the chemicals down. That will douse the blaze if my plans go right."

Ned was silent a moment, considering Tom's daring plan and project. Then, as it became clearer, the young banker cried:

"Blamed if I don't think that's just the thing, Tom! It ought to work, and, if it does, it will save a lot of lives, to say nothing of property! A fire in a sky-scraper ought to be fought from above. Then the extinguisher element, whether chemicals or water, could be dropped where they'd do the most good. As it is now, with water, a lot of it is wasted. Some of it never reaches the heart of the fire, being splashed on the outside of the building. A lot more turns to steam before it hits the flames, and only a small percentage is really effective."

"That's my notion," Tom said.

"Then go ahead and do it!" urged his friend. "You have my permission!"

"Thanks," commented Tom dryly. "But there are several things to be worked out before we can start. I've got to devise some scheme for carrying a sufficient quantity of chemicals, and invent some way of releasing them from an airship over the blaze. But that last part ought to be easy, for I think I can alter my warfare bomb-dropping attachment to serve the purpose.

"What I really need, however, is some new chemical combination that will quickly put a really big blaze out of business. There are any number of these chemicals, but most of them depend on the production of carbon dioxide. This is the product of some solution of a carbonate and sulphuric acid, and I suppose, eventually, I'll work out something on that order. But I hope I may get something better."

"You haven't delved much into chemistry, have you?"

"No. And I wish now that I had. I see my limitations and realize my weakness. But I can brush up a little on my chemistry. As for the mechanical part, that of dropping the extinguisher on the blaze, I'm not worrying over that end."

"No," agreed Ned. "You have enough types of airships to be able to select just the best one for the purpose. But, say, Tom!" he suddenly cried, "why not ask him to help you?"

"Who?"

"Mr. Baxter. He's a chemist. And though he says his formulae are about dyes and fireworks, maybe he can put you in the way of inventing a chemical solution that will be death to fires."

"He might," Tom agreed. "But I think he'll be out of business for some time. This shock—being overcome by smoke and his secret formulae having been stolen—seem to have affected his mind. I don't know that I could depend on him."

"It's worth trying," declared Ned. "What do you suppose he means, Tom, saying that Field and Melling stole his formulae?"

"Haven't the least idea. I only know those fireworks firm members slightly, if at all. I'm not sure I'd recognize them if I met them. But they are reputed to be wealthy, and I hardly think they would stoop to stealing some inventor's formulae.

"We inventors are a suspicious lot, Ned, as you probably have found out," he added with a smile. "We imagine the rest of the world is out to cheat us, and I presume Josephus Baxter is no exception. Still, there may be some truth in his story. I'll give him all the help I can. But I'm going into the aerial fire-fighting game. I've been waiting for something new, and this may be it."

"You may count on me!" declared Ned. "And now, unless you're going to sit up all night and start studying chemistry, you'd better come to bed."

"That's right. Tomorrow is another day. I hope Mr. Baxter gets some rest. Sleep will improve him a lot, the doctor said."

"I know one friend of yours who will be glad to know that you are going to start something," remarked Ned, as he and Tom started for their rooms, for the young manager was staying with his friend for the night.

"Who?" Tom wanted to know.

"Mr. Wakefield Damon," was the answer. "He hasn't been over lately, Tom."

"No, he's been off on a little trip, blessing everything from his baggage check to his suspender buttons," laughed the young inventor, as he recalled his eccentric acquaintance. "I shall be glad to see him again."

"He'll be right over as soon as he learns what's in the wind," predicted Ned.

The hopes that Mr. Baxter would be greatly improved in the morning were doomed to disappointment. He was in no actual danger, the doctor said, but his recovery from the effects of the smoke he had breathed was not as rapid as desired or hoped for.

"He's suffering from some shock," said the physician, "and his mental condition is against him. He ought to be kept quiet, and if you can't have him here, Mr. Swift, I can arrange to have him sent to a hospital."

"I wouldn't dream of it!" Tom exclaimed. "Let him stay here by all means. We have plenty of room, and Mrs. Baggert has been wishing for some one to nurse. Now she has him."

So it was arranged that the chemist should remain at the Swift home, and he gave a languid assent when they spoke to him of the matter. He really was much more ill than seemed at first.

But as everything possible had been done, Tom decided to go ahead with the new idea that had come to him—that of inventing an aerial chemical fire-fighting machine.

"And if we get a chance, Ned, we'll try to get back those secret formulae Mr. Baxter claims to have lost," Tom declared. "I have heard some stories about that fireworks firm, which make me believe there may be something in Baxter's story."

"All right, Tom, I'm with you any time you need me," Ned promised.

The young inventor lost little time in beginning his operations. As he had said, the chief need was a fire extinguishing chemical solution or powder. Tom resolved to try the solution first, as it was easier to make. With this end in view he proceeded to delve into old and new chemistry books. He also sought the advice of his father.

And one day, when Ned called, Tom electrified his chum with the exclamation:

"Well, I'm going to give it a try!"

"What?"

"My aerial chemical fire-fighting apparatus. Of course I only have the chemical yet. I haven't worked on the carrying apparatus nor decided how I will attach it to an airship. But I'm going up now with some of my new solution and drop it on a blaze from above."

"Where are you going to get the fire?" asked Ned. "You can't have a sky-scraper blaze made to order, you know."

"No, but as this is only an experiment," Tom said, "a big bonfire will answer the purpose. I'm having Koku and Rad make one now down in our big meadow. As soon as it gets hot enough and fierce enough, I'll sail over it in my small machine, drop the extinguisher on it, and see what happens. Want to come?"

"Sure thing!" cried Ned. "And I hope the experiment is a success!"

"Thanks," murmured Tom. "I'm about ready to start. All I have to do is to take this tank up with me," and he pointed to one containing his new mixture. "Of course the arrangement for dumping it out of the aircraft is very crude," Tom said. "But I can work on that later."

Ned and he were busy putting the can of Tom's new chemical extinguisher in the airship when the door of the hangar was suddenly opened and a very much excited man entered crying:

"Fire! Fire! Bless my kitchen sink, your meadow's on fire, Tom Swift! It's blazing high! Fire! Fire!"

The Explosion

Tom and Ned were so startled by the entrance of the excited man with his cry of "Fire!" that the young inventor nearly dropped the tank of liquid extinguisher he was helping to hoist into the aeroplane. Then, as he caught sight of his visitor, Tom exclaimed:

"Hello, Mr. Damon! We were wondering whether you'd be along to witness our first experiment."

"Experiment, Tom Swift! Experiment! Bless my Latin grammar! but you'd much better be calling out the fire department to play on that blaze down in your meadow. What is it—your barns or one of your new shops?"

"Neither one, Mr. Damon," laughed Ned. "It's only a blaze that Koku and Rad started."

"And the fire department is here," added Tom.

"Where?" inquired the eccentric man.

"Here," and Tom pointed to his airship—one of the smaller craft—into which the tank of chemicals had been hoisted.

"Oh!" exclaimed Mr. Damon. "Something new, eh, Tom?" His eyes glistened.

"Yes. Fighting fires from the air. I got the idea after the fireworks factory went up in smoke. Will you come along? There's plenty of room."

"I believe I will," assented Mr. Damon. It was not the first time, by any means, that he had gone aloft with Tom. "I happened to be coming over in my auto," he went on to explain, "when I happened to see the fire down in the meadow. I was afraid you didn't know about it."

"Oh, yes," replied Tom. "I had Rad and Koku light a big pile of packing boxes, to represent, as nearly as possible, on a small scale, a burning building. I plan now to sail over it and drop the tins of chemicals. They are arranged to burst as they fall into the blaze, and I hope the carbon dioxide set loose will blanket out the fire."

"Sounds interesting," commented Mr. Damon. "I'll go along."

The airship was wheeled out of the hangar and was soon ready for the flight. A big cloud of black vapor down in the meadow told Tom and Ned that Koku and Eradicate had done their work well. The giant and the colored man had poured oil over the wood to make a fierce blaze that would give Tom's new chemical combination a severe test.

A mechanic turned the propeller of the airship until there was an accumulation of gas in the different cylinders. Then he stepped back while Tom threw on the switch. This was not one of the self-starting types, of which Tom possessed one or two.

"Contact!" cried Tom sharply, and the man stepped forward to give the big blades a final turn that would start the motor. There was a muffled roar and then a steady staccato blending of explosions. Tom raced the motor while his men held the machine in place, and then, satisfied that all was well, the young inventor gave the word, and the craft raced over the ground, to soar aloft a little later.

Tom, Ned and Mr. Damon could look down to the meadow where the bonfire was blazing. A crowd had collected, but the heat of the blaze kept them at a good distance. Then, as many of the throng caught sight of the airship overhead, there was a new interest for them.

Tom had told Ned and Mr. Damon, before the trio had entered the machine, what he wanted them to do. This was to toss the chemicals overboard at the proper time. Of course in his perfected apparatus Tom hoped to have a device by which he could drop the fire extinguishing elements by a mere pressure of his finger or foot, as bombs were released from aircraft during the war. But this would serve for the time being.

Nearer and nearer the blaze the airship approached until it was almost above it. Tom had had some experience in bomb-dropping, and knew when to give the signal.

At last the signal came. Mr. Damon and Ned heaved over the side the metal containers of the powerful chemicals.

Down they went, unerring as an arrow, though on a slant, caused by the impetus given them by the speed of the airship.

Tom and his friends leaned over the side of the machine to watch the effect. They could see the chemicals strike the blaze, and it was evident from the manner in which the fire died down that the containers had broken, as Tom intended they should to scatter their contents.

"Hurray!" cried Ned, forgetting that he could not be heard, for no head telephones were used on this occasion and the roar of the motor would drown any human voice. "It's working, Tom!"

Truly the effect of the chemicals was seemingly to cause the fire to go out, but it was only a momentary dying down. Koku and Rad had made a fierce, yet comparatively small, conflagration, and though for a time the gas generated by Tom's mixture dampened the blaze, in a few seconds—less than half a minute—the flames were shooting higher than ever.

Tom made a gesture of disappointment, and swung his craft around in a sharp, banking turn. He had no more chemicals to drop, as he had thought this supply would be sufficient. However, he had guessed badly. The fire burned on, doing no damage, of course, for that had been thought of when it was started in the meadow.

"Something wrong!" declared the young inventor, when they were back at the hangar, climbing out of the machine.

"What was it?" asked Ned.

"Didn't use the right kind of chemicals," Tom answered. "From the way the flames shot up, you'd think I had poured oil on the blaze instead of carbon dioxide."

"Bless my insurance policy, Tom!" cried Mr. Damon, "but I'd hate to trust to your apparatus if my house caught."

"Don't blame you," Tom assented. "But I'll do the trick yet! This is only a starter!"

During the next two weeks the young inventor worked hard in his laboratory, Mr. Swift sometimes helping him, but more often Koku and Eradicate. Mr. Baxter had recovered sufficiently to leave the Swift home. But though the chemist seemed well physically, his mind appeared to be brooding over his loss.

"If I could only get my secret formulae back!" he sighed, as he thanked Tom for his kindness. "I'm sure Field and Melling have them. And I believe they got them the night of the fireworks blaze; the scoundrels!"

"Well, if I can help you, please let me," begged Tom. And then he dismissed the matter from his mind in his anxiety to hit upon the right chemical mixture for putting out fires from the air.

One afternoon, at the end of a week in which he had been busily and steadily engaged on this work, Tom finally moved away from his laboratory table with a sigh of relief, and, turning to Eradicate, who had been helping him, exclaimed:

"Well, I think I have it now!"

"Good lan' ob massy, I hopes so!" exclaimed the colored man. "It sho' do smell bad enough, Massa Tom, to make any fire go an' run an' drown hisse'f! Whew-up! It's turrible stuff!"

"Yes, it isn't very pleasant," Tom agreed, with a smile. "Though I am getting rather used to it. But when it's in a metal tube it won't smell, and I think it will put out any fire that ever started. We'll give it a test now, Rad. Just take that flask of red stuff and pour it into this one of yellow. I'll go out and light the bonfire, and we'll make a small test."

Leaving Rad to mix some of the chemicals, a task the colored man had often done before, Tom went out into the yard near his laboratory to start a blaze on which his new mixture could be tested.

He had not got far from the laboratory door when he felt a sudden jar and a rush of air, and then followed the dull boom of an explosion. Like an echo came the voice of Eradicate:

"Oh, Massa Tom, I'se blowed up! It done sploded right in mah face!"

TOM IS WORRIED

Dropping what he had in his hands, Tom Swift raced back to the laboratory where he had left Eradicate to mix the chemicals. Again the despairing, frightened cry of the colored man rang out.

"I hope nothing serious has happened," was the thought that flashed through Tom's mind. "But I'm afraid it has. I should have mixed those new chemicals myself."

Koku, the giant, who was at work in another part of the shop yard, heard Rad's cry and came running up. As there was always more or less jealousy between Eradicate and Koku, the latter now thought he had a chance to crow over his rival, not, of course, understanding what had happened.

"Ho! Ho!" laughed Koku. "You much better hab me work, Master Tom. I no make blunderstakes like dat black fellow! I never no make him!"

"I don't know whether Rad has made a mistake or not," murmured Tom. "Come along, Koku, we may need your help. There has been an explosion."

"Yep, dat Rad he don't as know any more as to blow up de whole place!" chuckled Koku.

He thought he would have a chance to make fun of Eradicate, but neither he nor Tom realized how serious had been the happening. As the young inventor reached the laboratory, which he had left but a few seconds before, he saw the interior almost in ruins. All about were scattered various pieces of apparatus, test tubes, alembics, retorts, flasks, and an electric furnace.

But what gave Tom more concern than anything else was the sight of Eradicate lying in the midst of broken glass on the floor. The colored man was moaning and held his hands over his face, and the young inventor could see that the hands, which had labored so hard and faithfully in his service, were cut and bleeding.

"Rad! Rad! what has happened?" cried Tom quickly.

"It sploded! It done sploded right in mah face!" moaned Eradicate. "I—I can't see no mo', Massa Tom! I can't see to help yo' nevah no mo'!"

"Don't worry about that, Rad!" cried Tom, as cheerfully as possible under the circumstances. "We'll soon have you fixed up! Come in here, Koku, and help me carry Rad out!"

Though the fumes from the chemicals that had exploded were choking, causing both Tom and Koku to gasp for breath, they never hesitated. In they rushed and picked up the limp figure of the helpless colored man.

"Poor Rad!" murmured the giant Koku tenderly. "Him bad hurt! I carry him, Master Tom! I take him bed, an' I go for doctor! I run like painted pig!"

Probably Koku meant "greased pig," but Tom never thought of that. All his concern was for his faithful Eradicate.

"Me carry him, Master Tom!" cried Koku, all the petty jealousy of his rival passing away now. "Me take care ob Rad. Him no see, me see for him. Anybody hurt Rad now, got to hurt Koku first!"

It was a fine and generous spirit that the giant was showing, though Tom had no time to speculate on it just then.

"We must get him into the house, Koku," said the young inventor. "And two of us can carry him better than one. After we get him to a bed you can go for the doctor, though I fancy the telephone can run even quicker than you can, Koku."

"Whatever Master Tom say," returned the giant humbly, as he looked with pity at the suffering form of his rival—a rival no longer. It seemed that Rad's working days were over.

Tenderly the aged colored man was laid on a lounge in the living room, Mr. Swift and Mrs. Baggert hovering over him.

"Where are you worst hurt, Rad?" asked Tom, with a view to getting a line on which physician would be the best one to summon.

"It's all in mah face, Massa Tom," moaned the colored man. "It's mah eyes. Dat stuff done sploded right in 'em! I can't see —nevah no mo'!"

"Oh, I guess it isn't as bad as that," said Tom. But when he had a glimpse of the seared and wounded face of his faithful servant he could not repress a shudder.

A physician was summoned by telephone, and he arrived in his automobile at the same time that Mr. Damon reached Tom's house.

"Bless my bottle of arnica, Tom!" exclaimed the eccentric man, with sympathy in his voice. "What's this I hear? One of your men tells me old Eradicate is killed!"

"Not as bad as that, yet," replied Tom, as he came out, leaving the doctor to make his first examination. "It was an explosion of my new aerial fire-fighting chemicals that I left Rad to mix for me. If anything serious results to him from this I'll drop the whole business! I'll never forgive myself!"

"It wasn't your fault, Tom. Perhaps he did something wrong," said Mr. Damon.

"Yes, it was my fault. I should not have let him take the chance with a mixture I had tried only a few times. But we'll hope for the best. How is he, Doctor?" Tom asked a little later when the physician came out on the porch.

"He's doing as well as can be expected for the present," was the answer. "I have given him a quieting mixture. His worst injury seems to be to his face. His hands are cut by broken glass, but the hurts are only superficial. I think we shall have to get an eye specialist to look at him in a day or two."

"You mean that he—that he may go blind?" gasped Tom.

"Well, we'll not decide right away," replied the doctor, as cheerfully as he could. "I should rather have the opinion of an oculist before making that statement. It may be only temporary."

"That's bad enough!" muttered Tom. "Poor old Rad!"

"Me take care ob him," put in Koku, who had been humbly standing around waiting to hear the news. "Me never be mad at dat black man no more! Him my best friend! I lub him like I did my brudder!"

"Thank you, Koku," said Tom, and his mind went back to the time when he had escaped in his airship from the gigantic men, of whom Koku and his brother were two specimens. The brother had gone with a circus, and Koku, for several years, only saw him occasionally.

Everything possible was done for Eradicate, and the doctor said that it would be several days, until after the burns from the exploding chemicals had partly healed, before the eye-doctor could make an examination.

"Then we can only wait and hope," said Tom.

"And hope for the best!" advised Mr. Damon.

"I'll try," promised Tom. He went back to the laboratory with his eccentric friend and with Ned, who had come over as soon as he heard the news. Not much of an examination could be made, as the place was in such ruins. But it was surmised that in combining the two chemical mixtures a new one had been created, or at least one that Tom had not counted on. This had exploded, blowing Eradicate down, flaring a sheet of flame up into his face, scattering broken glass about, and generally creating havoc.

"I can't understand it," said Tom. "I was trying to make a fire extinguishing liquid, and it turned out to be a fire creator. I don't see what was wrong."

"One chemical might have been impure," suggested Ned.

"Yes," agreed Tom. "I'll check them over and try to find out where the mistake happened."

"This place will have to be rebuilt," observed Ned. "It's in bad shape, Tom."

"I don't mind that in the least, if Rad doesn't lose his eyesight," was the answer of the young inventor, and his friends could see that he was much worried, as well he might be.

In silence Tom Swift looked about the ruins of what had been a fine chemical laboratory.

"It will take a month to get this back in shape," he said ruefully. "I guess I shall have to postpone my experiments."

"Why not ask Mr. Baxter to help you?" suggested Ned.

"What can he do?" Tom wanted to know. "He hasn't any laboratory."

"He has a sort of one," Ned rejoined. "You know you told me to keep track of him and give him any help I could."

"Yes," Tom nodded.

"Well, the other day he came to me and said he had a chance to set up a small laboratory in a vacant shop near the river. He needed a little capital and I lent it to him, as you told me to."

"Glad you did," returned Tom. "But do you suppose his plant is large enough to enable me to work there until mine is in shape again?"

"It wouldn't do any harm to take a look," suggested Ned.

"I'll do it!" decided Tom, more hopefully than he had spoken since the accident.

A Forced Landing

Josephus Baxter seemed to have recovered some of his spirits after his narrow escape from death in the fireworks factory blaze. He greeted Tom and Ned with a smile as they entered the improvised laboratory he had been able to set up in what had once been a factory for the making of wooden ware, an industry that, for some reason, did not flourish in Shopton.

"I'm glad to see you, Mr. Swift," said the chemist, who seemed to have aged several years in the few weeks that had intervened since the fire. "I want to thank you for giving me a chance to start over again."

"Oh, that's all right," said Tom easily. "We inventors ought to help one another. Are you able to do anything here?"

"As much as possible without my secret formulae," was the answer. "If I only had those back from the rascals, Field and Melling, I would be able to go ahead faster. As it is, I am working in the dark. For some of the formulae were given to me by a Frenchman, and I had only one copy. I kept that in the safe of the fireworks concern, and after the fire it could not be found."

"Was the safe destroyed?" asked Tom.

"No. But the doors were open, and much of what had been inside was in ashes and cinders. Amos Field claimed that the explosion had blown open the safe and burned a lot of their valuable fireworks formulae too."

"And you believe they have yours?" asked Ned.

"I'm sure of it!" was the fierce answer. "Those men are unprincipled rogues! They had been at me ever since I was foolish enough to tell them about my formulae to get me to sell them a share. But I refused, for I knew the secret mixtures would make my fortune when I could establish a new dye industry. Field and Melling claimed they wanted the formulae for their fireworks, but that was only an excuse. The formulae were not nearly so valuable for pyrotechnics as for dyes. The fireworks business is not so good, either, since so many cities have voted for a 'Sane Fourth of July.'"

"I can appreciate that," said Tom. "But what we called for, Mr. Baxter, is to find if you have room enough to let me do a little experimenting here. I am working on a new kind of fire extinguisher, to be dropped on tall buildings from an airship."

"Sounds like a good idea," said the chemist, rather dreamily.

"Well, I have the airship, and I can see my way clear to perfecting a device to drop the chemicals in metal tanks or bombs," went on Tom. "But what bothers me is the chemical mixture that will put out fires better than the carbon dioxide mixtures now on the market."

"I haven't given that much study myself," said Mr. Baxter. "But you are welcome to anything I have, Mr. Swift. The whole place, such as it is, will be at your disposal at any time. I intend to have it in better shape soon, but I have to proceed slowly, as I lost nearly everything I owned in that fire. If I could only get those formulae back!" he sighed.

"Perhaps you may recall the combinations, suggested Ned. "Or can't you get them from that Frenchman?"

"He is dead," answered the chemist. "Everything seems to be against me!"

"Well, it's always darkest just before daylight," said Tom. "So let us hope for the best. We both have had a bit of bad luck. But when I think of Rad, who may lose his eyesight, I can stand my losses smiling."

"Yes," agreed Mr. Baxter, "you have big assets when you have your health and eyesight."

Three days later the eye specialist looked at Rad. Tom stood by anxiously and waited for the verdict. The doctor motioned to the young inventor to follow him out of the room, while Mrs. Baggert replaced the bandages on the colored man's eyes and Koku stood near him, sympathetically patting Rad on the back.

"Well?" asked Tom nervously, as he faced the physician.

"I am sorry, Mr. Swift, that I can not hold out much hope that your man will ever regain his sight," was the answer.

Tom could not repress a gasp of pity.

"I do not say that the case is altogether hopeless," the doctor went on; "but it would be wrong to encourage you to hope for much. I may be able to save partly the sight of one eye."

"Poor Rad!" murmured Tom. "This will break his heart."

"There is no need for telling him at once," Dr. Henderson said. "It will only make his recovery so much the slower. It will be weeks before I am able to operate, and, meanwhile, he should be kept as comfortable and cheerful as possible."

"We'll see to that," declared Tom. "Is he otherwise injured?"

"No, it is merely his eyesight that we have to fear for. And, as I said, that is not altogether hopeless, though it would not be honest to let you look for much success. I shall see him from time to time until his eyes are ready to operate on."

Tom and his friends were forced to take such comfort as they could from this verdict, but no hint of their downcast feelings were made manifest to Eradicate.

"Whut de doctor man done say, Massa Tom?" asked Eradicate when the young inventor went back into the sick room.

"Oh, he talked a lot of big Latin words, Rad—bigger words than you used to use on your mule Boomerang," and Tom forced a laugh. "All he meant was that you'd have to stay in bed a while and let Koku wait on you."

"Huh! Am dat—dat big—dat big nice man heah now?" asked Rad, feeling around with his bandaged hand; and a smile showed beneath the cloth over his eyes.

"I here right upsidedown by you, Rad," said Koku, and his big hand clasped the smaller one of the black man.

"Koku—yo'—yo' am mighty good to me," murmured Eradicate. "I reckon I been cross to yo' sometimes, but I didn't mean nuffin' by it!"

"Huh! me an' you good friends now," said the giant. "Anybody what hurt my Rad, I—I—bust 'im! Dat I do!" cried the big fellow.

"Come on," whispered Tom to Ned. "They'll get along all right together now."

But Eradicate caught the sound of his young employer's footsteps and called:

"Yo' goin', Massa Tom?"

"Yes, Rad. Is there anything you want?"

"No, Massa Tom. I jest wanted to ast if yo' done 'membered de time mah mule Boomerang got stuck in de road, an' yo' couldn't git past in yo' auto? Does yo' 'member dat?"

"Indeed I do!" laughed Tom, and Eradicate also chuckled at the recollection.

"That laugh will do him more good than medicine," declared the doctor, as he took his leave. "I'll come again, when I can make a more thorough examination," he added.

For Tom the following days, that lengthened into weeks, were anxious ones. There was a constant worry over Eradicate. Then, too, he was having trouble with his latest invention—his aerial fire-fighting apparatus. It was not that Tom was financially dependent on this invention. He was wealthy enough for his needs from other patented inventions he and his father owned.

But Tom Swift was a lad not easily satisfied. Once embarked on an enterprise, whether it was the creation of a gigantic searchlight, an electric rifle, a photo telephone or a war tank, he never rested until he had brought it to a successful consummation.

But there was something about this chemical fire extinguishing mixture that defied the young inventor's best efforts. Mixture after mixture was tried and discarded. Tom wanted something better than the usual carbonate and sulphuric combination, and he was not going to rest until he found it.

"I think you've struck a blind lead, Tom," said Ned, more than once.

"Well, I'm not going to give up," was the firm answer.

"Bless my shoe laces!" cried Mr. Damon, when he had called on Tom once at the Baxter laboratory and had been driven out, holding his breath, because of the chemical fumes, "I should think you couldn't even start a fire with that around, Tom, much less need to put one out."

"Well, it doesn't seem to work," said the young inventor ruefully. "Everything I do lately goes wrong."

"It is that way sometimes," said Mr. Baxter. "Suppose you let me study over your formulae a bit, Mr. Swift. I haven't given much thought to fire extinguishers, but I may be able, for that very reason, to approach the subject from a new angle. I'll lay aside my attempt to get back the lost formulae and help you."

"I wish you would!" exclaimed Tom eagerly. "My head is woozie from thinking! Suppose I leave you to yourself for a time, Mr. Baxter? I'll go for an airship ride."

"Yes, do," urged the chemist. "Sometimes a change of scene is of benefit. I'll see what I can do for you."

"Will you come along, Ned—Mr. Damon?" asked Tom, as he prepared to leave the improvised laboratory, the repairs on his own not yet having been finished.

"Thank you, no," answered Ned. "I have some collections to make."

"And I promised my wife I'd take her riding, Tom," said the jolly, eccentric man. "Bless my umbrella! she'd never forgive me if I went off with you. But I'll run you to your first stopping place, Ned, and you to your hangar, Tom."

His invitation was accepted, and, in due season, Tom was soaring aloft in one of his speedy cloud craft.

"Guess I'll drop down and get Mary Nestor," he decided, after riding about alone for a while and finding that the motor was running sweetly and smoothly. "She hasn't been out lately."

Tom made a landing in a field not far from the home of the girl he hoped to marry some day, and walked over to her house.

"Go for a ride? I just guess. I will!" cried Mary, with sparkling eyes. "Just wait until I get on my togs."

She had a leather suit, as had Tom, and they were soon in the machine, which, being equipped with a self-starter, did not need the services of a mechanician to whirl the propellers.

"Oh, isn't it glorious!" said Mary, as she sat at Tom's side. They were in a little enclosed cabin of the craft—which carried just two—and, thus enclosed, they could speak by raising their voices somewhat, for the noise of the motor was much muffled, due to one of Tom's inventions.

Other rides on other days followed this one, for Tom found more rest and better refreshment after his hours of toil and study in these rides with Mary than in any other way.

"I do love these rides, Tom!" the girl cried one day when the two were soaring aloft. "And this one I really believe is better than any of the rest. Though I always think that," she added, with a slight laugh.

"Glad you like it," Tom answered, and there was something in his voice that caused Mary to look curiously at him.

"What's the matter, Tom?" she asked. "Has anything happened? Is Rad's case hopeless?"

"Oh, no, not yet. Of course it isn't yet sure that he will ever see again, but, on the other hand, it isn't decided that he can't. It's a fifty-fifty proposition."

"But what makes you so serious?"

"Was I?"

"I should say so! You haven't told me one funny thing that Mr. Damon has said lately."

"Oh, haven't I? Well, let me see now," and he sent the machine up a little. "Well, the other day he—"

Tom suddenly stopped speaking and began rapidly turning several valve wheels and levers.

"What—what's the matter?" gasped Mary, but she did not clutch his arm. She knew better than that.

"The motor has stopped," Tom answered, and the girl became aware of a cessation of the subdued hum.

"Is it—does it mean danger?" she asked.

"Not necessarily so," Tom replied. "It means we have to make a forced landing, that's all. Sit tight! We're going down rather faster than usual, Mary, but we'll come out of it all right!"

Strange Talk

There was a rapid and sudden drop. Mary, sitting beside Tom Swift in the speedy aeroplane, watched with fascinated eyes as he quickly juggled with levers and tried different valve wheels. The girl, through her goggles, had a vision of a landscape shooting past with the speed of light. She glimpsed a brook, and, almost instantly, they had skimmed over it.

A jar, a nerve-racking tilt to one side, the creaking of wood and the rattle of metal, a careening, and then the machine came to a stop, not exactly on a level keel, but at least right side up, in the midst of a wide field.

Tom shut off the gas, cut his spark, and, raising his goggles, looked down at Mary at his side.

"Scared?" he asked, smiling.

"I was," she frankly admitted. "Is anything broken, Tom?"

"I hope not," answered the young inventor. "At least if it is, the damage is on the under part. Nothing visible up here. But let me help you out. Looks as if we'd have to run for it."

"Run?" repeated Mary, while proving that she did not exactly need help, for she was getting out of her seat unaided. "Why? Is it going to catch fire?"

"No. But it's going to rain soon—and hard, too, if I'm any judge," Tom said. "I don't believe I'll take a chance trying to get the machine going again. We'll make for that farmhouse and stay there until after the storm. Looks as if we could get shelter there, and perhaps a bit to eat. I'm beginning to feel hungry."

"It is going to rain!" decided Mary, as Tom helped her down over the side of the fusilage. "It's good we are so near shelter."

Tom did not answer. He was making a hasty but accurate observation of the state of his aeroplane. The landing wheels had stood the shock well, and nothing appeared to be broken.

"We came down rather harder than I wanted to," remarked Tom, as he crawled out after his inspection of the machine. "Though I've made worse forced landings than that."

"What caused it?" asked Mary, glancing up at the clouds, which were getting blacker and blacker, and from which, now and then, vivid flashes of lightning came while low mutterings of thunder rolled nearer and nearer. "Something seemed to be wrong with the carburetor," Tom answered. "I won't try to monkey with it now. Let's hike for that farmhouse. We'll be lucky if we don't get drenched. Are you sure you're all right, Mary?"

"Certainly, Tom. I can stand a worse shaking up than that. And you needn't think I can't run, either!"

She proved this by hastening along at Tom's side. And there was need of haste, for soon after they left the stranded aeroplane the big drops began to pelt down, and they reached the house just as the deluge came.

"I don't know this place, do you, Tom?" asked Mary, as they ran in through a gateway in a fence that surrounded the property. A path seemed to lead all around the old, rambling house, and there was a porch with a side entrance door. This, being nearer, had been picked out by the young inventor and his friend.

"No, I don't remember being here before," Tom answered. "But I've passed the place often enough with Ned and Mr. Damon. I guess they won't refuse to let us sit on the porch, and they may be induced to give us a glass of milk and some sandwiches—that is, sell them to us."

He and Mary, a little breathless from their run, hastened up on the porch, slightly wet from the sudden outburst of rain. As Tom knocked on the door there came a clap of thunder, following a burst of lightning, that caused Mary to put her hands over her ears.

"Guess they didn't hear that," observed Tom, as the echoes of the blast died away. "I mean my knock. The thunder drowned it. I'll try again."

He took advantage of a lull in the thundering reverberations, and tapped smartly. The door was almost at once opened by an aged woman, who stared in some amazement at the young people. Then she said:

"Guests must go to the front door."

"Guests!" exclaimed Tom. "We aren't exactly guests. Of course we'd like to be considered in that light. But we've had an accident—my aeroplane stopped and we'd like to stay here out of the storm, and perhaps get something to eat."

"That can be arranged—yes," said the old woman, who spoke with a foreign accent. "But you must go to the front door. This is the servant's entrance."

Mary was just thinking that they used considerable formality for casual wayfarers, when the situation dawned on Tom Swift.

"Is this a restaurant—an inn?" he asked.

"Yes," answered the old woman. "It is Meadow Inn. Please go to the front door."

"All right," Tom agreed good-naturedly. "I'm glad we struck the place, anyhow."

The porch extended around three sides of the old, rambling house. Proceeding along the sheltered piazza, Tom and Mary soon found themselves at the front door. There the nature of the place was at once made plain, for on a board was lettered the words "Meadow Inn."

"I see what has happened," Tom remarked, as he opened the old-fashioned ground glass door and ushered Mary in. "Some one has taken the old farmhouse and made it into a roadhouse—a wayside inn. I shouldn't think such a place would pay out here; but I'm mighty glad we struck it."

"Yes, indeed," agreed Mary.

The old farmhouse, one of the best of its day, had been transformed into a roadhouse of the better class. On either side of the entrance hall were dining rooms, in which were set small tables, spread with snowy cloths.

"In here, sir, if you please," said a white-aproned waiter, gliding forward to take Tom's leather coat and Mary's jacket of like material. The waiter ushered them into a room, in which at first there seemed to be no other diners. Then, from behind a screen which was pulled around a table in one corner, came the murmur of voices and the clatter of cutlery on china, which told of some one at a meal there.

"Somebody is fond of seclusion," thought Tom, as he and Mary took their places. And as he glanced over the bill of fare his ears caught the murmur of the voices of two men coming from behind the screen. One voice was low and rumbling, the other high-pitched and querulous.

"Talking business, probably," mused Tom. "What do you feel like eating?" he asked Mary.

"I wasn't very hungry until I came in," she answered, with a smile. "But it is so cozy and quaint here, and so clean and neat, that it really gives one an appetite. Isn't it a delightful place, Tom? Did you know it was here?"

"It is very nice. And as this is the first I have been here for a long while I didn't know, any more than you, that it had been made into a roadhouse. But what shall I order for you?"

"I should think you would have had enough experience by this time," laughed Mary, for it was not the first occasion that she and Tom had dined out.

Thereupon he gave her order and his own, too, and they were soon eating heartily of food that was in keeping with the appearance of the place.

"I must bring Ned and Mr. Damon here," said Tom. "They'll appreciate the quaintness of this inn," for many of the quaint appointments of the old farmhouse had been retained, making it a charming resort for a meal.

"Mr. Damon will like it," said Mary. "Especially the big fireplace," and she pointed to one on which burned a blaze of hickory wood. "He'll bless everything he sees."

"And cause the waiter to look at me as though I had brought in an escaped inmate from some sanitarium," laughed Tom. "No use talking, Mr. Damon is delightfully queer! Now what do you want for dessert?"

"Let me see the card," begged Mary. "I fancy some French pastry, if they have it."

Tom gazed idly but approvingly about as she scanned the list. The sound of the rumbling and the higher-pitched voices had gone on throughout the entire meal, and now, as comparative silence filled the room, the clatter of knives and forks having ceased, Tom heard more clearly what was being said behind the screen.

"Well, I tell you what it is," said the man whom Tom mentally dubbed Mr. High. "We got out of that blaze mighty luckily!"

"Yes," agreed he of the rumbly voice, whom Tom thought of as Mr. Low, "it was a close shave. If it hadn't been for his chemicals, though, there would have been a cleaner sweep."

"Indeed there would! I never knew that any of them could act as fire extinguishers."

Tom seemed to stiffen at this, and his hearing became more acute.

"They aren't really fire extinguishers in the real sense of the word," went on the other man behind the screen. "It must have been some accidental combination of them. But in spite of that we put it all over Josephus Baxter in that fire!"

"What's this? What's this?" thought Tom, shooting a glance at Mary and noting that apparently she had not heard what was said. "What strange talk is this?"

SUSPICIONS

"What's that?" exclaimed Mary Nestor, giving such a start as she sat opposite Tom at the restaurant table that she dropped the bill of fare she had been looking over.

A crash had resounded through the room, but it spoke well for the state of Tom's nerves that he gave no indication that he had heard the noise. It was caused by a waiter when he dropped a plate, which was smashed into pieces on the floor. The noise was startling enough to excuse Mary for jumping in her chair, and it seemed to put an end to the strange talk of "Mr. High" and "Mr. Low" back of the screen, for after the crash of china only indistinct murmurs came from there. But Tom Swift did not cease to wonder at the import of the talk about chemicals, fire, and the mention of the name of Josephus Baxter.

"I think I'll try some of those Murolloas, as they call them, Tom," announced Mary, having made her selection of the pastry. "And may I have another cup of tea?"

"Two if you like," answered the young inventor. "They say tea is good for the nerves, and you seem to need something, judging by the way you jumped when that plate fell."

"Oh, Tom, that isn't fair! After the way we had to come down in your 'plane!" objected Mary.

"That's right!" he conceded. "I forgot about that. My fault, entirely!"

Mary smiled, and seemed to have regained her composure. Tom glanced at her anxiously, not because of what he thought might be the state of her nerves, but to see if she had sensed anything the two men behind the screen had said. But the girl gave no indication that her mind had been occupied with anything more than the selection of her dessert.

"I wonder who they are, and what they meant by that talk," mused Tom, as the waiter served the Murolloas to him and Mary. "Poor Baxter! It looks as if he might have more enemies than the fireworks men he accuses of having taken his valuable formulae. I must see him soon, and have a talk with him. Yes, I must make a special point to see Josephus Baxter. But first I'd like to have a glimpse of these men."

Tom's wish in this respect was soon gratified, for before he and Mary had finished their pastry and tea there was a scraping of chairs back of the sheltering screen, and the two men, "Mr. Low" and "Mr. High," who had finished their meal, came forth.

Tom's judgment as to the statures of the men, based on the quality of their voices, was not exactly borne out. For it was the big man who had the high pitched, squeaky voice, and the little man who had the deep, rumbling tones.

They passed out, without more than a glance at Tom and his companion, but the young inventor peered at them sharply. As far as he could tell he had seen neither of them before, though he had an idea of their identity.

Tom took the chance to make certain this conjecture when Mary left her seat, announcing that she was going to the ladies' parlor to arrange her hair, which the run to escape from the rain had disarranged.

"Some storm," Tom observed to the waiter, who came up when the young inventor indicated that he wanted his check.

"Yes, sir, it came suddenly. Hope you didn't have to change a tire in it, sir."

"No, my machine isn't that kind," replied Tom, as he handed out a generous tip. "If I need a new tire I generally need a whole new outfit."

"Oh, then—" Obviously the man was puzzled.

"We came in an aeroplane," Tom explained. "But we had to make a forced landing. Is there a garage near here? I may need some help getting started."

"We accommodate a few cars in what was once the barn, and we have a good mechanic, sir. If you'd like to see him—"

"I would," interrupted Tom. "Tell the young lady to wait here for me. I'll see if I can get the Scud to work. If not, I'll have to telephone to town for a taxi. Did those men who just left come in a car?" and he nodded in the direction taken by the two who had dined behind the screen.

"Yes, sir. And they had engine trouble, I believe. Our man fixed up their machine."

"Then he's the chap I want to see," thought Tom. "I'll have a talk with him." He reasoned that he could get more about the identity of the two mysterious men from the mechanic than from the waiter. Nor was he wrong in this surmise.

"Oh, them two fellers!" exclaimed the mechanician, after he had agreed to go with Tom to where the airship Scud was stalled. "They come from over Shopton way. They own a fireworks factory— or they did, before it burned."

"Are they Field and Melling?" asked Tom, trying not to let any excitement betray itself in his voice.

"That's the names they gave me," said the man. "Little man's Field. He gave me his card. I'm going to get a job overhauling his car. There isn't enough work here to keep a man busy, and I told 'em I could do a little on the outside. This place just started, and not many folks know about it yet."

"So I judge," Tom said. "Well, I'll be glad to have you give me a hand. I fancy the carburetor is out of order."

And this, when the young inventor and the mechanician from Meadow Inn reached the stranded Scud, was found to be the case. The storm had passed, and Mary told Tom she would not mind waiting at the Inn until he found whether or not he could get his air craft in working order.

"There you are! That's the trouble!" exclaimed the mechanician, as he took something out of the carburetor. "A bit of rubber washer choked the needle valve."

"Glad you found it," said Tom heartily. "Now I guess we can ride back."

While preparations were being made to test the Scud after the carburetor had been reassembled, Tom's mind was busy with many thoughts, and chief among them were suspicions concerning Field and Melling.

"If their talk meant anything at all," reasoned the young inventor, "it meant that there was some deal in which Josephus Baxter got the worst of it. 'Putting it over on him in the fire,' could only mean that. Of course it isn't any of my business, in a way, but I don't think it is right to stand by and see a fellow inventor defrauded.

"Of course," mused Tom, while his helper put the finishing touches to the carburetor, "it may have been a business deal in which one took as many chances as the other. There are always two sides to every story. Baxter says they took his formulae, but he may have taken something from them to make it even. The only thing is that I'd trust Baxter sooner than I would those two fellows, and he certainly had a narrow squeak at the fire.

"But I have my own troubles, I guess, trying to perfect that fire-fighting chemical, and I haven't much time to bother with Field and Melling, unless they come my way."

"There, I reckon she'll work," said the mechanician, as he fastened the last valve in the carburetor. "It was an easier job than I expected. Wasn't as much trouble as I had over their car those two fellers you were speaking of—Field and Melling. They're rich guys!"

"Yes?" replied Tom, questioningly.

"Sure! They've started a big dye company."

"A dye company?" repeated the young inventor, all his suspicions coming back as he recalled that Baxter had said his formulae were more valuable for dyes than for fireworks.

"Yes, they're trying to get the business that used to go to the Germans before the war," went on the man.

"Yes, the Germans used to have a monopoly of the dye industry," said Tom, hoping the man would talk on. He need not have worried. He was of the talkative type.

"Well, if these fellers have their way they'll make a million in dyes," proceeded the mechanician, as he stepped down out of the airship. "They've built a big plant, and they have offices in the Landmark Building."

"Where's that?" asked Tom.

"Over in Newmarket," the man went on, naming the nearest large city to Shopton. "The Landmark Building is a regular New York skyscraper. Haven't you seen it?"

"No," Tom answered, "I haven't. Been too busy, I guess. So Field and Melling have their offices there?"

"Yes, and a big plant on the outskirts for making dyes. They half offered me a job at the factory, but I thought I'd try this out first; I like it here."

"It is a nice place," agreed Tom. "Well, now let's see if she'll work," and he nodded at the Scud.

It needed but a short test to demonstrate this and soon Tom went back to the Inn for Mary.

"Are you sure we shall not have to make an. other forced landing?" she asked with a smile, a she took her place in the cockpit.

"You can't guarantee anything about an aeroplane," said Tom. "But everything is in our favor, and if we do have to come down I have a better landing field than this." He glanced over the meadow near the wayside inn.

"I suppose I'll have to take a chance," said Mary.

However, neither of them need have worried, for the Scud tried, evidently, to redeem herself, and flew back to Shopton without a hitch. After making sure that his engine was running smoothly, Tom found his mind more at ease, and again he caught himself casting about to find some basis for his suspicious thoughts regarding the two men who had talked behind the screen.

"What is their game?" Tom found himself asking himself over and over again. "What did they 'put over' on poor Baxter?"

Tom had a chance to find out more about this, or at least start on the trail sooner than he expected. For when he landed he saw Koku, the giant, coming toward him with an appearance of excitement.

"Is Rad worse? Is there more trouble with his eyes?" asked the young inventor.

"No, him not much too bad," answered Koku. "I keep him good as I can. He sleep now, so I come out to swallow some fresh air. But man come to see you—much mad man."

"Mad?" queried Tom.

"Well, what you say—angry," went on Koku. "Man what was in Roman Skycracker blaze."

"Oh, you mean Mr. Baxter, who was in the fireworks blaze," translated Tom. "Where is he, and what's the matter?"

ANOTHER ATTEMPT

Koku managed to make Tom understand that the dye inventor was in the main office of the Swift plant talking to Tom's father. The young inventor sent Mary home in his electric runabout in company with Ned Newton, who, fortunately, happened along just then, and hurried to his office.

"Oh, Tom, I'm glad you have arrived," said his father. "You remember Mr. Baxter, of course."

"I should hope so," Tom answered, extending his hand. He noticed that the man whom he had helped save from the fireworks blaze was under the stress of some excitement.

"I hope he hasn't been getting on dad's nerves," thought Tom, as he took a seat. The elder Mr. Swift had been quite ill, and it was thought for a time that he would have to give up helping Tom. But there had been a turn for the better, and the aged inventor had again taken his place in the laboratory, though he was frail.

"What's the trouble now?" asked Tom. "At least I assume there has been some trouble," he went on. "If I am wrong—"

"No, you are right, unfortunately," said Mr. Baxter gloomily. "The trouble is that everything I do is a failure. Up to a little while ago I thought I might succeed, in spite of Field and Melling's theft of the formulae from me. I made a purple dye the other day, and tested it today. It was a miserable failure, and it got on my nerves. I came to see if you could help me."

"In what way?" asked Tom, wondering whether or not he had best tell Mr. Baxter what he had overheard at the Inn.

"Well, I need better laboratory facilities," the man went on. "I know you have been very kind to me, Mr. Swift, and it seems like an imposition to ask for more. But I need a different lot of chemicals, and they cost money. I also need some different apparatus. You have it in your big laboratory. That wouldn't cost you anything. But of course to go out and buy what I need—"

"Oh I guess we can stand that, can't we, Dad?" asked Tom, with a genial smile. "You may have free access to our big laboratory, Mr. Baxter, and I'll see that you get what chemicals you need."

"Oh, thank you!" exclaimed the inventor. "Now I believe I shall succeed in spite of those rascals. Just think, Mr. Swift! They have started a big new dye factory."

"So I have heard," replied Tom.

"And I'm almost sure they're using the secret formulae they stole from me!" exclaimed Mr. Baxter. "But I'll get the best of them yet! I'll invent a better dye than they ever can, even if they use the secrets the old

Frenchman gave me. All I need is a better place to work and all the chemicals at my disposal."

"Then we'll try to help you," offered Tom.

"And if I can do anything let me know," put in Mr. Swift. "I shall be glad to get in the harness again, Tom!" he added.

"Well, if you're so anxious to work, Dad, why not give me a hand with my fire extinguisher chemical?" asked Tom. "I haven't been able to hit on the solution, somehow or other."

"Perhaps I may be able to give you a hint or two after I get settled down," suggested Mr. Baxter.

"I shall be glad of any assistance you can give," replied Tom Swift. "And now I'm going to start right in. Dad, you can make the arrangements for Mr. Baxter to use our big laboratory. And let him have credit for any chemicals he needs. Have them put on my bill, for I am buying a lot myself."

"I'll never forget this," said Mr. Baxter, and there were tears in his eyes as he shook hands with Tom, who tried to make light of his generous act.

Tom, after the wrecking of his laboratory, in which accident poor Eradicate was injured, had built himself another—two others, in fact, after having shared Mr. Baxter's temporary one for a time. Tom put up the most completely equipped laboratory that could be devised, and he also erected a smaller one for his own personal use, the main one being at the disposal of his father and the various heads of the different departments of the Shopton plant.

The little conference broke up, and Tom was on his way to his own special private laboratory when there came the sound of some excitement in the corridor outside and Mr. Damon burst in.

"Bless my accident policy, Tom! what's this I hear?" he asked, all in a fluster.

"I'm sure I don't know," answered the young inventor, with a smile. "What about?"

"About you and Mary Nestor being killed!" burst out Mr. Damon. "I heard you fell in the aeroplane and were both dashed to pieces!"

"If you can believe the evidence of your own eyes, I'm far from being in that state," laughed Tom. "And as for Mary, she just left here with Ned Newton."

"Thank goodness!" sighed Mr. Damon, sinking into a chair. "Bless my elevator! I rushed over as soon as I heard the news, and I was almost afraid to come in. I'm so glad it didn't happen!"

"No gladder than I," said Tom. "We had to make a forced landing, that was all," and he made as light of the incident as possible when he saw the look of terror in his father's eyes.

"Some people in Waterford saw you going down," went on Mr. Damon, "and they told me."

"It was a false alarm," replied Tom. "And now, Mr. Damon, if you want to smell some perfumes come with me."

"Are you going into that line, Tom?" asked the eccentric man. "Bless my handkerchief, my wife will be glad of that!"

"I mean I'm going to experiment some more with fire-extinguishing chemicals," laughed the young inventor. "If you want to—"

"Bless my gas mask, I should say not!" cried Mr. Damon. "I don't see how you stand those odors, Tom Swift."

"Guess I'm used to 'em," was the answer. And then, leaving his father to entertain Mr. Damon and to make arrangements for Mr. Baxter's use of the main laboratory, he betook himself to his own private quarters.

The next week or so was a busy time for Tom; so busy, in fact, that he had little chance to see Mr. Baxter. All he knew was that the unfortunate man was also laboring in his own line, and Tom wished him success. He knew that if the man made any discoveries that would help with the fire-extinguishing fluid he would report, as he had promised.

"Well, Tom, how goes it?" asked Ned one day when he came over to call on his chum. "Are you ready to accept contracts for putting out skyscraper blazes in all big cities?"

"Not yet," was the answer. "But I'm going to make another attempt, Ned."

"You mean another experiment?"

"Yes, I have evolved a new combination of chemicals, using something of the carbonate idea as a basis. I found that I couldn't get away from that, much as I wanted to. But my application is entirely new, at least I hope it will prove so."

"When are you going to try it?" asked Ned.

"Right away. All I have to do is to put the chemicals in the metal tank."

"Then I'd better get my leather suit on," remarked Ned, starting to take off his street coat. Tom kept for his chum a full outfit of flying garments, one suit being electrically heated.

"Oh, we aren't going up in any airship," Tom said.

"Why, I thought you were going to test your aerial fire fighting dingus!" exclaimed Ned.

"So I am. But I want to stay on the ground and watch the effect on the blaze as the tank bursts and scatters the chemical fluid."

"Then you want me, and perhaps Mr. Damon to take the stuff up in the machine? Excuse me. I don't believe I care to run an airship myself."

"No," went on Tom, "there isn't any question of an airship this time. No one is going up. Come on out into the yard and I'll show you."

Ned Newton followed his chum out into the big yard near one of the shops. Erected in it, and evidently a new structure, was a large wooden scaffold in square tower shape with a long overhanging arm and a platform on the extremity. Beneath it was a pit dug in the earth, and in this pit, which was directly under the outstanding arm of the tower, was a pile of wood and shavings, oil-soaked.

"Oh, I see the game," remarked Ned. "You're going to drop the stuff from this height instead of doing it from an airship."

"Yes," Tom answered. "There will be time enough to go on with the airship end of it after I get the right combination of chemicals. And by having a metal container with the stuff in dropped from this frame work, I can station myself as near the burning pit as I can get and watch what happens."

"It's a good idea," decided Ned. "I wonder you didn't try that before."

"Mr. Baxter suggested it," replied Tom. "That helpful idea more than pays me for what I have done for him. So now, if you're ready, I'd like to have you watch with me and make some notes, one of us on one side of the pit, and one on the other. There are always two sides to a fire, the leeward and the windward, and I want to see how my chemicals act in both positions."

"I'm with you," said Ned. "Who's going to drop the stuff— Koku?"

"No, he is a bit too heavy for the framework, which I had put up in a hurry. I'd have Rad do it, but he's out of the game."

"Poor old Rad!" murmured Ned. "Do you think he'll ever get better, Tom?"

"I don't know," sighed the young inventor. "All I can do is to hope. He is very patient, and Koku is devoted to him. All their little bickerings and squabbles seem to have been forgotten."

Tom called some of his workmen, some of them to start the blaze of inflammable material in the pit, while one climbed up to the top of the tower of scantlings and made his way out on the extended arm, where there was a little platform for him to stand until it was time to drop the chemicals.

"Light her up!" cried Tom Swift, and a match was thrown in among the oiled wood. In an instant a fierce blaze shot up, as hot, in proportion, as would come from any burning building.

For the second time Tom was about to make a test on a fairly large scale of his experimental extinguisher mixture.

"All ready up there?" he called to his helper perched high in the air.

"All ready!" came back the answer above the roar and crackle of the flames that made Tom and Ned step back.

Would success or failure attend the young inventor's project?

THE BLAZING TREE

Tom Swift hesitated a moment before giving the final word that would send the metal container of powerful chemicals down into the midst of the crackling flames. He wanted to make sure, in his own mind, that he had done everything possible to insure the success of his undertaking. The young inventor never attempted the solution of any problem without going into it with his whole energy. So he wanted this experiment to succeed.

He quickly reviewed, mentally, the composition of the chemical compound. He had made it as strong as possible, and he had spared no pains to insure a hot fire, so that the test would not be too simple.

"What's the matter, Tom?" asked Ned, as his chum appeared to hesitate about giving the word that would send the chemicals hurtling down into the fire.

"Nothing. I was just making sure I hadn't forgotten anything," Tom answered. "I guess I haven't."

He paused a moment, looked up at his assistant on the overhanging arm of the tower, glanced down at the flames, now at their height, and then suddenly cried:

"Let her go!"

"Right!" came back the man's voice, and then a dark object, like a bomb, was seen descending from the skeleton framework above the flames.

There was a scattering of the fire in the pit as the extinguisher bomb fell among the blazing embers. Then followed a slight explosion when the bomb broke, as it was intended it should.

Tom and Ned leaned forward to peer through the pall of smoke which swirled this way and that. Here was to come the real test of the device. Would the fumes of the liberated chemicals choke the fire, or would it burn on in spite of them? That was the question to be settled for Tom Swift.

Almost immediately he had his answer. For after a fierce burst of the tongues of fire following the fall of the bomb, there was a distinct dying down of the conflagration in the pit. Great clouds of smoke arose, but the fire was quenched in a great measure, and as the fire-blanketing gas continued to be generated from the chemicals liberated from the bomb, there was a further dying down of the crackling fire.

"Tom, you've struck it!" yelled Ned in delight. "You have the right combination this time!"

Tom did not answer. He leaned forward and looked eagerly down into the pit. He was about to join with Ned in agreeing that he had, indeed, solved the problem, when, to his surprise, the flames started up again.

"What's this?" asked the young financial manager. Are you going to have a second test, Tom?"

"Not that I know of," was the puzzled answer. "I don't exactly understand this myself, Ned. By all calculations this fire ought to have died a natural death, but now it is breaking out again. I think what must have happened is that a quantity of the oil they poured on collected in a pool and didn't get all the effects of the chemicals from the bomb. Then the oil started to blaze."

"What can you do about it?" Ned wanted to know.

"Oh, I've got another bomb up there," and Tom pointed to his helper who was still perched on the overhanging arm. "I was prepared for some such emergency as this. Drop the other one!" Tom yelled, and again a dark object fell. bursting in the pit and again liberating the gas that was supposed to choke any fire.

The flames that had started up for the second time instantly died down, and Ned, leaning over the edge of the pit, cried:

"Hurray, Tom! That does the business!" But the young inventor shook his head. "I'm not quite satisfied," he remarked. "It didn't work quickly enough. What I want is a chemical combination that will choke the fire off first shot."

"Well, you pretty nearly have it," observed Ned.

"Yes. But 'good enough' isn't what I want," Tom said. "I've got to work on that chemical compound again. I think I know where I can improve it."

"Well, if I were a fire, and I had this happen to me," remarked Ned, laughing and pointing to the heap of blackened embers in the pit, "I should feel very much discouraged."

"But not enough," declared Tom. "I want the fire to be out more quickly than this one was. I think I can improve that chemical compound, and I'm going to do it."

"All right! Come on down!" he called to his helper, who was still perched on the overhanging arm. "We won't do any more today."

"What is your next move?" asked Ned, as Tom started for his small, private laboratory.

"Oh, I'm going to fiddle around among those sweet-smelling chemicals," answered the young inventor.

"Bless my vest buttons! then I'm not coming in, exclaimed a voice which could proceed from none other than Mr. Damon. And he it proved to be. He had driven over from Waterford in his automobile and had arrived just as the fire test was concluded.

"Oh, come on in!" called Tom. "You can visit with dad, and Eradicate will be glad to see you."

"Poor Rad! How is he?" asked Mr. Damon, walking along with Tom and Ned.

"No change," was the sad answer of the young inventor, for he felt responsible for the mishap to the colored man. "They can't operate on his eyes yet."

"And when they do will he be able to see?" asked Mr. Damon.

"That is what we are all hoping," answered Tom with a sigh. "But do go in to see him, Mr. Damon. It will cheer him up."

"I will," promised the eccentric man. "At any rate I'll not venture near your perfume shop, Tom Swift!"

"And I don't see that I can be of any service," added Ned, "so I'm off to my work."

"All right," assented Tom. "I've got several new schemes to try. Some of them ought to work."

Tom Swift was very busy for the next few days—so busy, in fact, that even Mary saw little of him. He was closeted with Mr. Baxter more than once, and that individual seemed to lose some of his bitter feelings over the loss of his formulae as he found he could be of service to the young inventor. For he was of service in suggesting new ways of combining fire-fighting chemicals, gained by his association with the fireworks concern.

"And that's about all the benefit I derived from being with those scoundrels, Field and Melling," said Mr. Baxter gloomily.

"You still think they took your dye formulae?"~ asked Tom.

"I'm positive of it, but I can't prove anything. They threatened to get the best of me when I would not sell them, for a ridiculously low sum, an interest in the secrets. And I believe they did get the best of me during that fire."

"I believe the same!" exclaimed Tom.

"How is that? What do you know? Can you help me prove anything against them?" eagerly asked the chemist.

"Well, I don't know," answered Tom slowly. "I'll tell you what I heard."

Thereupon he related the conversation he had overheard while with Mary at the wayside inn. The eyes of Josephus Baxter gleamed as he listened to this recital.

"So that was their game!" he cried, as he smote the table with his fist, thereby nearly upsetting a test tube of acid, which Tom caught just in time. "I knew something crooked was going on, and they thought I'd be so badly overcome in the fire that I wouldn't know, or wouldn't remember, what happened."

"What did happen?" asked Tom. "All I know is that you were overcome in the laboratory room."

"It's too long a story to tell in detail now," said Mr. Baxter. "But the main facts are that through misrepresentations I was induced to associate myself with Field and Melling. They had a good factory for the making of fireworks, and some of the chemicals used in that industry also enter into the manufacture of the kind of dyes I have in mind to make. So I associated myself with them, they agreeing to let me use their laboratory.

"One night they came to see me as I was working there over my formulae. They pretended to have discovered something in an expired patent that nullified what I had. I did not believe this to be so, and I brought out my formulae to compare with theirs— or what they said they had. The next thing I remember was that the fire broke out and my formulae disappeared. Then I was overcome, and I did not care what happened to me, for, having lost the valuable dye formulae, I did not think life worth living.

"Perhaps I was foolish," said Mr. Baxter, "but I had tried so many things and failed, and I counted so much on these formulae that it seemed as if the bottom dropped out of everything when I lost them."

"I know," said Tom sympathetically. "I've been in the same boat myself. But are you sure they took the papers which meant so much to you?"

"I don't see who else could," answered the chemist. "The papers were in a tin box on the table in the room where I was overcome by fire gases, or where, perhaps, they drugged me. I am not clear on this point. And afterward the tin box could not be found. There wasn't enough fire in that room to have melted it."

"No," agreed Tom, "it was mostly smoke in there, and smoke won't melt tin. Nor did I see any box on the table when we carried you out."

"Then the only other surmise is that Field and Melling got away with my formulae during the excitement and when I was half unconscious," Went on Mr. Baxter bitterly. "But you can see how foolish I would be to accuse them in court. I haven't a bit of proof."

"Not much, for a fact," agreed Tom. "Well, with what I heard and what you tell me, perhaps we can work up a case against them later. I'll go over it with Ned. He has a better head for business than I."

"Yes, we inventors need some business brains; or at least the time to give to business problems," agreed the chemist. "But enough of my troubles. Let's get at this chemical compound of yours."

Tom and Mr. Baxter spent many days and nights perfecting the fire-extinguisher chemical, and, after repeated tests, Tom felt that he was nearer his goal.

One afternoon Ned called, and Tom invited him to go for a ride in a small but speedy aeroplane.

"Anything special on?" asked the young manager.

"In a way, yes," Tom answered. "I'm having a firm in Newmarket make me some different containers, and they have promised me samples today. I thought I'd take a fly over and get them. I have the chemical compound all but perfected now, and I want to give it another test."

"All right, I'm with you," assented Ned. "Newmarket," he added musingly. "Isn't that where Field and Melling are now?"

"Yes. They have a factory on the outskirts of the place, and their offices are in the Landmark Building. But we aren't going to see them, though we may call on them later, when you have that case better worked up." For Ned's services had been enlisted to aid Mr. Baxter.

"I shall need a little more time," remarked Ned. "But I think we can at least bluff them into playing into our hands. I have a report to hear from a private detective I have hired."

"I hope we can do something to aid Baxter," remarked Tom. "He has done me good service in this chemical fire extinguisher matter."

A little later Tom and Ned were speeding through the air on their way to Newmarket. The rapid flier was making good time at not a great height when Ned, leaning forward, appeared to be gazing at something in the near distance.

"What's the matter?" asked Tom, for he had his silencer on this craft and it was possible for the occupants to converse. "Do you hear one of the cylinders missing, Ned?"

"No. But what's that smoke down there?" and Ned pointed. "It looks like a fire!"

"It is a fire!" exclaimed Tom, as he took an observation. "Not a big one, but a fire, just the same. If only—"

He did not finish what he started to say, but changed the direction of his air craft and headed directly toward a pall of smoke about a mile away.

In a few seconds they were near enough to make out the character of the blaze.

"Look, Tom!" cried Ned. "It's an immense tree on fire!"

"A tree!" exclaimed Tom, half incredulously, for he was leaning forward to look at one of the aeroplane gages and did not have a clear view of what Ned was looking at.

"Yes, as sure as Mr. Damon would bless something if he were here! It's a tree on fire up near the top!"

"That's strange!" murmured Tom. "But it may give me just the chance I've been looking for."

Ned wondered at this remark on the part of his chum as the airship drew nearer the blazing monarch in the patch of woods over which they were then hovering.

Tom Is Lonesome

"This is certainly the strangest sight I ever saw," remarked Ned, as he and his chum flew nearer and nearer to the smoking and blazing tree. "Is the world turning upside down, Tom, when fires start in this fashion?"

"I fancy it can easily be explained," answered the young inventor. "We'll go into that later. Here, Ned, grab hold of that tin can on the floor and take out the screw plug."

"What's the idea?"

"I want you to drop it as nearly as you can right into the midst of the tree that's on fire."

"Oh, I get your drift! Well, you can count on me."

Ned picked up from the floor of their aeroplane a metal can similar to those Tom used to hold oil or perhaps spare gasoline when he was experimenting on airship speed. The opening was closed with a screw plug, with wings to afford an easier grip. As Ned unscrewed this his nostrils were greeted by an odor that made him gasp.

"Don't mind a little thing like that," cried Tom. "Drop it down, Ned! Drop it down! We're going to be right over the tree in another second or two!"

Ned leaned over the side of the craft and had a good view of the strange sight. The tree that was on fire was a dead oak of great size, dwarfing the other trees in the grove in which it stood. In common with other oaks this one still retained many of its dried leaves, though it was devoid, or almost devoid, of life. Ned noticed in the branches many irregularly shaped objects, and it appeared to be these that were on fire, blazing fiercely.

"It looks as though some one had tied bundles of sticks in the tree and set them on fire," Ned thought as he poised the opened tin of the evil-smelling compound on the edge of the aeroplane's cockpit.

"Let her go, Ned!" cried Tom. "You'll be too late in another second!"

Ned raised himself in his seat and threw, rather than let fall, the can straight for the blazing tree. Like a bomb it shot toward earth, and Ned and Tom, looking down, could see it strike a limb and break open, the rupture of the can letting loose the liquid contained in it.

And then, before the eyes of Tom and Ned, the fire seemed to die out as a picture melts away on a moving picture screen. The smoke rolled away in a ball-like cloud, and the flames ceased to crackle and roar.

"Well, for the love of molasses! what happened, Tom?" cried Ned, as the young inventor guided his craft about in a big circle to come back again over the tree. He wanted to make sure that the fire was out.

It was!

"What sent that blaze to the happy hunting grounds?" asked Ned.

"My new aerial extinguisher," answered Tom, with justifiable pride in his voice. "This fire happened in the nick of time for me, Ned. I had a tin of my new combination in the car, not with any intention of using it, though. I intended to pour it in the new containers I am having made in Newmarket to see if it would corrode them, a thing I wish to avoid.

"But when I saw that tree on fire I couldn't resist the temptation to use my very latest combination of chemicals. It is so recent that I haven't actually tried it on a blaze yet, though I had figured out in theory that it ought to work. And it did, Ned! It worked!"

"Well, I should say so!" agreed his chum. "That blaze was doused for fair. The test could not have been better. But what in the name of a volunteer fire department set that tree to blazing, Tom?"

"I'll tell you in a moment. I want to make some notes before I forget. That combination seems to be just of the right strength. It did the trick. Here, take the wheel and hold her steady while I jot down some memoranda before they get away from me."

Ned was capable of managing an airship, especially under Tom's watchful eye, and as this craft was one with dual controls there was no difficulty in shifting from one steersman to the other.

So while Ned guided, now and then gazing down at the tree from which some smoke still arose, though the fire was all out, Tom made the necessary scientific notes for future amplification.

"And now," observed Ned, as his chum resumed the wheel, "suppose you enlighten me on how that tree came to be on fire—if you didn't set it yourself."

"No, I didn't do that," Tom said, with a laugh. "And I only have a theory as to the cause of the blaze. But suppose we go down and take a look. There's a good field around this grove, and we can get a fine take off. I'll have to go back to Shopton anyhow, to get some more of the chemical."

So the aeroplane made a landing, and then the mystery was explained. The dead oak, to which some of its last year's foliage still clung, was the abiding place of thousands of crows that had built their nests in it. There were hundreds of the big nests, made of dried sticks, mostly, and these made an ideal fuel for the fire.

"But where are the crows, and what started the fire?" asked Ned.

"I fancy the birds flew away as soon as they saw their homes on fire," said Tom. "Or they may not have been at home. Flocks of crows often go to some distant feeding ground for the day, returning at night. I fancy that is what happened here.

"As for the cause of the blaze, I believe it was set by some mischievous boys, who saw a good chance to have some fun without thought of doing any real damage. For the dead tree was of no value, and I imagine the farmers would be glad to see the flock of crows dispersed. Some boys probably climbed up and set fire to one of the nests, and then, when they saw the whole lot going, they became frightened and ran away."

And Tom's theory was, eventually, proved to be true. Some lads, wandering afield, had set fire to the crows' nests and then, frightened as they saw a bigger blaze than they intended, ran away.

Tom and Ned did not remain to see what the returning crows might think about the destruction of their homes, provided they saw fit to return, but, starting the aeroplane, were again on their way.

Tom had lingered long enough to make sure that his latest combination of chemicals had been just what was needed. He felt sure that by using a larger quantity, no fire, however fierce, could continue to blaze.

"But I want to give it a good trial, Ned, as we did from the tower," said Tom. "Though I don't believe there'll be a fizzle this time."

It did not take long for Tom to secure another supply of the new chemical. He then went with it to the firm in Newmarket that was making his containers, or "bombs" as he called them.

On his return he consulted with Mr. Baxter as to the ingredients of the fluid that had put out the blaze in the tree.

"I believe you have at last hit on the right combination," said the chemist. "You are on the road to success, Tom. I wish I could say the same of myself."

"Perhaps your formulae may come back to you as suddenly as they disappeared, or as quickly as I discovered that I had the right thing to put out the fire," said Tom hopefully.

Busy days followed for the young inventor. Now that he was convinced he had at last evolved the right mixture of chemicals, he prepared to make a test on a larger scale than merely a blazing tree.

"I'll try it with a fire in the pit," he said to his chum.

Preparations were made, and the day before Tom was to carry out his plans he received a letter.

"What's the matter? Bad news?" asked Ned, as he saw his friend's face change after reading the epistle.

"Nothing much. Only Mary is going away, and I had expected her to be at the test," Tom answered.

"Going away?" echoed Ned. For long?"

"Oh, no, only for a couple of weeks. She is going to visit an uncle and aunt in Newmarket, or just outside of that city. Another uncle, Barton Keith, has offices in the Landmark Building, I believe."

"Landmark Building," murmured Ned. "Isn't that where Field and Melling hang out?"

"Yes. But don't mention Mary's uncle in connection with them," laughed Tom. "He wouldn't like it."

"I should say not!"

Ned well remembered Mary's uncle, who had been associated with Tom in recovering the treasure in the undersea search.

"Well, if she can't be here, she can't," said Tom, as philosophically as possible. "I'd better run over and bid her goodbye."

This Tom did, though Ned noticed that his chum acted as though lonesome on his return.

"But when he gets to work testing his new chemical he'll be all right," decided Ned.

A Successful Test

"It took you long enough," Ned remarked as Tom entered the main office of the plant, having been to see Mary off on her trip to Newmarket. This was following his call of the night before to learn more particulars of her unexpected visit.

"Yes, I didn't plan to be gone so long," apologized Tom. "But I thought while I was there I might as well go all the way with her."

"And did you?"

"Yes. In the electric runabout. I wanted to come back and get the airship, but she said she wanted to look nice when she met her relatives, and as yet airship travel is a bit mussy. Though when I get my cabined cruiser of the clouds I'll guarantee not to ruffle a curl of the daintiest girl!"

"Getting poetical in your old age!" laughed Ned. "Well, here is that statement you said you wanted me to get ready. Want to go over it now?"

"No, I guess not, as long as you know it's all right. I'm going to start right in and get ready for a bang-up test."

"Of what—your new aerial fire fighting apparatus?"

"Yes. Mr. Baxter and I are going to make up a lot of the chemical compound that—we discovered through using it on the blazing tree—will best do the trick. Then I'm going to try it on a pit fire, and after that on a big blaze with an airship."

"Let me know when you do," begged Ned. "I want to see you do it."

"I'll send you word," promised the young inventor.

Then he began several days and nights of hard work. And he was glad to have the chance to occupy himself, for, though Tom professed not to be much affected by the departure of Mary Nestor, he really was very lonesome.

"How is her uncle, Barton Keith, by the way?" asked Ned, when he called on his chum one day, to find him reading a letter which needed but half an eye to tell was from Mary.

"About as usual," was the answer. "He sends word by Mary that he'll be glad to see us any time we want to call. He has some nice offices in the Landmark Building."

"Those papers proving his right to the oil land, which you recovered from the sunken ship for him, must have made his fortune."

"Well, yes—that and other things," agreed Tom. "Say, we had some exciting times on that undersea search, didn't we?"

"Did you call on Mr. Keith when you went to Newmarket with Mary?" Ned wanted to know, for he and Tom had taken quite a liking to Miss Nestor's uncle.

"No, I didn't get a chance. Besides, I wanted to keep away from the Landmark Building."

"Why?"

"Oh, I might run into Field and Melling, and I don't want to see them until I can accuse them, and prove it, of having taken Mr. Baxter's dye formulae."

"Oh, yes, they're in the same building with Mr. Keith, aren't they? Why do they call it the Landmark? Though I suppose the answer is obvious."

"Yes," assented Tom. "It's a big building—the tallest ever erected in that city, and a fine structure. Though while they were about it I don't see why they didn't make it fireproof."

"Didn't they?" asked Ned, in surprise. "Then the insurance rates must be unusually high, for the companies are beginning to realize how fire departments, even in big cities, are hampered in fighting blazes above the tenth or twelfth stories."

"Yes, it was a mistake not to have the Land mark Building fireproof," admitted Tom. "And Mr. Keith says the owners are beginning to realize that now. It is what is called the 'slow burning' construction."

"Insurance companies don't go much on that," declared Ned, who was in a position to know. "Well, let us hope it never catches fire."

These were busy days for the young inventor. He laid aside all his other activities in order to perfect the plans for manufacturing his new chemical fire extinguisher on a large scale. For Tom realized that while a small quantity of chemicals in a compound might act in a certain way on one occasion, if the bulk should happen to be increased the experimenter could not always count on invariably the same results.

There appeared to be at times a change engendered when a large quantity of chemicals were mixed which was not manifest in a small and experimental batch.

So Tom wanted to mix up a big tank of his new chemical compound and see if it would work in large quantities as well as it did with the small amount Ned had dropped on the blazing tree.

To this end Tom worked at night, as well as by day, and finally he announced to Ned and Mr. Damon, who called one evening, that he believed he had everything in readiness for an exhaustive test the next day.

"There's the stuff!" exclaimed Tom, not a little proudly, as he waved his hand toward an immense carboy in the main shop. "That's what I hope will do the trick. Just take a—"

"Hold on! Stop! That's enough! Bless my hair brush!" cried Mr. Damon, holding up a protesting hand. "If you take that cork out, Tom Swift, you and I will cease to be friends!"

"I wasn't going to open it," laughed the young inventor. "It has a worse odor and seems to choke you more in a big quantity than when there's only a little. I was just going to shake the carboy to let you realize how full it was."

"We'll take your word for it!" laughed Ned. "Now about your test. How are you going to work it?"

"There are to be two tests," answered Tom. "The first, and the smaller, will be in the pit, as before, only this time we shall have what, I believe, will be the successful combination of chemicals to drop on it.

"The second test will be the main one. In that I plan to have an old barn which I have bought set ablaze. Then Ned and I will sail over it in the airship and drop chemicals on it. The barn will be filled with empty boxes and barrels, to make as hot a fire as possible. You are invited to accompany us, Mr. Damon."

"Will there be any smell?" asked the eccentric man, who seemed to have a dislike for anything that was not as agreeable as perfume.

"No, the chemicals will be sealed in containers, which will be dropped from my airship as bombs were dropped in the war," said Tom.

"On those conditions I'll go along," agreed Mr. Damon. "But bless my wedding certificate, Tom! don't tell my wife. She thinks I'm crazy enough now, associating with you and flying occasionally. If she thought I would help you battle with flames from the air she'd likely never speak to me again."

"I'll not tell," promised Tom, laughing.

Preparations for the test went on rapidly. In the morning a fire was to be started in the same pit where the experiment had partly failed before.

From the platform over the blazing hole some of the new combination of chemicals was to be dropped. If it acted with success, as Tom believed it would, he proposed to go on with the more important test in the afternoon.

To this end he had purchased from a farmer the right to set on fire an old ramshackle barn, standing in the midst of a field about three miles outside of Shopton. The barn was on an untilled farm, the house having been destroyed some years before, and it was not near any other structures, so that, even in a high wind, no damage would result.

Tom had filled the barn with inflammable material, and was going to spare no effort to have the test as exhaustive as possible.

The time came for the preliminary trial, and there were a few anxious moments after the oil-soaked boards and boxes in the pit were set ablaze.

"Let her go!" cried Tom to his man on the elevated platform, and down fell the container of chemicals. It had no sooner struck and burst, letting loose a mass of flame-choking vapor, than the fire died out.

"You've struck it, Tom! You've struck it!" cried Ned.

"It begins to look so," agreed the young inventor. "But I'll not call myself out of the woods until this afternoon. Though we can consider it a success so far."

Quite a throng was on hand when the old barn was set ablaze. Tom and Ned and Mr. Damon were there with the airship which had been especially fitted to carry the bombs filled with the extinguisher.

In order to insure a quick, hot blaze the barn was fired on all four sides at once by Tom's men. When it was seen to be a veritable raging furnace of fire, Tom and his two friends took their places in the airship and rapidly mounted upward.

Necessarily they had to circle off away from the blaze to get to the necessary height, but Tom soon brought the airship around again and headed for the black pall of smoke which marked the place of the blazing barn.

"We'll all three send down bombs at the same time," Tom told his friends, as they darted forward. "When I give the word press the levers, and the chemical containers will drop. Then we'll hope for the best."

Higher mounted the flames, and more fiercely raged the fire. The heat of it penetrated even aloft, where Tom and his friends were scudding along in the airship.

"Now!" cried Tom, as his craft hovered for an instant in a favorable position for dropping the bombs. The young inventor, Mr. Damon, and Ned Newton pressed the levers. Looking over the sides of the craft, they saw three dark objects dropping into the midst of the burning barn.

OUT OF THE CLOUDS

Almost as though some giant hand had dropped an immense cloak over the fire in the barn, so did the blaze die down instantly after Tom Swift's extinguishing liquid had been dropped into the seething caldron of flame. For a moment there was even no smoke, but as the embers remained hot and glowing for a time, though the flames themselves were quenched, a rolling vapor cloud began to ascend shortly after the first cessation of the fire. But this only lasted a little while.

"You've turned the trick, Tom!" cried Ned, leaning far over to look at what was left of the barn and its contents.

"Bless my insurance policy, I should say so!" exclaimed Mr. Damon. "It was certainly neat work, Tom!"

"It does look as if I'd struck the right combination," admitted Tom, and he felt justifiable pride in his achievement.

"Look so! Why, hang it all, man, it is so!" declared Ned. "That fire went out as if sent for by a special delivery telegram to give a hurry-up performance in another locality. Look, there's hardly any smoke even!"

This was so, as the three occupants of the rapidly moving airship could see when Tom circled back to pass again over the almost destroyed structure. He had waited until it was almost consumed before dropping his chemicals, as he wished to make the test hard and conclusive. Now the fire was out except for a few small spots spouting up here and there, away from the center of the blaze.

"Yes, I guess she doesn't need a second dose," observed Tom, when he saw how effective had been his treatment of the fire. "I had an additional batch of chemicals on hand, in case they were needed," he added, and he tapped some unused bombs at his feet.

"I call this a pretty satisfactory test," declared Ned. "If you want to form a stock company, Tom, and put your aerial fire-fighting apparatus on the market, I'll guarantee to underwrite the securities."

"Hardly that yet," said Tom, with a laugh. "Now that I have my chemical combination perfected, or practically so, I've got to rig up an airship that will be especially adapted for fighting fires in sky-scrapers."

"What more do you want than this?" asked Ned, as his chum prepared to descend in the speedy machine.

"I want a little better bomb-releasing device, for one thing. This worked all right. But I want one that is more nearly automatic. Then I am going to put on a searchlight, so I can see where I am heading at night."

"Not your great big one!" cried Ned, recalling the immense electric lantern that had so aided in capturing the Canadian smugglers.

"No. But one patterned after that." Tom answered.

"Bless my candlestick!" exclaimed Mr. Damon, "what do you want with a searchlight at a fire, Tom? Isn't there light enough at a blaze, anyhow?"

"No," answered the young inventor, as he made his usual skillful landing. "You know all the big city fire departments have searchlights now for night work and where there is thick smoke. It may be that some day, in fighting a sky-scraper blaze from the clouds at night, I'll have need of more illumination than comes from the flames themselves."

"Well, you ought to know. You've made a study of it," said Mr. Damon, as he and Ned alighted with Tom, the latter receiving congratulations from a number of his friends, including members of the Shopton fire department who were present to witness the test.

"Mighty clever piece of work, Tom Swift!" declared a deputy chief. "Of course we won't have much use for any such apparatus here in Shopton, as we haven't any big buildings. But in New York, Chicago, Pittsburgh and other cities—why, it will be just what they need, to my way of thinking."

"And he needn't go so far from home," said Mr. Damon. "There is one tall building over in Newmarket—the Landmark. I happen to own a little stock in the corporation that put that up, along with other buildings, and I'm going to have them adopt Tom Swift's aerial fire-fighting apparatus."

"Thank you. But you don't need to go to that trouble," asserted Tom. "My idea isn't to have every sky-scraper equipped with an airship extinguisher."

"No? What then?" asked Mr. Damon.

"Well, I think there ought to be one, or perhaps two, in a big city like New York," Tom answered. "Perhaps one outfit would be enough, for it isn't likely that there would be two big fires in the tall building section at the same time, and an airship could easily cover the distance between two widely separated blazes. But if I can perfect this machine so it will be available for fires out of the reach of apparatus on the ground, I'll be satisfied."

"You'll do it, Tom, don't worry about that!" declared the deputy chief. "I never saw a slicker piece of work than this!"

And that was the verdict of all who had witnessed the performance.

With the successful completion of this exacting test and the knowledge that he had perfected the major part of his aerial fire-extinguisher—the chemical combination—Tom Swift was now able to devote his attention to the "frills" as Ned called them. That is, he could work out a scheme for attaching a searchlight to his airship and make better arrangements for a one-man control in releasing the chemical containers into the heart of a big blaze.

Tom Swift owned several airships, and he finally selected one of not too great size, but very powerful, that would hold three and, if necessary, four persons. This was rebuilt to enable a considerable quantity of the fire-extinguishing liquid to be stored in the under part of the somewhat limited cockpit.

This much done, and while his men were making up a quantity of the extinguisher, using the secret formula, and storing it in suitable containers, Tom began attaching a searchlight to his "cloud fire-engine," as Koku called it.

The giant was aching to be with Tom and help in the new work, but Koku was faithful to the blinded Eradicate, and remained almost constantly with the old colored man.

It was touching to see the two together, the giant trying, in his kind, but imperfect way, to anticipate the wishes of the other, with whom he had so often disputed and quarreled in days past. Now all that was forgotten, and Koku gave up being with Tom to wait on Eradicate.

While the colored man was, in fact, unable to see, following the accident when Tom was experimenting with the fire extinguisher, it was hoped that sight might be restored to one eye after an operation. This operation had to be postponed until the eyes and wounds in the face were sufficiently healed.

Meanwhile Rad suffered as patiently as possible, and Koku shared his loneliness in the sick room. Tom came to see Rad as often as he could, and did everything possible to make his aged servant's lot happier. But Rad wanted to be up and about, and it was pathetic to hear him ask about the little tasks he had been wont to perform in the past.

Rad was delighted to hear of Tom's success with the new apparatus, after having been told how quickly the barn fire was put out.

"Yo'—yo' jest wait twell I gits up, Massa Tom," said Rad. "Den Ah'll help make all de contraptions on de airship."

"All right, Rad, there'll be plenty for you to do when the time comes," said the inventor. And he could not help a feeling of sadness as he left the colored man's room.

"I wonder if he is doomed to be blind the rest of his life," thought Tom. "I hope not, for if he does it will be my fault for letting him try to mix those chemicals."

But, hoping for the best, Tom plunged into the work ahead of him. He did not want to offer his aerial fire extinguisher to any large city until he had perfected it, and he was now laboring to that end.

One day, in midsummer, after weary days of toil, Tom took Ned out for a ride in the machine which had been fitted up to carry a large supply of the chemical mixture, a small but powerful searchlight, and other new "wrinkles" as Tom called them, not going into details.

"Any special object in view?" asked Ned, as Tom headed across country. "Are you going to put out any more tree fires?"

"No, I haven't that in mind," was the answer. "Though of course if we come across a blaze, except a brush fire, I may put it out. I have the bombs here," and Tom indicated the releasing lever.

"What I want to try now is the stability of this with all I have on board," he resumed. "If she is able to travel along, and behave as well as she did before I made the changes, I'll know she is going to be all right. I don't expect to put out any fires this trip."

In testing the ship of the air Tom sent her up to a good height, heading out over the open country and toward a lake on the shores of which were a number of summer resorts. It was now the middle of the season, and many campers, cottagers and hotel folk were scattered about the wooded shore of the pretty and attractive body of water.

Tom and Ned had a glimpse of the lake, dotted with many motor boats and other craft, as the airship ascended until it was above the clouds. Then, for a time, nothing could be seen by the occupants but masses of feathery vapor.

"She's working all right," decided Tom, when he found that he could perform his usual aerial feats with his craft, laden as she was with apparatus, as well as he had been able to do before she was so burdened. "Guess we might as well go down, Ned. There isn't much more to do, as far as I can see."

Down out of the heights they swept at a rapid pace. A few moments later they had burst through the film of clouds and once more the lake was below them in clear view.

Suddenly Ned pointed to something on the water and cried:

"Look, Tom! Look! A motor boat in some kind of trouble! She's sinking!"

COALS OF FIRE

Tom Swift saw the craft almost as soon as did his chum. It was rather a large-sized motor boat, quite some distance out from shore, and there was no other craft near it at this time. From the quick, first view Tom and Ned had of it, they decided that a party of excursionists were on a pleasure trip.

But that an accident had happened, and that trouble, if not, indeed, danger, was imminent, was at once apparent to the young inventor and the other occupant of the swiftly moving airship.

For as Tom shut off his motor, to volplane down, thus reducing all noise on his craft, they could dimly hear the shouts and calls for help, coming from the water craft below them.

"Help! Help!" came the impassioned appeals, floating up to Tom and Ned.

"We're coming!" Tom answered, though it is doubtful if his voice was heard. Sound does not seem to carry downward as well as upward, and though Tom's craft was making scarcely any noise, save that caused by the rush of wind through the struts and wires, there was so much confusion on the motor boat, to say nothing of the engine which was going, that Tom's encouraging call must have been unheard.

"What are you going to do, Tom?" asked Ned, "You can't land on the water!"

"I know it; worse luck! If I only had the hydroplane, now, we could make a thrilling rescue—land right beside the other boat and take 'em all off. But, as it is, I'll have to land as near as I can and then we will look for a boat to go out to them in."

Ned saw, now, what Tom's object was. On one shore of the lake was a large, level field, suitable for a landing place for the craft of the air. At least it looked to be a suitable place, but Tom would be obliged to take a chance on that. This field sloped down to the beach of the lake, and as Ned and his chum came nearer to earth they could see several boats on shore, though no persons were near them. Had there been, probably they would have gone to the rescue.

Tom cast a rapid look across the sheet of water, to make sure his services were really needed. The motor boat was lower in the lake now, and was, undoubtedly, sinking. And no other craft was near enough to render help. Though distant whistles, seeming to come from approaching craft, told of help on the way.

"Hold fast, Ned!" cried Tom, as they neared the earth. "We may bump!"

But Tom Swift was too skillful a pilot to cause his craft to sustain much of a crash. He made an almost perfect "three point landing," and there would have been no unusual shaking, except for the fact that the field was a bit bumpy, and the craft more heavily laden than usual.

"Good work, Tom!" cried Ned, as the Lucifer slackened her speed, the young inventor having sent her around in a half circle so that she now faced the lake. Then Tom and Ned climbed from the cockpit, throwing off goggles and helmets as they ran to the shore where there were several rowboats moored.

"And a little old-fashioned naphtha launch! By all that's lucky!" cried Tom. "I didn't think they made these any more. If she only works now!"

There was a little dock at this point on the lake, and the boats appeared to be held at it for hire. But no one was in charge, and Tom and Ned made free with what they found. They considered they had this right in the emergency.

The naphtha launch was chained and padlocked to the dock, but using an oar Tom burst the chain.

"Get one of the rowboats and fasten it to the back of the launch!" Tom directed Ned. "I don't believe this craft will hold them all," and he nodded toward those aboard the sinking boat — for it was only too plainly sinking now.

"All right!" voiced Ned. "I'm with you. Can you get that engine to work?"

"She's humming now," announced Tom, as he turned on the naphtha, and threw in a blazing match to ignite it, this act saving his hand. Naphtha engines are a trifle treacherous.

A few moments later, though not as quickly as a gasoline craft could have been gotten under way, Tom was steering the small launch out and away from the dock, and toward the craft whence came the faint calls for help. Behind them Tom and Ned towed a large rowboat.

Tom speeded the naphtha craft to its limit, and, fortunately for those in danger, it was a fast boat. In less time than they had thought possible, the young inventor and his chum were near the boat that was now low in the water—so low, in fact, that her rail was all but awash.

"Oh, take us out! Save us!" screamed some of the girls.

"Take it easy now," advised Tom, approaching with care. "We've got room for you all. Ned, get back in the rowboat and bring that alongside—on the other side. We'll take you all in," he added.

"Girls first!" called Ned sternly, as he saw one young fellow about to scramble into the naphtha boat.

"Sure, girls first!" agreed the skipper of the disabled craft. "Hit a submerged log," he explained to Tom, as the work of rescue proceeded. "Stove a hole in the bow, but we stuffed coats and things in, and made it a slow leak. Kept the engine going as long as we could, but I thought no one would ever come! Lucky you happened to see us from up there!"

"Yes," assented Tom shortly. He and Ned were too busy to talk much, as they were aiding in getting some hysterical girls and young women into the two sound craft. And when the last of the picnic party had been taken off, the boat with a hole in it gave a sudden lurch, there was a gurgling, bubbling sound, and she sank quickly.

Tom and Ned had anticipated this, however, and had their craft well out of the way of the suction.

"You'll all have to sit quiet," Tom warned his passengers as he took Ned's boat, with her load, in tow. "I've got about all the law allows me to carry," he added grimly.

"Oh, what ever would we have done without you?" half sobbed one girl.

"I guess you could have managed to swim ashore," Tom answered, not wanting to make too much of his effort.

Then more rescue boats came up, but those in the naphtha craft, and Ned's smaller one, refused to be transferred, and remained with our friends until safely landed at the dock.

Receiving the half-hysterical thanks of the party, and leaving them to explain matters to the owner of the borrowed boats, Ned and Tom went back to the Lucifer, and were soon aloft again.

"Pretty slick act, Tom," remarked Ned.

"Oh, it's all in the day's work," was the answer. He had all but perfected his big fire-extinguishing aeroplane, and was contemplating means by which he could give a demonstration to the fire department of some big city, when Mr. Baxter asked to see Tom one day. There was a look on the face of the chemist that caused Tom to exclaim with a good deal of concern:

"What's the matter?"

"Only the same old trouble," was the discouraged answer. "I can't get on the track of my lost secret formulae. If I had Field and Melling here now I—I'd—"

He did not finish his threat, but the look on his face was enough to show his righteous anger.

"I wish we could do something to those fellows!" exclaimed Tom energetically. "If we only had some direct evidence against them!"

"I've got evidence enough—in my own mind!" declared Mr. Baxter.

"Unfortunately that doesn't do in law," returned Tom. "But now that I have this airship firefighter craft so nearly finished, I can devote more time to your troubles, Mr. Baxter."

"Oh, I don't want you bothered over my troubles," said the chemist. "You have enough of your own. But I'm at my wit's end what to do next."

"If it is money matters," began Tom.

"It's partly that, yes," said the other, in a low voice. "If I had those dye formulae, I'd be a rich man."

"Well, let me help you temporarily," begged Tom. And the upshot of the talk was that he engaged Mr. Baxter to do certain research work in the Swift laboratories until such time as the chemist could perfect certain other inventions on which he was working.

In return for his kindness to a fellow laborer, Tom received from Mr. Baxter some valuable hints about fire-extinguishing chemicals, one hint, alone, serving to bring about a curious situation.

It was several days after the accident to the motor boat from which the young inventor and Ned Newton had rescued the party of pleasure seekers that Tom was visited by Mr. Damon, who drove over in his car.

"Have you anything special to do, Tom?" asked the eccentric man. "If you haven't I wish you'd take a ride with me. Not for mere pleasure! Bless my excursion ticket, don't think that, Tom!" cried his friend quickly.

"I know better than to ask you out for a pleasure jaunt. But I have become interested in a certain candy-making machine that a man over in Newmarket is anxious to sell me a share in, and I'd like to get your opinion. Can you run over?"

"Yes," Tom answered. "As it happens I am going to Newmarket myself."

"Oh, I forgot about Mary Nestor being there!" laughed Mr. Damon. "Sly dog, Tom! Sly dog!" and he nudged the youth in the ribs.

"It isn't altogether Mary. Though I am going to see her," Tom admitted. "It has to do with a little apparatus I am getting up. I can capture several birds in the same auto, so I'll go along."

This pleased Mr. Damon, and he and Tom were soon speeding over the road. It was just outside Newmarket that they saw an automobile stalled at the foot of a hill which they topped. It needed but a glance to show that there was serious trouble. As Mr. Damon's car went down the slope two men could be seen leaping from the other machine. And, as they did so, flames burst out of the rear of the stalled machine.

"Fire! Fire!" cried Mr. Damon, rather needlessly it would seem, as any one could see the blaze.

"Another chance!" exclaimed Tom, reaching down between his feet for a wrapped object he had placed in Mr. Damon's car. "It's Field and Melling!" he cried. "The two men who boasted of having put it over on Mr. Baxter. Their car is blazing. Here's where I get a chance to heap coals of fire on their heads!"

VIOLENT THREATS

Tom Swift's companion in the automobile was sufficiently acquainted with this old expression to understand readily what it meant. And as he directed his car as close as was safe to the blazing car, Mr. Damon asked:

"Are you going to put out that fire for them, Tom?"

"I'm going to try," was the grim answer.

The young inventor was rapidly taking out of wrapping paper a metal cylinder with a short nozzle on one end and a handle on the other. It was, obviously, a hand fire extinguisher of a type familiar to all.

"Wait Tom, I'll slow up a little more," said Mr. Damon, as he applied the brakes with more force. "Bless my court plaster! don't jump and injure yourself."

But Tom Swift was sufficiently agile to leap from the automobile when it was still making good speed. He did not want Mr. Damon to approach too close to the burning car, for there might be an explosion. At the same time, he rather discounted the risk to himself, for he ran right in, while the two men, who had leaped from the blazing machine, hurried to a safe distance.

Tom held in readiness a small hand extinguisher. It was one he had constructed from an old one found in the shop, but it contained some of his own chemicals, the original solution having been used at some time or other. It was the intention of the young inventor to put on the market a house-size extinguisher after he had disposed of his big airship invention.

"Look out there! The gasoline tank may go up!" cried Field, the small man with the big voice.

Tom did not answer, but ran in as close as was necessary and began to play a small stream from his hand extinguisher on the blazing car. He was thus able to direct the white, frothy chemical better than when he had shot it from the airship, and in a few seconds only some wisps of curling smoke remained to tell of the presence of the fire. The automobile was badly charred, but the damage was not past redemption.

"Bless my check book! you did the trick, Tom," cried Mr. Damon, as he alighted and came up to congratulate his companion.

"Yes. But this wasn't much," Tom said. "I didn't use half the charge. Short circuit?" he asked Field and Melling who were now returning, having seen that the danger was passed.

"I—I guess so," replied Melling, in his squeaky voice. "We—we are much obliged to you."

"No thanks necessary," said Tom, a bit shortly, as he turned to go back with Mr. Damon to their car. "It's what any one would do under like circumstances."

"Only you did it very effectively," observed Field.

Tom was wondering if they knew who he was and of his association with Josephus Baxter. He did not believe the men recognized him as the person who had been at the Meadow Inn one day with Mary. They had hardly glanced at him then, he thought.

"That's a mighty powerful extinguisher you have there, young man," said Melling. "May I ask the make of it? We ought to carry one like it on our car," he told his companion.

"It is the Swift Aerial Fire Extinguisher," said Tom gravely, with a glance at Mr. Damon.

"The Swift—Tom Swift?" exclaimed Melling. "Do you mean—"

"I am Tom Swift," put in the young inventor quickly. "And this is one of my inventions. I might add," he said slowly, looking first Melling and then Field full in the face, "that I was aided in perfecting the chemical extinguisher by Josephus Baxter."

The effect on the two men, whom Tom believed were scoundrels, was marked.

"Baxter!" cried Field.

"Is he associated with you?" demanded Melling.

"Not officially," Tom answered, delighted at the chance to "rub it in," as he expressed it later. "I have been helping him, and he has been helping me since he lost his dye formulae in—in your fire!"

"Does he say he lost them in the fire of our factory?" demanded Field aggressively.

"He believes he did," asserted Tom. "I helped carry him out of the laboratory of your place when he was almost dead from suffocation. He remembers that he had the formulae then, but since has been unable to find them."

"He'd better be careful how he accuses us!" blustered Field, in his big voice.

"We could have the law on him for that!" squeaked the bigger Melling.

"He hasn't accused you," said Tom easily. "He only says the formulae disappeared during the fire in your place, and he is just wondering. that is all—just wondering!"

"Well, he—we, I—that is, we haven't anything from Baxter that we didn't pay for," declared Field. "And if he goes about saying such things he'd better be careful. I am going—"

But he suddenly became silent as his companion's elbow nudged him. And then Melling took up the talk, saying:

"We're much obliged to you, Mr. Swift, for putting out the fire in our car. But for you it would have been destroyed. And if you ever want to sell the extinguisher process of yours, you'll find us in the market. We are going into the dye business on a large scale, and we can always use new chemical combinations."

"My extinguisher is not for sale," said Tom dryly. "Come on, Mr. Damon. We can take you into town, I suppose," Tom went on, looking at his eccentric friend for confirmation, and finding it in a nod. "But I doubt if we could tow you, as we are in a hurry, and—"

"Oh, thank you, we'll look over our machine before we leave it," said Melling. "It may be that we can get it to go."

Tom doubted this, after a look at the charred section, but he easily understood the dislike of the men, upon whose heads he had heaped coals of fire, to ride with him and Mr. Damon.

So Field and Melling were left standing in the road near their stranded car, which, but for Tom Swift's prompt action, would have been only a heap of ruins.

Tom first visited the man who had a candy machine, in which the owner wanted to interest Mr. Damon. After seeing a demonstration and giving his opinion, he attended to his own affairs, in which his hand extinguisher played a part. Then he called on Mary Nestor at her relative's home.

"Oh, but it's good to see you again, Tom!" cried Mary, after the first greeting. "What have you been doing, and what's all that white stuff on your coat?"

"Fire extinguisher chemical," Tom answered, and he related what had happened.

"What's the matter with your aunt, Mary? She seems worried about something," he said, after the aunt with whom Mary was staying had come in, greeted Tom briefly, and gone out again.

"Oh, she and Uncle Jasper are worried over money matters, I believe," Mary said. "Uncle Jasper invested heavily in the Landmark Building here, and now, I understand, it is discovered that it was put up in violation of the building laws—something about not being fire-proof. Uncle Jasper is likely to lose considerable money.

"It isn't that it will make him so very poor," Mary went on. "But Uncle Barton Keith—you remember you went on the undersea search with him—Uncle Barton warned Uncle Jasper not to go into the Landmark Building scheme."

"And Uncle Jasper did, I take it," said Tom.

"Yes. And now he's sorry, for not only may he lose money, but Uncle Barton will laugh at him, and Uncle Jasper hates that worse than losing a lot. But tell me about yourself, Tom. What have you been doing? And is Eradicate going to get better?"

"I hope so," Tom said. "As for me—"

But he was interrupted by loud voices in the hall. He recognized the tones of Mary's Uncle Jasper saying:

"They're scoundrels, that's what they are! Just plain scoundrels! When I accuse them of swindling me and others in that Landmark Building deal they have the nerve to ask me to invest money in some secret dye formulae they claim will revolutionize the industry! Bah! They're scoundrels, that's what they are— Field and Melling are scoundrels, and I'm going to have them arrested!"

A TOWN BLAZE

Mary's uncle, Jasper Blake, always an impetuous man, opened the door so quickly that Tom, who was standing near it talking to Mary, barely had time to move aside.

"Oh, Tom, excuse me! Didn't see you!" bruskly went on Mr. Blake. "But this thing has gotten on my nerves and I guess I'm a bit wrought up."

"There isn't any guessing about it, Uncle Jasper," said Mary, with a laugh and a look at Tom to warn him not to tell her relative that he had just befriended Field and Melling. "For," as Mary said to Tom later, "he would positively rave at you."

Tom was wise enough to realize this, and so, after some laughing reference to the effect that he would have to wear protective armor if he stood near doors when Mary's uncle opened them so suddenly, the conversation became general.

"I hope you never get roped in as I have been," said Mr. Blake, as he sat down. "Those scoundrels, Field and Melling, would rob a baby of his first tooth if they had the chance!"

"No, I am not likely to have anything to do with them; though I have met them," and Tom gave Mary a glance. "But did I hear you say they are embarking on a dye enterprise?" he asked. "I couldn't help overhearing what you said in the hall," he explained.

"That's the story they tell," said Uncle Jasper. "I was foolish enough to invest in the Landmark Building, and now I'm likely to lose it all in a lawsuit."

"I mentioned it," said Mary.

"And that isn't the worst," went on Mr. Blake. "But Barton— that's your friend of the submarine—will give me the laugh, for he was asked to invest in the same building, and didn't."

"Oh, maybe it will all turn out right," said Tom consolingly. "My friend Mr. Damon has a little stock in the same structure."

"Nothing those two scoundrels have anything to do with will turn out right," declared Mary's uncle. "And to think of their nerve when they ask me to go in with them on a dye scheme!"

"That's what interests me," said Tom.

"Well, take my advice and don't become interested to the extent of investing any money," warned Mr. Blake. "I'm not going to."

"I didn't mean that way," said Tom. "But I happen to be acquainted with an expert dye maker who lost some secret formulae during a fire in Field and Melling's factory."

"You don't say so!" cried Mr. Blake. "Tom Swift, there's something wrong here! Let you and me talk this over. I begin to see how I may be able to take a peep through the hole in the grindstone," a colloquial expression which was as well understood by Tom as were some of Mr. Damon's blessing remarks.

"If you're going to talk business I think I'll excuse myself," said Mary.

"Don't go," urged Tom, but she said to him that she would see him before he left, and then she went out, leaving her uncle and the young inventor busily engaged in talking.

But though Mr. Blake had certain suspicions regarding Field and Melling, and though Tom Swift, too, believed they had something to do with the disappearance of Baxter's secret formulae, it was another matter to prove anything.

Impetuous as he often was, Mr. Blake was for calling in the police at once, and having the two men arrested. But Tom counseled delay.

"Wait until we get more evidence against them," he urged.

"But they may skip out!" objected Mary's uncle.

"They won't with that Landmark Building on their hands," said the young inventor.

"Their hands! Huh! They'll take precious good care that the trouble and responsibility of it are on other people's hands before they go," declared Mr. Blake. "However, I suppose you're right. Barton Keith sets a deal by your opinion since that undersea search, and while I don't always agree with him, I do in this case. Especially since he is likely to have the laugh on me."

"Oh, I wouldn't count everything lost in that building deal," said Tom. "A way may be found out of the trouble yet. But I must be getting back. Dr. Henderson was to give a report today on the condition of Eradicate's eyes, and I want to be there."

"Mary was saying something about your faithful old retainer being in trouble," said Mr. Blake. "I'm sorry to hear about it."

"We are all sorry for poor Rad," replied Tom slowly. "I only hope he gets his sight back. His last days will be very sad if he doesn't."

Tom found Mary waiting for him after he had left her uncle, and, after a short talk with her, he made ready to ride back with Mr. Damon, who, after having attended to several other matters, was now outside in his car.

"When are you coming home, Mary?" Tom asked.

"In a week or two," she answered. "I'll send word when I'm ready and you can come and get me."

"Delighted!" declared Tom. "Don't forget!" During the ride home the young inventor was unusually silent, so much so that Mr. Damon finally exclaimed:

"Bless my phonograph, Tom Swift! but what is the matter? Has Mary broken the engagement?"

"Oh, no, nothing like that," was the answer. "Only I'm wondering about Eradicate, and—other matters."

Other matters had to do with what Mary's uncle had told Tom about the interest manifested by Field and Melling in some dye industry.

Tom's forebodings regarding his colored helper were nearly borne out, for Dr. Henderson gloomily shook his head when asked for the verdict.

"It's too early to say for a certainty," replied the medical man, "but I am not as hopeful as I was, Tom, I'm sorry to say."

"I'm sorry to hear it," returned Tom. "Is there anything we can do—any hospital to which we can send him for special treatment?"

"No, he is doing as well as he can be expected to right here. Besides, he has his friends around him, and the companionship of that giant of yours, absurd as it may seem, is really a tonic to Eradicate. I never saw such devotion on the part of any one."

"Koku has certainly changed," said Tom. "He and Rad used always to be quarreling. But I guess that is all over," and Tom sighed.

"Oh, I wouldn't say that," declared the medical man. "I haven't given up, though there are some symptoms I do not like. However, I am going to wait a week and then make another test."

Tom knew that the week would be an anxious one for him, but, as it developed, he had so much to do in the next few days that, for the time being, he rather forgot about Eradicate.

Field and Melling, he heard incidentally, had their machine towed to a garage for repairs, but beyond that no word came from the two men. Josephus Baxter remained at work over his dye formulae in one of Tom's laboratories, but the young inventor did not see much of the discouraged old man.

Tom did not tell of the encounter with Field and Melling and of extinguishing the fire in their car, for he knew it would only excite Mr. Baxter, and do no good.

It was within a few days of the time when Tom was to call in a committee of fire insurance experts to give them a demonstration of the efficiency of his aerial fire-fighting machine. He was putting the finishing touches to his craft and its extinguishing-dropping devices when he received a call from Mr. Baxter.

"Well, how goes it?" asked Tom, trying to infuse some cheer into his voice.

"Not very well," was the answer. "I've tried, in every way I know, to get on the track of the missing methods perfected by that Frenchman, but I can't. I'd be a millionaire now, if I had that dye information."

"Do you really think they have them—actually have the formulae?" asked Tom.

"I certainly do. And the reason I believe so is that I was over at a chemical supply factory the other day when an order came in for a quantity of a very rare chemical."

"What has that to do with it?" asked Tom.

"This chemical is an ingredient called for by one of the dye formulae that were stolen from me. I never heard of its being used for anything else. I at once became suspicious. I learned that this chemical had been ordered sent to Field and Melling in their new offices in the Landmark Building."

"Maybe they intend to use it in making a new kind of fireworks," suggested Tom.

Mr. Baxter shook his head.

"That chemical never would work in a skyrocket or Roman candle," he said. "I'm sure they're trying to cheat me out of my dye formulae. If I could only prove it!"

"That's the trouble," agreed Tom. "But I'll give you all the help I can. And, come to think of it, I believe you might interest Mr. Blake. He has no love for Field and Melling, and he has several keen lawyers on his staff. I believe it would be a good thing for you to talk to Mr. Blake."

"Please give me a letter of introduction to him," begged Mr. Baxter. "What I need is legal talent and capital to fight these scoundrels. Mr. Blake may supply both."

"He may," agreed Tom. "I'll fix it so you can meet him. But what do you think of this combination, Mr. Baxter? It is my very latest solution for putting out fires. I'm loading an airship up with some of the bomb containers now, and—"

Tom's further remarks were interrupted by the noise of shouting and tumult in the street, and a moment later yells could be heard of:

"Fire! Fire! Fire!"

"Another blaze!" exclaimed Mr. Baxter, raising the shades which had been drawn, since night had fallen.

"And not far away," said Tom, as he caught the reflection of a red gleam in the sky.

There was a ring at the front doorbell, and almost at once Ned Newton's voice called:

"Tom! Tom Swift! There's quite a fire in town! Don't you want to try your new apparatus on it?"

"The very chance!" exclaimed the young inventor. "Come on, Mr. Baxter. There's room in the airship for you and Ned. I want you to see how my chemical works!"

Without waiting for a reply from the chemist, Tom caught him by the hand and led him toward the side door that gave egress to the yard where one of the airships was housed. Tom caught sight of Ned, who was hastening toward him.

"Big fire, Tom!" said the young manager again. "Fierce one!"

"I'm going to try to put it out!" Tom answered. "Want to come?"

"Sure thing!" answered Ned.

FINISHING TOUCHES

Tom Swift and Ned Newton were so accustomed to acting quickly and in emergencies that it did not take them long to run out the airship, which Tom had in readiness, not especially for this emergency, but to demonstrate his new apparatus to a committee of fire underwriters whom he had invited to call in a few days.

"Take this, if you will, Mr. Baxter!" cried Tom, giving the chemist a metal container. "It's a little different combination from the extinguisher I already have in the machine. Maybe I'll get a chance to try it."

"You're going to have all the chance you want, Tom, by the looks of that blaze," commented Ned Newton.

"It does look like quite a fire," observed Tom, as he gazed up at the sky, where the reflection was turning to a brighter red.

Outside in the streets near the Swift house and shops could be heard the rattle of fire apparatus, the patter of running feet, and many shouts from excited men and boys.

"Any idea what it is, Ned?" asked Tom, as he motioned to Mr. Baxter to climb into the aircraft.

"Some one said it was the new Normal School. But that's farther to the north," was Ned's answer. "By the way the blaze has increased since I first saw it, I'd take it to be the lumberyard."

"That would make a monster blaze!" observed Tom. "I don't believe I'll have chemicals enough for that," and he looked at the rather small supply in his craft. "However, I haven't time to get any more. Besides, they'll have the regular department on the job, and this isn't a skyscraper, anyhow."

"No, we'll have to go to New York or Newmarket for one of those," observed Ned. "All ready, Tom?"

"All ready," said the young inventor, as Ned took his place beside Mr. Baxter.

"What's the matter, Tom?" asked the voice of Mr. Swift, as he came out into the yard, having been attracted by the flashing lights and the noise of the aircraft motor, as Tom gave it a preliminary test.

"There's a fire in town," Tom answered. "I'm going to see if they need my services."

"Guess there isn't any question about that," said his business manager.

Tom's father, who was suffering the infirmities of age, was in the habit of retiring early, and he had dozed off in his chair directly after supper, to be awakened by the shouting and confusion about the place.

"Take care of yourself, my boy!" he advised, as there came a moment of silence before the throttle of the aircraft was opened to send it on its upward journey. "Don't take too many risks."

"I won't," Tom promised. "We'll be back soon."

Then came the roar of the motor as Tom cut out the muffler to gain speed and, a moment later, he and his two friends were sailing aloft with a load of fire-extinguishing chemicals.

Up and up rose the aircraft. It was not the first time Mr. Baxter had enjoyed the sensation, but he was not enough of a veteran to be immune to the thrills nor to be altogether void of fear. And it was his first night trip. Still he gave few evidences of nervousness.

"These she is!" cried Ned, for when the exhaust from the motor was sent through the new muffler Tom had attached it was possible to talk aboard the Lucifer. The young manager pointed down toward the earth, over which the craft was then skimming, though at no great height.

"It is the lumberyard!" exclaimed Mr. Baxter presently.

"It sure is," assented Tom. "I know I haven't enough stuff to cover as big a blaze as that, but I'll do my best. Fortunately there is no wind to speak of," he added, as he guided the craft in the direction of the fire.

"What has that to do with it—I mean as far as the working of your chemical extinguisher is concerned?" asked Mr. Baxter. "Can't you drop the bomb containers accurately in a wind?"

"Well, the wind has to be allowed for in dropping anything from an aeroplane," Tom answered. "And, naturally, it does spoil your aim to an extent. But the reason I'm glad there is no wind to speak of is that the chemical blanket I hope to spread over the fire won't be so quickly blown away."

"Oh, I see," said Mr. Baxter. "Well, I'm glad that you will be able to have a successful test of your invention."

"The regular land apparatus is on hand," observed Ned, for they were now so near the fire that they could look down and, in the reflection from the blaze, could see engines, hose-wagons and hook and ladder trucks arriving and deploying to different places of advantage, from which to fight the lumberyard fire that was now a roaring furnace of flames.

"No skyscraper work needed here," observed Tom. "But it will give me a chance to use the latest combination I worked out. I'll try that first. Are you ready with it, Mr. Baxter?"

"Yes," was the answer.

The young inventor, not heeding the cries of wonder that arose from below and paying no attention to the uplifted hands and arms pointing to him, steered his craft to a corner of the yard where there was a small isolated fire in a pile of boards. It was Tom's idea to try his new chemical first on this spot to watch the effect. Then he would turn loose all his other containers of the chemical mixture that had proved so effective in other tests.

Attention of those who had gathered to look at the fire was about evenly divided between the efforts of the regular department and the pending action by Tom Swift. The latter was not long in turning loose his latest sensation.

"Let it go!" he cried to Mr. Baxter, and down into the seething caldron of flame dropped a thin sheet-iron container of powerful chemicals. Leaning over the cockpit of the aircraft, the occupants watched the effect. There was a slight explosion heard, even above the roar of the flames, and the tongues of fire in the section where Tom's extinguisher had fallen died down.

"Good work!" cried Ned.

"No!" answered Tom, shaking his head. "I was a little afraid of this. Not enough carbon dioxide in this mixture. I'll stick to the one I found most effective." For the flames, after momentarily dying down, burst out again in the spot where he had dropped the bomb.

Tom wheeled the airship in a sharp, banking turn, and headed for the heart of the fire in the lumberyard. It was clearly getting beyond the control of the regular department.

"How about you, Ned?" called Tom, for he had given his chum charge of dropping the regular bombs containing a large quantity of the extinguisher Tom had practically adopted.

"All ready," was the answer.

"Let 'em go!" came the command, and down shot the dark, spherical objects. They burst as they hit the ground or the piles of blazing lumber, and at once the powerful gases generated by the mixture of several different chemicals were released.

Again the three in the airship leaned eagerly over the side of the cockpit to watch the effect. It was almost magical in its action.

The bombs had been dropped into the very fiercest heart of the fire, and it was only an instant before their action was made manifest.

"This will do the trick!" cried Ned. "I'm certain it will."

"I didn't have much fear that it wouldn't," said Tom. "But I hoped the other would be better, for it is a much cheaper mixture to make, and that will count when you come to sell it to big cities."

"But the fire is certainly dying down," declared Mr. Baxter.

And this was true. As container after container of the bomb type fell in different parts of the burning lumberyard, while Tom coursed above it, the flames began to be smothered in various sections.

And from the watching crowds, as well as from the hard-working members of the Shopton fire department, came cheers of delight and encouragement as they saw the work of Tom Swift's aerial fire-fighting machine.

For he had, most completely, subdued what threatened to be a great fire, and when the last of his bombs had been dropped, so effective was the blanket of fire-dampening gases spread around that the flames just naturally expired, as it were.

As Tom had said, the absence of wind was in his favor, for the generated gases remained just where they were wanted, directly over the fire like an extinguishing blanket, and were not blown aside as would otherwise have been the case.

And, by the peculiar manner in which his chemicals were mixed, Tom had made them practically harmless for human beings to breathe. Though the fire-killing gases were unpleasant, there was no danger to life in them, and while several of the firemen made wry faces, and one or two were slightly ill from being too close to the chemicals, no one was seriously inconvenienced.

"Well, I. guess that's all," said Tom, when the final bomb had been dropped. "That was the last of them, wasn't it, Ned?"

"Yes, but you don't need any more. The fire's out—or what isn't can be easily handled by the hose lines."

"Good!" cried Tom. "But, all the same, I wish I had been able to make the first mixture work."

"Perhaps I can help you with that," suggested Mr. Baxter.

And the following day, after Tom had received the thanks of the town officials and of the fire department for his work in subduing the lumberyard blaze, the young inventor called Josephus Baxter in consultation.

"I feel that I need your help," said the young inventor. "You have been at this chemical study longer than I, and I am willing to pay you well for your work. Of course I can't make up to you the loss of your dye formulae. But while you are waiting for something to turn up in regard to them, you may be glad to assist me."

"I will, and without pay," said the chemist.

But Tom would not hear of that, and together he and Mr. Baxter set about putting the finishing touches to Tom's latest invention.

ON THE TRAIL

"There, Tom Swift, it ought to work now!"

Josephus Baxter held up a large laboratory test tube, in which seethed and bubbled some strange mixture, turning from green to purple, then to red, and next to a white, milky mixture.

"Do you think you've hit on the right combination?" asked the young inventor, whose latest idea, the plan of fighting fires in skyscrapers from an airship as a vantage point, was taking up all his spare moments.

"I'm positive of it," said Mr. Baxter. "I've dabbled in chemicals long enough to be certain of this, even if I can't get on the track of the missing dye formulae."

"That certainly is too bad," declared Tom. "I wish I could help you as much as you have helped me."

"Oh, you have helped me a lot," said the chemist. "You have given me a place to work, much better than the laboratory I had in the old fireworks factory of Field and Melling. And you have paid me, more than liberally, for what little I have done for you."

"You've done a lot for me," declared Tom. "If it had not been for your help this chemical compound would not be nearly as satisfactory as it is, nor as cheap to manufacture, which is a big item."

"Oh, you were on the right track," said Mr. Baxter. "You would have stumbled on it yourself in a short time, I believe. But I will say, Tom Swift, that, between us, we have made a compound that is absolutely fatal to fires. Even a small quantity of it, dropped in the heart of a large blaze, will stop combustion."

"And that's what I want," declared Tom. "I think I shall go ahead now, and proceed with the manufacture of the stuff on a large scale."

"And what do you propose doing with it?" asked Mr. Baxter.

"I'm going to sell the patent and the idea that goes with it to as many large cities as I can," Tom answered. "I'll even manufacture the airships that are needed to carry the stuff over the tops of blazing skyscrapers, dropping it down. I'll supply complete aerial fire-fighting plants."

"And I think you'll do a good business," said the chemist.

It was the conclusion of the final tests of an improved chemical mixture, and the reaction that had taken place in the test tube was the end of the experiment. Success was now again on the side of Tom Swift.

But when that has been said there remains the fact that it was just the other way with the unfortunate Mr. Baxter.

Try as he had, he could not succeed in getting the right chemical combination to perfect the dye process imparted to him by his late French friend. With the disappearance of the secret formulae went the good luck of Josephus Baxter.

He had worked hard, taking advantage of Tom's generosity, to bring back to his memory the proper manner of mixing certain ingredients, so that permanent dyes of wondrous beauty in coloring would be evolved. But it was all in vain.

"I know who have those formulae," declared the chemist again and again. "It is those scoundrels, Field and Melling. And they are planning to build up their own dye business with what is mine by right!"

And though Tom, also, believed this, there was no way of proving it.

As the young inventor had said, he was now ready to put his own latest invention on the market. After many tests, aided in some by Mr. Baxter, a form of liquid fire extinguisher had been made that was superior to any known, and much cheaper to manufacture. Veteran members of fire departments in and about Shopton told Tom so. All that remained was to demonstrate that it would be as effective on a large scale as it was on a small one, and big cities, it was agreed, must, of necessity, add it to their equipment.

"Well, I think I'll give orders to start the works going," said Tom, at the conclusion of the final test. "I have all the ingredients on hand now, and all that remains is to combine them. My airship is all ready, with the bomb-dropping device."

"And I wish you all sorts of luck," said Mr. Baxter. "Now I am going to have another go at my troubles. I have just thought of a possible new way of combining two of the chemicals I need to use. It may be I shall have success."

"I hope so," murmured Tom. He was about to leave the room when Koku, the giant, entered, with a letter in his hand. The big man showed some signs of agitation, and Tom was at once apprehensive about Eradicate.

"Is Rad—has anything happened—shall I get the doctor?"

"Oh, Rad, him all right," answered Koku. "That is him not see yet, but mebby soon. Only I have to chase boy, an' he make faces at me—boy bring this," and the giant held out the envelope.

"Oh!" exclaimed Tom, and he understood now. Messenger boys frequently came to Tom's house or to the shops, and they took delight in poking fun at Koku on account of his size, which made him slow in getting about. The boys delighted to have him chase them, and something like this had evidently just taken place, accounting for Koku's agitation.

"This is for you, Mr. Baxter, not for me," said Tom, as he read the name on the envelope.

"For me!" exclaimed the chemist. "Who could be writing to me? It's a big firm of dye manufacturers," he went on, as he caught a glimpse of the superscription in the upper left hand corner.

Quickly he read the contents of the epistle, and a moment later he gave a joyful cry.

"I'm on the trail! On the trail of those scoundrels at last!" exclaimed Josephus Baxter. "This gives me just the evidence I needed! Now I'll have them where I want them!"

A Heavy Load

Josephus Baxter was so excited by the receipt of the letter which Koku delivered to him that for some seconds Tom Swift could get nothing out of him except the statement:

"I'm on their trail! Now I'm on their trail!"

"What do you mean?" Tom insisted. "Whose trail? What's it all about?"

"It's about Field and Melling! That's who it's about!" exclaimed Mr. Baxter, with a smothered exclamation. "Look, Tom Swift, this letter is addressed to me from one of the biggest dye firms in the world—a firm that is always looking for something new!"

"But if you haven't anything new to give them, of what use is it?" Tom asked, for he knew that the chemist had said his process, stolen, as he claimed, by Field and Melling, was his only new project.

"But I will have something new when I get those secret formulae away from those scoundrels!" declared Mr. Baxter.

"Yes, but how are you going to do it, when you can't even prove that they have them?" asked Tom.

"Ah, that's the point! Now I think I can prove it," declared Mr. Baxter. "Look, Tom Swift! This letter is addressed to me in care of Field and Melling at the office I used to have in their fireworks factory."

"The office from which you were rescued nearly dead," Tom added.

"Exactly. The place where you saved me from a terrible death. Well, if you will notice, this letter was written only two days ago. And it is the first mail I have received as having been forwarded from that address since the fire. I know other mail must have come for me, though."

"What became of it?" asked Tom.

"Those scoundrels confiscated it!" declared the chemist. "But, in some manner, perhaps through the error of a new clerk, this letter was remailed to me here, and now I have it. It is of the utmost importance!"

"In what way?" asked Tom.

"Why, it is directed to me, outside and in, and it makes an inquiry about the very dyes of the lost secret formulae, one dye in particular."

"I don't quite understand yet," said Tom.

"Well, it's this way," went on Mr. Baxter. "I had, in the office of Field and Melling, all the papers telling exactly how to make the dyes. After the fire, in which I was rendered unconscious, those papers disappeared.

"The only way in which any one could make the dyes in question was by following the formulae given in those papers. And now here is a letter, addressed to me from a big firm, asking my prices on a certain dye, which can only be made by the process bequeathed to me by the Frenchman."

"Which means what?" asked Tom.

"It means that Field and Melling must have been writing to this firm on their own hook, offering to sell them some of this dye. But, in some way, my name must have appeared on the letter or papers sent on by the scoundrels, and this big firm replies to me direct, instead of to Field and Melling! Even then I would not have benefited if they had confiscated this letter as I am sure, they have done in the case of others. But, by some slip, I get this.

"And it proves, Tom Swift, that Field and Melling are in possession of my dye formulae, and that they have tried to dispose of some of the dye to this firm. Not knowing anything of this, the firm replies to me. So now I have direct evidence—just what I wanted—and I can get on the trail of the scoundrels who have cheated me of my rights."

Tom looked at the letter which, it appeared, had been left with Koku by a special delivery boy from the post office. It was an inquiry about certain dyes, and was addressed to Mr. Baxter in care of Field and Melling, the former fireworks firm, which now had started a big dye plant, with offices in the Landmark Building in Newmarket.

"It does look as though you might get at them through this," Tom said, as he handed back the letter. "But I'm afraid you'll have to get further evidence before you could convict them in a court of law—you'll have to show that they actually have possession of your formulae."

"That's what I wish I could do," said the chemist, somewhat wistfully. His first enthusiasm had been lessened.

"I'll help you all I can," offered Tom. And events were soon to transpire by which the young inventor was to render help to the chemist in a most sensational manner.

"Just now," Tom went on, "I must arrange about getting a large supply of these chemicals made, and then plan for a test in some big city."

"Yes, you have done enough for me," said Mr. Baxter. "But I think now, with this letter as evidence, we'll be able to make a start."

"I agree with you," Tom said. "Why don't you go over to see Mr. Damon? He's a good business man, and perhaps he can advise you. You might also call on that lawyer who does work for Mr. Keith and Mr. Blake. And that reminds me I must call Mary Nestor up and find out when she is coming home. I promised to fetch her in one of the airships."

"I will go and see Mr. Damon," decided Mr. Baxter. "He always gives good advice."

"Even if he does bless everything he sees!" laughed Tom. "But if you're going to see him I'll run you over. I'm going to Waterfield."

"Thanks, I'll be glad to go with you," said the chemist.

Mr. Damon was glad to see his friends, and, when he had listened to the latest developments, he exclaimed with unusual emphasis:

"Bless my law books, Mr. Baxter! but I do believe you're on the right trail at last. Come in, and we'll talk this over."

So Tom left them, traveling on to a distant city where he arranged for a large supply of the chemicals he would need in his extinguisher.

For several days Tom was so busy that he had little time to devote to Mr. Baxter, or even to see him. He learned, however, that the chemist and Mr. Damon were in frequent consultation, and the young inventor hoped something would come of it.

Tom's own plans were going well. He had let several large cities know that he had something new in the way of a fire-fighting machine, and he received several offers to demonstrate it.

He closed with one of these, some distance off, and agreed to fly over in his aircraft and extinguish a fire which was to be started in an old building which had been condemned. and was to be destroyed. This was in a city some four hundred miles away and when Ned Newton called on him one afternoon he found Tom busily engaged in loading his sky-craft with a heavy cargo of the newest liquid extinguisher.

"You aren't taking any chances, are you, Tom?" asked Ned.

"What do you mean?"

"I mean you seem to have enough of the liquid 'fire-discourager' to douse any blaze that was ever started."

"No use sending a boy on a man's errand," said Tom. "I'm counting on you to go with me, Ned—you and Mr. Baxter. We leave this afternoon for Denton."

"I'll be with you. Couldn't pass up a chance like that. But here comes Koku, and it looks as if he had something on his mind."

The giant did, indeed, seem to be laboring under the stress of some emotion.

"Oh, Master Tom!" the big man exclaimed when he had got the attention of the young inventor. "Rad—he—he—"

"Has anything happened?" asked Tom, quickly. "No, not yet. But dat pill man—he say by tomorrow he know if Rad ever will see sunshine more!"

"Oh, the doctor says he'll be able to decide about Rad's eyesight tomorrow, does he?"

"Yes. What so pill man say," repeated Koku.

"Um," mused Tom, "I wish I were going to be here, but I don't see how I can. I must give this test." But it was with a sinking heart as he thought of poor Eradicate that the young inventor proceeded to pile into his airship the largest and heaviest load of chemicals it had ever carried.

THE LIGHT IN THE SKY

"Well, what do you say, Tom?" asked Ned, in a low voice.

"She's all right as far as I can see, though she may stagger a bit at the take off."

"It's a pretty heavy load," agreed the young manager, as he and Tom Swift walked about the big fire-fighting airship Lucifer, which had been rolled outside the hangar. "But still I think she'll take it, especially since you've tuned up the motor so it's at least twenty per cent. more powerful than it was."

"Perhaps you'd better leave me out," suggested Mr. Baxter, who had been helping the boys. "I'm not a feather weight, you know."

"I need you with us," said Tom. "I want your expert opinion on the effect the new chemicals have on the flames."

"Well, I'd like to come," admitted the chemist, "for it will be a valuable experience for me. But I don't want an accident up in the air."

"Trust Tom Swift for that!" cried Ned. "If he says his aircraft will do the trick, it positively will."

"How about leaving me out?" asked Mr. Damon. "I'm not an expert in anything, as far as I know."

"You are in keeping us cheerful. And we may need you to bless things if there's a slip-up anywhere," laughed Tom, for Mr. Damon had been invited to be one of the party.

"I don't so much mind a slipup," said Mr. Damon, "as I do a slip down. That's where it hurts! However, I'll take a chance with you, Tom Swift. It won't be the first one—and I guess it won't be the last."

The work of getting the big airship ready for what was to be a conclusive test of her fire-fighting abilities from the clouds proceeded rapidly. As has been related, Tom had perfected, with the help of Mr. Baxter, a combination of chemicals which was effective in putting out a fire when dropped into the blaze from above. Quantities of this combination had been stored in metal containers which Tom had at first styled "bombs," but which he now called "aerial grenades."

The manner of dropping the grenades was, on the whole, similar to the manner in which bombs were dropped from airships during the Great War, but Tom had made several improvements in this plan.

These improvements had to do with the releasing of the bombs, or, in this case, grenades. It is not easy to drop or throw something from a swiftly moving airship so that it will hit an object on the ground. During the war aviators had to train for some time before becoming even approximately accurate.

Tom Swift decided that to leave this matter to chance or to the eye of the occupant of an airship was too indefinite. Accordingly he invented a machine, something like a range-finder for big guns. With this it was a comparatively easy matter to drop a grenade at almost any designated place.

To accomplish this it was necessary to take into consideration the speed of the airship, its height above the ground, the velocity of the wind, the weight of the grenades, and other things of this sort. But by an intricate mathematical process Tom solved the problem, so that it was only necessary to set certain pointers and levers along a slide rule in the cockpit of the craft. Then when the releasing catch was pressed, the grenades would drop down just about where they were most needed.

"I think everything is ready," said Tom, when he had taken a last look over his craft, making sure that all the chemical grenades were in place. "If you will be ready, gentlemen, we will take our places and start in about half an hour," he added. "I want to say goodbye to my father, and cheer up Rad—if I can."

"The doctor will know tomorrow, will he?" asked Mr. Damon.

"Yes. And I'm sorry I will not be here to listen to the report," said Tom. "Though I am almost afraid to receive it," he added in a low voice. "I shall blame myself if Rad is to go through the remainder of his life blind."

"It couldn't be helped," said Ned. "We'll hope for the best."

"Yes," agreed Tom, "that's all we can do—hope for the best. By the way," he went on, turning to Mr. Baxter, "are you any nearer fastening the guilt on those two rascals, Field and Melling?"

"Bless my prosecuting attorney, no!" exclaimed Mr. Damon. "Those are the slickest scoundrels I ever tackled! They're like a flea. Once you think you have them where you want them, and they're on the other side of the table, skipping around."

"I've about given up," said Mr. Baxter, in discouraged tones. "I guess my dye formulae are gone forever."

"Don't say that!" exclaimed Tom. "Once I get this fire matter off my hands, I'm going to tackle the problem myself. We'll either make those fellows sorry they ever meddled in this matter, or we'll get up a new combination of dyes that will put them out of business!"

"Bless my Easter eggs, I'm glad to hear you talk that way!" cried Mr. Damon.

"Well, Rad, I'll expect to see you up and around when I get back," said Tom to his old servant, as he stepped into the sick room to say goodbye.

"Oh, is yo' goin', Massa Tom?" asked the colored man, turning his bandaged head in the direction of the beloved voice.

"Yes. I'm going to try out a new scheme of mine—the fire extinguisher, you know."

"De same one whut fizzed up, an'—an' busted me in de eyes, Massa Tom?"

"Yes, Rad, I'm sorry to say, it's the same one."

"Oh, shucks now, Massa Tom! whut's use worryin'?" laughed Rad. "I suah will be all right when yo' gits back. De doctor man—de 'pill man' dat giant calls him—says I'll suah be better."

"Of course you will," declared Tom, but his heart sank when he saw Mrs. Baggert remove the bandages and he caught sight of Rad's burned face and the eyes that had to be kept closed if ever they were again to look on the sunshine and flowers. "And when I come back, Rad, I'll stage a little fire for your benefit, and show you how quickly I can put it out."

"Ha! dat's whut I wants to see, Massa Tom, I suah does like to see fires!" chuckled Eradicate. "Mah ole mule, Boomerang—does yo' 'member. him, Massa Tom?"

"Of course, Rad!"

"Well, Boomerang he liked fires, too. Liked 'em so much I jest couldn't git him past 'em lots ob times I But run 'long, Massa Tom. Yo' ain't got no time to waste on an ole culled man whut's seen his best days. Yas-sir, I reckon I'se seen mah best days," and the smile died from the honest, black face.

"Oh, don't talk like that!" cried Tom, as cheerfully as he could. "You've got a lot of work in you yet, Rad. Hasn't he, Koku?" and the young inventor appealed to the giant, who seldom left the side of his former enemy.

"Rad good man—him an' me do lots work—next week mebby," said Koku, smiling very broadly.

"That's the way to talk!" exclaimed Tom, and he laughed a little though his heart was far from light.

And then, having seen to the final details, he took his place in the big airship with Ned, Mr. Damon and Josephus Baxter. The craft carried the largest possible load of fire extinguishing chemicals.

As Tom had feared, the Lucifer staggered a bit in "taking off" late that afternoon when the start was made for the distant city of Denton, where the first real test was to be made under the supervision and criticism of the fire department. But once the craft was aloft she rode on a level keel.

"I guess we're all right," Tom said. But to make certain he circled several times over his own landing field, that a good place to come down might be assured if something unforeseen developed.

However, all went well, and then the course was straightened for the distant city.

"We'll go right over Newmarket, sha'n't we, Tom?" asked Ned, as the speed of the Lucifer increased.

"Yes. And I wish I had time to stop and see Mary, but I haven't. It's getting dark fast, and we ought to arrive at our destination early in the morning. The test has been set by the committee for ten o'clock."

They settled themselves comfortably in the big craft for a long night trip, and Mr. Damon was just going to bless something or other when he pointed off into the distance.

"Look, Tom!" cried the eccentric man. "See that light in the sky!"

"Seems to be a fire," observed Ned.

"It is a fire!" shouted Mr. Baxter. "And it's in Newmarket, if I'm any judge."

Tom Swift did not answer, but he shoved forward the gasolene lever of his controls, and the Lucifer shot ahead through the air while the red, angry glow deepened in the evening sky.

TRAPPED

While Tom Swift was loading the Lucifer for her trip and the fire extinguishing test to occur the next morning, quite a different scene was taking place in the home of Jasper Blake, the uncle of Mary Nestor, where she had gone to spend a few weeks.

"Well, are you all ready, Mary?" asked her aunt, and it was about the same time that Ned Newton asked that same question of Tom Swift. Only Tom was in Shopton, and Mary was in Newmarket, and Tom was setting off on an air voyage, while Mary was only preparing to take a car downtown to do some shopping.

"Yes, Aunt, I'm all ready," Mary answered. "But I may be a bit late getting home."

"Why?" asked Mrs. Blake.

"I promised Uncle Barton I'd stop and call on him at his office," Mary replied. "He has something he wants me to take home to mother when I go tomorrow."

"I shall be sorry to see you go back," said Mrs. Blake. "But I imagine there will be those in Shopton who will be glad to see you return, Mary."

"Yes, mother wrote that she and dad were getting a bit lonesome," the girl casually replied, as she adjusted her veil.

"Yes, and some one else. Ah, Mary, you are a very lucky girl!" laughed her aunt, while Mary turned aside so she would not see her own blushes in the mirror.

"I thought Tom was going to call and take you home in his airship, Mary," went on her relative.

"So he is, I believe, on his way back from a city where he is going to be tomorrow making a big fire test. I am to wait for him until tomorrow afternoon. But now I really must go shopping, or all the bargains will be taken. Is there any word you want to send to Uncle Barton?"

"No," answered Mrs. Blake. "Though you might tell him to stop poking fun at your Uncle Jasper for having invested money in the Landmark Building. It's getting on your Uncle Jasper's nerves," she added.

"Uncle Barton never can give up a joke, once he thinks he has one," said Mary. "But I'll tell him to stop pestering Uncle Jasper."

"Please do," urged Mary's aunt, and then the girl left.

Mary's uncle, Barton Keith, with whom Tom Swift had been associated during the undersea search, had offices in the Landmark Building, but his home was in an adjoining suburb.

The girl was pleased with the results of her shopping, and at the close of the afternoon she stopped at the Landmark Building and was soon being shot up in the elevator to the floor where Barton Keith had his offices.

Though Mr. Keith had refrained from investing in the Landmark Building and though he laughed at Mary's Uncle Jasper for having done so, this did not prevent him from having a suite of offices in the big structure which, as we already know, was owned in large part by Field and Melling.

"Ah, Mary! Come in!" exclaimed Mr. Keith, welcoming Tom Swift's sweetheart. "It is so late I was afraid you weren't coming, and I was about to close the office and go home."

"You must blame the bargain sales for my delay," laughed Mary. "I hope I haven't kept you waiting."

"No, I still had a few things to do. One was to write a letter to your Uncle Jasper, telling him I had heard of another fire trap that was open to investors."

"Oh, and that reminds me I must tell you not to push Uncle Jasper too far!" warned Mary.

"Ha! Ha!" laughed Uncle Barton. "He made fun of me for going on the undersea search with Tom Swift. But I made good on that, and that's more than he can say about his Landmark Building deal!"

"But don't exasperate him too much!" begged Mary. "By the way, what are they doing to this building? I see the stairways and some of the elevator shafts all littered with building material."

"They are trying to make it fireproof," answered her uncle. "It's rather late to try that now, but they've got either to do it or stand a big increase in insurance rates. I'm glad I'm out of it. But now, Mary, take an easy chair until I finish some work, and then I'll walk out with you."

Mary took a seat near one of the front windows, whence she could look down into the now fast-darkening streets. She could see the supper crowds hurrying home, and out in the corridor of the big skyscraper could be heard the banging of elevator doors as the office tenants, one after another, left for the day.

Suddenly there was more commotion than usual, followed by the sound of broken glass. Then came a cry of:

"Fire! Fire!"

Mary sprang to her feet with a gasp of alarm, and her uncle rushed past her to the door leading into the hall outside his offices. As he opened the door a cloud of smoke rushed toward him and Mary, causing them to choke and gasp.

Mr. Keith closed the door a moment, and when he opened it again the smoke in the hall seemed less dense.

"It probably is only a slight blaze among some of the material the workmen are using," he said. "Come, Mary, we'll get out."

Pausing only to swing shut the door of his heavy safe and to stuff some valuable papers into his pocket, Mr. Keith advanced and, taking Mary by the arm, led her into the hall. The smoke was increasing again, and distant shouts and cries could be heard, mingled with the breaking of glass.

Mr. Keith rang the elevator buzzer several times, but when no car came up the shaft in response to his summons he turned to his niece and said:

"We'll try the stairs. It's only ten stories down, and going down isn't anything like coming up."

"Oh, indeed I can walk!" said Mary. "Let's hurry out!"

They turned toward the stairway, which wound around the elevator shafts, but such a cloud of hot, stifling smoke rolled up that it sent them back, choking and gasping for breath.

And then, as they stood there, up the elevator shafts, which were veritable chimneys, came more hot smoke, mingled with sparks of fire.

"Trapped!" gasped Mr. Keith, and he pulled Mary back toward his offices to get away from the choking, stifling smoke. "We're trapped!"

To the Rescue

"Uncle! Uncle Barton!" faltered Mary, as she clung to Mr. Keith. "Can't we get down the stairs?"

"I'm afraid not, Mary," he answered, and he closed the door of his office to keep out the smoke that was ever increasing.

"And won't the elevators come for us?"

"They don't seem able to get up," was his reply. "Probably the fire started in the bottom of the shafts, and they act just like flues, drawing up the flames and smoke."

"Then we must try the fire escapes!" exclaimed Mary, and she started toward the front window, pulling her uncle across the room after her.

"Mary, there aren't—aren't any fire escapes!" he said hoarsely.

"No fire escapes!" The girl turned paler than before.

"No, not an escape as far as I know. You see, this was thought to be a fireproof building at first and small attention was given to escapes. Then the law stepped in and the owners were ordered to put up regular escapes. They have started the work, but just now the old escapes have been torn down and the new ones are not yet in place."

"Oh, but Uncle Barton! can't we do something?" cried Mary. "There must be some way out! Let's try the elevators again, or the stairs!"

Before Mr. Keith could stop her Mary had opened the door into the hall. To the agreeable surprise of her uncle there seemed to be less smoke now.

"We may have a chance!" he cried, and he rushed out. "Hurry!"

Frantically he pushed the button that summoned the elevators. Down below, in the elevator shafts, could be heard the roar and crackle of flames.

"Let's try the stairs!" suggested Mary. "They seem to be free now."

She started down the staircase which went in square turns about the battery of elevators, and her uncle followed. But they had not more than reached the first landing when a roll of black, choking smoke, mingled with sparks of fire, surged into their faces.

"Back, Mary! Back!" cried Mr. Keith, and he dragged the impetuous girl with him to their own corridor, and back into his offices which, for the time being, were comparatively free from the choking vapor.

"We must try the windows, Uncle Barton! We must!" cried Mary. "Surely there is some way down—maybe by dropping from ledge to ledge!"

Her uncle shook his head. Then he opened the window and looked out. As he did so there arose from the streets below the cries of many voices, mingled with the various sounds of fire apparatus — the whistles of engines, the clang of gongs, and the puffing of steamers.

"The firemen are here! They'll save us!" cried Mary, as she heard the noises in the street below. "We can leap into the life nets."

"There isn't a life net made, nor men who could retain it, to hold up a person jumping from the tenth story," said her uncle. "Our only chance is to wait for them to subdue the fire."

"Isn't there a back way down, Uncle Barton?" "No, Mary!" He closed the window for, open as it was, the draft created served to suck smoke into the office, and Mary was coughing.

Uncle and niece faced each other. Trapped indeed they were, unless the fire, which was now raging all through the building, with the stairs and elevator shafts as a center. could be subdued. That the city fire department was doing its best was not to be doubted.

"We can only wait—and hope," said Mr. Keith solemnly.

Mary gave a gasp. Her uncle thought she was going to burst into tears, but she bravely conquered herself and faced him with what was meant to be a smile. But it is difficult to smile with quivering lips, and Mary soon gave up the attempt.

Mr. Keith went over to the water cooler—one of those inverted large glass bottles—and looked to see how much water it contained.

"It's nearly full," he said.

"What good will it do?" asked Mary. "This fire is beyond a little water like that."

"Yes, but it will serve to keep our handkerchiefs wet so we can breathe through them if the smoke gets too thick," was his reply.

"It begins to look as if we'd need to try that soon," said Mary, and she pointed to thick smoke curling in under the door.

"Yes," agreed her uncle. "It's getting worse." Hardly had he spoken when there came a rush of feet in the corridor outside his office door. Then a voice exclaimed:

"We're trapped! We can't get down either the stairs or the elevators!"

"It can't be possible!" said another voice. "Something must be done! Help! Help! Take us out of here!"

"Foolish cowards!" murmured Mr. Keith, and then the door of his office was violently opened and two men rushed in. They were strangers to Mary and her uncle.

"Isn't there any way out of this fire trap?" cried one of the men. "Are there any fire escapes at your windows?"

"None," said Mr. Keith.

"This is all your fault, Melling!" cried the smaller of the two men, whose voice, in loudness and depth of pitch, was out of all proportion to his size. "All your fault! I told you we should have those new fire escapes!"

"And you were the one, Field, who objected to the cost of fire escapes when you found what the charge would be," retorted the other. "You said we didn't need to waste that money, if the building was fire-proof."

"But it isn't, Melling! It isn't!" yelled the other.

"We're finding that out too late!" came the retort. "But I'm not going to die here like a rat in a trap!" And he raised the window and leaned out and yelled, "Help! Help! Help!"

"Don't do that," said Mr. Keith, coming over to close the casement. "They can't hear you down below, and opening the window will only fill this place with smoke. Are you Field and Melling?"

"Yes, of the Consolidated Dye Company," was the answer from the big man. "We are also part owners of this building, but I wish we weren't."

"It is a pretty poor specimen of a modern building," said Mr. Keith. "You have offices here, haven't you?" he went on. "I remember to have seen your names on the directory."

"We're on the floor above," was the answer from Field. "We were in a rear room, going over some accounts, and we didn't know anything was wrong until we smelled smoke. We tried to get down, and managed to come, by way of the stairs, as far as this floor," he explained quickly.

"You can't go any farther," said Mr. Keith. "All there is to do is to wait for the firemen."

"Suppose they never come?" whined Melling. "Oh, they'll come!" asserted Mary's uncle, but he spoke more to quiet her alarm than because he really believed it, for the Landmark Building was a seething furnace of flame centering in and about the elevator shafts and stairs.

Meanwhile Tom and his companions in the airship had seen the red glow in the evening sky, and in another minute the young inventor had turned his craft more directly toward it.

"It surely is in Newmarket," said Mr. Damon. "Right in the center of the city, too. There's one big building there—the Landmark."

"Looks as if that was afire," said Ned quickly. "Hasn't some relative of Mary's an office there, Tom?"

"Yes. Mr. Keith. And her other uncle, Jasper Blake, is also interested in the building. It's the Landmark all right!" cried Tom, as his craft rose higher and advanced nearer the blaze.

"What are you going to do?" yelled Mr. Damon, as he saw the young inventor head directly toward a spouting mushroom of flame, which showed that the fire had broken through the roof. "What are you going to do?"

"Go to the rescue!" answered Tom Swift. "I couldn't ask a better opportunity to try my new extinguisher! Sit tight, every one!"

A Strange Discovery

Once it became evident to the occupants of the airship what Tom Swift's plans were, they all prepared to help him. Previous to the trip certain duties had been assigned to each one, duties which were to be exercised when Tom gave the exhibition of his new aerial fire-fighting apparatus at the set fire before the fire department of Denton.

This preparation now stood the young inventor in good stead, for there was no confusion aboard the Lucifer when she winged her way toward the burning Landmark Building, where the flames were continually spouting higher and higher as they rushed through the roof, directly above the stairway well and elevator shafts.

So far the flames had confined themselves to this central part of the big structure, but it was only a question of time when they would spread out on all sides, licking up the remainder of the pile. And, for the most part, the firemen on the ground were at a great disadvantage.

They had run in lines as near as they could get to the center of the blaze, and had also attached hose to the standpipes inside the building. But this last effort was wasted, as developed later, for there was no one in the building to direct the nozzle ends of the hose attached to the standpipes on the different floors. Also the fierce heat fairly melted the pipes themselves in the vicinity of the elevator shafts, and there was no automatic sprinkling system in the building.

This was the situation, then, when Tom in his airship loaded with fire-extinguishing chemicals headed for the blaze. And this, also, was the desperate situation that confronted Mary Nestor and her uncle, Barton Keith, as well as Amos Field and Jason Melling. Those unscrupulous and cowardly men were in a veritable panic of fear, which contrasted strangely with the calm, resigned attitude of Mary and her uncle.

"We must get out! Some one must save us!" yelled Field.

"Jump from the window!" cried Melling.

"No, I can't permit that!" declared Mr. Keith, standing in their path. "It would be sure death! As it is, there may be a chance."

"A chance? How?" asked Field. "Listen to that!"

Through the closed door of Mr. Keith's office could be heard the roar and crackle of flames, while the very air was now stifling and hot, filled with acrid smoke.

"We can only wait," said Mr. Keith, and he wet Mary's handkerchief in the water and handed it to her to bind over her face.

"Is everything all right, Ned?" called Tom, as he turned on a little more power, so that the Lucifer lunged ahead toward the great pillar of fire that now reddened the sky for miles around.

"All ready," was the answer. "You only have to give the word when you want us to let go."

"Let go!" cried Mr. Damon. "Bless my umbrella, Tom! We don't have to jump out, do we?"

"He means to let go the extinguisher grenades," said Mr. Baxter. "Shall we let them all go at once, Tom?" asked the chemist.

"No, drop half when I shoot over the first time. We'll see what effect they have, and then come back with the rest."

"That's the idea!" cried Ned. "Well, give us the word when you're ready, Tom."

"I will," was the answer of the young inventor, and with keen eyes he began to set the automatic gages so those in charge of the grenades would be able to drop them most effectively.

The flames were mounting higher and higher above the ill-fated Landmark Building. It was a "land-mark" now, for miles around—a fearsome mark, indeed.

"I hope every one is out of the place," said Ned, as the airship approached nearer and the fierceness of the fire was more manifest.

"Bless my thermometer, you're right!" exclaimed Mr. Damon. "I don't see how any one could live in that furnace."

Seen from above it appeared that the fire was engulfing the whole building, while, as a matter of fact, only the central portion was yet blazing. But it was only a question of time when the remainder would ignite.

And it was to this fact—that the fire was rushing up the stairway and elevator shafts as up a chimney—that Mary and her uncle, as well as Field and Melling, owed their temporary safety.

Had Tom known that the girl he loved was in such direful danger, it is doubtful if his hand would have been as steady as it was on throttle and steering wheel. But not a muscle or nerve quivered. To Tom it was but carrying out a prearranged task. He was going to extinguish a great blaze, or attempt to do so, by means of his aerial fire-fighting apparatus. And his previous tests had given him confidence in his device. His one regret was that the fire department of the city that was contemplating the purchase of certain rights in his invention could not witness what he was about to do.

"But they'll hear of it," declared Ned, when Tom voiced this idea to his chum.

Nearer and nearer to the up-spouting column of flames the airship winged her way. Tense and alert, Tom sat at the wheel guiding his craft with her load of fire-defying chemicals. Behind him were Ned, Mr. Damon and Mr. Baxter, ready to drop the grenades at the word.

"Getting close, Tom!" called Ned, as they could all feel the heat of the conflagration in the Landmark Building, which now seemed doomed.

"You'll not dare cross it too low down, will you?"

"No, I'll have to keep pretty well up," was the answer. "There's a current of air over that fire which might turn us turtle."

Heat creates a draft, sucking in colder air from below, and making an upward-rushing column which, in the case of a big blaze, is very powerful. Tom knew he had to avoid this.

It was now almost time to act. In another few seconds they would be sailing directly into the path of the up-spouting flames. Realizing that to do this at too low an elevation would result in disaster, Tom sent his craft upward at a sharp angle. Then he turned to call to his companions.

"Be ready when I give the word!"

"All set and ready!" answered Ned, and the others signified their attention to the command that soon was to be given.

Having attained what he considered a sufficient elevation, Tom headed the Lucifer straight toward the up-spouting column of fire and smoke. If ever his craft of the air was to justify her name it was now!

Straight and true as an arrow she headed for the fiery pillar! Hotter and hotter grew the air! The darkness of the night was lighted by the awful fire, which rendered objects in the street clear and distinct. But Tom and his friends had little time for such observation.

"Get ready!" cried the young inventor, as he felt a rush of heat across his face, partly protected, as it was, by great goggles.

"All ready!" shouted Ned.

"Let go!" cried Tom, and with a click of springs the fire extinguishers dropped from the bottom of the Lucifer into the very heart of the flames in the Landmark Building.

There was a blast as from a furnace seventy times heated, a choking and gasping for breath on the part of the occupants of the airship, a shriveling, as it seemed, of the naked flesh, and then, when it appeared that all of them must be engulfed in the great heat, the airship passed out of the zone of fire.

A rush of cool air followed, reviving them all, and then, when out of the swirls of smoke, Ned, looking back, cried:

"Good work, Tom! Good work!"

"Did we hit it?" cried the young inventor. "She's half gone!" declared Mr. Baxter. "Can you give her the rest of the load?"

"I'm going to try!" declared Tom.

"Bless my bank balance!" shouted Mr. Damon, "are we going through that awful furnace again?"

"It will not be so bad this time," observed Ned. "The fire is half out now. Tom's stuff did the trick!"

Indeed it was evident, as Tom sent the Lucifer around in a sharp turn, that the fire had been largely smothered by the gas that now lay over it like a wet blanket. But there was still some fire spouting up.

"Give her all we have!" yelled Tom, as, once more, he prepared to cross the zone of fire.

"Right," sang out Ned.

Once more the Lucifer swept over the burning building. Down shot the remaining grenades, falling into the mass of flames and bursting, though the reports could not be heard because of the tumult in the streets below. For the firemen and spectators had seen the sudden dying down of the fire, they had caught sight of a shadowy shape in the night, hovering over the blazing building, and they wondered what it all meant.

"How is it?" asked Tom, as he guided the craft back to get a view of his work.

"That settles it!" answered Ned. "There isn't fire enough now to broil a beefsteak!"

This was not exactly true, for the blaze was not entirely subdued. But the flames had all been killed off in the higher parts of the Landmark Building, and what remained could easily be dealt with by the firemen on the ground. They proceeded to make short work of the remainder of the conflagration, the while wondering who had so effectively aided them from the clouds.

"Well," observed Tom, as he saw how effectively he had smothered the great fire, "it's of no use to go on now. I haven't an ounce of chemical left on board. I can't give the demonstration that I planned for tomorrow."

"You've given a better demonstration here than you ever could have in the other city," declared Mr. Baxter. "I fancy this will be all the test needed, Tom Swift!"

"Perhaps. I hope so. But we may as well land and see from the ground the effect of our work. I'd also like to inquire if any one was hurt. Let's go down."

It was rather ticklish work, making a landing in the midst of a populous city, and at night. But as it happened, there had been a number of buildings razed in the vicinity of the Landmark structure, and there was a large, vacant level space. Also several of the city's fire department searchlights were focused around the burning structure, and when it became evident that an airship was going to land—though as yet none guessed whose it was—the searchlights were turned on the vacant spot and Tom was able to make a good landing, his own powerful searchlight giving effective aid.

"What did you do that put out the fire?" demanded the chief of the Newmarket department, as he rushed up with a crowd of others when Tom and his friends alighted.

"I dropped a few grenades down that chimney," modestly answered the young inventor.

"A few grenades! Say, you must have turned a whole river of them loose!" cried the delighted chief. "It doused the fire quicker than I ever saw one put out in all my life!"

"I'm glad I was successful," said Tom. "But was any one in the building?"

"Yes, a few," answered a policeman, who was trying to keep the crowd back from the airship. "They're bringing them out now."

"Killed?" gasped Tom.

"No. But some of them are badly hurt," the officer answered. "There was one young lady and a man named Barton Keith—"

"Barton Keith!" shouted Tom, springing forward. "Was he—Who was the young lady? I—I—"

But at that moment there was a stir in the crowd about the building, in which only a little fire flow remained, and through the throng came a disheveled and smoke-blackened young lady and a man whose clothing was also greatly disarrayed.

"Mary!" cried the young inventor.

"Tom!" gasped Mary Nestor. "How did you get here?"

"I came to put out the fire," was the answer, and Tom cooled down now that he saw Mary was unharmed. "How did you happen to be in the building?"

"I was in Uncle Barton's office when the fire broke out," answered Mary, "and we were trapped. We had to stay there, with two men from the floor above."

"Yes, and if they had stayed with us they wouldn't have been hurt," said Mr. Keith. "But, as it was, they rushed out and tried to get down the stairs. They were caught in the draft and badly burned, I believe. They are bringing them out now."

Two stretchers, on which lay inert forms, were borne through the now silent crowd by firemen and police officers, and taken to waiting ambulances.

"That's Field and Melling," said Mr. Keith to Tom. "They had offices just above me, and they were trapped, as were Mary and I. They acted like big cowards, too, though I hope they're not badly hurt. We stayed inside my office, and we were just giving up the hope of rescue when the fire seemed suddenly to die down."

"I should say it was sudden!" cried the enthusiastic local chief. "It was the chemicals from this young man's airship that did the trick!"

"Oh, Tom, was it your new machine?" asked Mary.

"Yes," was the answer. "I was on my way to give a test tomorrow in Denton when I saw this fire. I didn't know you were in it, though, Mary."

"Oh, but I'm glad you came," she said. "It was just—awful!" and she clung to Tom's arm, trembling.

When Field and Melling, whose rash conduct had caused them to be severely but not fatally burned, had been taken to a hospital and the fire was declared to be practically out, Tom made arrangements to leave his airship in the city field all night.

"And you and your friends can come to Uncle Jasper's house," said Mary.

"Of course!" said Uncle Jasper himself, who had arrived on the scene, attracted to the fire by the news that his niece and Mr. Keith were in danger. "Lots of room! Come along! We'll celebrate your rescue

So the crew of the fire-fighting Lucifer went with Mary, while the firemen, after again thanking Tom most enthusiastically, kept on playing, as a precaution, their streams of water on the still hot building.

Only the central portion of the structure, the stairs and elevator shafts, were burned away. The strong upward draft had kept the fire from spreading much to either side.

"It certainly was a fierce blaze, and I'm glad my chemicals took such prompt effect," said Tom. "I shall not fear any test after this."

It was the day following the night of excitement, and Tom and his friends, at the invitation of the fire department of Newmarket, were inspecting what was left of the Landmark Building —and there was considerable left—though access to the upper floors was to be had only by ladders, down which Mary and her uncle, Barton Keith, had been carried.

"Here are my offices," said Mr. Keith, who accompanied Tom, Ned, Mr. Damon and Mr. Baxter, as he ushered them into his suite of rooms.

"Bless my fountain pen! nothing is burned here," cried the eccentric man.

"No, the flames just shot upward," explained the fire chief, who was leading the party. "But I think those chemicals of yours would have been just as effective, Mr. Swift, if the fire had mushroomed out more."

"It was hot enough as it was," answered Tom, with a grim laugh.

"Bless my thermometer, too hot—too hot by far!" exclaimed Tom Swift's eccentric friend, and to this Ned nodded an amused agreement.

An exclamation from Mr. Baxter attracted the attention of all in Mr. Keith's office. The chemist picked up from the floor a bundle of papers.

"Here is a bundle of documents that some one has dropped, Mr. Keith," he said. "I guess you forgot to put it in your safe. Why —why—no—they aren't yours! They're mine. Here are my missing dye formulae! The secret papers I've been searching for so long! The ones I thought Field and Melling had!" cried Mr. Baxter. "How—how did they get here?" and, wonderingly, he looked at the bundle of papers he had discovered in such a strange manner.

THE LIGHT OF DAY

"What's that? Your dye formulae here in my office?" cried Mr. Keith, for he had heard something of the chemist's loss, though he did not directly associate Field and Melling with it.

"That's what this is! The very papers, containing all the rare secrets, for which I have been so at a loss!" cried the delighted old man. "Now I can give to the world the dyes for which it has long been waiting! Oh, Tom Swift, you did more than you knew when you put out this fire!" and he hugged the bundle of smoke-smelling papers to his breast.

"But how did they get here?" asked the young inventor. "I know that Field and Melling had offices in this building. They were starting a new dye concern, and, though Mr. Baxter and I suspected them of having stolen his secret, we couldn't prove it."

"But we can now!" cried Mr. Baxter. "Though I don't know that I'll bother even to accuse them, as long as I have back my previous papers. I see how it happened. They had the formulae in their office. They rushed out with the documents, and, when they found they couldn't get past this floor, they went into Mr. Keith's office. There, in their excitement, they dropped the papers, and you put the fire out just in time, Tom, or they'd have been burned beyond hope of saving. You have given me back something almost as valuable as life, Tom Swift!"

"I'm glad I could render you that service," said the young inventor. "And I had no idea, when I dropped the chemicals, that I was saving someone even more valuable than your secret formulae," and they all knew he referred to Mary Nestor.

An examination of the papers found on Mr. Keith's office floor showed that not one of the dye secrets was missing. Thus Mr. Baxter came into possession of his own again, and when Field and Melling were sufficiently recovered they were charged with the theft of the papers. The charge was proved, and, in addition, other accusations were brought against them which insured their remainder in jail for a considerable period.

As Mr. Baxter had suspected, Field and Melling had, indeed, robbed him of his dye formulae papers. They learned that he possessed them, and they invited him to a night conference with the purpose of robbing him. The fire in their factory was an accident, of which they took advantage to make it appear that the chemist lost his papers in the blaze. But they had taken them, and though they did not mean to leave poor Baxter to his fate, that would have been the result of their selfish action had not Tom and Ned come to the rescue. And it was of this "putting over" that Field and Melling had boasted, the time Tom overheard their talk at Meadow Inn.

As Mr. Baxter guessed, the letter delivered to him at Tom's place was one that the two scoundrels would have retained, as they had others like it, if they had seen it. But a new clerk forwarded it, and the evidence it contained helped to convict Field and Melling.

As for the Landmark Building, while badly damaged, it would have been worse burned but for Tom's prompt action. And though he was more than glad that he had been on hand, he rather regretted that he could not give the test for which he had set out.

Eventually the building was made more nearly fire-proof and the fire-escapes were rebuilt, and Mr. Blake did not lose his money, as he had feared, though Barton Keith said it was more owing to Tom Swift's good luck than to Mr. Blake's management.

But, as it developed, nothing could have been more opportune than Tom's action, for word of his quenching a bigger blaze than he would have had to encounter in the official test reached the Denton fire department. As a result there was a conference, and, after only a nominal showing of his apparatus, it was adopted by a unanimous vote.

But this occurred some time afterward, for, following his rescue of Mary Nestor and her uncle and the saving of the lives of Field and Melling, as well as others in the building, by his prompt smothering of the fire, Tom returned to Shopton.

He and his companions went in the Lucifer, minus, now, the big load of chemicals, and on landing near the hangar Tom was surprised to see Koku the giant running toward him. The big man showed every symptom of great excitement as he cried:

"Oh, Master Tom! He see the light ob day! he see the light ob day now! Oh, so glad! So glad!"

"Who sees the light of day?" asked the young inventor.

"Black Rad! Eradicate! Him eyes all better now! Pill man take off cloth. Rad—he see light ob day!"

"Oh, I'm so glad! So thankful!" cried Tom. "How I've wished for this! Is it really true, Koku?"

"Sure true! Pill man say Rad see K O now." The giant, doubtless, meant "O K," but Tom understood. And it was true, as he learned more directly a little later.

When Tom entered the room where Rad had been kept in the dark ever since the explosion, the colored man looked at his master with seeing eyes, though the apartment was still but dimly lighted.

"I's all right ag'in now, Massa Tom!" cried Rad. "See fine! I's all ready to make more smellin' stuff to put out fires!"

"You won't have to, Rad!" cried Tom joyfully. "My chemical extinguisher is completed, and you did your share in making it a success. But I never would have felt like claiming credit for it if you had been—had been left in the dark."

"No mo' dark, Massa Tom!" said Eradicate. "I kin see now as good as eber, an' yo'-all won't hab to 'pend on dat lazy good-fo'-nuffin cocoanut!" and he chuckled as he looked at the giant.

"Huh! Lazy!" retorted the big man. "I show you—black coon!"

"By golly!" laughed Rad. "Him an' me good friends now, Massa Tom. Neber I fuss wif Koku any mo'! He suah was good to me when I had to stay in de dark!"

Of course it would be too much to hope that Koku and Eradicate never again quarreled, but for a long time their warm friendship was a thing at which to marvel, considering the past.

"Well, I guess this settles it," said Tom to Ned one day, after going over the day's mail.

"Settles what, Tom?"

"My aerial fire-fighting apparatus. Here's word from the National Fire Underwriters Association that they have adopted it, and there will be a big reduction of rates in all cities where it is a part of the fire department equipment. It's been as great a success as Mr. Baxter's new dye."

"Yes, and he has had wonderful success with that. But what are you going to do now, Tom? What new line of endeavor are you going to aim at?"

Tom arose and reached for his hat.

"I am now going," he said, with a grin, "to see somebody on private business."

"You are going to see Mary Nestor!" broke out Ned.

"I am," said Tom.

And he did.

Tom Swift and His Electric Locomotive
Or Two Miles a Minute on the Rails

TABLE OF CONTENTS:

A Tempting Offer

"An electric locomotive that can make two miles a minute over a properly ballasted roadbed might not be an impossibility," said Mr. Barton Swift ruminatively. "It is one of those things that are coming," and he flashed his son, Tom Swift, a knowing smile. It had been a topic of conversation between them before the visitor from the West had been seated before the library fire and had sampled one of the elder Swift's good cigars.

"It is not only a future possibility," said the latter gentleman, shrugging his shoulders. "As far as the Hendrickton and Pas Alos Railroad Company goes, a two mile a minute gait—not alone on a level track but through the Pas Alos Range—is an immediate necessity. It's got to be done now, or our stock will be selling on the curb for about two cents a share."

"You do not mean just that, do you, Mr. Bartholomew?" asked Tom Swift earnestly, and staring at the big-little man before the fire.

Mr. Richard Bartholomew was just that—a "big-little man." In the railroad world, both in construction and management, he had made an enviable name for himself.

He had actually built up the Hendrickton and Pas Alos from a narrow-gauge, "jerkwater" road into a part of a great cross-continent system that tapped a wonderfully rich territory on both sides of the Pas Alos Range.

For some years the H. & P. A. had a monopoly of that territory. Now, as Mr. Bartholomew intimated, it was threatened with such rivalry from another railroad and other capitalists, that the H. & P. A. was being looked upon in the financial market as a shaky investment.

But Tom Swift repeated:

"You do not mean just that, do you, Mr. Bartholomew?"

Mr. Bartholomew, who was a little man physically, rolled around in his chair to face the young fellow more directly. His own eyes sparkled in the firelight. His olive face was flushed.

"That is much nearer the truth, young man," he said, somewhat harshly because of his suppressed emotion, "than I want people at large to suspect. As I have told your father, I came here to put all my cards on the table; but I expect the Swift Construction Company to take anything I may say as said in confidence."

"We quite understand that, Mr. Bartholomew," said the elder Swift, softly. "You can speak freely. Whether we do business or not, these walls are soundproof, and Tom and I can forget, or remember, as we wish. Of course if we take up any work for you, we must confide to a certain extent in our close associates and trusted mechanics."

"Humph!" grunted the visitor, turning restlessly again in his chair. Then he said: "I agree as the necessity of that last statement; but I can only hope that these walls are soundproof."

"What's that?" demanded Tom, rather sharply. He was a bright looking young fellow with an alert air and a rather humorous smile. His father was a semi-invalid; but Tom possessed all the mental vigor and muscular energy that a young man should have. He had not neglected his Athletic development while he made the best use of his mental powers.

"Believe me," said the visitor, quite as harshly as before, "I begin to doubt the solidity of all walls. I know that I have been watched, and spied upon, and that eavesdroppers have played hob with our affairs.

"Of late, there has been little planned in the directors' room of the H. & P. A. that has not seeped out and aided the enemy in foreseeing our moves."

"The enemy?" repeated Mr. Swift, with mild surprise.

"That's it exactly! The enemy!" replied Mr. Bartholomew shortly. "The H. & P. A. has got the fight of its life on its hands. We had a hard enough time fighting nature and the elements when we laid the first iron for the road a score of years ago. Now I am facing a fight that must grow fiercer and fiercer as time goes on until either the H. & P. A. smashes the opposition, or the enemy smashes it."

"What enemy is this you speak of?" asked Tom, much interested.

"The proposed Hendrickton & Western. A new road, backed by new capital, and to be officered and built by new men in the construction and railroad game.

"Montagne Lewis—you've heard of him, I presume—is at the head of the crowd that have bought the little old Hendrickton & Western, lock, stock and barrel.

"They have franchises for extending the road. In the old days the legislatures granted blanket franchises that allowed any group of moneyed men to engage in any kind of business as side issues to railroading. Montagne Lewis and his crowd have got a 'plenty-big' franchise.

"They have begun laying iron. It parallels, to a certain extent, our own line. Their surveyors were smarter than the men who laid out the H. & P. A. I admit it. Besides, the country out there is developed more than it was a score of years ago when I took hold.

"All this enters into the fight between Montagne Lewis and me. But there is something deeper," said the little man, with almost a snarl, as he thrashed about again in his chair. "I beat Montagne Lewis at one big game years ago. He is a man who never forgets—and who never hesitates to play dirty politics if he has to, to bring about his own ends.

"I know that I have been watched. I know that I was followed on this trip East. He has private detectives on my track continually. And worse. All the gunmen of the old and wilder West are not dead. There's a fellow named Andy O'Malley—well, never mind him. The game at present is to keep anybody in Lewis's employ from getting wise to why I came to see you."

"What you say is interesting," Mr. Swift here broke in quietly. "But I have already been puzzled by what you first said. Just why have you come to us—to Tom and me—in reference to your railroad difficulties?"

"And this suggestion you have made," added Tom, "about a possible electric locomotive of a faster type than has, ever yet been put on the rails?"

"That is it, exactly," replied Bartholomew, sitting suddenly upright in his chair. "We want faster electric motor power than has ever yet been invented. We have got to have it, or the H. & P. A. might as well be scrapped and the whole territory out there handed over to Montagne Lewis and his H. & W. That is the sum total of the matter, gentlemen. If the Swift Construction Company cannot help us, my railroad is going to be junk in about three years from this beautiful evening."

His emphasis could not fail to impress both the elder and the younger Swift. They looked at each other, and the interest displayed upon the father's countenance was reflected upon the features of the son.

If there was anything Tom Swift liked it was a good fight. The clash of diverse interests was the breath of life to the young fellow. And for some years now, always connected in some way with the development of his inventive genius, he had been entangled in battles both of wits and physical powers. Here was the suggestion of something that would entail a struggle of both brain and brawn.

"Sounds good," muttered Tom, gazing at the railroad magnate with considerable admiration.

"Let us hear all about it," Mr. Swift said to Bartholomew. "Whether we can help you or not, we're interested."

"All right," replied the visitor again. "Whether I was followed East, and here to Shopton, or not doesn't much matter. I will put my proposition up to you, and then I'll ask, if you don't want to go into it, that you keep the business absolutely secret. I have got to put something over on Montagne Lewis and his crowd, or throw up the sponge. That's that!"

"Go ahead, Mr. Bartholomew," observed Tom's father, encouragingly.

"To begin with, four hundred miles of our road is already electrified. We have big power stations and supply heat and light and power to several of the small cities tapped by the H. & P. A. It is a paying proposition as it stands. But it is only paying because we carry the freight traffic—all the freight traffic—of that region.

"If the H. & W. breaks in on our monopoly of that, we shall soon be so cut down that our invested capital will not earn two per cent.—No, by glory! not one-and-a-half per cent.—and our stock will be dished. But I have worked out a scheme, Gentlemen, by which we can counter-balance any dig Lewis can give us in the ribs.

"If we can extend our electrified line into and through the Pas Alos Range our freight traffic can be handled so cheaply and so effectively that nothing the Hendrickton & Western can do for years to come will hurt us. Get that?"

"I get your statement, Mr. Bartholomew," said Mr. Swift. "But it is merely a statement as yet."

"Sure. Now I will give you the particulars. We are using the Jandel locomotives on our electrified stretch of road. You know that patent?"

"I know something about it, Mr. Bartholomew," said the younger inventor. "I have felt some interest in the electric locomotive, though I have done nothing practical in the matter. But I know the Jandel patent."

"It is about the best there is—and the most recent; but it does not fill the bill. Not for the H. & P. A., anyway," said Mr. Bartholomew, shortly.

"What does it lack?" asked Mr. Swift.

"Speed. It's got the power for heavy hauls. It could handle the freight through the Pas Alos Range. But it would slow up our traffic so that the shippers would at once turn to the Hendrickton & Western. You understand that their rails do not begin to engage the grades that our engineers thought necessary when the old H. & P. A. was built."

"I get that," said Tom briskly. "You have come here, then, to interest us in the development of a faster but quite as powerful type of electric locomotive as the Jandel."

"Stated to the line!" exclaimed Mr. Bartholomew, smiting the arm of his chair with his clenched fist. "That is it, young man. You get me exactly. And now I will go on to put my proposition to you."

"Do so, Mr. Bartholomew," murmured the old inventor, quite as much interested as his son.

"I want you to make a study of electric motive power as applied to track locomotives, with the idea of utilizing our power plants and others like them, and even with the possibility in mind of the continued use of the Jandel locomotives on our more level stretches of road.

"But I want your investigation to result in the building of locomotives that will make a speed of two miles a minute, or as near that as possible, on level rails, and be powerful enough to snake our heavy freight trains through the hills and over the steep grades so rapidly that even two engines, a pusher and a hauler, cannot beat the electric power."

"Some job, that, I'll say," murmured Tom Swift.

"Exactly. Some job. And it is the only thing that will save the H. & P. A.," said Mr. Bartholomew decidedly. "I put it up to you Swifts. I have heard of some of your marvelous inventions. Here is something that is already invented. But it needs development."

"I see," said Mr. Swift, and nodded.

"It interests me," admitted Tom. "As I say, I have given some thought to the electric locomotive."

"This is the age of speed," said Mr. Bartholomew earnestly. "Rapidity in handling freight and kindred things will be the salvation, and the only salvation, of many railroads. Tapping a rich territory is not enough. The road that can offer the quickest and cheapest service is the road that is going to keep out of a receivership. Believe me, I know!"

"You should," said Mr. Swift mildly. "Your experience should have taught you a great deal about the railroad business."

"It has. But that knowledge is worth just nothing at all without swift power and cheap traffic. Those are the problems today. Now, I am going to take a chance. If it doesn't work, my road is dished in any case. So I feel that the desperate chance is the only chance."

"What is that?" asked Tom Swift, sitting forward in his chair. "I, for one, feel so much interested that I will do anything in reason to find the answer to your traffic problem."

"That's the boy!" ejaculated Richard Bartholomew. "I will give it to you in a few words. If you will experiment with the electric locomotive idea, to develop speed and power over and above the Jandel patent, and will give me the first call on the use of any patents you may contrive, I will put up twenty-five thousand dollars in cash which shall be yours whether I can make use of a thing you invent or not."

"Any time limit in this agreement, Mr. Bartholomew?" asked Tom, making a few notes on a scratch pad before him on the library table.

"What do you say to three months?"

"Make it six, if you can," Tom said with continued briskness. "It interests me. I'll do my best. And I want you to get your money's worth."

"All right. Make it six," said Mr. Bartholomew. "But the quicker you dig something up, the better for me. Now, that is the first part of my proposition."

"All right, sir. And the second?"

"If you succeed in showing me that you can build and operate an electric locomotive that will speed two miles a minute on a level track and will get a heavy drag over the mountain grades, as I said, as surely as two engines of the coal-burning or oil-burning type, I will pay you a hundred thousand dollars bonus, besides buying all the engines you can build of this new type for the first two years. I've got to have first call; but the hundred thousand will be yours free and clear, and the price of the locomotives you build can be adjusted by any court of agreement that you may suggest."

Tom Swift's face glowed. He realized that this offer was not only generous, but that it made it worth his while dropping everything else he had in hand and devoting his entire time and thought for even six mouths to the proposition of developing the electric locomotive.

He looked at his father and nodded. Mr. Swift said, calmly:

"We take you on that offer, Mr. Bartholomew. Tom has the facts on paper, and we will hand it to Mr. Newton, our financial manager, in the morning. If you will remain in town for twenty-four hours, the contract can be signed."

"Suits me," declared. Richard Bartholomew, rising quickly from his chair. "I confess I hoped you would take me up quite as promptly as you have. I want to get back West again.

"We will see you in the office of the company at two o'clock tomorrow," said Tom Swift confidently.

"Better than good! And now, if that trailer that I am pretty sure Montagne Lewis sent after me does not get wise to the subject of our talk, it may be a slick job we have done and will do. I admit I am rather afraid of the enemy. You Swifts must keep your plans in utter darkness."

After a little talk on more ordinary affairs, Mr. Bartholomew took his departure. It was getting late in the evening, and Tom Swift had an engagement. While old Rad, their colored servant, was helping him on with his coat preparatory to Tom's leaving the house, his father called from the library:

"Got those notes in a safe place, Tom?"

"Safest in the world, Dad," his son replied. But he did not go into details. Tom considered the "safest place in the world" just then was his own wallet, which was tucked into an inside pocket of his vest "I'm going to see Mary Nestor, Father," said Tom, as he went to the front door and opened it.

He halted a moment with the knob of the door in his hand. The porch was deep in shadows, but he thought he had seen something move there.

"That you, Koku?" asked Tom in an ordinary voice. Sometimes his gigantic servant wandered about the house at night. He was a strange person, and he had a good many thoughts in his savage brain that even his young master did not understand.

There was no reply to Tom's question, so he walked down the steps and out at the gate. It was not a long distance to the Nestor house, and the air was brisk and keen, in spite of the fact that threatening clouds masked the stars.

Two blocks from the house he came to a high wall which separated the street from the grounds of an old dwelling. Tom suddenly noticed that the usual street lights on this block had been extinguished—blown out by the wind, perhaps.

Involuntarily he quickened his steps. He reached the archway in the wall. Here was the gate dividing the private grounds from the street. As he strode into the shadow of this place a voice suddenly halted Tom Swift.

"Hands up! Put 'em up and don't be slow about it!" A bulky figure loomed in the dark. Tom saw the highwayman's club poised threateningly over his head.

TROUBLE STARTS

The fact that he was stopped by a footpad smote Tom Swift's mind as not a particularly surprising adventure. He had heard that several of that gentry had been plying their trade about the outskirts of the town. To a degree he was prepared for this sudden event.

Then there flashed into Tom's mind the thought of what Mr. Richard Bartholomew had said regarding the spy he believed had followed him from the West. Could it be possible that some hired thug sent by Montagne Lewis and his crooked crowd of financiers considered that Tom Swift had obtained information from the president of the H. & P. A. that might do his employers signal service?

Tom Swift had fallen in with many adventures—and some quite thrilling ones—since, as a youth, he was first introduced to the reader in the initial volume of this series, entitled "Tom Swift and His Motor Cycle." His first experiences as an inventor, coached by his father, who had spent his life in the experimental laboratory and workshop, was made possible by his purchase from Mr. Wakefield Damon, now one of his closest friends, of a broken-down motor cycle.

Through a series of inventions, some of them of a marvelous kind, Tom Swift, aided by his father, had forged ahead, building motor boats, airships, submarines, monoplanes, motion picture cameras, searchlights, cannons, photo-telephones, war tanks. Of late, as related in "Tom Swift Among the Fire Fighters," he had engaged in the invention of an explosive bomb carrying flame-quenching chemicals that would, in time, revolutionize fire-fighting in tall buildings.

The matter that Mr. Richard Bartholomew, the railroad magnate, had brought to Tom's and his father's attention had deeply interested the young inventor. Thought of the electric locomotive, the development of which the railroad president stated was the only salvation of the finances of the H. & P. A., had so held Tom's attention as he walked along the street that being stopped in this sudden way was even more startling than such an incident might ordinarily have been.

Tom was a muscular young fellow; but a club held over one's head by a burly thug would have shaken the courage of anybody. Dark as it was under the archway the young fellow saw that the bulk of the man was much greater than his own.

"That's right, sonny," said the stranger, in a sneering tone. "You got just the right idea. When I say 'Stick 'em up' I mean it. Never take a chance. Ah—ah!"

The fellow ripped open Tom's overcoat, almost tearing the buttons off. Another masterful jerk and his victim's jacket was likewise parted widely.

He did not lower the club for an instant. He thrust his left hand into the V-shaped parting of the young fellow's vest.

It was then that Tom was convinced of what the fellow was after. He remembered the notes he had made regarding the contract that was to be signed on the morrow between the Swift Construction Company and President Richard Bartholomew of the H. & P. A. Railroad. He remembered, too, the figure he thought he had seen in the dark porch of the house as he so recently left it.

Mr. Bartholomew had considered it very possible that he was being spied upon. This was one of the spies—a Westerner, as his speech betrayed. But Tom was suddenly less fearful than he had been when first attacked.

It did not seem possible to him that Mr. Bartholomew's enemies would allow their henchman to go too far to obtain information of the railroad president's intentions. This fellow was merely attempting to frighten him.

A sense of relief came to Tom Swift's assistance. He opened his lips to speak and could the thug have seen his face more clearly in the dark he would have been aware of the fact that the young inventor smiled.

The fellow's groping hand entered between Tom's vest and his shirt. The coarse fingers seized upon Tom's wallet. Nobody likes to be robbed, no matter whether the loss is great or small. There was not much money in the wallet, nor anything that could be turned into money by a thief.

These facts enabled Tom, perhaps, to bear his loss with some fortitude. The highwayman drew forth the wallet and thrust it into his own coat pocket. He made no attempt to take anything else from the young inventor.

"Now, beat it!" commanded the fellow. "Don't look back and don't run or holler. Just keep moving—in the way you were headed before. Vamoose."

More than ever was Tom assured that the man was from the West. His speech savored of Mexican phrases and slang terms used mainly by Western citizens. And his abrupt and masterly manner and speech aided in this supposition. Tom Swift stayed not to utter a word. It was true he was not so frightened as he had at first been. But he was quite sure that this man was no person to contend with under present conditions.

He strode away along the sidewalk toward the far corner of the wall that surrounded this estate. Shopton had not many of such important dwellings as this behind the wall. Its residential section was made up for the most part of mechanics' homes and such plain but substantial houses as his father's.

Prospering as the Swifts had during the last few years, neither Tom nor his father had thought their plain old house too poor or humble for a continued residence. Tom was glad to make money, but the inventions he had made it by were vastly more important to his mind than what he might obtain by any lavish expenditure of his growing fortune.

This matter of the electric locomotive that had been brought to his attention by the Western railroad magnate had instantly interested the young inventor. The possibility of there being a clash of interests in the matter, and the point Mr. Bartholomew made of his enemies seeking to thwart his hope of keeping the H. & P. A. upon a solid financial footing, were phases of the affair that likewise concerned the young fellow's thought.

Now he was sure that Mr. Bartholomew was right. The enemies of the H. & P. A. were determined to know all that the railroad president was planning to do. They would naturally suspect that his trip East to visit the Swift Construction Company was no idle jaunt.

Tom had turned so many fortunate and important problems of invention into certainties that the name of the Swift Construction Company was broadly known, not alone throughout the United States but in several foreign countries. Montagne Lewis, whom Tom knew to be both a powerful and an unscrupulous financier, might be sure that Mr. Bartholomew's visit to Shopton and to the young inventor and his father was of such importance that he would do well through his henchmen to learn the particulars of the interview.

Tom remembered Mr. Bartholomew's mention of a name like Andy O'Malley. This was probably the man who had done all that he could, and that promptly, to set about the discovery of Mr. Bartholomew's reason for visiting the Swifts.

Without doubt the man had slunk about the Swift house and had peered into one of the library windows while the interview was proceeding. He had observed Tom making notes on the scratch pad and judged correctly that those notes dealt with the subject under discussion between the visitor from the West and the Swifts.

He had likewise seen Tom thrust the paper into his wallet and the wallet into his inside vest pocket. Instead of dogging Mr. Bartholomew's footsteps after that gentleman left the Swift house, the man had waited for the appearance of Tom. When he was sure that the young fellow was preparing to walk out, and the direction he was to stroll, the thug had run ahead and ensconced himself in the archway on this dark block.

All these things were plain enough. The notes Tom had taken regarding the offer Mr. Bartholomew had made for the development of the electric locomotive might, under some circumstances, be very important. At least, the highwayman evidently thought them such. But Tom had another thought about that.

One thing the young inventor was convinced about, as he strode briskly away from the scene of the hold-up: There was going to be trouble. It had already begun.

Tom Swift's Friends

Tom was still walking swiftly when he arrived in sight of Mary Nestor's home. He was so filled with excitement both because of the hold-up and the new scheme that Mr. Richard Bartholomew had brought to him from the West, that he could keep neither to himself. He just had to tell Mary!

Mary Nestor was a very pretty girl, and Tom thought she was just about right in every particular. Although he had been about a good deal for a young fellow and had seen girls everywhere, none of them came up to Mary. None of them held Tom's interest for a minute but this girl whom he had been around with for years and whom he had always confided in.

As for the girl herself, she considered Tom Swift the very nicest young man she had ever seen. He was her beau-ideal of what a young man should be. And she entered enthusiastically into the plans for everything that Tom Swift was interested in.

Mary was excited by the story Tom told her in the Nestor sitting room. The idea of the electric locomotive she saw, of course, was something that might add to Tom's laurels as an inventor. But the other phase of the evening's adventure—" Tom, dear!" she murmured with no little disturbance of mind. "That man who stopped you! He is a thief, and a dangerous man! I hate to think of your going home alone."

"He's got what he was after," chuckled Tom. "Is it likely he will bother me again?"

"And you do not seem much worried about it," she cried, in wonder.

"Not much, I confess, Mary," said Tom, and grinned.

"But if, as you suppose, that man was working for Mr. Bartholomew's enemies

"I am convinced that he was, for he did not rob me of my watch and chain or loose money. And he could have done so easily. I don't mind about the old wallet. There was only five dollars in it."

"But those notes you said you took of Mr. Bartholomew's offer?"

"Oh, yes," chuckled Tom again. "Those notes. Well, I may as well explain to you, Mary, and not try to puzzle you any longer. But that highwayman is sure going to be puzzled a long, long time."

"What do you mean, Tom?"

"Those notes were jotted down in my own brand of shorthand. Such stenographic notes would scarcely be readable by anybody else. Ho, ho! When that bold, bad hold-up gent turns the notes over to Montagne Lewis, or whoever his principal is, there will be a sweet time."

"Oh, Tom! isn't that fun?" cried Mary, likewise much amused.

"I can remember everything we said there in the library," Tom continued. "I'll see Ned tonight on my way home from here, and he will draw a contract the first thing in the morning."

"You are a smart fellow, Tom!" said Mary, her laughter trilling sweetly.

"Many thanks, Ma'am! Hope I prove your compliment true. This two-mile-a-minute stunt—"

"It seems wonderful," breathed Mary.

"It sure will be wonderful if we can build a locomotive that will do such fancy lacework as that," observed Tom eagerly. "It will be a great stunt!"

"A wonderful invention, Tom."

"More wonderful than Mr. Bartholomew knows," agreed the young fellow. "An electric locomotive with both great speed and great hauling power is what more than one inventor has been aiming at for two or three decades. Ever since Edison and Westinghouse began their experiments, in truth."

"Is the locomotive they are using out there a very marvelous machine?" asked the girl, with added interest.

"No more marvelous than the big electric motors that drag the trains into New York City, for instance, through the tunnels. Steam engines cannot be used in those tunnels for obvious, as well as legal, reasons. They are all wonderful machines, using third-rail power.

"But that Jandel patent that Mr. Bartholomew is using out there on the H. & P. A. is probably the highest type of such motors. It is up to us to beat that. Fortunately I got a pass into the Jandel shops a few months ago and I studied at first hand the machine Mr. Bartholomew is using."

"Isn't that great!" cried Mary.

"Well, it helps some. I at least know in a general way the 'how' of the construction of the Jandel locomotive. It is simple enough. Too simple by far, I should say, to get both speed and power. We'll see," and he nodded his head thoughtfully.

Tom did not stay long with the girl, for it was already late in the evening when he had arrived at her house. As he got up to depart Mary's anxiety for his safety revived.

"I wish you would take care now, Tom. Those men may hound you."

"What for?" chuckled the young inventor. "They have the notes they wanted."

"But that very thing—the fact that you fooled them—will make them more angry. Take care."

"I have a means of looking out for myself, after all," said Tom quietly, seeing that he must relieve her mind. "I let that fellow get away with my wallet; but I won't let him hurt me. Don't fear."

She had opened the door. The lamplight fell across porch and steps, and in a broad white band even to the gate and sidewalk. There was a motor-car slowing down right before the open gate.

"Who's this?" queried Tom, puzzled.

A sharp voice suddenly was raised in an exclamatory explosion.

"Bless my breakshoes! is that Tom Swift? Just the chap I was looking for. Bless my mileage-book! this saves me time and money."

"Why, it's Mr. Wakefield Damon," Mary cried, with something like relief in her tones. "You can ride home in his car, Tom."

"All right, Mary. Don't be afraid for me," replied Tom Swift, and ran down the walk to the waiting car.

"Bless my vest buttons! Tom Swift, my heart swells when I see you—"

"And is like to burst off the said vest buttons?" chuckled the young fellow, stepping in beside his eccentric friend who blessed everything inanimate in his florid speech.

"I am delighted to catch you—although, of course," and Tom knew the gentleman's eyes twinkled, "I could have no idea that you were over here at Mary's, Tom."

"Of course not," rejoined the young inventor calmly. "Seeing that I only come to see her just as often as I get a chance."

"Bless my memory tablets! is that the fact?" chuckled Mr. Damon. "Anyway, I wanted to see you so particularly that I drove over in my car tonight—"

"Wait a minute," said Tom, hastily. "Is this important?"

"I think so, Tom."

"Let me get something else off of my mind first, then, Mr. Damon," Tom Swift said quickly. "Drive around by Ned's house, will you, please? Ned Newton's. After I speak a minute with him I will be at your service."

"Surely, Tom; surely," agreed the gentleman.

The automobile had been running slowly. Mr. Damon knew the streets of Shopton very well, and he headed around the next corner. As the car turned, a figure bounded out of the shadow near the house line. Two long strides, and the man was on the running board of the car upon the side where Tom Swift sat. Again an ugly club was raised above the young fellow's head.

"You're the smart guy!" croaked the coarse voice Tom had heard before. "Think you can bamboozle me, do you? Up with 'em!"

"Bless my spark-plug!" gasped Mr. Wakefield Damon.

Either from nervousness or intention, he jerked the steering wheel so that the car made a sudden leap away from the curb. The figure of the stranger swayed.

Instantly Tom Swift struck the man's arm up higher and from under his own coat appeared something that bulked like a pistol in his right hand. He had intimated to Mary Nestor that he carried something with which to defend himself from highwaymen if he chose to. This invention, his ammonia gun, now came into play.

"Bless my failing eyesight!" exclaimed Mr. Damon, as he shot the motor-car ahead again in a straight line.

The man who had accosted Tom so fiercely fell off the running board and rolled into the gutter, screaming and choking from the fumes from Tom's gun.

"Drive on!" commanded the young inventor. "If he keeps bellowing like that the police will pick him up. I guess he will let us alone here-after."

"Bless my short hairs and long ones!" chuckled Mr. Damon. "You are the coolest young fellow, Tom, that I ever saw. That man must have been a highwayman. And it is of some of those gentry that I drove over to Shopton this evening to talk to you about."

Much to Think About

Although it was now nearing ten o'clock on this eventful evening, Tom knew that he would find Ned Newton at home. When Mr. Damon's car stopped before the house there was a light in Ned's room and the front door opened almost as soon as Tom rang. Mr. Damon left the car and entered with the young inventor at his invitation.

"What's up?" was Ned's greeting, looking at the two curiously as he ushered them in. "I see this isn't entirely a social call," and he laughed as he shook the older man's hand.

"Bless my particular star!" exclaimed the latter excitedly. "Of all the thrilling adventures that anybody ever got into, it is this Tom Swift who cooks them up! Why, Newton! do you know that we have been held up by a highwayman within two blocks of this very house?"

"And that of course was Tom's fault?" suggested Ned, still smiling.

"It wouldn't have happened if he had not been with me," said Mr. Damon.

"I am curious," said Ned, as they seated themselves. "Who was the footpad? What drew his attention to you two? Tell me about it."

"Bless my suspender buckles!" exclaimed Mr. Damon. "You tell him, Tom. I don't understand it myself, yet."

"I think I can explain. But whatever I tell you both, you must hold in secret. Father and I have been entrusted with some private information tonight and I am going to take you, Ned, and Mr. Damon, into the business in a confidential way."

"Let's have it," begged Newton. "Anything to do with the works?"

"It is," answered Tom gravely. "We are going to take up a proposition that promises big things for the Swift Construction Company."

"A big thing financially?"

"I'll say so. And it looks as though we were mixing into a conspiracy that may breed trouble in more ways than one."

Tom went on to sketch briefly the situation of the Hendrickton & Pas Alos Railroad as brought to the attention of the Swifts by the railroad's president. First of all his two listeners were deeply interested in the proposition Mr. Richard Bartholomew had made the inventors. Ned Newton jotted down briefly the agreement to be incorporated in the contract to be drawn and signed, by the Swift Construction Company and the president of the H. & P. A. road.

"This looks like a big thing for the company, Tom," the young manager said with enthusiasm, while Mr. Damon listened to it all with mouth and eyes open.

"Bless my watch-charm!" murmured the latter. "An electric locomotive that can travel two miles a minute? Whew!"

"Sounds like a big order, Tom," added Ned, seriously.

"It is a big order. I am not at all sure it can be done," agreed Tom, thoughtfully. "But under the terms Mr. Bartholomew offers it is worth trying, don't you think?"

"That twenty-five thousand dollars is as good as yours anyway," declared his chum with finality. "I'll see there is no loophole in the contract and the money must be placed in escrow so that there can be no possibility of our losing that. The promise of a hundred thousand dollars must he made binding as well."

"I know you will look out for those details, Ned," Tom said with a wave of his hand.

"That is what I am here for," agreed the financial manager. "Now, what else? I fancy the building of such a locomotive looks feasible to you and your father or you would not go into it."

"But two miles a minute!" murmured Mr. Damon again. "Bless my prize pumpkins!"

"The idea of speed enters into it, yes," said Tom thoughtfully. "In fact electric motor power has always been based on speed, and on cheapness of moving all kinds of traffic.

"Look here!" he exclaimed earnestly, "what do you suppose the first people to dabble in electrically driven vehicles were aiming at? The motor-car? The motor boat? Trolley cars? All those single motor sort of things? Not much they weren't!"

"Bless my glove buttons!" exclaimed Mr. Damon, dragging off his gauntlets as he spoke. "I don't get you at all, Tom! What do you mean?"

"I mean to say that the first experiments in the use of electricity as a motive power were along the electrification of the steam locomotive. Everybody realized that if a motor could be built powerful enough and speedy enough to drag a heavy freight or passenger train over the ordinary railroad right of way, the cost of railroad operation would be enormously decreased.

"Coal costs money—heaps of money now. Oil costs even more. But even with a third-rail patent, a locomotive successfully built to do the work of the great Moguls and mountain climbers of the last two decades, and electrically driven, will make a great difference on the credit side of any rails road's books."

"Right-o!" exclaimed Ned. "I can see that."

"That was the object of the first experiments in electric motive power," repeated Tom. "And it continues to be the big problem in electricity. The Jandel locomotive is undoubtedly the last word so far as the construction of an electric locomotive is concerned. But it falls down in speed and power. I thought so myself when I saw that locomotive and looked over the results of its work. And this Mr. Bartholomew has assured father and me this evening that it is a fact.

"It has a record of a mile a minute on a level or easy grade; but it can't show goods when climbing a real hill. It slows up both freight and passenger traffic on the Hendrickton & Pas Alos road. That range of hills is too much for it.

"So the Swift Construction Company is going to step in," concluded the young inventor eagerly. "I believe we can do it. I've the nucleus of an idea in my head. I never had a problem put up to me, Ned and Mr. Damon, that interested me more. So why shouldn't I go at it? Besides, I have dad to advise me."

"That's right," agreed Ned. "Why shouldn't you? And with such a contract as you have been offered—"

"Bless my bootsoles!" ejaculated Mr. Damon, getting up and tramping about the room in his excitement. "I thought the trolley cars that run between Shopton and Waterfield were about the fastest things on rails."

"Not much. The trolley car is a narrow and prescribed manner of using electricity for motive power. The motor runs but one car— or one and a trailer, at most," said Tom. "As I have pointed out, the problem is to build a machine that will transmit power enough to draw the enormous weight of a loaded freight train, and that over steep grades.

"A motor for each car is a costly matter. That is why trolley car companies, no matter how many passengers their cars carry, are so often on the verge of financial disaster. The margin of profit is too narrow.

"But if you can get a locomotive built that will drag a hundred cars! Ah! how does that sound?" demanded Tom. "See the difference?"

"Bless my volts and amperes!" exclaimed Mr. Damon. "I should say I do! Why, Tom, you make the problem as plain as plain can be."

"In theory," supplemented Ned Newton, although he meant to suggest no doubt of his chum's ability to solve almost any problem.

"You've hit it," said Tom promptly. "I only have a theory so far regarding such a locomotive. But to the inventor the theory always must come first. You understand that, Ned?"

"I not only appreciate that fact," said his chum warmly; "but I believe that you are the fellow to show something definite along the line of an improved electric locomotive. But, whether you can reach the high mark set by the president of that railroad—"

"Two miles a minute!" breathed Mr. Damon in agreement. "Bless my wind-gauge! It doesn't seem possible!"

Tom Swift shrugged his shoulders. "It is the impossible that inventors have to overcome. If we experimenters believed in the impossible little would be done in this world, to advance mechanical science at least. Every invention was impossible until the chap who put it through built his first working model."

"That's understood, old boy," said Ned, already busily scratching off the form of the contract he proposed to show the company's legal advisers early in the morning.

When he had read over the notes he had made Tom O.K.'d them. "That is about as I had the items set down myself on the sheet that fellow stole from me."

"Wait!" exclaimed Ned, as Tom arose from his chair. "Do you know what strikes me after your telling me about your second hold-up?"

"What's that?" asked his chum.

"Are you sure that was the same fellow who stole your wallet?"

"Quite sure."

"Then his second attack on you proves that he got wise to the fact that your notes were in shorthand. He had a chance to study them while you visited with Mary Nestor."

"Like enough."

"I wonder if it doesn't prove that the fellow has somebody in cahoots with him right here in Shopton?" ruminated Ned.

"Bless my spare tire!" ejaculated Mr. Damon, who had already started for the door but now turned back.

"That's an idea, Ned," agreed Tom Swift. "It would seem that he had consulted with some superior," said the young manager of the Swift Construction Company. "This hold-up man may be from the West; but perhaps he did not follow Bartholomew alone."

"I'd like to know who the other fellow is," said Tom thoughtfully. "I would know the man who attacked me, both by his bulk and his voice."

"Me, too," put in Mr. Damon. "Bless my indicator! I'd know the scoundrel if I met him again."

"The thing to do," said Ned Newton confidently, "is to identify the man who robbed you tonight as soon as possible and then, if he hangs around Shopton, to mark well anybody he associates with."

"Perhaps they will not bother me any more," said Tom, rather carelessly.

"And perhaps they will," grumbled Mr. Damon. "Bless my self-starter! they may try something mean again this very night. Come on, Tom. I want to run you home. And on the way, I tell you, I've got something to put up to you myself. It may not promise a small fortune like this electric locomotive business; but bless my barbed wire fence! my trouble has more than a little to do with footpads, too."

He led the way out of the house and to the motor car again. In a minute he had started his engine, and Tom, jumping in beside him, was borne away toward his own home.

BARBED WIRE ENTANGLEMENTS

"This gets us to your particular trouble, Mr. Damon," Tom Swift said, while the motor car was rolling along. "You intimated that you had something to consult me about."

"Bless my windshield! I should say I had," exclaimed the eccentric gentleman, swinging around a corner at rather a fast clip.

"And has it to do with highwaymen?" asked Tom, much amused.

"Some of the same gentry, Tom," declared Mr. Damon. "I haven't any peace of my life, I really haven't!"

"Who is troubling you, sir?"

"Why, what nonsense that is, to ask that!" ejaculated the gentleman. "If I knew who they were I wouldn't ask odds of anybody. I'd go after them. As it is, I've left my servant with a gun loaded with rock-salt watching for them now."

"Burglars?" exclaimed Tom, with real interest.

"Chicken-house burglars! That's the kind of burglars they are," growled Mr. Damon. "Two or three times they have tried to get my prize buff Orpingtons. Last night they got me out of bed twice fooling around the chicken house and yard. Other neighbors have lost their hens already. I don't mean to lose mine. Want you to help me, Tom."

"Is that all that is worrying you, Mr. Damon?" laughed the young fellow.

"Bless my radiator! isn't that enough?"

"I know you set your clock by those buff Orpingtons," agreed Tom.

"That's right. That ten-months cockerel, Blue Ribbon Junior, never fails to crow at three-thirty-three to the minute. Bless my combs and spurs; a wonderful bird!"

"But let's see how I can help you regarding the chicken thieves," Tom said, as they sighted the lights of the Swift house beyond the long stockade fence that surrounded the Construction Company's premises.

"You know I have a barbed wire entanglement around the whole yard and hen-house. I don't take any more chances than I can help. Those prize huff Orpingtons are a great temptation to chicken lovers—both blond and brunette," and in spite of his anxiety, Mr. Damon could chuckle at his own joke. "Even your old Eradicate's friend fell for chickens, you know"

"And Rad promptly cured him of the disease," laughed Tom.

"And I'm trying to cure these others. I've charged my shotgun with rock-saltÄas he did. My servant has orders to shoot anybody who tampers with my chicken house tonight.

"But bless my shirt!" exclaimed Mr. Damon, "I'll never be able to sleep comfortably until I know that no thief can get at my buff Orpingtons. I want you to fix it so I can sleep in peace, Tom."

He slowed to a stop in front of the Swift's door. Tom stared at his eccentric friend questioningly.

"Bless my gaiters!" ejaculated Mr. Damon, "don't you see what I want? And your head already full of this electrified locomotive you are going to build?"

"Hush!" murmured Tom, with his hand upon his companion's arm. "But what do you want me to do?"

"I want you to fix it so that I can turn a current of electricity into that barbed wire chicken fence at night that will shock any thief that touches the wires. Not kill 'em—though they ought to be killed!" declared the eccentric man. "But shock 'em aplenty. Can't you do it for me, Tom Swift?"

"Of course it can be done," said the young fellow. "You use electricity in your house. There is a feed cable in the street. We will have to change your lighting switch for another. Fix it with the Electric Supply Company. It will cost you more—"

"Bless my pocketbook! I don't care how much it costs. It will be ample satisfaction to see just one low-down chicken thief squirming on those wires.

Tom laughed again. He meant to help his friend; but he did not propose to rig the wires so that anybody, even a chicken thief, would be seriously injured by the electric current passing through the strands.

"I'll come down to Waterfield tomorrow in the electric runabout and fix things up for you. Get a permit from the Electric Supply Company early in the morning. Tell them I will rig the thing myself. They can send their inspector afterward."

"That's fine, Tom! What—Ugh! what's this? Another footpad?"

Out of the darkness beside the fence a bulky figure started. For a moment Tom thought it was the same man who had attacked him twice. Then the very size of this new assailant proved that suspicion to be unfounded.

"Koku!" exclaimed Tom. "What's the matter with you, Koku?"

The huge and only half-tamed giant gained the side of the car in seemingly a single stride. In the dark they could not see his face, but his voice distinctly showed excitement.

"Master come good. 'Cause there be enemy. Koku find—Koku kill!"

"Bless my magnifying glass!" ejaculated Mr. Damon. "That fellow is the most bloodthirsty individual that I ever saw."

"All in his bringing up," chuckled Tom who knew, as the saying is, that Koku's bark was a deal worse than his bite. "Killing and maiming his enemies used to be Koku's principal job. But he has his orders now. He doesn't kill anybody without consulting me first."

"Bless my buttons!" murmured Mr. Damon. "That is certainly a good thing too. What's the matter with him now?"

That is exactly what Tom himself wanted to know. He had dropped a hand upon the arm of the giant as he stood beside the car.

"Who is the enemy, Koku?" he asked.

"Not know, Master. See him footmarks. Follow him footmarks. Not find. When do find—kill!"

"That is, after first obtaining my permission," said Tom dryly.

"It is so," agreed the imperturbable Koku. "See! Show Master footmarks. Him look in at window. See! Koku have got the wonder lamp."

He flashed the electric torch in his hand. He left the car and strode into the yard. Tom followed him, and Mr. Damon's curiosity brought him along.

The giant pointed the ray of the flashlight at the ground below the porch. Several footprints —the marks of boots at least number twelve in size—were imbedded in the soil. Koku went around the house to the other side, following repeated marks of the same boots.

"How came you to find them, Koku?" asked Tom softly.

"Me look. All around stockade," and he waved a generous gesture with his free hand including the fence about the works. "Enemy may come. Anytime he come. Now he come."

"Bless my slippery shoes!" exclaimed Mr. Damon, who had hard work to keep up both physically and mentally with the giant. "What does he mean

"Koku has always had it in his head," explained Tom, "that we built that fence about the works to keep out enemies. And, to tell the truth, we did! But all that is over—"

"Is it?" asked Mr. Damon pointedly. "Enemy here," added Koku, flashing the lamplight upon the footprints on the ground.

"Those bootmarks," added Mr. Damon, "are doubtless those of that fellow who jumped upon the running board of the car."

"Humph! And who robbed me of my wallet," added Tom musingly. "Well, it might be. And, if so, Koku is right. The enemy has come."

"Me kill!" exclaimed the giant, stretching himself to his full height.

"We'll consider the killing later," said Tom, who well knew his influence with this big fellow. "You are forbidden to kill anybody, or chase anybody away from here, until I have a talk with them. Enemy or not—understand?"

"Me understand," said Koku in his deep voice. "Master say—me do."

"Just the same," Tom said, aside to Mr. Damon, "there has been somebody around here. I guess Mr. Bartholomew was right. He is being spied upon. And now that we Swifts are going to try to do something for him, we are likely to be spied upon too."

"Bless my statue of Nathan Hale!" murmured the eccentric gentleman. "I believe you. And you've been already attacked twice by some thug! You are positively in danger, Tom."

"I don't know about that. Save that the fellow who robbed me was sore because I fooled him. Naturally he might like to get square about those shorthand notes. He knows no more now about Mr. Bartholomew's business with us than he did before he held me up."

"That is a fact," agreed Mr. Damon.

"And that brings me to another warning, Mr. Damon," added Tom earnestly, as his friend climbed into the motor car again. "Keep all that has happened, and all that I told you and Ned about the H. & P. A. railroad, to yourself."

"Surely! Surely!"

"If Mr. Bartholomew's rivals continue to keep their spies hanging around the works here, we'll handle them properly. Trust Koku for that," and Tom chuckled.

"And don't forget my barbed wire entanglements," put in Mr. Damon, starting his engine. "I want to fix those chicken thieves."

"All right. I'll be over tomorrow," promised Tom Swift.

Then he stood a minute on the curb and looked after the disappearing lights of Mr. Damon's car. The latter's problem dovetailed, after all, into this discovery of possible marauders lurking about the Swift premises. Koku had made no mistake in bringing his attention to the matter of the footprints. Tom had seen somebody dodging into the darkness outside the house when he had come out on his way to visit Mary Nestor.

"And sure as taxes," muttered Tom, as he finally turned toward the front door again, "the fellow who twice attacked me this evening wore the boots the prints of which Koku found.

"Those fellows, whoever they are, whether Montagne Lewis and his associates, or not, have bitten off several mouthfuls that they may be unable to chew. Anyhow, before they get through they may learn something about the Swifts that they never knew before."

THE CONTRACT SIGNED

Tom Swift went to bed that night without the least fear that the man who had twice attacked him in the streets of Shopton would be able to trouble him unless he went abroad again. Koku was on guard.

The giant whom Tom had brought home from one of his distant wanderings was wholly devoted to his master. Koku never had, and he never would, become entirely civilized.

He was naturally a born tracker of men. For generations his people had lived amid the alarms of threat and attack. He could not be made to understand how so many "tribes," as he called them, of civilized men could live in anything like harmony.

That somebody should prowl about the Swift house at night with a desire to rob his young master or injure him, did not surprise Koku in the least. He accepted the fact of the marauder's presence as quite the expected thing.

But the man who had robbed Tom and later tried to repay him for playing what appeared to be a practical joke on the robber, did not trouble the Swift premises with his presence before morning. Koku, thrusting Eradicate Sampson aside and striding to his bedroom to report this fact, was what awoke Tom at eight o'clock.

"Hey! What you want, tromping in here for, man?" demanded old Rad angrily. "An' totin' that spear, too. Where you t'ink yo' is? In de jungle again? Go 'way, chile!"

Both Rad and Koku were rapidly outliving the sudden friendship of Rad's sick days, when it was thought he might be blind for life, and were dropping back into their old ways of bickering and rivalry for Tom's attention.

"I report to the Master," declared the giant, in his deep voice.

"You tell me, I tell him," Rad said pompously. "No need yo' 'sturbing Massa Tom at dis hour."

"Koku go in!" declared the giant sternly.

"Jes' stay out dere on de stair an' res' yo'self," said Rad.

Koku lost his temper with old Rad. There was a feud between them, although deep in their hearts they really were fond of each other. But the two were jealous of each other's services to young Tom Swift.

Suddenly Tom heard the old negro utter a frightened squeal. The door which had been only ajar, burst inward and banged against the door-stop with a mighty smash.

Rad went through the big bedroom like a chocolate-colored streak, entered Tom's bathroom, and the next moment there was the sound of crashing glass as Eradicate Sampson went through the lower sash of the window, headfirst, out upon the roof of the porch!

"What do you mean by this?" shouted Tom, sitting up in bed.

Koku paused in the doorway, bulking almost to the top of the door. His right arm was drawn back, displaying his mighty biceps, and he poised a ten foot spear with a copper head that he had seized from a nest of such implements which was a decoration of the lower hall.

Had the giant ever flung that spear at poor Rad's back, half the length of the staff might have passed through his body. Little wonder that the colored man, having roused the giant's rage to such a pitch, had given small consideration to the order of his going, but had gone at once!

"You want to scare Rad out of half a year's growth?" Tom pursued sternly, slipping out of bed and reaching for his robe and slippers. "And he's broken that window to smithereens."

"Koku come make report, Master," said the giant.

"You go put that spear back where you found it and come up properly," commanded the young fellow, with difficulty hiding his amusement. "Go on now!"

He shuffled into the bathroom while the giant disappeared. He peered out of the broken window. It was a wonder Rad had not carried the sash with him! The broken glass was scattered all about the roof of the porch and the old colored man lay groaning there.

"What did you do this for, Eradicate?" demanded Tom. "You act worse than a ten-year-old boy."

"I's done killed, Massa Tom!" groaned Rad with confidence. "I's blood from haid to foot!"

There was a scratch on his bald crown from which a few drops of blood flowed. But with all his terror, Eradicate had put both arms over his head when he made his dive through the window, and he really was very little injured.

"Come in here," repeated Tom. "Fix something over this broken window so that I can take my bath. And then go and put something on that scratch. Don't you know better yet, than to cross Koku when he is excited?"

"Dat crazy ol' cannibal!" spat out Rad viciously. "I'll fix him yet. I'll pizen his rations, dat's what I'll do."

"You wouldn't be so bad as that, Rad!"

"Well, mebbe not," said the colored man, crawling in through the bathroom window. "It would take too much pizen, anyway, to kill that giant. Take as much as dey has to give an el'phant to kill it. Anyways, I's bound to fix him proper some time, yet."

These quarrels between Eradicate and Koku were intermittent. They almost always arose, too, because of the desire of the two servants to wait upon Tom or his father. They were very jealous of each other, and their clashes afforded Tom and his friends a good deal of amusement.

While the young inventor was in his bath the giant strode back into the bedroom, out of which Rad had scurried by another door, and proceeded to report the result of his night watch about the premises.

He had not much to tell. In fact, after Tom had gone into the house Koku had seen nobody lurking about at all. The fact remained that, earlier in the evening, somebody had made a close surveillance of the Swift house, but the mysterious marauder had not come back.

"All right, Koku. Keep your eyes open. I expect that enemy may return sometime. Too bad," he added to himself, "that I didn't get a better look at him."

"Koku know him next time," declared the giant.

"Why! you didn't even see him this time," cried Tom.

"See him boots. See marks him boots make. Know him boots. Waugh!"

"'Waugh!' yourself," returned Tom, shaking his head. "You are altogether too sure, Koku. You couldn't tell a man from his bootprints in the mud."

"Koku know," said the giant, just as confidently. "Wait. Him catch—see—show Master."

"Don't you go to grabbing every stranger who comes around the house or the works for a spy, and make me trouble. Remember now."

Koku nodded gravely and went away. When he met Rad suddenly in the hall with Mr. Swift's breakfast tray, the giant said "boo!" and almost cost the old colored man the loss of the tray.

"Dat big el'phant ought to be livin' in a barn," declared Rad. "Look at dat spear he come near runnin' me t'rough wid! If he had, yo' could ha' driv a tipcart full o' rubbish in after it. Lawsy me!"

But an hour later when Tom and his father started for the offices of the Swift Construction Company down the street, Rad and Koku were sitting before an enormous breakfast in the back kitchen and chatting together as companionably as ever.

The old inventor and his son arrived at the offices of the Swift Construction Company not long ahead of Mr. Richard Bartholomew. Tom had merely found time to read over the contract that had been jointly prepared by Ned Newton and the firm's legal advisers, before the railroad man came.

"No getting out of the provisions of that paper, Tom," Ned had whispered, when he saw Mr. Bartholomew coming into the outer office. "Is this your man

"Yes."

"A sharp looking little fellow," commented Ned. "But even if he were bent on tricking us, this contract would hold him. He is solvent and so is his road—as yet. If it has a bad name in the market that is more because of slander by the Montagne Lewis crowd than from any real cause. I've found that out this morning."

"Faithful Nero!" chuckled Tom. "Aren't going to let the Swifts get done, are you?"

"Not if I can help it," declared Ned Newton emphatically.

A clerk brought Mr. Bartholomew into the private office and he was introduced to Newton. If he considered the financial manager of the Swift Construction Company very young for his responsible position, after he had read the contract he felt considerable respect for Ned Newton.

"You've got me here, young man, hard and fast," Mr. Bartholomew said. "If I was inclined to want to wriggle out, I see no chance of it. But I don't. You have set forth here exactly my meaning and intent. I want your best efforts in this matter, Mr. Swift, and if you give them to me I'll foot the bill as agreed."

"You've got me interested, I confess," said Tom. "By the way, were your friends following you when you came here this morning?"

"My friends?" repeated Mr. Bartholomew, for a moment puzzled.

"The spy that you mentioned," said Tom, smiling.

"That Andy O'Malley?" exclaimed Bartholomew. "Haven't spotted him today."

"He spotted me last night," said Tom grimly, and proceeded to relate what had happened.

"You fooled 'em that time, young man!" exclaimed the railroad president, with satisfaction. "I am convinced that Montagne Lewis is behind it. Look out for these fellows when you get to work, Mr. Swift. They will stop at nothing. I tell you that the fight is on between the Hendrickton & Pas Alos and the Hendrickton & Western. I have either got to break them or they will break me."

"You seem very sure that there is a conspiracy against you, Mr. Bartholomew," said the senior Swift reflectively.

"I am sure," was the reply. "And I am likewise sure that this scheme of electrification of my road through the Pas Alos Range is the only salvation for my railroad."

"I should call it a big contract," Ned Newton said, thoughtfully.

"You have said it! But it is not a visionary scheme I have in mind. You must know—you Swifts—how successful such an electrification through the Rockies has been made by the Chicago, Milwaukee & St. Paul Railway."

"I've looked that up," confessed Tom, with enthusiasm. "That was a great piece of work."

"It is. It is. But I hope for even a greater outcome of your experiments, Mr. Swift. Of course, I do not expect to compete with that great road. They had millions to spend, and they spent them. Those Baldwin-Westinghouse locomotives the Chicago, Milwaukee & St. Paul built in nineteen hundred and nineteen are wonderful machines. They have got forty-two freight locomotives, fifteen passenger locomotives and four switchers of that new type.

"The Jandel patent that my road uses is, in some degree, the equal of those Baldwin-Westinghouse locomotives. At least, our machines equal the C., M. & St. P. on our level road. They can reach a mile-a-minute gait. But when it comes to speed and pull on steep grades—Ah! that is where they fail."

"You will have to get power in the hills for your stations," suggested Tom, thoughtfully.

"I know that. I know where the power is coming from. I gathered those waterfalls in years ago. Lewis and his crowd can't shut me off from them. But I have got to have a speedier and more powerful type of electric locomotive than has ever yet been built to protect the Hendrickton & Pas Alos Railroad from any rivalry.

"I am looking to you Swifts to give me that. I am risking this twenty-five thousand dollars upon your succeeding. And I am offering you the hundred thousand dollars bonus for the right to purchase the first successful locomotives that can be built covered by your patents. Is it plain?"

"It is eminently satisfactory," said Mr. Swift, quietly.

"I will do my very best," agreed Tom, warmly. "There isn't a thing the matter with the agreement," declared Ned Newton, with confidence. "Gentlemen, sign on the dotted line."

Five minutes later the twin contracts were in force. One went into the safe of the Swift Construction Company. The other, Mr. Richard Bartholomew bore away with him.

THE MAN WITH BIG FEET

The consultation in the private office of the Swift Construction Company after the departure of Mr. Richard Bartholomew between the two Swifts and Ned Newton had more to do with a vision of the future than with mere present finances.

"I expect you know just about how you are going to work on this new invention, Tom?" suggested the financial manager, and Tom's chum.

"Haven't the first idea," rejoined the young inventor, promptly.

"What do you mean?" ejaculated Ned. "You talked just now as though you knew all about electric locomotives."

"I know a good deal about those that have been built, both under the Jandel patent and those built for the Chicago, Milwaukee & St. Paul in the great Philadelphia shops.

"But when you ask me if I know how I am going to improve on those patents so as to make my locomotive twice as speedy and quite as powerful as those other locomotives—well, I've got to tell you flat that I have not as yet got the first idea."

"Humph!" grumbled Ned. "You say it coolly enough."

"No use getting all heated up about it," returned his friend. "I have got to consider the situation first. I must look over the field of electrical invention as applied to motive power. I must study things out."

"I don't just see myself," Ned Newton remarked thoughtfully, "why there should be such a great need for the electrification of locomotives, anyway. Those great mountain-hogs that draw most of the mountain railroad trains are very powerful, aren't they? And they are speedy."

"Locomotives that use coal or oil have been developed about as far as they can be," said Mr. Swift, quietly. "A successful electric locomotive has many advantages over the old-time engine."

"What are those advantages?" asked the business manager, quickly. "I confess, I do not understand the matter, Mr. Swift."

"For instance," proceeded the old gentleman, "there is the coal question alone. Coal is rising in price. It is bulky. Using electricity as motive power for railroads will do away with fuel trains, tenders, coal handling, water, and all that. Of course, Mr. Bartholomew will generate his electricity from water power— the cheapest power on earth."

"Humph! I've got my answer right now," said Ned Newton. "If there is no other good reason, this is sufficient."

"There are plenty of others," drawled Tom, smiling. "Good ones. For instance, heat or cold has nothing to do with the even running of an electric locomotive. It can bore right through a snowbank—a thing a steam engine can't do. It runs at an even speed. Really, grade should have nothing to do with its speed. There is a fault somewhere in the construction of the Jandel machine or the H. & P. A. would have little trouble with those locomotives on its grades.

"Then, all you have to do to start an electrified locomotive is to turn a handswitch. No stoking or water-boiling. Does away with the fireboy. One man runs it!"

"Why!" cried Ned, "I never stopped to think of all these things."

"No ashes to dump," went on Tom. "No flues to clean, no boilers to inspect, and none to wear out. And they say that on the Chicago, Milwaukee & St. Paul, at least, their freight locomotives handle twice the load of a steam locomotive at a greatly reduced cost."

"Sounds fine. Don't wonder Mr. Bartholomew is eager to electrify his entire tine."

"On the side of passenger traffic," continued Tom Swift, "the electric locomotive is smokeless, noiseless, dirtless, and doesn't jerk the coaches in either stopping or starting. And in addition, the electric locomotive is much easier on track and roadbed than the old 'iron horse' driven by steam generated either from coal or oil."

"It is a great field for your talents, Tom!" cried Ned, warmly.

"It is a big job," admitted Tom, and he said this with modesty. "I don't know what I may be able to do—if anything. I would not feel right in taking Mr. Bartholomew's twenty-five thousand dollars for nothing."

"Quite right, my boy," said Mr. Swift, approvingly.

"Never mind that," said the financial manager, rather grimly. "It was his own offer and his risk. That twenty-five thousand comes to our account."

Tom laughed. "All business, Ned, aren't you? But there is more than business for the Swift Construction Company in this. Our reputation for fair dealing as well as for inventive powers is linked up with this contract.

"I want to show the Jandel people—to say nothing of the bigger firms—that the Swifts are to be reckoned with when it comes to electric invention. Other roads will be electrifying their lines as fast as it is proved that the electric-driven locomotive has the bulge on the steam-driven.

"In the case of the Hendrickton & Pas Alos there are very steep grades to overcome. Supposedly an electric motor-drive should achieve the same speed on a hill as on the level. But there is the weight of the train to be counted on.

"The H. & P. A. has a two per cent. grade in more than one place. Mr. Bartholomew confessed as much to me last night. The electric-driven locomotive of the powerful freight type, which the Jandel people built for Mr. Bartholomew, can make about sixteen miles an hour on those grades, although they can hit it up to thirty miles an hour on level track.

"His passenger locomotives turn off a mile a minute and more, on the level road; but they can not climb those steep grades at a much livelier pace than the freight engines. That is why he is talking about two-mile-a-minute locomotives. He must get a mighty speedy locomotive, for both freight and passenger service, to keep ahead of Montagne Lewis's rival road, the Hendrickton & Western."

"You don't suppose it can be done, do you?" demanded Ned. "The two-mile-a-minute locomotive, I mean, Tom."

"That is the target I am to aim for," returned his friend, soberly. "At any rate, I hope to improve on the type of locomotive Mr. Bartholomew is now using, so that the hundred thousand dollars bonus will come our way as well as this first twenty-five thousand."

"That wouldn't pay for one engine, would it?" cried Ned.

"Nor is it expected to. The bonus has nothing to do with payment for any model, or patent, or anything of the kind. To tell you the truth, Ned, I understand those big locomotives used by the Chicago, Milwaukee & St. Paul cost them about one hundred and twelve thousand dollars each."

"Whew! Some price, I'll tell the world!" murmured the youthful financial manager of the Swift Construction Company.

When the conference was over, and Tom had been through the workshop to overlook several little jobs that were in process of completion by his trusted mechanics, it was lunch time. He left word that he would not be back that day, for this new task he was to attack was not to be approached with any haphazard thought.

Tom knew quite as well as his father knew that the idea of improving the Jandel patent on electric locomotives was no small thing. The Jandel people had claimed that their patent was the very last word in electric motor-power. And Tom was quite willing to acknowledge that in some ways this claim was true.

But in invention, especially in the field of electric invention, what is the last word today may be ancient history tomorrow.

It was because this field is so broad and the possibility of improvement in every branch of electrical science so exciting, that Tom had accepted Mr. Bartholomew's challenge with such eagerness.

Tom went back to the house for lunch, and as he joined his father in the dining room he remarked to Eradicate:

"I want the electric runabout brought around after lunch. I am going to Waterfield. Tell Koku, will you, Rad?"

"Tell that crazy fellow?" demanded the old colored man heatedly. "Why should I tell him, Massa Tom? Ain't I able to bring dat runabout out o' de garbarge? Shore I is!"

"You can't do everything, Rad," said Tom, soberly. "That is humanly impossible."

"But dat Koku can't do nothin' right. Dat's inhumanly possible, Massa Tom."

"Give him a chance, Rad. I have to take Koku with me this afternoon. You must give your attention to the house and to father."

"Huh! Umm!" grunted Eradicate.

Rad was jealous of anybody who waited on Tom besides himself. Yet he was proud of responsibility, too. He teetered between the pride of being in charge at home and accompanying his young master, and finally replied:

"Well, in course, you ain't going to be gone long, Massa Tom. And yo' father does like to get his nap undisturbed. And he'll want his pot o' tea afterwards. So I'll let dat irresponsible Koku go wid yo'. But yo' got to watch him, Massa Tom. Dat giant don't know what he's about half de time."

As Koku was not within hearing to challenge that statement, things went all right. When Tom came out of the house after eating, he found his very fast car waiting for him, with the giant standing beside it at the curb.

"Get in at the back, Koku," said Tom. "I am going to take you with me."

"Master is much wise," said Koku. "That man with big feet will not hurt Master while Koku is with him."

To tell the truth Tom had quite forgotten the supposed spy that had attacked him the night before. He needed Koku for a purpose other than that of bodyguard. But he made no comment upon the giant's remark.

They stopped at one of the gates of the works, and Tom instructed Koku to bring out and put into the car certain boxes and tools that he wished to take with him. Then he drove on, taking the road to Waterfield.

This way led through farmlands and patches of woods, a rough country in part. A mile out of the limits of Shopton the road edged a deep valley, the sidehill sparsely wooded.

Almost at once, and where there was not a dwelling in sight, they saw a figure tramping in the road ahead, a big man, roughly dressed, and wearing a broad-brimmed hat. Somehow, his appearance made Tom reduce speed and he hesitated to pass the pedestrian.

The man did not hear the runabout at first; or, at least, he did not look over his shoulder. He strode on heavily, but rapidly. Suddenly the young inventor heard the giant behind him emit a hissing breath.

"Master!" whispered the giant.

"What's up now?" demanded Tom, but without glancing around.

"The big feet!" exclaimed Koku.

The giant's own feet were shod with difficulty in civilized footgear, but compared with his other physical dimensions his feet did not seem large. The man ahead wore coarse boots which actually looked too big for him! Koku started up in the back of the car as the latter drew nearer to the stranger.

The man looked back at last and Tom gained a clear view of his features—roughly carved, dark as an Indian's, and holding a grim expression in repose that of itself was far from breeding confidence. In a moment, too, the expression changed into one of active emotion. The man glared at the young inventor with unmistakable malevolence.

"Master!" hissed Koku again. "The big feet!" The fellow must have seen Koku's face and understood the giant's expression. In a flash he turned and leaped out of the roadway. The sidehill was steep and broken here, but he went down the slope in great strides and with every appearance of wishing to evade the two in the motor-car.

The giant's savage war cry followed the fugitive. Koku leaped from the moving car. Tom yelled:

"Stop it, Koku! You don't know that that is the man."

"The big feet!" repeated the giant. "Master see the red mud dried on Big Feet's boots? That mud from Master's garden."

Again Koku uttered his savage cry, and in strides twice the length of those of the running man, started on the latter's trail.

AN ENEMY IN THE DARK

The situation offered suggestions of trouble that stung Tom to immediate action. The impetuousness of his giant often resulted in difficulties which the young inventor would have been glad to escape.

Now Koku was following just the wrong path. Tom Swift knew it.

"Koku, you madman!" he shouted after the huge native. "Come back here! Hear me? Back!"

Koku hesitated. He shot a wondering look over his shoulder, but his long legs continued to carry him down the slope after the dark-faced stranger.

"Come back, I say!" shouted Tom again. "Have I got to come after you? Koku! If you don't mind what you're told I'll send you back to your own country and you'll have to eat snakes and lizards, as you used to. Come here!"

Whether it was because of this threat of a change of diet, which Koku now abhorred, or the fact that he had really become somewhat disciplined and that he fairly worshiped Tom, the giant stopped. The man with the big shoes disappeared behind a hedge of low trees.

"Get back up here!" ejaculated Tom sternly. "I'll never take you away from the house with me again if you don't obey me."

"Master!" ejaculated the giant, slowly approaching. "That Big Feet—"

"I don't care if he made those footprints in the yard last night or not. I don't want him touched. I didn't even want him to know that we guessed he had been sneaking about the house. Understand?"

"Of a courseness," grumbled Koku. "Koku understand everything Master say."

"Well, you don't act as though you did. Next time when I want any help I may have to bring Rad with me."

"Oh, no, Master! Not that old man. He don't know how to help Master. Koku do just what Master say."

"Like fun you do," said Tom, still apparently very angry with the simple-minded giant. "Get back into the car and sit still, if you can, until we get to Mr. Damon's house." Then to himself he added: "I don't blame that fellow, whoever he is, for lighting out. I bet he's running yet!"

He knew that Koku would say nothing regarding the incident. The giant had wonderful powers of silence! He sometimes went days without speaking even to Rad. And that was one of the sources of irritation between the voluble colored man and the giant.

"'Tain't human," Rad often said, "for nobody to say nothin' as much as dat Koku does. Why, lawsy me! if he was tongue-tied an' speechless, an' a deaf an' dumb mute, he couldn't say nothin' more obstreperously dan he does—no sir! 'Tain't human."

So Tom had not to warn the giant not to chatter about meeting the stranger on the road to Waterfield. If that person with dried red mud on his boots was the spy who had followed Mr. Richard Bartholomew East and was engaged by Montagne Lewis to interfere with any attempt the president of the H. & P. A. might make to pull his railroad out of the financial quagmire into which it was rapidly sinking, Tom would have preferred to have the spy not suspect that he had been identified after his fiasco of the previous evening.

For if this Western looking fellow was Andy O'Malley, whose name had been mentioned by the railroad man, he was the person who had robbed Tom of his wallet and had afterward attempted reprisal upon the young inventor because the robbery had resulted in no gain to the robber.

Of course, the fellow had been unable to read Tom's shorthand notes of the agreement that he had discussed with Mr. Bartholomew. Just what the nature of that agreement was, would be a matter of interest to the spy's employer.

Having failed in this attempt to learn something which was not his business, the spy might make other and more serious attempts to learn the particulars of the agreement between the railroad president and the Swifts. Tom was sorry that the fellow had now been forewarned that his identity as the spy and footpad was known to Tom and his friends.

Koku had made a bad mess of it. But Tom determined to say nothing to his father regarding the discovery he had made. He did not want to worry Mr. Swift. He meant, however, to redouble precautions at the Swift Construction Company against any stranger getting past the stockade gates.

Arrived at Mr. Damon's home in Waterfield, Tom got quickly to work on the little job he had come to do for his old friend. Of course, Tom might have sent two of his mechanics from the works down here to electrify the barbed wire entanglements that Mr. Damon had erected around his chicken run. But the young inventor knew that his eccentric friend would not consider the job done right unless Tom attended to it personally.

"Bless my cracked corn and ground bone mixture!" ejaculated the chicken fancier. "We'll show these night-prowlers what's what, I guess. One of my neighbors was robbed last night. And I would have been if I hadn't set a watch while I drove over to see you, Tom. Bless my spurs and hackles! but these thieves are getting bold."

"We'll fix 'em," said Tom, cheerfully, while Koku brought the tools and wire to the hen run. "After we link up your supply of the current with this wire fence it will be an unhappy chicken burglar who interferes with it."

"That was an unhappy fellow who got your charge of ammonia last evening," whispered Mr. Damon. "Heard anything more of him?"

"I think I have seen him. But Koku spoiled everything by trying to eat him up," and Tom laughingly related what had occurred on the way from Shopton.

"Bless my boots!" said Mr. Damon. "You'd better see the police, Tom."

"What for?"

"Why, they ought to know about such a fellow lurking about Shopton. If he followed that Western railroad president here—"

"We'll hope that he will follow Mr. Bartholomew away again," chuckled Tom. "Mr. Bartholomew won't stay over today. When that chap finds he has gone he probably will consider that there is no use in his bothering me any further."

Whether Tom believed this statement or not, he was destined to realize his mistake within a very short time. At least, the fact that he was being spied upon and that the enemy meant him anything but good, seemed proved beyond a doubt that very week.

Having done the little job for Mr. Damon, Tom allowed no other outside matter to take up his attention. He shut himself into his private experimental workshop and laboratory at the works each day. He did not even come out for lunch, letting Rad bring him down some sandwiches and a thermos bottle of cool milk.

"The young boss is milling over something new," the men said, and grinned at each other. They were proud of Tom and faithful to his interests.

Time was when there had been traitors in the works; but unfaithful hands had been weeded out. There was not a man who drew a pay envelope from the Swift Construction Company who would not have done his best to save Tom and his father trouble. Such a thing as a strike, or labor troubles of any kind, was not thought of there.

So Tom knew that whatever he did, or whatever plans he drew, in his private room, he was safely guarded. Yet he always took a portfolio home with him at night, for after dinner he frequently continued his work of the day. Naturally during this first week he did not get far in any problem connected with the proposed electric locomotive. There were, however, rough drafts and certain schedules that had to do with the matter jotted down.

It was almost twelve at night. Tom had sat up in his own room after his father had retired, and after the household was still.

Eradicate was in bed and snoring under the roof, Tom knew. Just where Koku was, it would have been hard to tell. Although a fine and penetrating rain was falling, the giant might be roaming about the waste land surrounding the stockade of the works. The elements had no terrors for him.

Tom locked his portfolio and stepped into his bathroom to wash his hands before retiring. Before he snapped on the electric light over the basin he chanced to glance through the newly set windowpane which had replaced the one Rad had shattered in escaping threatened impalement on Koku's spear.

Although the clouds were thick and the rain was falling, there was a certain humid radiance upon the roof of the porch under the bathroom window. At least, the wet roof glistened so that any moving figure on or beyond it was visible,

"What's that?" muttered Tom, and he sank down lower than the sill and crept slowly to the window. He merely raised himself until his eyes were on a level with the sill.

Coming up over the edge of the porch roof was a bulky figure. It was so dimly outlined at first that Tom could scarcely be sure that it was that of a man.

However, it was not possible that any creature but a man would be able to mount the lattice supporting the honeysuckle vines and so creep out upon the porch roof. Once making secure his footing, the enemy in the dark approached directly the bathroom window at which Tom crouched.

WHERE WAS KOKU?

Tom reached up swiftly and pushed over the lever that locked the two window sashes. In doing this he set his own patent burglar alarm. If that lever was turned back again, or broken, the buzzers would be set ringing all over the house, and in Koku's room over the garage.

He did not believe that the marauder on the roof of the porch could have seen the flash of his shirt-sleeved arm. But he took no chance of being observed from outside by rising to his feet.

On his hands and knees he crept away from the window, and out of the bathroom. Once there, he stood up, grabbed the portfolio, and without coat or vest and as he was, dashed out of the bedroom. He had been positive that nobody but himself was astir in the big house, and he was right.

He did not punch the light button when he entered the library. He knew where to put his hand upon an electric torch in the table drawer, and he gained possession of this.

Then he went to the safe and twirled the knob and watched the indicator find the four numbers which were the "open sesame" to the burglar and fire-proof door.

He flung the portfolio into the inner compartment, closed both doors, and twirled the combination-knob. Then Tom tiptoed to the foot of the front stairs to listen. He could hear no sound from above.

He did not want his father to be startled, if the enemy did break in; and he knew that old Rad, awakened out of a sound sleep, would be worse than useless at such a time.

After all, the giant, Koku, was his main dependence under these circumstances. Tom crept to the outer door, opened it carefully, and slipped out, letting the spring lock click behind him. For the first time he realized that he was in his shirt and trousers and wore only felt slippers on his feet.

But he was locked out now. He had no key. He must run the risk of the fine rain and the chill of the night air.

He stepped. off the end of the porch and ran around the house. It was to the roof of the rear porch that the marauder had climbed. But peer as he might from down in the yard, Tom could see no moving figure up there near the bathroom window. It was pitch dark against the wall of the house.

He turned to glance up at the window of the sleeping room over the garage where Koku was supposed to spend the night. But Tom knew the giant was seldom there during the dark hours. He was as much of a night-prowler as a wildcat or an owl.

There was no light there in any case. But Koku did not use a light much. He could see in the dark, like a wild animal. Tom did not want to call him. If he must have Koku's help, he would have to climb the stairs to his bedside. The giant always aroused as wide awake as at noonday.

But while the young inventor hesitated a sudden, but muffled, snap—the breaking of metal—sounded. Tom knew instantly the direction from which the sound came.

Although he could see nothing up there at the bathroom window because of the rain and the deep shadow, he knew that the snapping sound meant the severing of the window lock that he had so recently closed. Some instrument had been forced under the bottom of the lower sash and pressure enough been brought to bear to break the thin steel lever.

On the heels of this sound came another. A muffled buzzing somewhere in the house—again! again! And then, startlingly clear from the room over the garage, the burglar alarm went off in Koku's chamber.

"It's all off now!" gasped Tom, and he ran to the foot of the honeysuckle ladder up which he knew the enemy had climbed to get to the roof of the porch. "If he comes down I'll have him!" muttered Tom, staring up into the mist and gloom.

"Fo' de lawsy's sake! 'Tain't mawnin', is it?" Rad's sleepy voice was heard to announce. "No, it's da'k as—" And the voice trailed off into silence.

"Tom! Tom!" the young fellow heard his aroused father shouting.

Tom knew that his father was in no danger. In fact Mr. Swift's voice did not even betray apprehension. It was. to the garage Tom looked for an explosion. But none came.

If Koku was up there the prolonged buzzing of the alarm did not awake him. Therefore he could not be there. Tom realized that if the burglar was to be taken the whole affair fell upon his shoulders.

"And I've got my hands full, if it is the fellow with the big feet that we saw on the Waterfield Road the other day," muttered the young inventor.

Nothing stirred on the porch roof. Moment after moment slipped by. Tom began to grow more than amazed. He was worried. What would happen next?

His father had not cried out again. Stepping around to the end of the roofed porch, Tom saw a light in Mr. Swift's room. Rad had evidently gone to sleep again. It would take more than an intermittent buzzer to rouse fully that colored man.

"When old Morpheus has a strangle hold on Rad, Gabriel's trump would scarcely awaken him," Tom muttered.

What had become of the enemy? If it was an ordinary burglar he would have feared the electric alarm instantly. The buzzers were still working. But there was no sign of the man who had set them off at the bathroom window.

Suddenly Tom heard a door slam. It was from the front of the house. Had his father come downstairs to look around and see what the matter was?

The young fellow started around the house on a run. He heard heavy bootsoles spurning the gravel of the path to the front gate. He arrived at the far corner of the house in time to see a man dash through the gateway and run down the street, disappearing finally into the fast-driving rain.

"Fooled me! He went in and right through and down the stairs! Out the front door!" gasped Tom. "Did he get anything? I wonder!"

He sprang up to the front porch and tried the door. It was locked again, of course. Should he ring the bell and get Rad or his father down to the door?

And then, of a sudden, the principal mystery of all this affair bit into Tom Swift's mind. The burglar had made his escape. He could relieve his father's anxiety later. It was his own puzzlement of mind that he first wished to ease.

Where was Koku?

Even had the giant been circling the stockade around the shops he surely must have come up to the home premises by this time. His keen ears could not fail to hear the buzzers. They were still going and would go until the switch was turned.

If the giant was in his room—Tom turned suddenly and started on a run for the rear premises. He still carried the hand-lamp and it lit his way into the garage door and up the narrow stairway. He shot the round beam of the lamp into Koku's room.

He had been obliged to have an iron bedstead made to order for the giant. It stood against one wall of the room. The buzzer was snarling like a huge bumblebee above the head of the couch. Below it sprawled the giant, eyes tightly closed and mouth slightly ajar. From the lips of Koku were emitted sounds worthy of Rad Sampson in his deepest slumbers!

"Asleep?" gasped Tom, stepping cat-like into the room.

And then he was suddenly aware of a sickish, heavy odor in the chamber. The window had been closed. But it was something more than stale air that Tom smelled.

A folded cloth lay on the floor beside the couch. The young fellow saw at once that it had been originally placed over the giant's face, but had slid off. And lucky for Koku that it had been dislodged!

"Chloroform!" muttered Tom. "He's drugged. It is no wonder he did not hear the burglar alarm."

In any event, the incident made one deep impression on Tom's mind. The spies who he believed were working for the Hendrickton & Western Railroad and its owner, Montagne Lewis, were desperate men. Tom could not believe that the fellow with the big feet was alone in Shopton and was unaided in his attempts to find out what Tom was doing.

This attempt to burglarize the house betrayed the caliber of the enemy. In chloroforming Koku he had taken the risk of murdering the giant. Only the fact that the pad of saturated cloth had fallen off Koku's face had, perhaps, saved the man from suffocation.

Tom did not tell the giant when he aroused what the matter with him was. Koku was ill enough! He was wrenched by interior spasms that seemed almost to tear his huge body to pieces.

"What done got into dat big lump o' bone an' grizzle?" demanded Eradicate. "He looks like, he swallowed a volcano, and it just got to wo'kin' right. My lawsy!"

"He is a sick man, all right," admitted Tom. "Looks like he wouldn't try to stab me to deaf wid no spear no mo'," went on Rad, inclined to approve of Koku's sufferings.

"If he died you'd be mighty sorry, old man," declared Tom, sternly.

"Sho' would. Be a mighty hard job to bury him," was the callous response.

Just the same, the crotchety old colored man began to hop around in lively fashion with hot water, and later with coffee and other stimulants; and he nursed Koku all day as though he were a big baby.

Koku, who had never been ill before in his life, was inclined to lay the trouble to an evil genius of some kind. Perhaps, in spite of his half-civilized state, he was still a devil-worshiper. At any rate, he had a vital respect for the forces of evil.

Naturally he considered this unknown and unexpected misery he suffered the result of malignant influences of some kind. Tom did not want him to suspect that the man with the big feet had any possible part in the mystery. Had Koku suspected this, and had he got his hands on the spy, the latter could never have been successfully used in that sort of work again. In all probability he would have said that he had had enough.

Meanwhile Tom made a point of considering each step he took alone thereafter with particular care. He had a bodyguard— usually the giant after the latter had recovered—between the works and the house. He did not bring home any more the schedules or drawings connected with the electric locomotive that he proposed to have built and to test inside the stockade of the Swift Construction Company.

He even put a private detective to work on the matter of finding a man named Andy O'Malley who might be lurking around Shopton. He had a pretty clear description of the fellow, for he had not only seen him once, face to face by daylight, but Tom had written to the president of the H. & P. A. and had got from that gentleman a clear picture in words of the spy whom Mr. Bartholomew believed was working in the interests of Montagne Lewis.

"If O'Malley appears in Shopton, look out. He is a bad character. He is not only a notorious gunman, with several warrants out for him in these parts, but he is a cruel and desperate man in any event. The minute you mark him, have him arrested and telegraph me. We'll get him extradited and put him through for ten years or more right in this county." The private investigator, however, as the weeks went by, could not find any man who filled O'Malley's description.

Meanwhile Tom Swift had got what he called "a lead" and was working day and night upon the invention that he believed might make even the Jandel people respectful, if not a bit envious.

First of all Tom had arranged to have built all around inside the stockade a track of rails heavy enough to stand the wear and tear of the heaviest locomotive built. Meanwhile the various parts of his locomotive were being built in several shops, but would be shipped to the Swift Construction Company and assembled in Tom's try-out shed.

Great secrecy was of course maintained. Aside from the fact that the new invention had something to do with electric motive power, nobody about the shops could say what the new industry portended. Save, of course, the Swifts themselves, Ned Newton, and Mr. Damon, who was the Swifts' closest friend and sometimes had furnished additional capital for Tom's experiments.

There was a thing that Mr. Damon furnished Tom at this time that proved in the end to be of much importance. Before Tom had seized upon this idea of his eccentric friend, and had made proper use of it, something happened that came near to wrecking utterly Tom's invention and completely putting an end to Tom himself as an inventor.

A Strange Conversation

Mr. Wakefield Damon frequently came to the shops, for he was not alone very friendly with the Swifts, but he was greatly interested in Tom's new invention.

"If it goes as good as what you did for my chicken run," he declared, chuckling, "bless my dampers! you'll beat all the electric locomotives in the market."

"That is easy, perhaps," said Tom smiling. "There are not many in the market at the present time. But I don't know what mine will be. This is going to be some job."

"Bless my flues and clinkers!" cried Mr. Damon, "you are not losing hope, Tom Swift? Look what you did for my chicken run. And believe me, that entanglement will give a shock that makes a man stand right up and shake."

"Have you tried it yourself?" asked Tom.

"No. But my servant did. I saw him through the window of my study doing some kind of a shimmy with the shovel. Thought he'd gone crazy. Then I saw what he had done. It was early in the morning and I hadn't turned the current off, and he had put one hand against the wires. When he dropped the shovel as I told him to, bless my plyers and nippers! he was all right."

"The current would not seriously hurt him," said Tom. "I was careful about that."

"It killed two tomcats," said Mr. Damon. "I certainly was glad of that, for those two ash-barrel cats kept the whole neighborhood awake. Bless my claws and whiskers! how those two cats did use to yell. But when one tried to climb the wires and the other sprang on him, it was all over! That is, all over but the burial party."

Mr. Damon was on the ground when the mechanical equipment and a part of the electrical equipment of the new locomotive arrived and was set up in the erection shed. The length of the machine was what first impressed Ned Newton as well as Mr. Damon.

"Bless my yardstick!" exclaimed the eccentric man, it's as long as a gossip's tongue. What a monster it will he!"

"How long is it, Tom?" asked Ned Newton.

"When completed, and standing on its drivers and bogie truck and trailer truck, from cow-catcher to rear bumper it will be a few inches over ninety feet. And that is slightly longer than the biggest electric locomotive so far built. But length does not so much enter into the value of the machine. I would have it built more compactly if I could."

"What is the horsepower?" asked Mr. Damon.

"I figure on forty-four hundred horsepower. The power must be received from a three thousand-volt direct-current trolley. There are twelve driving-wheels, as you can see. Each pair of drivers will be driven by a twin-motor geared to the axles through a system of flexible spring drive. Remember, I have got to obtain both speed as well as power in this locomotive, for it is being built to pull a passenger train—a fast cross-continent express—to compete with the best passenger equipment in the country."

"Bless my combination ticket!" murmured Mr. Damon. "You have picked out some task, and no mistake, Tom Swift."

"He'll do it," cried Ned, with his usual optimism when Tom had once started on any experimental work. "Of course he will. Just as she stands there now, only half put together, I would be willing to bet a farm that she is a better locomotive than the Jandel patent."

"Three cheers!" laughed Tom. "Ned is as enthusiastic as usual. But believe me, friends, we are not going to turn out a better locomotive than the Jandel without both thought and work."

His friends' enthusiasm was heartening, however. No doubt of that. He never let them into his experiment room, any more than he allowed his workmen in there. Aside from his own father, nobody really knew what Tom Swift was doing behind that always-locked door.

The huge structure of the locomotive was set up on the driving wheels and leading and trailing trucks by Tom's chief foreman and a picked crew. Just such another locomotive had never been seen anywhere about Shopton. Naturally the men at work on the monster began to speak of it outside the works.

Not that they betrayed any secrets regarding the locomotive. In fact, as yet none of them knew anything about what Tom intended to do with the big machine. But the story soon circulated that Tom Swift, the young inventor, was about to show all the previous builders of electric locomotives how such machines should be built.

It was even whispered that Tom's objective was a two-mile-a-minute locomotive. And when this was publicly known the information was not long in seeping to the ears of certain men who had been keeping as close a watch as they dared on the Swift Construction Company and the activities of Tom himself.

Ned Newton went to the bank one Friday for money for the payroll of the working and clerical force of the Swift Company. It was an errand he never relegated to any employee.

Ned had once worked himself in the bank, and naturally he knew many of its employees as well as the officials. With his back to the general waiting room, he sat at the vice president's desk discussing some minor matter. Only a railing divided the vice president's enclosure from the long settee on which waiting customers of the bank were seated.

Ned knew that there were two men directly behind him, whispering together; but he paid no attention to them until he heard this phrase:

"It's time to explode in just five hours; then good-night to that invention, whatever it is."

This statement might mean almost anything—or nothing. Ordinarily Ned Newton might not have paid any consideration to the words. But "invention" was a term that he could not over-look. His mind then was fixed upon Tom's invention almost as closely as the mind of the young inventor himself.

Ned turned around slowly, as though idly, indeed, and tried to see the faces of the two men behind him. One was a small, neatly dressed man of professional appearance. He wore a Vandyke beard and eyeglasses. The other's face Ned could not see; but as they both rose just then and strolled toward the door of the bank he could observe that the fellow was big and burly.

Ned wheeled to his friend, the vice president, and asked:

"Who are those men, Mr. Stanley? Do you know them?"

The pair were just going out through the revolving door. The vice president craned his neck for a look at them.

"Don't know the small man, Ned. But the other is named O'Malley, I believe. Somebody introduced him here and he gets a check cashed occasionally. Not a customer of the bank."

At that moment the name "O'Malley" did not mean anything to Ned Newton. But he bade his friend good-bye and went out after the two men. They had disappeared.

Rad was in the electric runabout, waiting for him. The words spoken by O'Malley (Ned thought it must have been he who spoke of the invention because of his deep voice) continued to disturb Ned's thought.

"Rad," he said, as he got into the runabout, "did you ever hear the name O'Malley?"

"Sure has," declared the colored man. "And it's a bad name and a bad man owns it."

"Do you mean that?" exclaimed the financial manager of the Swift Construction Company, with increasing apprehension. "Who is he?"

"Why, Mr. Newton, don't you 'member dat man?"

"Who is he?" repeated Ned.

"Dat Andy O'Malley is de one what tried to hold up Massa Tom dat time. O'Malley is de man what's been spyin' on Massa Tom—"

"Great grief!" exclaimed Ned, breaking in with excitement. "I'll drive as fast as I can, Rad. There is something wrong at the works, I do believe!"

"What's wrong, Mr. Ned?" demanded Rad. "We just come from dere, and everyt'ing was all right."

"I just heard something that O'Malley said. I want to get back in a hurry. I believe that scoundrel is attempting to blow up Tom's locomotive. We've got to get to the works just as quick as we can."

Touch and Go

The mechanical equipment of the new locomotive was now complete and Tom was establishing the electrical equipment as rapidly as possible. He not only acted as overseer of this work, but in overalls and jumper he was doing a good share of the work himself.

The weight of the electrical equipment when it was finally set up was not far from two hundred thousand pounds. Altogether, when the oil, sand, and water tanks were filled, the great machine would weigh two hundred and eighty-five tons—a monster indeed!

"She is going to take a lot of current to run her," said Tom to his father, who was standing by. "When I come to arrange with the Shopton Electric Company for power, it's a question if they can give me all I need. And I must have plenty of current to make sure that my motors till the bill."

"As your tests will be made in the daytime, the company should be able to furnish the power you need," rejoined Mr. Swift. "At night, of course, when they must furnish so much light as well as power, it might be difficult for them to give you the proper current."

"Forty-four hundred horsepower is a big demand," went on Tom. "I've got to have at least a three-thousand-volt direct-current to feed my motors. I will soon have to take up the matter with the Electric Company."

The heavy work of setting the electrical parts of the locomotive had been finished the day previous, and the track-derrick was removed. Tom was engaged in adjusting the more delicate parts of the equipment and had merely stepped down from the cab to speak to Mr. Swift.

Now he climbed back into the interior of the great machine which, in a general way, looked like a box car. An electric locomotive has not much of the appearance of a steam engine. The machinery is all boxed in and the entire floor of the locomotive is above even the drivers.

These six pairs of driving wheels were about seventy inches in diameter, while the diameter of the leading and following truck-wheels was but half that number of inches.

Mr. Swift had turned away from the locomotive when Tom put his head out of the door again.

"Do you hear that, father?" he demanded in a puzzled tone.

"Hear what, Tom?" asked the old inventor, looking up.

"That ticking sound? I declare, I'd think it was one of those death-watch beetles had got in here. Sounds like a big watch ticking. I can't make it out."

"Where is it? What is it?" repeated Mr. Swift. "I hear nothing down here on the floor of the shed."

"Well, it gets me," muttered Tom, and disappeared again. In a moment he called out: "Say, you fellows! who left his bundle of overalls in here? Better take 'em out to be manicured. Whose are these?"

Two or three of the mechanics working near looked up from their tasks. Mr. Swift turned back to the door of the cab again.

"What is the matter now, Tom?" he asked, in added curiosity.

"That bundle, Dad."

Tom once more appeared and addressed the workmen: "Whose bundle of dirty overalls is this in here? Come and take 'em away. They shouldn't have been left here."

"Why, Mr. Tom," said the foreman who was near, "I didn't see any soiled overalls in there when I left last evening. Any of you fellows," he asked the group of hands, "know anything about any overalls?"

"The bundle is here all right. Pushed back against the third series motors. Come up here, one of you fellows

Suddenly there was a noise at the end of the shed where the door to the offices lay. Two figures burst through from the glass doors and charged down the lanes between the lathes and cranes. Ned Newton led, Rad Sampson, his face a mouse-gray with fear, followed.

"Massa Tom! Massa Tom!" shouted the colored man. "Look out fo' de bomb! Look out fo' de bomb!"

The foreman sprang toward the high door of the locomotive where Tom stood, staring out. The young inventor, quick as his mind usually functioned, did not understand at all what Eradicate meant.

"There's something wrong in there, Mr. Tom!" shouted the foreman. "Come down, sir, and let me get up there and see what it is."

But Mr. Barton Swift grasped the meaning of what was going on more quickly than anybody else. Tom's father, Tom frequently said, had spent so many years investigating chemical and mechanical mysteries that he saw more clearly and more exactly into and through most problems than other people.

His raised voice now cut through the rumble of machinery and all the other noises of the shop. Even Rad Sampson's delirious cry was dwarfed by Mr. Swift's sharp tone:

"Tom! The ticking of that watch! That means danger!"

The declaration seemed to rip away a curtain from Tom's thoughts. Perhaps Rad's cry about "de bomb" aided the young inventor to understand the peril that threatened.

The faint ticking sound that had begun to annoy him during the past few minutes betrayed the nature of the threatening peril. Tom swung back from the open doorway of the locomotive cab, reached in to the space between the motors, and seized the bundle of overall stuff that he had previously spied.

He knew instantly that the rapid ticking came from that bundle. It could be nothing but a time bomb. He had heard of such things and, indeed, had seen one before, an infernal machine which, set like an alarm clock, would go off at a certain time. That indicated time might be an hour hence, or might be within a few seconds! Ned Newton, almost at the spot, shouted to Tom when the latter reappeared with the bundle in his hands:

"Get down out of that, Tom Swift! Quick! For your life!"

But Tom was cool enough now. He saw his father's white, strained face at one side and the young inventor could even smile at him. Behind the foreman was set a barrel of water in which tools were cooled and tempered.

"Stoop, McAvoy!" Tom shouted, and tossed the bundle from him.

Had the infernal machine exploded in midair Tom would not have been surprised. But McAvoy dodged, Rad clapped his hands over his ears, and, even Ned Newton halted like a bird-dog at point.

The bundle splashed into the barrel of water. It sank to the bottom. There was no explosion. When a few seconds had passed the group of excited men began to relax. The barrel was carried carefully to a neighboring field.

"Fo' de lawsy sake!" gasped Rad, and got a full breath again.

"That was touch and go, sure enough," muttered Ned Newton.

"Those overalls sure went to the wash, Boss," declared the foreman. "What was in 'em? And who put 'em in the cab up there?"

But Tom dropped down the ladder and went to his father. Their hands sought each other and gripped, hard.

"Better not tell Mary about this," whispered Tom. "She's worried enough as it is."

"Right, Tom," agreed the old inventor. "From this time on we cannot be too careful. If there proves to be an infernal machine in that package we may be sure that we are dealing with desperate men. We've got to keep our eyes open."

"Wide open," added Ned.

"I'll say we have," said Tom.

THE TRY-OUT DAY ARRIVES

It did not need Ned Newton's story of what he had overheard at the bank to prove that an attempt had been made to blow to pieces Tom Swift's electric locomotive before even it had been tested.

An examination of the water-soaked package in the open yard of the shops of the Swift Construction Company, proved that there was enough explosive in the bomb to blow the shed itself to pieces. But the stopping of the clockwork attachment of course made the bomb harmless.

"The main thing to be explained," Tom said, when he and his father and Ned discussed the particulars of the affair, "is not who did it, or what it was done for. Those are comparatively easy questions to answer."

"Yes," agreed Ned. "O'Malley did it, or caused it to be done; and it was an attempt to balk Mr. Bartholomew and the H, & P. A. rather than a direct attack upon the Swift Construction Company."

"I am afraid, however," remarked Mr. Swift, "that Tom has aroused the personal antagonism of this spy from the West. We must not overlook that."

"I don't," replied the young inventor. "O'Malley has it in for me. No doubt of that. But he could not be sure that I would be hurt by the explosion he arranged for."

"True," said his father.

"The attempt was against my invention. And O'Malley was doubtless urged to destroy the locomotive that I am building because my success will aid Mr. Bartholomew and his railroad."

"Quite agreed," said Ned. "But—"

"But the important question," interrupted Tom, "is this: How did the bomb get into the interior of the electric locomotive? That is the first and most important problem. Its having been done once warns us that it can be done again until our system of guarding the works is changed."

"We have five watchmen on the job at night, and the gates are never opened in the daytime to anybody for any purpose without a pass," declared Ned. "I don't see how that fellow got in here with the time bomb."

"Exactly. It shows that there is a fault in our system somewhere," said Tom grimly. "We cannot surround the place at night with an armed guard. It would cost too much. Even Koku cannot be everywhere. And I have reason to know that he was wandering about the stockade last night as usual."

"The fellow was pretty sharp to slip by," Ned observed.

"The stockade is no mean barrier, especially with the rows of barbed wire at the top," said Mr. Swift.

"Barbed wire! That's it!" exclaimed Tom. It was just here that Mr. Damon's idea for guarding his prize buff Orpingtons came into play in

Tom's scheme of things. "Barbed wire doesn't seem to keep out spies," he added slowly. "But believe me, something else will!"

For Tom to think of a thing was to start action without delay. Immediately he called a gang from the shops and set them to work stringing copper wire along the top of the stockade.

He was sure that the man who had set the time bomb in place had got into the enclosure over the fence. If he tried the same trick again he was very apt to have the surprise of his life!

Each night when the shops closed and the watchmen went on duty, a current of electricity was turned into those copper wires entwined with the barbed wire entanglement at the top of the stockade that would certainly double up any marauder who sought to get over the top.

However, no further attempt was made against Tom's peace of mind and against his invention during the immediate weeks that followed. The young inventor was so closely engaged in his work that he scarcely left the house or the confines of the shops. Even Mary Nestor saw very little of him.

But Mary realized fully that at such a time as this Tom must give all his thought and energy to the task in hand. She was proud of Tom's ability and took a deep interest in his inventions.

"I want to see the test when you try the locomotive, Tom," she told him, when she came to the shops the first time to look at the monster locomotive. "What a wonderful thing it is!"

"Its wonder is yet to be proved," rejoined the young inventor. "I believe I've got the right idea; but nothing is sure as yet."

In addition to his mechanical contrivances inside the locomotive, Tom had to arrange for an increased supply of electric power to drive the huge machine around the track that was being built inside the stockade.

A regular station had to be built for receiving the electricity in a 100,000-volt alternating current and delivering it to the locomotive in a 3,000-volt direct current. Therefore, this station had two functions to perform—reducing the voltage and changing the current from alternating to direct.

The reduction of the voltage was accomplished as follows: The 100,000-volt alternating current was received through an oil switch and was conveyed to a high-tension current distributor made up of three lines of copper tubing, thus forming the source of power for this station.

From the current distributor the current was conducted through other oil switches to the transformers—entering at 100,000 volts and emerging at 2,300 volts. Then the current was conducted from the transformers through switches to the motor-generator sets and became the power employed to operate them.

The motor generator consisted of one alternating current motor driving two direct current generators. The motor Tom established in his station was of the 60-cycle synchronous type, which means that the current changes sixty times each second.

There were two sets, each generating a 1,500 or 2,000 volt direct current; and the two generators being permanently connected, delivered a combined direct current of 3,000 volts—as high a direct voltage current, Tom knew, as had ever been adopted for railroad work. The current voltage for ordinary street railway work is 550 volts.

"I could run even this big machine," Tom explained to Ned Newton, "with a much lighter current. But out there on the Hendrickton & Pas Alos line the transforming stations deliver this high voltage to the locomotives. I want to test mine under similar conditions."

"This is going to be an expensive test, Tom," said Ned, grumbling a little. "The cost-sheets are running high."

"We are aiming at a big target," returned the inventor. "You've got to bait with something bigger than sprats to catch a whale, Ned."

"Humph! Suppose you don't catch the whale after all?"

"Don't lose hope," returned Tom, calmly. "I am going after this whale right, believe me! This is one of the biggest contracts—if not the very biggest—we ever tackled."

"It looks as if the expense account would run the highest," admitted the financial manager.

"All right. Maybe that is so. But I'll spend the last cent I've got to perfect this patent. I am going to beat the Jandels if it is humanly possible to do so."

"I can only hope you will, Tom. Why, this track and the overhead trolley equipment is going to cost a small fortune. I had no idea when you signed that contract with Mr. Bartholomew that so much money would have to be spent in merely the experimental stage of the thing."

Ned Newton possessed traits of caution that could not be gainsaid. That was one thing that made him such a successful financial manager for the Swift Company. He watched expenditures as closely now as he had when the business was upon a much more limited footing.

The rails laid along the inside of the stockade made a two-mile track, as well ballasted as any regular railroad right of way. In addition the overhead equipment was costly.

To eliminate any possibility of the trolley wire breaking, a strong steel cable, called a catenary, was slung just above the trolley wire. To this catenary the trolley wire was suspended by hangers at short intervals.

These cables were strung from brackets so that a single row of poles could be used, save at the curves, at which cross-span construction was used. The trolley wire itself was of the 4/0 size, and was the largest diameter copper wire ever employed for railroad purposes.

Several weeks had now passed since the great locomotive had been assembled in the erection shed and the cab of the locomotive completed. It really was a monster machine, and any stranger coming into the place and seeing it for the first time must have marveled at the grim power suggested by the mere bulk of the structure.

When the day of the first test arrived Tom allowed only his most intimate friends to be present. Mary Nestor accompanied Mr. Swift into the shops at the time appointed, and she was as excited over the outcome of the test as Tom himself.

Ned Newton and the mechanical force of the shops knocked off work to become spectators at the exhibition. The only other outsider was Mr. Damon.

"Bless my alternating current!" cried the eccentric gentleman. "I would not miss this for the world. If you tried to shut me out, Tom, I'd climb over the stockade to get in."

"You'd better not," Tom told him, dryly. "If you tried that you'd get a worse shock than any chicken thief will get that tries to steal your buff Orpingtons."

Hopes and Fears

Tom climbed into the huge cab of the electric locomotive. In fact, the cab was the most of it, for every part of the mechanism save the drivers was covered by the eighty-odd foot structure. From the peak of the pilot to the rear bumper the length was ninety feet and some inches.

As Tom slid the monster out upon the yard track the small crowd cheered. At least, the locomotive had the power to move, and to the unknowing ones, at least, that seemed a great and wonderful thing.

What they saw was apparently a box-car—like a mail coach, only with more high windows—ten feet wide, its roof more than fourteen feet from the rails, its locked pantagraph adding two feet more to its height.

Just what was in the cab—the water and oil tanks, the steam-heating boiler to supply heat and hot water to the train the monster was to draw, the motors and the many other mechanical contrivances—was hidden from the spectators.

In fact, since completing the electrical equipment of the Hercules 0001, as Tom had named the locomotive, the young inventor had allowed nobody inside the cab, any more than he allowed visitors inside his private workshop. Even Mr. Swift did not know all the results of Tom's experimental work. In a general way the older inventor knew the trend of his son's attempts, but the details and the results of Tom's experiments, the latter told to nobody.

But as the huge locomotive rolled into the yard and followed the more or less circular track inside the yard fence, it was plain to all of the onlookers that the motive-power was there all right! Just what speed could be coaxed from the feed-cable overhead was another question.

Nor did Tom Swift try for much speed on this first test of the Hercules 0001. He went around the two-mile track several times before bringing his machine to a stop near the crowd of onlookers. He came to the open door of the cab.

"One thing is sure, Tom!" shouted Ned. "It do move!"

"Bless my slippery skates!" exclaimed Mr. Damon, "it slides right along, Tom. You've done it, my boy—you've done it!"

"It looks good from where I stand, my son," said Mr. Barton Swift.

It was Mary who suspected that Tom was not wholly satisfied—as yet, at least—with the test of the Hercules 0001. She cried:

"Tom! is it all right?"

"Nothing is ever all right—that is, not perfect —in this old world, I guess, Mary," returned the young inventor. "But I am not discouraged. As Ned says, the old contraption 'do move.' How fast she'll move is another thing."

"What time did you make?" asked Mr. Swift.

"Not above fifteen miles an hour."

"Whew!" whistled Ned dolefully. "That is a long way from—"

Tom made an instant motion and Ned's careless lips were sealed. It was not generally known among the men the speed which Tom hoped to obtain with his new invention.

"It is a wide shoot at the target, that is true," Tom said, soberly. "But remember I cannot test it for speed on this short and almost circular track. Right at the start, however, I see that something about the power-feed must be changed."

"What is that?" asked Mary, curiously.

"I have only had rigged here one trolley wire. There must be two attached alternately to the catenary cable. Such a form of twin conductor trolley will permit the collection of a heavy current through the twin contact of the pantagraph with the two trolley wires, and should assure a sparkless collection of the current at any speed. You noticed that when I took the sharper curves there was an aerial exhibition. I want to do away with the fireworks."

The fact that the Hercules 0001 was a going and apparently powerful draught engine satisfied most of the onlookers that Tom Swift was on the road to final and overwhelming success. The mechanics, indeed, saw no reason why the locomotive could not be run right out of the yard on the freight track and coupled to the first train going West. Of course, the Hercules 0001 could not be delivered to the Hendrickton & Pas Alos under its own power.

When the locomotive was run back into the shed and stood once more on the erection track, Tom confessed to Mary and Ned, while Mr. Damon and Mr. Swift were looking through the huge cab, that he was not at all pleased with the action of the machine.

"I have the best equipment of any electric locomotive on the rails today. I am sure of that," he said. "The Hercules Three-Oughts-One is not as long as those electric locomotives of the C. M. &. St. P. But that's all right. I have built mine more compactly and, properly geared, it should have all the power of either the Baldwin-Westinghouse or the Jandel locomotive."

"Then, Tom dear, what is wrong?" cried Mary.

"Speed. That is what troubles me. Have I got anything like the speed I am aiming for?"

"Two miles a minute!" breathed Ned Newton. "Some speed, boy!"

"And must you have such great speed, Tom?" repeated Mary.

"That is in my contract. Not only that, but to be of much use to the H. & P. A. this locomotive must have such speed—or mighty near it. Of course, under ordinary conditions, two miles a minute for a locomotive and train of heavy freights would burn up the track—maybe melt the flanges and throw everything out of gear."

"Why try for it, then?" demanded Mary.

"It is the power suggested by the possession of such speed that we want in the Hercules Three-Oughts-One. That two miles a minute is a fiction of the imagination, cannot be claimed. It is possible. It is humanly possible. It is coming."

"Then you must be the fellow to first accomplish it, Tom Swift," Ned declared.

"Of course, if anybody can do it, you can, Tom," agreed the girl complacently.

"Thanks—many, many thanks," laughed the young inventor. "I'd be able to harness the sun and stars, and put a surcingle around the moon if I came up to my friends' opinion of my ability.

"Nevertheless, two-miles-a-minute is my objective point, and I do not believe it is visionary. Consider the motor-cycle. Ninety miles an hour has long been possible with that, and some tests have shown a speed of over a hundred and ten. That is not far from my mark.

"Some Mallet locomotives of the oil-burning type have achieved from eighty-five to ninety-five miles an hour with a heavy load behind them. They are very powerful machines. The Mogul mountain climbers are powerful, too, although they are not built for speed.

"The electric Goliaths built for the C. M. & St. P., and the Jandels, are both very speedy under certain conditions. The former has a maximum speed of sixty-five miles and the Jandel slightly faster."

"But that is only half what that Mr. Bartholomew demands of your invention, Tom!" Mary cried.

"That is a fact. I must reach twice sixty miles an hour, anyway, to meet his demand and gain that hundred thousand bonus. But I have the advantage of a knowledge of all that has been done before my time in the matter of electrical locomotive construction."

"The world do move," repeated Ned. "You believe that you have the edge on all the other inventors?"

"Along the line of this development—yes," said Tom. "I am taking up the work where former experimenters ended theirs. Why shouldn't I find the right combination to bring about a two-miles-a-minute drive?"

"Oh, Tom!" cried Mary, with clasped hands, "I hope you do."

"I hope I do, too," said Tom, grimly. "At least, if trying will bring it, success is going to come my way."

SPEED

More than four months had passed since the contract had been signed, when Tom made his first yard-test of the Hercules 0001. For a month nothing had been seen or heard of Andy O'Malley, whose identity as the spy, set by Montagne Lewis to cripple Tom's attempt to help the Hendrickton & Pas Alos Railroad, had been determined beyond any doubt.

The private inquiry agent that Tom had engaged to find O'Malley had been unsuccessful in his work. The spy had disappeared from Shopton and the vicinity. Nevertheless, the inventor did not for a moment overlook the possibility that the enemy might again strike.

Every night the electric current was turned into the wires that capped the stockade of the Swift Construction Company enclosure. Koku beat a path around the enclosure at night, getting such short sleep as he seemed to need in the forenoon.

"Dat crazy cannibal," grumbled Rad, "got it in his haid dat he's gwine to he'p Massa Tom by walkin' out o' nights like he was dis here Western, de great sprinter, Ma lawsy me! Koku ain't got brains enough to fill up a hic'ry nut shell. Dat he ain't."

Nothing anybody else could do for Tom ever satisfied Rad. The colored man fully believed that he was the only person really necessary for Tom's success and peace of mind. In fact, Rad thought that even Ned Newton's duties as financial manager of the firm were scarcely of as much importance.

When he heard that Tom was going West, after a time, with the electric locomotive, to try it out on the tracks of the H. & P. A., Rad was quite sure that if he did not go along, the test would not come out right.

"O' course yo'll need me, Massa Tom," he said, confidently. "Couldn't git along widout me nohow. Yo' knows, sir, I allus has to go 'long wid yo' to fix things."

"Don't you think father will need you here, Rad?" Tom asked the faithful old fellow. "You're getting old—"

"Me gittin' old?" cried, the colored man. "Huh! Yo' don't know 'bout dis here chile. I don't purpose ever to git old. I been gray-haided since befo' yo' was born; but I ain't old yit!"

Mr. Damon chanced to be present at this conversation, and he was highly amused, yet somewhat impressed, too, by the colored man's statement.

"Bless my own antiquity!" he exclaimed. "I agree with Rad, Tom. It's us old fellows who know what to do when an emergency of any kind arises. Experience teaches more than inspiration."

"Oh," said Tom, laughing, "I do not deny the value of old friends at any stage of the game."

"Bless my roving nature! I am glad to hear you say that. For I tell you right now, Tom, I want to be out there when you make your final test of the locomotive."

"Do you mean that you will go West when I take out the Hercules Three-Oughts-One?" cried Tom.

"It's just what I want to do. Bless my traveling bag, Tom! I mean to be present at your final triumph."

"What will happen to your buff Orpingtons while you are gone?" asked the young inventor, gravely.

"I have got my servant trained to look after those chickens," declared Mr. Damon. "And this invention of yours is really more important than even my buff Orpingtons."

"Just the same," remarked Tom to his eccentric friend, when Rad had left the room,. "I've got to fix it so that Eradicate stays at home with father. He doesn't really know how old and broken he is—poor fellow."

"His heart is green, Tom. That's what is the matter with Rad."

"He is a loyal old fellow. But I shall take Koku with me, not Rad," and the young inventor spoke decidedly. "And that is going to trouble poor Rad a lot."

The prospect of going West, however, was not the main subject of Tom's thoughts at this time. As the weeks passed and the end of the six months of experiment came nearer, the inventor was more and more troubled by the principal difficulty which had from the first confronted him. Speed.

That was the mark he had set himself. A maximum speed of two miles a minute on a level track for the Hercules 0001. With the speed already attained by both steam and electric locomotives in the more recent past, this was by no means an impossible attainment, as Tom quite well knew.

But he became convinced that the conditions under which he labored made it impossible for him to be positive of just how great a speed on a straight, level track his invention would attain.

There was no electrified stretch of railroad near Shopton on which the Hercules 0001 might be tested. The track inside the Swift Company's enclosure did not offer the conditions the inventor needed. He felt balked.

"I believe I have hit the right idea in my improvements on the Jandel patents," he told Ned Newton when they were discussing the matter. "But believing is one thing. Knowing is another!"

"Theoretically it works out all right, I suppose?" questioned Ned.

"Quite. I can prove on paper that I've got the speed. But that isn't enough. You can see that."

"Impossible to be sure on the trackage already built here, Tom?"

"I haven't dared give her all she'll take," grumbled Tom. "If I did, I fear she'd jump the rails and I'd have a wreck on my hands."

"And maybe kill yourself!" exclaimed Ned. "You want to have a care."

"Oh, that's all right! I've taken risks before. I don't want to risk the safety of the locomotive, which is more important. That machine has cost us a lot of money."

"I'll say so!" agreed Ned. "You'll have to wait till you can get the locomotive out there on the H. & P. A. tracks before you get a fair speed-test."

"And suppose instead of a triumph it is a fiasco?" Tom said, doubtfully. "I tell you straight, Ned: I never was so uncertain about the outcome of one of my inventions since I began dabbling with motive—power."

"We could build several miles of straight track in the waste ground behind the works," Ned said, thoughtfully.

"Not a chance! There is neither time nor money for such work. Besides, I should have to rebuild my transforming station if I supplied longer conduit wires with current."

"You don't really consider that you have failed, do you, Tom?" and Ned's anxiety made his voice sound very woeful indeed.

"I tell you that my belief doesn't satisfy me. I hate to go West without being sure—positive. I want to know! I have tried the locomotive out in the yard half a dozen times. It runs like a fine watch. There doesn't seem to be a thing the matter with it now. But what speed can I attain?"

"I don't see but you'll have to risk it, Tom."

"I mean to give her one more test. I'll run her out tonight when there is nobody about but the watchmen—and you, if you want to come. I'll arrange with the Electric Company for all the current they can spare. By ginger! I've got to take some risk."

"By the way, Tom," said his chum, "did it ever strike you as odd that that private detective agency never got any trace of O'Malley?"

"Well, he's gone away. We needn't worry about him. Maybe the detective wasn't very smart, at that."

"And yet he was here in town after you put the inquiry on foot. I saw him in the bank. He came there occasionally. And either he, or somebody he hired, placed that bomb in the locomotive."

"All those being facts, what of it?"

"Besides, there was that other fellow—the man with the Vandyke beard. Might be a shyster lawyer, or something of the kind. He wasn't spotted, either."

"To tell the truth, I didn't bother to give the Detective Agency the description of that fellow, although you gave it to me," and Tom laughed. "I must confess that I depend more upon my man-trap electric wires to protect the invention than I do on the private inquiry agent."

"It's funny, just the same. If I had another job for a detective I should not submit it to the Blatz Agency," grumbled Ned.

"I fancy Montagne Lewis and his crowd called off their Wild West gunman," said Tom. "In any case, every attempt he made to bother us turned out a fizzle. I am not, however, forgetting precautions, my boy."

Ned Newton realized that his chum had determined to make this night test of the electric locomotive the pivotal trial of the whole affair. He came back to the works after dinner and was let in by the office watchman at about nine o'clock.

"Mr. Tom here yet?" he asked the man.

"Yes, Mr. Newton. The young boss didn't go home to supper, even. That colored man brought something down for him, and he's in the shed yet."

"Rad is here, you mean?"

"Yes, sir. At least, he didn't go out this way, and we watchmen have instructions to let nobody in or out by the yard gates at night."

"I'll say Tom is being careful," thought Ned, as he stepped out through the runway toward the erection shed.

Before he reached the entrance to the huge shed, however, Ned chanced to look down the enclosure. There were several arc lights burning, but even these only furnished a dim illumination for the whole yard.

He supposed that four watchmen were tramping their several beats along the inside of the stockade and close to the trolley-track. But when he saw an instant gleam of light down there, close to the ground, Ned did not believe that it was the flash of a torch in the hand of any sentry.

"Funny," he muttered. "That's outside the fence, or I'm much mistaken. I wonder now—"

He turned from the door of the shed, left the runway, and began walking toward the distant point at which he had seen the mysterious flash of light.

THE ENEMY STILL ACTIVE

Ned was dressed in a dark business suit, so he was not likely to be observed from a distance, for it was a starless night. Half way to the end of the great yard he began to wonder if the light he had seen might not have been an hallucination.

He doubted very much if anybody was creeping about outside the fence. The boards were close together, with scarcely a crack half an inch wide anywhere. A light out there—

It flashed again. He was positive of it this time, and of its locality as well. It could be nobody who had any honest business about the Swift Construction Company's premises. It was not Koku, for ordinarily the giant would not use an electric torch.

Ned did not know where any of the watchmen were who were acting as sentinels. In fact, as it appeared later, three of them had been called off their beats by Tom himself to help in some necessary task inside the shed. The young inventor was getting ready to run the huge locomotive out upon the yard-track.

Remembering vividly the attempt which had been made some weeks before to blow up the Hercules 0001, it was only natural that Ned should suspect that the flash of light he had seen revealed the presence of some ill-conditioned person lurking just beyond the fence.

A man might be crouching there prepared to hurl an explosive bomb over the fence when the locomotive was brought around as far as that spot. Or was the villain foolish enough to attempt to enter the enclosure by surmounting the fence?

Ned, keeping close to the ground, crossed the rails in the fortunate shadow of one of the posts. There he found a place where, with his back to a pole-prop right at this curve in the trolley system, the shadow enfolded him completely.

Had his movements been marked by the person outside the fence? Ned waited several long and anxious minutes for some move from out there. Then something rather unexpected occurred. For the past ten minutes he had forgotten about the test of the Hercules 0001 which Tom had promised.

With a blast of its siren the huge electric locomotive burst out of the shed and thundered around the track. It smote Ned Newton's mind suddenly that the inventor was going to "take a chance" on this evening and try to get some speed out of the huge machine.

The electric headlight cast a broad cone of white and dazzling light across the yard. It suddenly struck full upon the spot where Ned Newton crouched; but the upright against which he leaned was broad enough to hide him completely.

Looking up at the top of the stockade at that moment of illumination, the young financial manager of the Swift Construction Company beheld a crawling figure nearing the wire entanglements on the summit of the fence.

The unknown man was climbing by means of a notched pole. Ned could not see that he bore any bulky object in his hands; indeed, he needed both of them to aid him to climb. But the man's right hand was reaching upward, above his head.

The Hercules 0001 came roaring on. Its cone of light passed beyond Ned's station. In a few seconds it reached the spot, and roared on. Ned had not made a move. It seemed to him that he could not move or speak.

The onrush of the electric locomotive all but swept the young fellow from his feet. It had come and gone in an instant!

"He's making more than fifteen or twenty miles an hour, all right," muttered Ned.

Then he flashed another glance up at the figure outside the fence. The man's cap showed above the top of the boards. He seemed to be dragging something up to him from below—something that hung and swung around and around a few feet from the ground.

Ned was about to dart out of concealment and hail the fellow. He was not armed, nor could he get out of the stockade near this point. He feared what the marauder intended, and he felt that he must frighten him away.

"Suppose that is a bomb and he means to fling it in front of Tom's locomotive?" thought the anxious Ned.

He again saw the stranger's right hand reach up above his head. But he had no bomb in his hand. Ned suddenly shrieked a word of warning! It had come to him what the man was doing and what the result of his act would be.

The wire-cutters bit on one of the copper wires. There followed a flash of blue flame, and the man screamed. He dropped the thing swinging below him and involuntarily grabbed at the wires with his left hand.

He was caught, then! The crackling intermittent shocks of electric fluid passed through his body in fiery sequence. His limbs writhed. He mouthed horribly, and croaking gasps came from between his wide open jaws.

The Hercules 0001 had rounded the enclosure and was coming down upon its second lap. The cone of white radiance from the headlight fell upon the writhing body of the victim on the wires. The locomotive siren emitted a blast that almost deafened Ned.

The monster ground to a stop. Tom swung himself half out of the cab window beside the controller.

"Who's that?" he yelled. Then he saw Ned below him. "Who is that fellow?"

"No friend of yours, Tom, I believe," returned his financial manager in a shaking voice.

"Where's Rad? Rad!" Tom shouted at the top of his voice.

"I's comm', Massa Tom," rejoined the colored man.

"Never mind coming here! Get a move on, and get to the switchboard. Turn the current out of the fence wires.

"Yis, sir, I'll go Massa Tom," declared the old man.

"Is he a spotter, Ned?" demanded the inventor.

"He's no friend. I am going out by the gate. He's got something there that means harm, I believe. Do you think he's killed, Tom?"

"Only ought to be. Not enough current to kill him. But he's badly burned and—and—well! I bet he won't care to fool around the works again."

Ned dashed away to an entrance. A watchman came running, opened the small gate, and followed Ned into the open.

Before they arrived at the vicinity of the accident Rad had got to the switchboard. The electricity was shut out of the stockade wires.

Ned uttered another shout. He saw the writhing body of the shocked man fall from the stockade. When he and the watchman got to the spot the fellow lay upon his back, groaning and sobbing; but Ned saw at once that he was more frightened than hurt.

"Well, you did it that time!" exclaimed the young financial manager. "And I hope you got enough."

"You—you demons!" gasped the man. "I'll have the law on you—"

"Sure you will," cackled the watchman. "You had every right in the world to try to cut those wires, of course, and get into the yard of the works. Sure! The judge will believe you all right."

Ned was, meanwhile, staring closely at the fallen man. Tom had come down from the locomotive and was close to the fence.

"Who is he?" demanded the inventor. "Not O'Malley?"

Ned stepped to the fence and whispered:

"It's the other fellow. The little chap with the Vandyke. He's dressed like a tramp, but it's the same man."

"Is he badly hurt?" demanded Tom.

"His temper is, Boss," said the watchman callously. "And say! I know this fellow. He works for the Blatz Detective Agency. I used to work for those folks myself. His name is Myrick—Joe Myrick."

"Ned," said Tom sternly, "go to the office and call the police. I'll make him tell why he was here. And I'll make the Blatz people explain, too. Hullo! what's that?"

Ned had seized the rope he had seen in Myrick's hand, and from a patch of weeds drew a two-gallon oil-can.

"What you got there, Ned?" repeated the young inventor.

"Whatever it is, I am going to be mighty easy with it. I think this scoundrel was trying to get it over the fence and into the way of the locomotive."

"You can't hang anything on me," said Myrick, suddenly. "I was just climbing up to the top of the fence to get a squint at that contraption you've built. You can't hang anything on me."

"He's evidently feeling better," said Tom, scornfully. "Nugent, don't let him get away from you. Go call the police, Ned. And take care of that can until we can find out what's in it."

Later, when the police had removed Joe Myrick and the mysterious can had been deposited in a tub of water in the open lot until its contents could be examined, Tom said to his chum:

"I was just working up some speed on the locomotive. The speedometer indicated fifty-five when I saw that fellow sprawling up there on the fence. I would not have dared go much faster in any case."

"Why, you weren't half trying, Tom!" cried the delighted Ned.

"She did slide around easy, didn't she? Fifty-five on an almost circular track is a good showing. I am not so scared as I was, my boy."

"You think that on a straight track you might accomplish what you set out to do?"

"It looks like it. At any rate, I shall risk a trial on the H. & P. A. tracks. I'm going to take her West. Be ready on Monday, Ned, for I shall want you with me," declared Tom Swift.

OFF FOR THE WEST

Of course, as Tom supposed they would, the Blatz Detective Agency denied that Joe Myrick, their one-time operative, had been engaged through their bureau either to spy upon the Swift Construction Company or to injure Tom's invention of the electric locomotive.

Nevertheless, three points were indisputable: Myrick had been caught spying; in his possession was a can of explosive which could be set off by concussion; and it was a fact that to Myrick had been first entrusted the matter of hunting for Andy O'Malley when Tom had put the search for the Westerner up to the Blatz people.

"He played traitor both to you, Mr. Swift, and to our agency," declared Blatz to Tom. "I wash my hands of him. I hope the police send him away for life!"

"He'll go to prison all right," said Tom, confidently. "But the main point is that one of your operatives fell down on a simple job. I wanted that Andy O'Malley traced. He's out of the way, now, of course. If you had put an honest man to work for me, O'Malley would be behind the bars himself."

"Some doubt of that, Mr. Swift," grumbled Blatz.

"Why?"

"Where's your evidence that this O'Malley was connected with the attempt to blow up your locomotive the first time? Mr. Newton's testimony would need corroboration."

"Never mind that," rejoined the young inventor, with a smile. "I'd have him for highway robbery. I recognized him. He robbed me of a wallet. Guess we could put O'Malley away for awhile on that charge. And by the time he got out again my job for that Western railroad would be completed."

"Humph! Nothing personal in your going after the fellow, then?" queried the head of the detective agency.

"No. But I frankly confess that I am afraid of O'Malley. He is undoubtedly in the employ of men who will pay him well if he wrecks my invention. But there really is no personal grudge between O'Malley and me. At least, I feel no particular enmity against the fellow."

There was a pause.

"If you say so we will give you a couple of good men as bodyguards on your trip West," suggested Blatz, licking his lips hungrily.

"As good men as Myrick?" retorted Tom, rather scornfully. "No, thank you. Just make your bill out to the Swift Construction Company to date, and a check will be sent you the first of the month. I will take my own precautions hereafter."

And those precautions Tom considered sufficient. When the Hercules 0001 was towed out of the enclosure belonging to the Swift Construction Company early on Monday morning, each door and window of the huge cab was barred and locked. Inside the cab rode Koku, the giant.

Koku had his orders to allow nobody to enter the Hercules 0001 until Tom or Ned Newton came to relieve him of his responsibility as guard. The giant had a swinging cot to sleep on and sufficient food—of a kind—to last him for a fortnight if necessary.

He was not armed, for Tom did not often trust him with weapons. The young inventor, however, did not expect that any armed force would attack the electric locomotive.

If Montagne Lewis desired to wreck the new invention which might mean so much to Mr. Bartholomew and the H. & P. A., he surely would not allow his hirelings to attack openly the locomotive while it was en route.

On the other hand, Tom did not really believe that Andy O'Malley would attempt any reprisal against him personally. Of course, the Western desperado might feel himself abused by Tom, especially in the matter of Tom's use of his ammonia pistol.

But that had happened months ago. O'Malley had undoubtedly been hired by Mr. Bartholomew's enemies to obtain knowledge of the contract signed between the young inventor and the railroad president; and later it was certain that the spy had tried his best to wreck the electric locomotive.

As for any personal assault so many weeks after O'Malley had clashed with him Tom Swift did not expect it. With Ned in his company on this journey to Hendrickton, the young inventor had good reason to consider that he was perfectly safe.

Mary Nestor and Mr. Swift came to the station to see the two young men off on Monday evening. Mary had heard about the second attempt made to blow up the Hercules 0001 and she begged Tom to take every precaution while he was in the West.

"You will be in the enemy's country out there, Tom dear," she warned him. "You won't be careless?"

"I know I shall be mighty busy," he told her, laughing. "I'll let Ned play watch-dog. And you know, his is a cautious soul, Mary."

"I've every confidence in Ned's faithfulness," the girl said, still with anxious tone. "But those men who are trying to ruin Mr. Bartholomew's road will stop at nothing. I must hear from you frequently, Tom, or I shall worry myself ill."

"Don't lose your courage, Mary," rejoined the inventor, more gravely. "I do not think they will attack me personally again. Remember that Koku is on the job, as well as Ned. And Mr. Damon declares he will follow us West very shortly," and again Tom chuckled.

"Even Mr. Damon may be a help to you, Tom," declared Mary, warmly. "At least, he is completely devoted to you."

"So is Rad Sampson," said Tom, with a little grimace. "I certainly had my hands full convincing him that father needed him here at home. At that, Rad is pretty warm over the fact that I sent Koku on with the locomotive. If anything should chance to happen to my invention, Eradicate Sampson is going to shout 'I told you so!' all over the shop."

Mary dabbed her eyes a little with her handkerchief, and Tom patted her shoulder.

"Don't worry, Mary," he said more cheerfully. "There won't a thing happen to me out there at Hendrickton. I'll keep the wires hot with telegrams. And I'll write to both you and father, and give you the full particulars of how we get along. You'll keep your eye on father, Mary, won't you?"

"You may be sure of that," said the girl. "I will not leave him entirely to the care of Rad," and she tried hard to smile again. But it was a difficult matter.

Such a parting as this is always hard to endure. Tom wrung his father's hand and warned him to be careful of his health. The train came along and the two young men boarded it with their personal luggage.

They had a flash of the two faces—that of Mr. Swift's and Mary's blooming countenance—as the express started again, and then the outlook from the Pullman coach showed them the fast-receding environs of Shopton.

"We're on our way, my boy," said Tom to his chum.

"We certainly are," said Ned, thoughtfully. "I wonder what the outcome of the trip will be? It may not be all plain sailing."

"Don't croak," rejoined the young inventor, with a grin.

"I don't see how you can appear so cheerful., Why! you don't even know if that electric locomotive is safe. Something may have already happened to it. The freight train might be wrecked. A dozen things might happen."

"I am not crossing any bridges before I come to them," declared Tom. "Besides, I propose to keep in touch with the Hercules Three-Oughts-One in a certain way—Hullo! Here it is."

"Here what is?" demanded Ned.

The Pullman conductor at that moment came in through the forward corridor. He had a telegram in his hand, and intoned loudly as he approached:

"Mr. Swift! Mr. Thomas Swift! Telegram for Mr. Swift."

"That is for me, Conductor," said Tom briskly, offering his card.

"All right, Mr. Swift. Just got it at Shopton. Operator said you had boarded my car. This is railroad business, you'll notice. Have you any reply, sir?"

Tom ripped open the envelope and unfolded the telegram. He held it so that Ned could read, too. It was signed: "N. G. Smith, Conductor, Number 48."

"What's that?" exclaimed Ned, reading the message.

"'Locomotive and crazy man in it all right at Lingo,'" repeated Tom aloud, and chuckled.

"No, Conductor, there is no answer."

"Good!" exclaimed Ned. "You arranged to get reports en route from the conductors handling the Hercules Three-Oughts-One?"

"Surest thing you know," replied Tom. "And I guess, from the wording of this message, that the crew of Forty-eight have already found out that Koku is not an ordinary guard."

"He's a great boy," smiled Ned. "Glad he is on the job."

THE WRECK OF FORTY-EIGHT

The two chums sought their berths that night in high fettle. Even Ned sloughed off his mood of apprehension which he had worn on boarding the train at Shopton.

For, true to the arrangement Tom had made with the railroad people, another reassuring telegram was brought to him before bedtime. The second conductor responsible for the management of the Western bound freight to which the Hercules 0001 was attached, sent back a brief statement of the safety of the electric locomotive.

Naturally the two chums would have passed the freight and got well ahead of it before reaching Hendrickton. But Tom had business in Chicago, and they stayed over in that city for twenty-four hours. The freight train went around the city, of course. But the telegrams continued to reach Tom promptly, even at the hotel where he and Ned stopped in the city.

Occasionally the trainmen in charge of the freight mentioned Koku. His eccentric behavior doubtless somewhat puzzled the railroaders.

"That's all right," chuckled Ned. "Let them think Koku is dangerous if they want to. That O'Malley person believed he was!"

"I'll say so!" replied Tom. "The way he ran when Koku started after him that time on the Waterfield Road seemed to prove that he didn't want to mix with Koku."

"If he—or other spies—learns that Koku is with the Hercules Three-Oughts-One, it ought to warn them away from the locomotive."

This was Ned's final speech before getting into his berth. He, as well as Tom, slept quite as calmly on this first night out of Chicago as they had before.

They knew exactly where the electric locomotive was. It was on the same road as this train they were traveling in, and, although on a different track, it was not many miles ahead. In fact, if the two trains kept to schedule, the transcontinental passenger train would pass the freight in question about five o'clock in the morning.

It lacked half an hour of that time when the Pullman train came suddenly to a jolting stop. Both Tom and Ned were awakened with the rest of the passengers in their coach.

Heads were poked out between curtains all along the aisle and a chorus of more or less excited voices demanded:

"What's the matter?"

"Nothin's the matter wid dis train, gen'lemens an' ladies," came in the porter's important voice. "Jest nothin' at all's happened. It's done happened up ahead of us, das all."

"Well, what has happened ahead of us, George?" asked Ned.

"Jest another train, Boss, been splatterin' itself all ober de right of way. We sort o' bein' held up, das all," replied the porter.

"That's good news—for us," said Ned, preparing to climb back into his berth. But he halted where he was when he heard his chum ask:

"What train left the track, George?"

"A freight train, sah. Yes, sah. Number Forty-eight. She jumped de rails, side-swiped de accommodation dat was holdin' us back, and has jest done spread herself all over de right of way."

"My goodness!" gasped Ned.

"Hear that, Ned?" exclaimed Tom. "Scramble into your clothes, boy. The Hercules Three-Oughts-One is hitched to Forty-eight."

"Suppose she's off the track?" murmured Ned.

"It's lucky if she isn't smashed to matchwood," groaned Tom, and almost immediately left the Pullman coach on the run.

Ned was not far behind him. When they reached the cinder path beside the freight train it was just sunrise. Long arms of rosy light reached down the mountain side to linger on the tracks and what was strewed across them. A glance assured the two young fellows from the East that it was a bad smash indeed.

Several of the rear boxcars were slung athwart the passenger tracks. The passenger train that had been ahead of the Pullman train on which Tom and Ned rode, had been badly beaten in all along its side. Scarcely a whole window was left on the inner side of the five cars. But those cars were not derailed. It was merely some of the freight cars that retarded the further progress of the transcontinental flyer. A derrick car must be brought up to lift away the debris before the fast train could move on.

Tom and Ned walked forward along the length of the wreck. Suddenly the anxious young inventor seized Ned's arm.

"Glory be!" he ejaculated. "It's topside up, anyway."

"The Hercules Three-Oughts-One?" gasped Ned.

"That's what it is!"

Tom quickened his pace, and his financial manager followed close upon his heels. The forward end of Forty-eight had not left the track and the electric locomotive stood upright upon the rails, being near the head end of the train.

"If this wreck was intentional, and aimed at your invention, Tom," whispered Ned Newton, "it did not result as the wreckers expected."

Tom scouted the idea suggested by his chum. And in a few moments they learned from a railroad employee that a broken flange on a boxcar wheel had caused the wreck.

"So that disposes of your suspicion, Ned," said Tom, approaching the huge electric locomotive.

"Hey, gents!" exclaimed another railroad man, one of the crew of the wrecked freight. "Better keep away from that locomotive."

"What's the matter with it?" Ned asked, curiously.

"Got some kind of an aborigine caged up in it. You put your hand on any part of it and he's likely to jump out and bite your hand off, or something. Believe me, he's some savage."

Both Tom and Ned burst into laughter. The former went forward to the door of the cab and knocked in a peculiar way. It was a signal that the giant recognized instantly.

"Master!" Koku cried from inside the cab. "Master! Him come in?"

"No, Koku," said Tom. "I'm not coming in. Are you all right?"

"Yes. Koku all right. Him come out?"

"No, no!" laughed Tom. "You are not at your journey's end yet, Koku. Keep on the job a while longer."

"Sure. Koku stay here forever, if Master say so."

"Forever is a long word, Koku," said Tom, more seriously. "I'll tell you when to open the door. I'll be at the end of the journey to meet you."

"It all right if Master say so. But Koku no like to travel in box," grumbled the giant.

Tom turned from the electric locomotive to see Ned staring across the tracks at a man who was talking to several of the train crew of the side-swiped accommodation train. That train was about to be moved on under its own power. None of the wreckage of the freight interfered with the progress of the accommodation.

Tom stepped to Ned's side and touched his arm. "Who is he?" the inventor asked.

The man who had attracted Ned's attention and now held Tom's interest as well was a solid looking man with gray hair and a dyed mustache. He was chewing on a long and black cigar, and he spoke to the train hands with authority.

"Well, why can't you find him?" he wanted to know in a hoarse and arrogant voice.

"Who is he?" asked Tom again in Ned's ear.

"I've seen him somewhere. Or else I've seen somebody that looks like him. Maybe I've seen his picture. He's somebody of importance."

"He thinks he is," rejoined the young inventor, with some disdain.

In answer to something one of the railroad men said the important looking individual uttered an oath and added:

"There's nobody been killed then? He's just missing? He was sitting in the coach ahead of me. I saw him just before the wreck. You know O'Malley yourself. Do you mean to say you haven't seen him, Conductor?"

"I assure you he disappeared like smoke, sir," said the passenger conductor. "I haven't an idea what became of him."

"Humph! If you see him, send him to me, and the solid man stepped heavily aboard the nearest coach and disappeared inside.

Tom and Ned stared at each other with wondering gaze. O'Malley! The spy who had represented Montagne Lewis and the Hendrickton & Western Railroad in the East.

"What do you know about that?" demanded Ned, wonderingly.

"Hold on!" exclaimed Tom. He sprang across the rails after the conductor of the accommodation train that was just starting on. "Let me ask you a question."

"Yes, sir?" replied the conductor

"Who was that man who just spoke to you?" "That man? Why, I thought everybody out this way knew Montagne Lewis. That is his name, sir—and a big man he is. Yes, sir," and the conductor, giving the watching engineer of his train the "highball," caught the hand-rail of the car and swung himself aboard as the train started.

ON THE HENDRICKTON & PAS ALOS

The transcontinental was delayed three hours by the strewn wreckage of the rear of Number Forty-eight. When she went on the two young fellows from Shopton gazed anxiously at the Hercules 0001, which stood between two gondolas in the forward end of the freight train.

"Just by luck nothing happened to it," muttered Ned.

"Just luck," agreed Tom Swift. "It was a shock to me to learn that Andy O'Malley was right there on the spot when the accident happened."

"And his employer, too," added Ned. "For we must admit that Mr. Montagne Lewis is the man who sicked O'Malley on to you." "True."

"And they were both in the accommodation that was sideswiped by the derailed cars of Number Forty-eight."

"That, likewise is a fact," said Tom, nodding quickly.

"But what puzzles me, as it seemed to puzzle Lewis, more than anything else, is what became of O'Malley?"

"I guess I can see through that knot-hole," Tom rejoined.

"Yes?"

"I bet O'Malley got a squint at me—or perhaps at you—as we walked up the track from this coach, and he lit out in a hurry. There stood the Three-Oughts-One, and there were we. He knew we would raise a hue and cry if we saw him in the vicinity of my locomotive."

"I bet that's the truth, Tom."

"I know it. He didn't even have time to warn his employer. By the way, Ned, what a brute that Montagne Lewis looks to be."

"I believe you! I remember having seen his photograph in a magazine. Oh, he's some punkins, Tom."

"And just as wicked as they make 'em, I bet! Face just as pleasant as a bulldog's!"

"You said it. I'm afraid of that man. I shall not have a moment's peace until you have handed the Hercules Three-Oughts-One over to Mr. Bartholomew and got his acceptance."

"If I do," murmured Tom.

"Of course you will, if that Lewis or his henchmen don't smash things up. You are not afraid of the speed matter now, are you?" demanded Ned confidently.

"I can be sure of nothing until after the tests," said Tom, shaking his head. "Remember, Ned, that I have set out to accomplish what was never done before—to drive a locomotive over the rails at two miles a minute. It's a mighty big undertaking."

"Of course it will come out all right. If Koku is faithful

"That is the smallest 'if' in the category," Tom interposed, with a laugh. "If I was as sure of all else as I am of Koku, we'd have plain sailing before us."

Two days later Tom Swift and Ned Newton were ushered into the private office of the president of the H. & P. A. at the Hendrickton terminal. The two young fellows from the East had got in the night before, had become established at the best hotel in the rapidly growing Western municipality, and had seen something of the town itself during the hours before midnight.

Now they were ready for business, and very important business, too.

Mr. Richard Bartholomew sat up in his desk chair and his keen eyes suddenly sparkled when he saw his visitors and recognized them.

"I did not expect you so soon. Your locomotive arrived yesterday, Mr. Swift. How are you, Mr. Newton?"

He motioned for them to take chairs. His secretary left the room. The railroad magnate at once became confidential.

"Nothing happened on the way?" he asked, pointedly. "There was a freight wreck, I understand?"

"And we chanced to be right at hand when that happened," said Tom.

"So was your friend, Mr. Lewis," remarked Ned Newton.

"You don't mean to say that Montagne Lewis—"

"Was there. And Andy O'Malley," put in Tom.

Then he detailed the incident, as far as he and Ned knew the details, to Mr. Bartholomew, who listened with close attention.

"Well, it might merely have been a coincidence," murmured the railroad president. "But, of course, we can't be sure. Anyhow, it is just as well if your servant, Mr. Swift, keeps close watch still upon that locomotive."

"He will," said Tom, nodding. "He is down there in the yard with the Hercules Three-Oughts-One, and I mean to keep Koku right on the job."

"Good! Let's go down and look at her," Mr. Bartholomew said, eagerly.

But first Tom wanted to go into the theoretical particulars of his invention. And he confessed that thus far his tests of the locomotive had not been altogether satisfactory.

"I have got to have a clear track on a stretch of your own line here, Mr. Bartholomew, and under certain conditions, before I can be sure as to just how much speed I can get out of the machine."

"Speed is the essential point, Mr. Swift," said the railroad man, seriously.

"That is what I have been telling Ned," Tom rejoined. "I believe my improvements over the Jandel patents are worthy. I know I have a very powerful locomotive. But that is not enough."

"We have got to shoot our trains through the Pas Alos Range faster than trains were ever shot over the grades before, or we have failed," said Mr. Bartholomew, with decision.

"But—" began Ned; but Tom put up an arresting hand and his financial manager ceased speaking.

"I have not forgotten the details of our contract, Mr. Bartholomew," he said, quietly. "Two-miles-a-minute is the target I have aimed for. Whether I have hit it or not, well, time will show. I have got to try the locomotive out on the tracks of the H. & P. A. in any case. The Hercules Three-Oughts-One has been dragged a long distance, and has been through at least one wreck. I want to see if she is all right before I test her officially."

"I'll arrange that for you," said Mr. Bartholomew, briskly, putting away his papers. "I will go with you, too, and take a look at the marvel."

"And a marvel it is," grumbled Ned. "Don't let him fool you, Mr. Bartholomew. Tom never does consider what he's done as being as great as it really is."

"Everything must be proved," Tom said, cautiously. "If it was a financial problem, Mr. Bartholomew, believe me it would be Ned who displayed caution. But I have seldom built anything that could not—and has not—later been improved."

"You do not consider your electric locomotive, then, a completed invention?" asked Mr. Bartholomew, as the three walked down the yard.

"I have too much experience .to say it is perfect," returned Tom. "I can scarcely believe, even, that it is going to suit you, Mr. Bartholomew, even if the speed test is as promising as I hope it may be."

"Humph!"

"But before I shall be willing to throw up the sponge and say that I have failed, I shall monkey with the Hercules Three-Oughts-One quite a little on your tracks."

"Your six months isn't up yet," said Mr. Bartholomew, more cheerfully. "And it doesn't matter if it is. If you see any chance of making a success of your invention, you are welcome to try it out on the tracks of the H. & P. A. for another six months."

"All right," Tom said, smiling. "Now, there is the Hercules Three-Oughts-One, Mr. Bartholomew. And there is Koku looking longingly through the window."

In fact, the giant, the moment he saw Tom, ran to unbar and open the door of the cab on that side.

"Master! If no let Koku out, Koku go amuck -Äcrazy! No can breathe in here! No can eat! No can sleep!"

"The poor fellow!" ejaculated Ned.

"What's the matter with him?" asked Mr. Bartholomew, curiously.

"Get out, if you want to, Koku. I'll stay by while you kick up your heels."

No sooner had the inventor spoken than the giant leaped from the open door of the locomotive and dashed away along the cinder path as though he actually had to run away. Tom burst into a laugh, as he watched the giant disappear beyond the strings of freight cars.

"What is the matter with him?" repeated the railroad president.

"He's got the cramp all right," laughed Tom Swift. "You don't understand, Mr. Bartholomew, what it means to that big fellow to be housed in for so many days, and unable to kick a free limb. I bet he runs ten miles before he stops."

"The police will arrest him," said the railroad man.

It was then Ned's turn to chuckle. "I am sorry for your railroad police if they tackle Koku right now," he said. "He'd lay out about a dozen ordinary men without half trying. But, ordinarily, he is the most mild-mannered fellow who ever lived."

"He will come back, if he is let alone, as harmless as a kitten," Tom observed. "And when I am not with the Hercules Three-Oughts-One, and while I continue making my tests, Koku will be on guard. You might tell your police force, Mr. Bartholomew, to let him alone. Now come aboard and let me show you what I have been trying to do."

They spent two hours inside the cab of the great locomotive. Mr. Richard Bartholomew was possessed of no small degree of mechanical education. He might not be a genius in mechanics as Tom Swift was, but he could follow the latter's explanations regarding the improvements in the electrical equipment of this new type of locomotive.

"I don't know what your speed tests will show, Mr. Swift," said the railroad president, with added enthusiasm. "But if those parts will do what you say they have already done, you've got the Jandels beat a mile! I'm for you, strong. Yes, sir! like your friend, Newton, here, I believe that you have hit the right track. You are going to triumph."

But Tom's triumph did not come at once. He knew more about the uncertainties of mechanical contrivances than did either Mr. Bartholomew or Ned Newton.

The very next day the Hercules 0001 was got out upon a section of the electrified system of the Hendrickton & Pas Alos Railway, and the pantagraphs of the huge locomotive for the first time came into connection with the twin conductor trolleys which overhung the rails.

Ned accompanied Tom as assistant. Koku was allowed by the inventor to roam about the hills as much as he pleased during the hours in which his master was engaged with the Hercules 0001. Tom did not think any harm would come to Koku, and he knew that the giant would enjoy immensely a free foot in such a wild country. The two young fellows, dressed in working suits of overall stuff, spent long hours in the cab of the electric locomotive. Their try-outs had to be made for the most part on sidetracks and freight switches, some miles outside Hendrickton, where the invention would not be in the way of regular traffic.

Speed on level tracks had been raised in one test to over ninety-five miles an hour and Mr. Bartholomew cheered wildly from the cab of a huge Mallet that paced Tom's locomotive on a parallel track. No steam locomotive had ever made such fast time.

But Tom was after something bigger than this. He wanted to show the president of the H. & P. A. that the Hercules 0001 could drag a load over the Pas Alos Range at a pace never before gained by any mountain-hog.

Therefore he coaxed the electric locomotive out into the hills, some hundred or more miles from headquarters. He had to keep in touch with the train dispatcher's office, of course; the new machine had often to take a sidetrack. Nor was much of this hilly right-of-way electrified. The Jandels locomotive had been found to be a failure on the sharp grades; so the extension of the trolley system had been abandoned.

But there was one steep grade between Hammon and Cliff City that had been completed. The current could be fed to the cables over this stretch of track, and for a week Tom used this long and steep grade just as much as he could, considering of course the demands of the regular traffic.

The telegraph operator at Half Way (merely a name for a station, for there was not a habitation in sight) thrust his long upper-length out of the telegraph office window one afternoon and waved a "highball" to the waiting electric locomotive on the sidetrack.

"Dispatcher says you can have Track Number Two West till the four-thirteen, westbound, is due. I'll slip the operator at Cliff City the news and he'll be on the lookout for you as well as me, Mr. Swift. Go to it."

Every man on the system was interested, and most of them enthusiastic, about Tom's invention. The latter knew that he could depend upon this operator and his mate to watch out for the western-bound flyer that would begin its climb of the grade at Hammon less than half an hour hence.

The electric locomotive was coaxed out across the switch. Tom was earnestly inspecting the more delicate parts of the mechanism while Ned (and proud he was to do it) handled the levers. Once on the main line he moved the controller forward. The machine began to pick up speed.

The drumming of the wheels over the rail joints became a single note—an increasing roar of sound. The electric locomotive shot up the grade. The arrow on the speedometer crept around the dial and Ned's eye was more often fastened on that than it was on the glistening twin rails which mounted the grade.

Black-green hemlock and spruce bordered the right of way on either hand. Their shadows made the tunnel through the forest almost dark. But Tom had not seen fit to turn on the headlight.

"How is she making out?" asked the inventor, coming to look over his chum's shoulder.

"It's great, Tom!" breathed Ned Newton, his eyes glistening. "She eats this grade up."

And it's within a narrow fraction of a two per cent.," said the inventor proudly. "She takes it without a jar—Hold on! What's that ahead?"

The locomotive had traveled ten miles or more from Half Way. The summit of the grade was not far ahead. But the forest shut out all view of the station at Cliff City and the structures that stood near it.

Right across the steel ribbons on which the hercules 0001 ran, Tom had seen something which brought the question to his lips. Ned Newton saw it too, and he shouted aloud:

"Tree down! A log fallen, Tom!"

He did not lose completely his self-control. But he grabbed the levers with less care than he should. He tried to yank two of them at once, and, in doing so, he fouled the brakes!

He had shut off connection with the current. But the brake control was jammed. The locomotive quickly came to a halt. Then, before Tom could get to the open door, the wheels began spinning in reverse and the great Hercules 0001 began the descent of the steep grade, utterly unmanageable!

Peril, the Mother of Invention

Tom Swift's first thought was one of thankfulness. Thankfulness that he did not have a drag of fifty or sixty steel gondolas or the like to add their weight to the down-pull. The locomotive's own weight of approximately two hundred and seventy tons was enough.

For when the inventor pushed Ned aside and tried to handle the controllers properly, he found them unmanageable. There was not a chance of freeing them and getting power on the brakes. The Hercules 0001 was hacking down the mountain side with a speed that was momentarily increasing, and without a chance of retarding it!

The young inventor at that moment of peril, knew no more what to do to avert disaster than Ned Newton himself.

It flashed across his mind, however, that others beside themselves were in peril because of this accident. The fast express from the East that should pass Half Way at four-thirteen, might already be climbing the hill from Hammon. Hammon, at the foot of the grade, was twenty-five miles away. Nor was the track straight.

If the operator at Half Way did not see the runaway locomotive and telephone the danger to the foot of the grade, when the Hercules 0001 came tearing down the track it might ram something in the Hammon yard, if it did not actually collide with the approaching westbound express.

Such an emergency as this is likely either to numb the brains of those entangled in the peril or excite them to increased activity. Ned Newton was apparently stunned by the catastrophe. Tom's brain never worked more clearly.

He seized the siren lever and set it at full, so that the blast called up continuous echoes in the forest as the locomotive plunged down the incline. He ran to the door again, on the side where Half Way station lay, and hung out to signal the operator who had so recently given him right of way on this stretch of mountain road.

"We're going to smash! We're going to smash!" groaned Ned Newton.

Tom read these words on his chum's lips, rather than heard them, for the roar of the descending locomotive drowned every other sound. Tom waved an encouraging hand, but did not reply audibly.

Meanwhile his brain was working as fast as ever it had. He had instantly comprehended all the danger of the situation. But in addition he appreciated the fact that such an accident as this might happen at any time to this or any other locomotive he might build.

Automatic brakes were all right. If there had been a good drag of cars behind the Hercules 0001, on which the compressed air brakes might have been set, the present manifest peril might have been obliterated. The brakes on the cars would have stopped the whole train.

But to halt this huge monster when alone, on the grade, was another matter. Once the locomotive brake lever was jammed, as in this case, there was no help for the huge machine. It had to ride to the foot of the grade—if it did not chance to hit something on the way!

And with this realization of both the imminent peril and the need of averting it, to Tom's active brain came the germ of an idea that he determined to put into force, if he lived through this accident, on each and every electric locomotive that he might in the future build.

This monster, flying faster and faster down the mountain side, was a menace to everything in its track. There might be almost anything in the way of rolling stock on the section between Half Way and Hammon at the foot of the grade. If this thunderbolt of wood and steel collided with any other train, with the force and weight gathered by its plunge down the mountain, it would drive through such obstruction like a projectile from Tom's own big cannon.

Tom realized this fact. He knew that whatever object the Hercules 0001 might strike, that object would be shattered and scattered all about the right of way. What might happen to the runaway was another matter. But the inventor believed that the electric locomotive would be less injured than anything with which it came into collision.

At any rate, thought of the peril to himself and his invention had secondary consideration in Tom Swift's mind. It was what the monster which he could not control might do to other rolling stock of the H. & P. A. that rasped the young fellow's mind.

The grade above Half Way had few curves. Tom soon caught the first glimpse of the station. Would the operator hear the roar of the descending runaway and understand what had happened?

He leaned far out from the open doorway and waved his cap madly. He began to shout a warning, although he saw not a soul about the station and knew very well that his voice was completely drowned by the voice of the siren and the drumming of the great wheels.

Suddenly the tousled head of the operator popped out of his window. He saw the coming locomotive, the drivers smoking!

To be a good railroad man one has to have his wits about him. To be a good operator at a backwoods station one has to have two sets of wits—one set to tell what to do in an emergency, the other to listen and apprehend the voice of the sounder.

This Half Way man was good. He knew better than to try the telegraph instrument. He grabbed the telephone receiver and jiggled the hook up and down on the standard while the Hercules 0001 roared past the station.

It did not need Tom's frantically waving cap to warn him what had happened. And he remembered clearly the fact of the expected westbound flyer.

"Hammon? Get me? This is Half Way. That derned electric hog has sprung something and is coming down, lickity-split!

"Yes! Clear your yard! Where's Number Twenty-eight? Good! Side her, or she'll be ditched. Get me?"

The voice at the other end of the wire exploded into indignant vituperation. Then silence. The Half Way operator had done his best—his all. He ran out upon the platform. The electric locomotive had disappeared behind the woods, but the roar of its wheels and the shrill voice of its siren echoed back along the line.

The sound faded into insignificance. The operator went back into his hut and stayed close by the telephone instrument for the next ten minutes to learn the worst.

If the operator's nerves were tense, what about those of Tom Swift and his chum? Ned staggered to the door and clung to Tom's arm. He shrilled into the latter's ear:

"Shall we jump?"

"I don't see any soft spots," returned Tom, grimly. "There aren't any life nets along this line."

Ned Newton was frightened, and with good reason. But if his chum was equally terrified he did not show it. He continued to lean from the open door to peer down the grade as the Hercules 0001 drove on.

Around curve after curve they flew. It entered Ned's tortured mind that if his chum had wanted speed, he was getting it now! He realized that two miles a minute was a mere bagatelle to the pace now accomplished by the runaway locomotive.

THE RESULT

As Ned Newton, fumbling at the controls when he saw the fallen tree across the tracks, had jammed the brakes, the station master at Hammon, at the bottom of this long grade on the Hendrickton & Pas Alos, had stepped out to the blackboard in the barnlike waiting room and scrawled with a bit of chalk:

"No. 28—Westbound—due 3:38 is is 15 m. late."

The fact, thus given to the general public or to such of it as might be interested, averted what would have been a terrible catastrophe.

The fast express was late. When the babbling voice of the Half Way operator over the telephone warned Hammon of the coming of the runaway electric locomotive, there was time to shift switches at the head of the yard so that, when Number Twenty-eight came roaring in, she was shunted on to a far track and flagged for a stop before she hit the bumper.

Thirty seconds later, from the west, the Hercules 0001 roared down the grade and shot into the cleared west track in a halo of smoke and dust. Speed! No runaway had ever traveled faster and kept the rails. The story of the incident was embalmed in railroad history, and no history is so full of vivid incident as that of the rail.

When the first relay of excited railroad men reached the electric locomotive after it had stopped on the long level, even Ned Newton had pulled himself together and could look out upon the world with some measure of calmness. Tom Swift was making certain notes and draughting a curious little diagram upon a page of his notebook.

"What happened to you, Mr. Swift?" was the demand of the first arrival.

"Oh, my foot slipped," said the young inventor, and they got nothing more out of him than that.

But to Ned, after the crowd had gone, the inventor said:

"Ned, my boy, they used to say that necessity was the mother of invention. Therefore a loaf of bread was considered the maternal parent of the locomotive. I've got one that will beat that."

"Whew!" gasped Ned. "How can you? I haven't got my breath back yet."

"It is peril that is the mother of invention," Tom went on, still jotting down his notes. "Believe me! that jolt gave me a new idea—an important idea. Suppose that operator at Half Way had been out back somewhere, and had not seen or heard us flash by?"

"Well, suppose he had? What's the answer?" sighed Ned.

"Like enough we would have rammed something down here."

"And I hardly understand even now why we didn't do just that," muttered his chum, with a shake of his head.

"Wake up, Ned! It's all over," laughed Tom. "While it was happening I admit I was guessing just as hard as you were about the finish. But—"

"Your recovery is better," grumbled his friend. "I'm scared yet."

"And it might happen again—"

"No—not—ever!" exclaimed Ned. "I shall never touch those controllers again. I'll drive your airscout, or your fastest automobile, or anything like that. But me and this electric locomotive have parted company for good. Yes, sir!"

"All right. It wasn't your fault. It might happen to any motor-engineer. And the very fact that it can happen has given me my idea. I tell you that danger is the mother of invention."

"As far as I am concerned, it can be father and grandparents into the bargain," Ned declared, with a smile.

"Wake up!" cried his friend again. "I have got a dandy idea. I wouldn't have missed that trip for anything

"You are crazy," interrupted Ned. "Suppose we had bumped something?"

"But we didn't bump anything, except my brain tank. An idea bumped it, I tell you. I am going to eliminate any such peril as that here-after."

"You mean you are going to make it impossible for this locomotive ever to slide down such a hill again if the brakes won't work? Humph! Meanwhile I will go out and make the nearest water-fall begin to run upward."

"Don't scoff. I do not mean just what you mean."

"I bet you don't!"

"But although I cannot be sure that a locomotive will never again fall downhill," said Tom patiently, "I'm going to fix it so that warning need not be given by some operator along the line. The engineer must be able to send warning of his accident, both up and down the road."

"Huh? How are you going to do that?" demanded Ned.

"Wireless telephone. I may make some improvements on the present models; but it is practicable. It has been used on submarines and cruisers, and lately its practicability has been proved in the forestry service.

"Every one of these electric locomotives I turn out will be supplied with wireless sets. The expense of making certain telegraph offices along the line into receiving stations will be small. I am going to take that up with Mr. Bartholomew at once. And I am going to fix these brake controls so that nobody need ball them up again."

If, out of such a desperate adventure, Tom could bring to fruition really worthwhile improvements in relation to his invention, Ned acknowledged the value of the incident. Just the same, he had a personal objection to having any part in a similar experience.

He was brave, but he could not forget danger. Tom seemed to throw the effect of that terrible ride off his mind almost instantly. Ned dreamed of it at night!

However, from that time things seemed to go with a rush. Mr. Bartholomew approved of the young inventor's suggestion regarding the use of the wireless telephone as a method of averting a certain quality of danger in the use of the proposed monster locomotive. The railroad man was convinced that Tom's ideas were finally to culminate in success, and he was ready to spend money, much money, in pushing on the work.

It was not long before a private test of the Hercules 0001 up the grade from Hammon to Cliff City showed Mr. Bartholomew that the speed he had required in his contract was attainable. With a drag fully as heavy as any two locomotives had been able to get over the same sector, the new locomotive alone marked a forty-five mile an hour pace.

This attainment was kept quiet; not even the train crew knew what the monster had done when they reached the summit of the mountain. But Mr. Bartholomew, who rode with Tom and Ned in the cab, had held his own watch on the test and compared it every minute with the speedometer.

"I am satisfied that you are going to do more than I had really hoped, Mr. Swift," the railroad president said at the end of the run. "Already you could drive this locomotive at a two-mile-a-minute clip on level rails, I am sure. Keep at it! Nobody will be more delighted than I shall be if you pull down that hundred thousand dollars' bonus."

"That's a fine way to talk, sir," cried Ned, with enthusiasm.

"I mean every word of it, Mr. Newton. The money is his as soon as he makes good."

Both Tom and his financial manager left the president's office in a satisfied state of mind.

"Great news to send home, Tom," remarked Ned, when they were alone.

"Righto, Ned. My father will be glad to hear it."

"And what about Mary?" And Ned poked his chum in the ribs.

"I guess she'll he glad too," Tom replied, his face reddening.

That night Tom sent word to Mary and also a telegram, in code, to his father, saying the prospects were now bright for a quick finish of the task that had brought him West.

THE OPEN SWITCH

Meanwhile the work of electrifying another division of the Hendrickton & Pas Alos Railroad had been pushed to completion. As Mr. Bartholomew had in the first place stated, the road controlled water rights in the hills which would supply any number of electric power stations, and his enemies could not shut his road off from these waterfalls.

Tom had not warned his faithful servant, the giant Koku, to watch out for Andy O'Malley in particular; the inventor knew that the giant would be as cautious about any stranger as could be wished. But personally Tom was amazed that either O'Malley or some other henchman of the president of the Hendrickton & Western did not make an attempt to injure the electric locomotive.

"Perhaps Mr. Bartholomew's police are really of some good," said Ned Newton, when his chum mentioned his surprise on this point. "Has Koku seen nobody lurking about at night?"

"He certainly has not seen the man he calls 'Big Feet,'" chuckled Tom. "If he had spotted O'Malley, there certainly would have been an explosion."

"Tell you what," Ned said reflectively, "the longer Lewis keeps off you, the more suspicious I should be."

"You think he is a bad citizen, do you?"

"And then some, as the boys say out here," replied Ned. "I wouldn't trust that man any farther than I would a nest of hornets or a shedding rattlesnake."

"I am inclined to believe, with you, Ned, that Lewis is hatching up something and is keeping mighty whist about it. I sounded Mr. Bartholomew on the idea and he, too, is puzzled."

"I guess he knows that hombre," grumbled Ned.

"Mr. Bartholomew admits that several roads have sent representatives to make inquiries about my locomotive. They have got wind of it, and, after all, most railroads work in unison. What means progress for one is progress for all."

"That same rule does not seem to apply in the case of the H. & P. A. and the H. & W.," remarked Ned.

"No. They are out and out rivals. And Lewis and his gang have done this road dirt—no two ways about that. But when I am convinced that my locomotive has got all the speed and power contracted for, Mr. Bartholomew wants to invite a bunch of his brother railroaders to see the tests—to ride in the Hercules Three-Oughts-One, in fact."

"How about it? You going to agree? Suppose they have some inventive sharp along who will be able to steal some of your mechanical contrivances—in his head, I mean," and Ned seemed quite suddenly anxious.

"I had thought of that. But before the test I shall send my blueprints to Washington. Our patent attorney there has already filed tentative plans and applied for certain patents that I consider completed. Don't fret. I'll make it impossible for anybody to steal our patents legally."

"Yes! But illegally?"

"That we cannot help in any case, and you know it," Tom said. "If some road tries to build anything like the Hercules Three-Oughts-One for the first two years without arranging with the Swift Construction Company, you know that that railroad can be made to suffer in the courts, and you are the boy, Ned, to put them over the jumps for it."

"Sure," grumbled his chum. "It's always up to me to save the day."

"Exactly," chuckled Tom. "And in your character of life saver, do look out for anybody who looks suspicious hanging about the Hercules Three-Oughts-One. I'll take care of rival inventors. You and Koku keep your eyes peeled for the H. & W. spies. Especially for that Andy O'Malley. I feel that he will again show up. Maybe by 'the pricking of my thumb' as Macbeth's witch used to remark."

Every day save Sunday the electric locomotive had some kind of try-out. On a level track Tom was sure of his monster invention's qualities; but in the hills, at a distance from the Hendrickton terminal, it was another matter.

The grades were steep; but the road was well ballasted. There was plenty of power. He saw the Jandel locomotives hurry back and forth with the local trains and realized that this rival invention was by no means to be despised.

It was at about this time, too, that Mr. Damon appeared in Hendrickton. Early one forenoon, when Tom and Ned were preparing to take the Hercules 0001 out of the yard, and Koku was going to his lodgings to get a little sleep, Tom's eccentric friend came across the tracks, waving his cane at Tom.

"Bless my frogs and switch-targets!" he ejaculated, "I've walked a mile from that station to get here. Where are you going with that big contraption? How does it work? Does it make all the speed you want, Tom Swift? Bless my rails and sleepers!'

"We're going about a hundred miles out on the road to a good, stiff grade," Tom told him, having shaken hands in welcome. "If you want to, get aboard."

"They haven't blown you up yet, or otherwise wrecked the locomotive," remarked Mr. Damon, grinning broadly. "I'll have to write right back to your father—and to a certain young lady who shows a remarkable interest in your welfare—that you are all right."

"They should already be sure of that," laughed Tom. "Ned and I have kept the post-office department and the telegraph company very busy."

"They are waiting for my report," announced Mr. Damon, with confidence. "And I am waiting for yours. Tell me, Tom: Is the locomotive a success

"It's going to be," declared the inventor, with decision.

"Bless my trolley wires!" cried Mr. Damon, "I am glad to hear that. Then you will surely pull down the extra hundred thousand dollars?"

"I believe I shall fulfill every clause of the contract Mr. Bartholomew and I signed," said Tom.

"Then it's more than a success!" cried his friend. "You have invented another marvel, Tom Swift!"

"Marvel or not," rejoined Tom, "I believe that the Hercules Three-Oughts-One will top anything so far built in the way of electric locomotives."

"Hurrah!" cried Mr. Damon. "Bless my controller! But your father and Mary Nestor will be glad to hear that!"

Mr. Damon was quite as much interested in this invention as he always was in anything the young inventor worked upon. When he had once seen the Hercules 0001 work on an up-grade he was doubly enthusiastic. To his sanguine mind the locomotive was already completed. He could see no possibility of failure.

Tom, however, had to prove to his own satisfaction the success of every detail of his invention before he was willing to tell Mr. Bartholomew that he was ready for a public test. Mr. Damon, nor even Ned, could scarcely see the reason for Tom's caution.

Tom's favorite try-out grade was between Hammon and Cliff City. He could obtain a right of way order from the train dispatcher on that grade, sometimes of an hour's duration. He often snaked a load of gondolas or cattle cars up the grade, relieving both the puller and pusher steam locomotive. By this time the H. & P. A. system had stopped using the Jandel machines on any grades. They had proved their lack of power for such work

"But the Hercules Three-Oughts-One shows at every test that it has the kick," Mr. Damon cried.

In his enthusiasm he was out every day with Tom and Ned. And sometimes Koku remained in the cab during the trial runs as well.

On one such occasion Tom had drawn a heavy train over the mountain, taking it down the grade beyond Cliff City to Panboro in the farther valley. This was over a newly built stretch of the electrified road. The power station charged the trolley cables with an abundance of current, and the Hercules 0001 made a splendid trip.

"Bless my cuff-links!" ejaculated Mr. Damon, his rosy face one beaming smile. "You couldn't expect to do better than this. You save one locomotive on the haul, and you beat the schedule ten minutes, so that you had to lay by to get right of way into the yard here. Why linger longer, Tom?"

"I agree with Mr. Damon," Ned said. "It seems to work perfectly. And you have, I believe, established your required speed."

"Can't be too perfect," said the young inventor, smiling. "But I will tell Mr. Bartholomew when we get back that he can set his time for the big test whenever he pleases. I have already sent our patent attorney in Washington the final blueprints. Now, if nothing happens—"

"Bless my stickpin!" exclaimed Mr. Damon, "What can happen now that the locomotive is practically perfect?"

That question was answered in one way, and a most startling way, within the hour. Tom got right of way back over the mountain and pushed the electric locomotive up-grade at almost top speed. He drew no train on this occasion, and the speed made by the Hercules 0001 was really remarkable.

They topped the rise at Cliff City and got orders from the dispatcher to proceed on the time of Number Eighty-seven, which chanced to be late. With that release Tom might have made the entire distance of a hundred and ten miles to Hendrickton had it not been for the accident—the unexpected something that so often happens in the railroad business.

Tom was a careful driver; the chatter of Ned and Mr. Damon did not take the inventor's mind off his business for one instant. He was quite alert at his window, looking ahead, as Koku was at the open doorway of the cab.

Not a mile outside of Cliff City, and on this eastbound side of the right of way, was a long siding and a shipping point for timber. It was sometimes a busy point; but at this time of year there were no lumbermen about and no activities in the adjacent forest.

The Hercules 0001 came spinning along from the Cliff City yards, and Tom Swift gave scarcely a glance to the joint of the switch ahead. He had been over it so many times of late, and knew that it was always locked. The railroad did not even keep a man here at this season.

Suddenly Koku emitted a wild yell. He startled everybody else in the cab, as he flung his huge body more than half out of the doorway and prepared to jump—or so it seemed.

Ned shrieked a warning to the big fellow. Mr. Damon began to bless everything in sight. But it was Tom, quite as excited as his friends, who understood what Koku shouted:

"Big Feet! Big Feet! I see um Big Feet, Master!"

The next moment he threw himself from the rapidly moving locomotive. He might have been killed easily enough. But fortunately he landed feet first in the drift beside the rails, and remained upright as he slid down into the ditch.

Tom, glancing ahead again, saw the flash of a man in a checked Mackinaw running up through the open wood and away from the right of way. He could not be sure of Andy O'Malley's figure at that distance; but he could be pretty confident of Koku's identification.

And then, with a shock that gripped and almost paralyzed his mind, Tom saw again the switch ahead of the pilot of the Hercules 0001. The switch was open, and at the speed the electric locomotive had attained, if she did not jump the rails, it seemed scarcely possible that she could be stopped before hitting the bumper at the end of the siding!

A Desperate Chase

These moments were fraught with peril, and not alone peril to the huge machine that Tom Swift had built, but peril to those who remained in the cab of the electric locomotive, as her forward trucks struck the open switch.

There was a mighty jerk that brought a shout from Ned Newton's lips and a grunt from Mr. Damon. Tom clung to his swivel-seat, staring ahead.

The pilot of the electric locomotive shot over on the siding; the forward trucks followed, then the great drivers. The whole locomotive swerved into the siding, but for several breathless seconds Tom was not at all sure that the monster would not jump the rails and head into the ditch!

Meanwhile his gaze measured the speed of that flying figure in the Mackinaw as it scuttled up the slope through the open grove of hard wood and pine. He could not at first see Koku, but he knew the giant was headed for the fugitive, whether the latter proved to be Andy O'Malley or not.

Tom's gaze flashed to what lay ahead of the electric locomotive. As it seemed to joggle back into balance, gain its uprightness, as it were, the inventor saw the great, log-braced bumper between the two rails at the end of the siding. With what force would the locomotive hit that obstruction?

Until the trailers were over the switch Tom dared not give her the brakes. To lock the brake shoes upon the wheels might easily throw the locomotive off the rails. But the instant he felt the tail of the long locomotive swerve off the switch he jabbed the compressed air lever and the wild shriek of the brake shoes answered to his effort.

Then the bumper was but a few yards ahead. The electric locomotive was bound to collide with it. And under the speed at which it had been running, now scarcely reduced by half, the collision was apt to be a tragic happening!

Weeks of effort might be ruined in that moment! If the crash was serious, thousands of dollars might be lost! In truth, Tom Swift apprehended the possibility of a disaster, the complete results of which might put the test of his invention forward for weeks—perhaps for months.

Nor could he do a thing to avert the disaster. He had reversed and set the brakes immediately after the last wheel of the trailer was on the siding. Nothing more could he do as the great electric locomotive bore down upon the solid timber at the far end of this short track.

Those few seconds, as the locked wheels slid toward the end of the siding, were about as hard to bear as any experience the young inventor had ever gone through. It was not so much the peril of the accident, it was the possibility of what might happen to the locomotive.

Within those few moments, however, Tom considered more than the safety of his companions and himself, and more than the peril of wreck to his locomotive. He considered the schedule of the trains on this division of the Hendrickton & Pas Alos and remembered all those that might be within this sector at this time.

If the locomotive smashed into the bumper with force enough to wreck the structure, would some approaching train on the westbound track not be endangered?

The thought was parent to Tom's act before the collision occurred. With a single swift motion he reached for the signaling apparatus which he had established in connection with his wireless telephone.

Just the moment before the head of the locomotive rammed that seemingly immovable barrier at the end of the siding there flashed into the air from Tom's annunciator the code word agreed upon announcing a wreck, and the number of the sector on which the electric locomotive was then running.

The next moment the crash occurred.

Tom had leaped up with a shout of warning. "Hang on!" was his cry. But when the locomotive had struck and rebounded Ned, from far down the aisle of the locomotive, wanted to know in a very peevish tone what he should have hung on to?

"My elbows!" he groaned. "I've skinned 'em, and my back has got a twist in it like the Irishman thought he had when he put on his overalls hindside to. What's happened?"

"Bless my radiolite!" growled Mr. Damon. "My watch crystal is broken all to finders, if you want to know. Bless my shock-absorbers! you won't do this locomotive a bit of good, Tom Swift, if you stop it so abruptly."

"And that's the surest word you ever said" responded Tom, hurrying to the door. "I don't know what's broken, but we're still on the rails. The most immediate thing to learn, is the where-abouts of the fellow who did this."

"Who opened the switch?" cried Ned.

"I believe it was Andy O'Malley. Come on, Ned! Koku is after him and I don't want him to tear O'Malley apart before I get there."

"O'Malley has got powerful interests behind him, and it might go hard with Koku if he injured the spy and some of these Westerners caught him," suggested Mr. Damon.

"They ought to thank Koku for manhandling the fellow—if he does," said Ned.

"As a matter of fact," replied Tom, "Koku will merely hold to the fellow until we get there. But my giant's strength is enormous, and he does not always know the strength of his grasp. he might hurt the fellow. Come on," and Tom leaped from the doorway of the electric locomotive.

Ned leaped down the ladder after his chum.

"Which way did they go?" he asked.

"Across the ditch and up the hill," said Tom. "Mr. Damon!" he called back to that eccentric man, "will you please remain there and watch the locomotive?"

"I certainly will. And I'm armed, too," shouted Mr. Damon. "Don't fear for this locomotive, Tom. I am right on the job."

Tom waved his hand in reply, leaped the ditch, and started up through the wood. Ned was close behind him, and the two young men ran as hard as they could in the direction Tom had seen Andy O'Malley, followed by the giant, running.

In places the earth was slippery with pine needles, and the ground was elsewhere rough. Therefore the chums did not make much speed in running after the giant and his quarry. But Tom was sure of the direction in which the two had disappeared, and he and Ned kept doggedly on.

They went over the crest of the hill and lost sight of the siding and the locomotive. Here was a sharp descent into a gulch, and some rods away, in the bottom of this gully, the young fellows obtained their first sight of Koku. He was still running with mighty strides and was evidently within sight of the man he had set out after in such haste.

"Hey! Koku!" shouted Tom Swift.

The giant's hearing was of the keenest. He glanced back and raised his arm in greeting. But he did not slacken his pace.

"He must see O'Malley, Tom," cried Ned Newton.

"I am sure he does. And I want to get there about as soon as Koku grabs the fellow," panted Tom.

"He'll maul O'Malley unmercifully," said Ned.

"I don't want Koku to injure him," admitted Tom, and he increased his own stride as he plunged down into the gully.

The young inventor distanced his chum within the next few moments. Tom ran like a deer. He reached the bottom of the gully and kept on after Koku's crashing footsteps. At every jump, too, he began to shout to the giant:

"Koku! Hold him!"

The giant's voice boomed back through the heavy timber: "I catch him! I hold him for Master! I break all um bones! Wait till Koku catch him!"

"Hold him, Koku!" yelled Tom again. "Be careful and don't hurt him till I get there!"

He could not see what the giant was doing. The timber was thicker down here. It might be that the giant would seize the man roughly. His zeal in Tom's cause was great, and, of course, his strength was enormous.

Yet Tom did not want to call the giant off the trail. Andy O'Malley must be captured at this time. He had done enough, too much, indeed, in attempting the ruin of Tom's plans. Before the matter went any further the young inventor was determined that Montagne Lewis' spy should be put where he would be able to do no more harm.

But he did not want the man permanently injured. He knew now that Koku was so wildly excited that he might set upon O'Malley as he would upon an enemy in his own country.

"Koku! Stop! Wait for me!" Tom finally shouted.

Now the young inventor got no reply from the giant. Had the latter got so far ahead that he no longer heard his master's command?

Tom pounded on, working his legs like pistons, putting every last ounce of energy he possessed into his effort. This was indeed a desperate chase.

Mr. Damon at Bat

Mr. Wakefield Damon was a very odd and erratic gentleman, but he did not lack courage. He was much more disturbed by the possible injury to Tom Swift's invention by this collision with the bumper at the end of the timber siding than he had been by his own danger at the time of the accident.

He did not understand enough about the devices Tom had built in the forward end of the locomotive cab to understand, by any casual examination, if they were at all injured. But when he climbed down beside the track he saw at once that the forward end of the locomotive had received more than a little injury.

The pilot, or cow-catcher, looked more like an iron cobweb than it did like anything else. The wheels of the forward trucks had not left the track, but the impact of the heavy locomotive with the bumper had been so great that the latter was torn from its foundations. A little more and the electric locomotive would have shot off the end of the rails into the ditch.

While Mr. Damon was examining the front of the locomotive, and Tom and Ned remained absent, he suddenly observed a group of men hurrying out of the forest on the other side of the H. & P. A. right of way. They were not railroad men—at least, they were not dressed in uniform—but they were drawn immediately to the locomotive.

The leader of the party was a squarely built man with a determined countenance and a heavy mustache much blacker than his iron gray hair. He was a bullying looking man, and he strode around the rear of the locomotive and came forward just as though he was confident of boarding the machine by right.

Mr. Damon, knowing himself in the wilderness and not liking the appearance of this group of strangers, had retired at once to the cab, and now stood in the doorway.

"Where's that young fool Swift?" growled the man with the dyed mustache, looking up at Mr. Damon and laying one hand upon the rail beside the ladder.

"Don't know any such person," declared Mr. Damon promptly.

"You don't know Tom Swift?" cried the man.

"Oh! That's another matter," said Mr. Damon coolly. "I don't know any fool named Swift, either young or old. Bless my blinkers! I should say not."

"Isn't he here?" demanded the man, gruffly.

"Tom Swift isn't here just now—no."

"I'm coming up," announced the stranger, and started to put his foot on the first rung of the iron ladder.

"You're not," said Mr. Damon, promptly.

"What's that?" ejaculated the man.

"You only think you are coming up here. But you are not. Bless my fortune telling cards!" ejaculated Mr. Damon, "I should say not."

At this point the black-mustached man began to splutter words and threats so fast that nobody could quite understand him. Mr. Damon, however, did not shrink in the least. He stood adamant in the doorway of the cab.

Finding little relief in bad language, the enemy made another attempt to climb up. For one thing, he was physically brave. He did not call on his companions to go where he feared to.

"I'll show you!" he bawled, and scrambled up the rungs of the ladder.

Mr. Damon did show him. He drew from some pocket a black object with a bulb and a long barrel. Somebody below on the cinder path shouted:

"Look out, boss lie's got a gun!"

At that moment the marauder reached out to seize Mr. Damon's coat. Then the object in Mr. Damon's hand spat a fine spray into the florid face of the enemy!

"Whoo! Achoo! By gosh!" bawled the big man, and he fell back screaming other ejaculations.

"Bless my face and eyes!" cried Mr. Damon. "What did I tell you? And you other fellows want to notice it. Tom Swift isn't here just at this precise moment; but he is guarding his locomotive just the same. He invented this ammonia pistol, and I should say it was effectual. Do you?"

The eccentric man was shrewd enough now to keep behind the jamb of the cab door. For some of these fellows, he realized, might be armed with more deadly weapons than his own.

"Hey, Mr. Lewis!" cried one big fellow, "d'you want we should get that fellow for you?"

"I want to know how badly that blamed thing is smashed," replied the big man with the dyed mustache savagely. "Where's O'Malley?"

"O'Malley's lit out, Boss, like I told you. That giant and them other fellows is after him."

"Break into that cab! Oh! My eyes! I'll kill that old fool! Break a way in there—What's that?"

In pain as he was, his other senses were alert. He was first to hear the screeching whistle of the on-coming freight.

"Think they got wind of this so quick?" demanded Montagne Lewis, for it was he. "Are they sending help from Cliff City?"

"It's a regular freight," returned one of his men.

"She's comm' a-whizzin'," added another. "Right down the eastbound track. If the crew see us—"

"Wait!" commanded Lewis. "Isn't that switch open?"

"You bet it is, Boss."

"Let it be, then," cried the chief plotter. "Let 'em run into it. That freight will smash up this electric locomotive more completely than we could possibly do it. Stand away, men, and let her go!"

A sharp curve in the right of way hid the siding, as well as the open switch into it, from the gaze of the engineer who held the throttle of the coming freight. His locomotive drew a string of empties, eastbound, and having had a heavy pull of it coming up the grade to Cliff City, as soon as he had got the highball from the yardmaster there, he had "let her out," and was now coming to the head of the down grade to Hammon at high speed.

As it chanced, the wireless receiving station of Tom's new telephone system was not yet completed at Cliff City. The news of the wreck of the Hercules 0001 and her position had not been relayed to the master of the Cliff City yards.

That employee of the H. & P. A. had taken a chance in letting the string of empties through his block. He knew the electric locomotive was somewhere ahead, but he thought it would be making its usual time and would have already passed Half Way.

But the situation was serious. The freight was coming along at top speed and the switch into the siding was still open. Montagne Lewis and his crew of ruffians might well stand back and let what seemed sure to happen, happen! The driving freight must do more harm to Tom Swift's invention than they could have hoped to do with the sledges and bars they had brought with them to the spot.

Mr. Wakefield Damon had shown his courage already. He would have been glad to do more to save Tom's locomotive from further injury, but he did not realize what was threatening. He did not hear the shriek of the freight engine's whistle.

PUTTING THE ENEMY TO FLIGHT

The pilot and headlight of the freight locomotive came around the turn and the freight thundered on toward the switch. Seeing the group of men standing by the stalled electric locomotive, and the locomotive itself in the clear of the siding, the driver of the freight did not suppose the switch was open. Nobody who was not a criminal would have stood by idly in such an emergency and let the freight run into an open switch.

Therefore, for the first minute, the coming engineer did not observe his danger. Lewis and his gang stared at the head of the freight and did nothing. They had moved hastily back from the siding so as to be clear of the wreckage. Mr. Damon was in the front of the cab of Hercules 0001 and had no idea of the approaching menace.

But of a sudden a loud shout echoed through the wood. Tom Swift came over the ridge and started toward his invention at top speed. From that height he saw the freight train coming, he observed the men standing at the siding, and he recognized Montagne Lewis, roughly as the railroad magnate was dressed.

Instantly Tom realized what was about to happen—what would surely occur—and he saw what must be done if the utter wreck of his locomotive was to be averted. Yelling at the top of his voice, he leaped down the slope.

"That's Swift!" shouted Lewis. "Stop him!" But the men he had hired to do his wicked work fell back instead of trying to halt the young inventor. It was not Tom's appearance that made them quail. Over the ridge there appeared a second figure—and a more fearful or threatening apparition none of them had ever before seen!

Koku came running with the limp body of Andy O'Malley slung over his shoulder like a bag of meal. The fellows knew it was Andy from his dress.

The giant came down the slope after Tom as though he wore the seven-league boots. The fellows Lewis had hired to wreck the electric locomotive shrank back from before both Tom and the giant.

"Get him!" yelled the half blinded Lewis again.

"Get your grandmother!" bawled one of the men suddenly. "Good-night!"

He turned tail and ran, disappearing almost instantly into the thicker woods. And his mates, after a moment of wavering, sped after him. Lewis was left alone, quite helpless because of the ammonia fumes.

As a matter of fact not all of O'Malley's predicament was due to Koku. The rascal, exhausted by his run and half blind through fright and rage, had stumbled, fallen, and struck his head on a root, which rendered him unconscious.

This, of course, Lewis and his ruffians did not know. All the men of the railroad president's gang saw was the gigantic Koku coming along in great strides, bearing the unconscious O'Malley, who was a burly fellow, as though he were a featherweight. No wonder they fled from such a monster.

Tom had reached the switch, and he was several seconds ahead of the freight locomotive. The engineer saw the open switch then; but he was too late to stop his train.

Going into reverse, however, helped some. Tom seized the switch lever and threw it over, locking it in place, just as the forward trucks thundered upon the joint. The train swept by in safety, and the engineer leaned from his cab window to wave a grateful hand at the young inventor.

Neither the engineer nor the crew of the freight understood the meaning of the scene at the timber siding. All they learned was that Tom Swift had saved the freight from a possible wreck.

The young inventor turned sharply from the switch and motioned with his hand to Koku.

"Throw that fellow into the cab, Koku," he commanded.

The giant did as he was told, just as Ned Newton came panting to the spot.

"Did they do any harm, Tom?" he cried. Then he saw Montagne Lewis standing by, and he seized his chum's arm. "Do you see what I see, Tom?" he demanded, earnestly.

"I guess we both see the same snake," rejoined his chum. "And I mean to scotch it."

"Montagne Lewis!" murmured Ned. "And we've got his chief tool."

Tom said nothing to his chum, hut he approached Lewis with determined mien.

"I can see something has happened to you, Mr. Lewis, and I can guess what it is. The effect of that ammonia will blow away after a time. Ask your friend, Andy O'Malley. He knows all about it, for he sampled it back East, in Shopton."

"I'm going to get square for this, young man," growled the railroad magnate. "You know who I am. And that fellow in the cab knew me, too. How dared he shoot that stuff into my face and eyes?"

"I fancy it didn't take much daring on Mr. Damon's part," and Tom actually chuckled. "A big crook isn't any more important in our eyes than a little crook. We've got your henchman, O'Malley—"

"And you'd better let him go. I'm telling you," snarled Lewis. "I'll ruin you in this country, Tom Swift. I've got influence—"

"You won't have much after this thing comes out. And believe me, I mean to spread it abroad. I've got nothing to win or lose from you, Mr. Lewis. As for O'Malley, I'll put him behind the bars for a good long term."

"You'll do a lot—"

"More than you think," said Tom. "Koku!" The giant had pitched O'Malley, who was still senseless, into the cab, and now was coming up behind Lewis.

"Yes, Master," said the giant.

"Get him!"

"Yes, Master," said Koku, and to Lewis' startled amazement, the next instant he was in the hands of the giant!

He screamed and threatened, and even kicked, to no avail. When he was pitched into the electric locomotive he was held under the threat of Mr. Damon's ammonia pistol until Tom and Ned and the giant entered and the door was shut. Then Koku proceeded to tie both the prisoners by wrist and ankle while the others examined the mechanism of the Hercules 0001.

The pantagraph had been torn off the trolley wires when the locomotive had gone on the siding. But now Tom climbed to the roof of the locomotive, and with Koku's aid managed to set the rear pantagraph at such an angle that its wheels caught the trolley cables again, and once more the current was pumped into the Hercules 0001.

Tom tried out the several parts of the mechanism and found that, despite the jar of the collision, nothing was really injured.

"I built this thing to withstand hard usage," he declared with pride. "The Swift Hercules Electric Locomotives will not be built for parlor ornaments. She is going to run into Hendrickton under her own power, in spite of a smashed cows catcher and target lights."

"Is nothing really injured, Tom?" asked Mr, Damon. "Bless my dinner set! I thought everything had gone to smash when she hit that bumper."

"She will be as good as new in a week," declared Tom, with conviction.

This prophecy of the young inventor proved to be true. A week from that day the public test of the electric locomotive on the Hendrickton & Pas Alos Railroad was held. A picked delegation of railroad men was present to observe and marvel, with Mr. Bartholomew; but Montagne Lewis, the president of the H. & W., was not one of those who attended.

Of course, Lewis soon got out of jail on bail. But the accusation against him was a serious one. His guilt would be proved by his own employee, Andy O'Malley, who was in a hospital for the time being.

O'Malley had got enough. He had turned State's evidence and implicated his employer. Influential and wealthy as Lewis was, he could not escape trial with O'Malley when the time came.

"One thing sure, Lewis has got all he wants. He isn't likely to try any more crooked work against the H. & P. A.," Mr. Bartholomew said. "I can thank you for that, Torn. Swift, as well as for your invention. You have saved the day for my railroad."

"You can thank Koku," chuckled Tom. "If he hadn't spied and identified 'Big Feet,' we might not have caught O'Malley, and, through O'Malley, implicated Montagne Lewis. You give Koku a new suit of clothes, Mr. Bartholomew, and we will call it square. But be sure and have the pattern of the goods loud enough."

This conversation took place while the party of guests was gathering to board Mr. Bartholomew's private car, attached to the Hercules 0001. Mr.

Damon was one of the guests and so was Ned Newton. Tom took into the cab a crew of H. & P. A. men who would hereafter drive the huge locomotive and take care of her.

The semaphore signal dropped and the electric locomotive started as quietly as a baby going to sleep! There was not a jar as the train moved off the siding and over the switches to the main line.

The dispatcher had arranged a clear road for them. Tom knew that he had a free track ahead of him—a level of ninety-odd miles to the Hammon yards. As he passed the Hendrickton shops he touched the siren lever for a moment, and the shrill voice of the Hercules 0001 bade the town good-bye.

The next minute the visitors in the private car grabbed out their split-second watches and began to murmur. The electric locomotive had begun to travel!

SPEED AND SUCCESS

"What town is that?"

"Looks like a splotch of paint on a board fence, we went by so quick."

"I've lost count, Bartholomew. Where are we?"

Ned Newton listened to these comments from the visiting railroad men with delight. In reply to a question of his neighbor, the grinning financial manager of the Swift Construction Company paid:

"No, sir. That isn't a picket fence. It's the telegraph poles you see, and they are no nearer together than on another railroad. But we're going some."

"Bless my railroad stock!" shouted Mr. Damon, "I should say we were."

The electric, locomotive and the private car were hurled toward the Pas Alos Range at a speed that almost frightened some of the guests.

"Three-quarters of an hour!" gasped one man as they began to see the outskirts of Hammon. "And ninety-six miles? Great Scott, Bartholomew! that's over two miles a minute!"

"That is the speed we set out to get," Mr. Richard Bartholomew said, with quite as much pride as though he had done it all himself.

But it had been his suggestion and his money that had accomplished this wonder. Tom Swift was willing to give the railroad president his share of the fame.

The train scarcely slackened speed at Hammon, for Tom got the signal announcing a clear track ahead, and he bucked the grade with all the power he could get from the feed wires. This hill, so well known to him now, was surmounted at a slightly decreased speed; but it was a wonderful display of power after all.

They went down the other side to Panboro and there linked up with an eastbound freight that the Hercules 0001 snatched over the mountain to Hammon at a pace slightly exceeding forty-five miles an hour—at least twice the speed that any two oil-burning locomotives could attain. As for the Jandels, they were not in the same class at all with Tom Swift's locomotive!

"Bless my speedometer!" exclaimed Mr. Damon, when the train pulled down and stopped again at the Hendrickton terminal. "This is the greatest test of speed and power I ever heard of. Why, a coal burner or an oil burner isn't in it with this Hercules locomotive! What do you say, Mr. Bartholomew?"

"I'll say I am satisfied—completely and thoroughly satisfied, Mr. Damon," said the president of the Hendrickton & Pas Alos Railroad frankly. "Mr. Swift has fulfilled his contract in every particular."

An hour later the young inventor and his two friends were in conference with Mr. Bartholomew over a new contract. The bonus of a hundred thousand dollars would be paid at once to the Swift Construction Company. But as the elder Swift's name would be needed on the new contract for the building of other Hercules locomotives, Tom had an idea.

"We won't send the papers East for father to sign," he said. "I want him to see the locomotive in real action. And I know where he can borrow a private car and come out here in comfort. Rad can come with him."

"Bless my valentines!" ejaculated Mr. Damon, "I bet somebody else will come too."

Mr. Damon must have been a prophet, for a fortnight later, when the borrowed car got in to the Hendrickton terminal at the tail of the transcontinental flyer, Tom Swift saw first of all Mary Nestor's rosy face on the platform of the car.

"Tom! are you all right?" she cried, beaming down upon the young inventor.

"No. Half of me is left," he said, grinning up at her. "You look great, Mary!"

"Do you think so?" she cried, dimpling. "Well, if anybody should ask you, Mr. Tom Swift, you look very good to me."

"Don't make me swell all up, Mary," he laughed. "How's father?"

"Splendid! And Rad—"

"Eradicate Sampson is sho' 'nough puffectly all right," broke in the voice of the old colored man, eager to make himself heard and seen. "Here I is, Massa Tom. What dat lizard doin' here? Ain't he a sight?"

The old man had caught sight of Koku in the wonderful new suit Mr. Bartholomew had ordered made for the giant. A Navajo blanket had nothing on that suit for a mixture of colors, and Koku strutted like a turkey-gobbler.

"My lawsy!" gasped Rad again, "he's as purty as a sunset. Is dat de way de tailors out here build a man up? Sure's yo live, Massa Tom, I needs a new suit of clo'es myself."

And before he got away from Hendrickton, Rad Sampson sported a suit off the same piece of goods as that of Koku's. Otherwise there might have been a lasting feud between the giant and the Swift's ancient serving man.

Mr. Barton Swift had stood the easy journey in the private car very well. Before he would sign the contract that Mr. Bartholomew offered, he wished to see for himself just how good his son's invention was.

They made another test from Hendrickton to Panboro, over the "official route," as Ned called it. The time made by Hercules 0001 was even a little better than before.

That the invention was well nigh perfect, and that it could do even more than Mr. Bartholomew had hoped or Tom had claimed, was Mr. Swift's conviction.

"Tom," he said to his son, "you have done a wonderful thing. Not only have you completed a marvelous invention and gained thereby a lot of money, and more in prospect, but you have aided in the world's progress to no small degree.

"Speed in transportation is the big problem before the world of commerce today. To move goods from point to point safely and cheaply, as well as rapidly, is the great task of this age. We are entering the Age of Speed. The railroads must solve the problem to compete with motor-truck traffic and fast boats on the lakes and rivers of our land.

"You have, by your invention, shoved the clock of progress forward. I am proud of you, my boy. I know now that, no matter what may happen to me, you will make an enviable mark in the world of invention.

"You have done much before for the Government in time of stress. But war engines of any kind are not worthy examples of inventive genius beside such a thing as this.

"It is the inventions of peace, rather than those of war, that stand for human progress."

Coming back over the mountain, Mary Nestor rode in the cab with Tom. She sat on the swivel stool, in fact, and handled the controls for part of the way. But she gave up the driver's place to Tom before they reached the timber siding east of Cliff City.

"I cannot go by that place without a shudder," Mary said to the inventor. "Ned and Mr. Damon told me all about that accident. Suppose you had been killed, Tom!"

"I see I'll have to build an invention that will make that impossible," chuckled the young fellow. "Make what impossible?"

"Some invention that will make it positively certain that no matter what I do or where I go, nothing can harm me. Nothing else will suit you, Mary, I plainly see."

"Well," returned the girl, smiling fondly at him. "I admit that would satisfy me completely!"

www.ingramcontent.com/pod-product-compliance
Lightning Source LLC
Chambersburg PA
CBHW030801260626
47169CB00001B/141